THE ATROCITY ARCHIVES

By Charles Stross

THE ATROCITY ARCHIVES

CHARLES STROSS

www.orbitbooks.net

ORBIT

First published in the United States in 2004 by Golden Gryphon Press
First published in Great Britain in 2007 by Orbit
This paperback edition published in 2013 by Orbit
Reprinted 2014

A CIP catalogue record for this book
is available from the British Library.

ISBN 978-0-356-50239-7

Typeset in Garamond by M Rules
Printed and bound by CPI Group (UK) Ltd, Croydon, CR0 4YY

Papers used by Orbit are from well-managed forests
and other responsible sources.

MIX
Paper from
responsible sources
FSC
www.fsc.org   FSC® C104740

Orbit
An imprint of
Little, Brown Book Group
100 Victoria Embankment
London EC4Y 0DY

An Hachette UK Company
www.hachette.co.uk

www.orbitbooks.net

For my parents,
David and Cecilie Stross

ACKNOWLEDGMENTS

Authors write, but not in a vacuum. Firstly, I owe a debt of gratitude to the usual suspects — members of my local writers workshop all — who suffered through first-draft reading hell and pointed out numerous headaches that needed fixing. Paul Fraser of *Spectrum SF* applied far more editorial muscle than I had any right to expect, in preparation for the original magazine serialization; likewise Marty Halpern of Golden Gryphon Press, who made this longer edition possible. Finally, I stand on the shoulders of giants. Three authors in particular made it possible for me to imagine this book and I salute you, H. P. Lovecraft, Neal Stephenson, and Len Deighton.

CONTENTS

CONTENTS

INTRODUCTION
CHARLIE'S DEMONS

'The Atrocity Archive' is a science fiction novel. Its form is that of a horror thriller with lots of laughs, some of them uneasy. Its basic premise is that mathematics can be magic. Its lesser premise is that *if* the world contains things that (as Pratchett puts it somewhere) even the dark is afraid of, *then* you can bet that there'll be a secret government agency covering them up for our own good. That last phrase isn't ironic; if people suspected for a moment that the only thing Lovecraft got wrong was to underestimate the power and malignity of cosmic evil, life would become unbearable. If the secret got out and (consequently) other things got in, life would become impossible. Whatever then walked the Earth would not be life, let alone human. The horror of this prospect is, in the story, linked to the horrors of real history. As in any good horror story, there are moments when you cannot believe that anyone would dare put on paper the words you are reading. Not, in this case, because the words are gory, but because the history is all too real. To summarise would spoil, and might make the writing appear to make light of the worst of human accomplishments. It does not. Read it and see.

Charlie has written wisely and well in the Afterword about the uncanny parallels between the Cold War thriller and the horror story. (Think, for a moment, what the following phrase would call to mind if you'd never heard it before: 'Secret intelligence.') There is, however, a third side to the story. Imagine a world where speaking or writing words can literally and directly make things happen, where getting one of those words wrong can wreak unbelievable havoc, but where with the right spell you can summon immensely powerful agencies to work your will. Imagine further that this world is administered: there is an extensive division of labour, among the magicians themselves and between the magicians and those who coordinate their activity. It's bureaucratic, and also (therefore) chaotic, and it's full of people at desks muttering curses and writing invocations, all beavering away at a small part of the big picture. The coordinators, because they don't understand what's going on, are easy prey for smooth-talking preachers of bizarre cults that demand arbitrary sacrifices and vanish with large amounts of money. Welcome to the IT department.

It is Charlie's experience in working in and writing about the Information Technology industry that gives him the necessary hands-on insight into the workings of the Laundry. For programming is a job where Lovecraft meets tradecraft, all the time. The analyst or programmer has to examine documents with an eye at once skeptical and alert, snatching and collating tiny fragments of truth along the way. His or her sources of information all have their own agendas, overtly or covertly pursued. He or she has handlers and superiors, many of whom don't know what really goes on at the sharp end. And the IT worker has to know in their bones that if they make a mistake, things can go horribly wrong. Tension and cynicism are constant companions, along with camaraderie and competitiveness. It's a lot like being a spy, or necromancer. You don't get out much, and when you do it's usually at night.

Charlie gets out and about a lot, often in daylight. He has no demons. Like most people who write about eldritch horrors, he has a cheerful disposition. Whatever years he has spent in the cellars haven't dimmed his enthusiasm, his empathy, or his ability to talk and write with a speed, range of reference, and facility that makes you want to buy the bastard a pint just to keep him quiet and slow him down in the morning, before he gets too far ahead. I know: I've tried. It doesn't work.

I first encountered Charles Stross when I worked in IT myself. It was 1996 or thereabouts, when you more or less had to work in IT to have heard about the Internet. (Yes, there was a time not long ago when news about the existence of the Internet spread by *word of mouth*.) It dawned on me that the guy who was writing sensible-but-radical posts to various newsgroups I hung out in was the same Charles Stross who'd written two or three short stories I'd enjoyed in the British SF magazine *Interzone:* 'Yellow Snow,' 'Ship of Fools,' and 'Dechlorinating the Moderator' (all now available in his collection *TOAST*, Cosmos Books, 2002).

'Dechlorinating the Moderator' is a science fiction story about a convention that has all the trappings of a science fiction convention, but is (because this is the future) a science *fact* convention, of desktop and basement high-energy fundamental physics geeks and geekettes. Apart from its intrinsic fun, the story conveys the peculiar melancholy of looking back on a con and realising that no matter how much of a good time you had, there was even more that you missed. (All right: as subtle shadings of emotion go this one is a bit low on universality, but it was becoming familiar to me, having just started going to cons.) 'Ship of Fools' was about the Y2K problem (which as we all know turned out not to be a problem, but BEGIN_RANT that was entirely thanks to programmers who did their jobs properly in the first place back when only geeks and astronomers believed the twenty-first century would actually arrive END_RANT) and it was also full of the funniest and most authentic-sounding insider yarns about IT I'd ever read. This Stross guy sounded like someone I wanted to meet, maybe at a con. It turned out he lived in Edinburgh. We were practically neighbours. I think I emailed him, and before too long he materialised out of cyberspace and we had a beer and began an intermittent conversation that hasn't stopped.

He had this great idea for a novel: 'It's a techno-thriller! The premise is that Turing cracked the NP-Completeness theorem back in the forties! The whole Cold War was really about preventing the Singularity! The ICBMs were there in case godlike AIs ran amok!' (He doesn't really talk like this. But that's how I remember it.) He had it all in his head. Lots of people do, but he (and here's a tip for aspiring authors out there) actually wrote it. That one, *Burn Time*, the first of his novels I read, remains unpublished – great concept, shaky execution – but the raw talent was there and so was the energy and application and the astonishing range of reference. Since then he has written a lot more novels and short stories. The short stories kept getting better and kept getting published. He had another great idea: 'A family saga about living through the Singularity! From the point of view of the cat!' That mutated into the astonishing series that began with 'Lobsters,' published in *Asimov's SF*, June 2001. That story was short-listed for three major SF awards: the Hugo, the Nebula, and the Sturgeon. Another, 'Router,' was short-listed for the British Science Fiction Association (BSFA) Award. The fourth, 'Halo,' has been short-listed for the Hugo.

Looking back over some of these short stories, what strikes me is the emergence of what might be called the Stross sentence. Every writer who contributes to, or defines, a stage in the development of SF has sentences that only they could write, or at least only they could write *first*. Heinlein's dilating door opened up a new way to bypass explication by showing what is taken for granted; Zelazny's dune buggies beneath the racing moons of Mars introduced an abrupt gear-change in the degrees of freedom allowed in handling the classic material; Gibson's television sky and Ono-Sendai decks displayed the mapping of virtual onto real spaces that has become the default metaphor of much of our daily lives. The signature Stross sentence (and you'll come to recognise them as you read) represents just such an upward jump in compression and comprehension, and one that we need to make sense not only of the stories, but of the world we inhabit: a world sentenced to Singularity.

The novels kept getting better too, but not getting published, until quite recently and quite suddenly three or four got accepted more or less at once. The only effect this has had on Charlie is that he has written another two or three while these were in press. He just keeps getting faster and better, like computers. But the first of his novels to be published is this one, and it's very good.

We'll be hearing, and reading, a lot more from him.

Read this now.

Ken MacLeod
West Lothian, UK
May 2003

1: ACTIVE SERVICE

GREEN SKY AT NIGHT; HACKER'S DELIGHT.

I'm lurking in the shrubbery behind an industrial unit, armed with a clipboard, a pager, and a pair of bulbous night-vision goggles that drench the scenery in ghastly emerald tones. The bloody things make me look like a train-spotter with a gas-mask fetish, and wearing them is giving me a headache. It's humid and drizzling slightly, the kind of penetrating dampness that cuts right through waterproofs and gloves. I've been waiting out here in the bushes for three hours so far, waiting for the last workaholic to turn the lights out and go home so that I can climb in through a rear window. Why the hell did I ever say 'yes' to Andy? State-sanctioned burglary is a lot less romantic than it sounds – especially on standard time-and-a-half pay.

(You bastard, Andy. 'About that application for active service you filed last year. As it happens, we've got a little job on tonight and we're short-staffed; could you lend a hand?')

I stamp my feet and blow on my hands. There's no sign of life in the squat concrete-and-glass block in front of me. It's eleven at night and there are still lights burning in the cubicle hive: Don't these people have a bed to go home to? I push my goggles up and everything goes dark, except the glow from those bloody windows, like fireflies nesting in the empty eye sockets of a skull.

There's a sudden sensation like a swarm of bees throbbing

around my bladder. I swear quietly and hike up my waterproof to get at the pager. It's not backlit, so I have to risk a precious flash of torchlight to read it. The text message says, MGR LVNG 5 MINS. I don't ask how they know that, I'm just grateful that there's only five more minutes of standing here among the waterlogged trees, trying not to stamp my feet too loudly, wondering what I'm going to say if the local snouts come calling. Five more minutes of hiding round the back of the QA department of Memetix (UK) Ltd. – subsidiary of a multinational based in Menlo Park, California – then I can do the job and go home. Five more minutes spent hiding in the bushes down on an industrial estate where the white heat of technology keeps the lights burning far into the night, in a place where the nameless horrors don't suck your brains out and throw you to the Human Resources department – unless you show a deficit in the third quarter, or forget to make a blood sacrifice before the altar of Total Quality Management.

Somewhere in that building the last late-working executive is yawning and reaching for the door remote of his BMW. The cleaners have all gone home; the big servers hum blandly in their air-conditioned womb, nestled close to the service core of the office block. All I have to do is avoid the security guard and I'm home free.

A distant motor coughs into life, revs, and pulls out of the landscaped car park in a squeal of wet tires. As it fades into the night my pager vibrates again: GO GO GO. I edge forward.

No motion-triggered security lights flash on. There are no Rottweiler attack dogs, no guards in coal-scuttle helmets: this ain't that kind of movie, and I'm no Arnold Schwarzenegger. (Andy told me: 'If anyone challenges you, smile, stand up straight, and show them your warrant card – then phone me. I'll handle it. Getting the old man out of bed to answer a clean-up call will earn you a black mark, but a black mark's better than a cracked skull. Just try to remember that Croxley Industrial Estate isn't Novaya Zemlya, and getting your head kicked in isn't going to save the world from the forces of evil.')

I squish through the damp grass and find the designated window. Like the briefing said, it's shut but not locked. A good tug and the window hinges out toward me. It's inconveniently high up, a good four feet above the concrete gutter. I pull myself up and over the sill, sending a tiny avalanche of disks scuttering across the floor. The room is ghostly green except for the bright hot spots of powered-down monitors and fans blowing air from hot CPU cases. I stumble forward over a desk covered in piles of kipple, wondering how in hell the owner is going to fail to notice my great muddy boot-print between the obviously confidential documents scattered next to a keyboard and a stone-cold coffee mug. Then I'm on the floor in the QA department, and the clock is ticking.

The pager vibrates again. SITREP. I pull my mobile out of my breast pocket and dial a three-digit number, then put it back again. Just letting them know I've arrived and everything's running smoothly. Typical Laundry – they'll actually include the phone bill in the event log to prove I called in on schedule before they file it somewhere secret. Gone are the days of the impromptu black-bag job . . .

The offices of Memetix (UK) Ltd. are a typical cubicle hell: anonymous beige fabric partitions dividing up little slices of corporate life. The photocopier hulks like an altar beneath a wall covered with devotional scriptures – the company's code of conduct, lists of compulsory employee self-actualization training courses, that sort of thing. I glance around, hunting cubicle D14. There's a mass of Dilbert cartoons pinned to the side of his partition, spoor of a mildly rebellious mind-set; doubtless middle managers prowl round the warren before any visit from the upper echelons, tearing down such images that signal dissent. I feel a minor shiver of sympathy coming on: Poor bastard, what must it be like to be stuck here in the warren of cells at the heart of the new industrial revolution, never knowing where the lightning's going to strike next?

There's a desk with three monitors on it: two large but otherwise ordinary ones, and a weird-ass piece of machinery that looks at least a decade old, dredged out of the depths of the computer revolution. It's probably an old Symbolics Lisp machine or something. It tweaks my antique gland, but I don't have time to rubberneck; the security guard's due to make another round in just sixteen minutes. There are books leaning in crazy piles and drifts on either side: Knuth, Dijkstra, Al-Hazred, other less familiar names. I pull his chair back and sit down, wrinkling my nose. In one of the desk drawers something's died and gone to meet its maker.

Keyboard: check. Root account: I pull out the filched S/Key smartcard the Laundry sourced from one of Memetix's suppliers and type the response code to the system's challenge. (One-time passwords are a bitch to crack; once again, give thanks to the Laundry's little helpers.) Then I'm logged in and trusted and it's time to figure out just what the hell I'm logged in *to*.

Malcolm – whose desk I sit at, and whose keyboard I pollute – is running an ant farm: there are dead computers under the desk, scavenged for parts, and a dubious Frankenstein server – guts open to the elements – humming like a generator beside it. For a moment I hunt around in panic, searching for silver pentacles and glowing runes under the desktop – but it's clean. Logged in, I find myself in a maze of twisty little automounted filesystems, all of them alike. *Fuck shit curse dammit*, I recite under my breath; it was never like this in *Cast a Deadly Spell*. I pull out the phone and dial.

'Capital Laundry Services, how may we help you?'

'Give me a hostname and target directory, I'm in but I'm lost.'

'One sec . . . try "auto slash share slash fs slash scooby slash netapp slash user slash home slash malcolm slash uppercase-R slash catbert slash world-underscore-domination slash manifesto."'

I type so fast my fingers trip over each other. There's a faint clicking as the server by the desk mounts scooby's gigantic drive array and scratches its read/write heads, looking for what has got to be one of the most stupidly named files anywhere on the company's intranet.

'Hold on . . . yup, got it.' I view the sucker and it's there in plaintext: *Some Notes Toward a Proof of Polynomial Completeness in Hamiltonian Networks*. I page through the text rapidly, just skimming; there's no time to give it my full in-depth attention, but it looks genuine. 'Bingo.' I can feel an unpleasant slimy layer of sweat in the small of my back. 'I've got it. Bye for now.'

'Bye yourself.' I shut the phone and stare at the paper. Just for a moment, I hesitate . . . What I'm here to do isn't fair, is it? The imp of perversity takes over: I bang out a quick command, mailing the incriminating file to a not-so-dead personal account. (Figure I'll read it later.) Then it's time to nuke the server. I unmount the netapp drive and set fire to it with a bitstorm of low-level reformatting. If Malcolm wants his paper back he'll have to enlist GCHQ and a scanning tunneling microscope to find it under all the 0xDEADBEEF spammed across the hard disk platters.

My pager buzzes again. SITREP. I hit three more digits on the phone. Then I edge out of the cubicle and scramble back across the messy desk and out into the cool spring night, where I peel off those damned latex gloves and waggle my fingers at the moon.

I'm so elated that I don't even remember the stack of disks I sent flying until I'm getting off the night bus at home. And by then, the imp of perversity is chuckling up his sleeve.

I'm fast asleep in bed when the cellphone rings.

It's in my jacket pocket, where I left it last night, and I thrash around on the floor for a bit while it chirps merrily. 'Hello?'

'Bob?'

It's Andy. I try not to groan. 'What time is it?'

'It's nine-thirty. Where are you?'

'In bed. What's—'

'Thought you were going to be in at the debrief? When can you come in?'

'I'm not feeling too wonderful. Got home at about two-thirty. Let me think . . . eleven good enough?'

'It'll have to be.' He sounds burned. Well, Andy wasn't the one freezing his butt off in the woods last night, was he? 'See you there.' The implicit *or else* doesn't need enunciating. Her Majesty's Extra-Secret Service has never really been clear on the concept of flexitime and sensible working hours.

I shamble into the bathroom and stare at the thin rind of black mold growing around the window as I piss. I'm alone in the house; everyone else is either out – working – or *out* – gone for good. (That's out, as in working, for Pinky and the Brain; *out*, as in fucked off, for Mhari.) I pick up my senescent toothbrush and perform the usual morning ritual. At least the heating's on. Downstairs in the kitchen I fill a percolator with nuclear-caffeinated grounds and nudge it onto the gas ring. I figure I can make it into the Laundry by eleven and still have time to wake up first. I'll need to be alert for that meeting. Did last night go off properly, or not? Now that I can't do anything about them I remember the disks.

Nameless dread is all very well when you're slumped in front of the TV watching a slasher movie, but it plays havoc with your stomach when you drop half a pint of incredibly strong black coffee on it in the space of fifteen minutes. Brief nightmarish scenarios flit through my head, in order of severity: written reprimands, unemployment, criminal prosecution for participating in a black-bag job for which authorisation is unaccountably retroactively withdrawn; worst of all, coming home to find Mhari curled up on the living room sofa again. Scratch that latter vision; the short-lived sadness gives way to a deeper sense of relief, tempered by a little loneliness. The loneliness of the long-distance spook? Damn, I need to get my head in order. I'm no James Bond, with a sexy KGB minx trying to seduce me in every hotel room. That's about the first thing they drum into you at Capital Laundry Services ('Washes cleaner than clean!'): life is not a spy movie, work is not romantic, and there's nothing particularly exciting about the job. Especially when it involves freezing your balls off in a corporate shrubbery at eleven o'clock on a rainy night.

Sometimes I regret not having taken the opportunity to study accountancy. Life could be so much more fun if I'd listened to the right recruiting spiel at the university milk round . . . but I need the money, and maybe one of these days they'll let me do something interesting. Meanwhile I'm here in this job because all the alternatives are worse.

So I go to work.

The London underground is famous for apparently believing that human beings go about this world owning neither kidney nor colon. Not many people know that there's precisely one public toilet in Mornington Crescent station. It isn't signposted, and if you ask for it the staff will shake their heads; but it's there all the same, because we asked for it.

I catch the Metropolitan line to Euston Square – sharing a squalid rattle-banging cattle car with a herd of bored commuters – then switch to the Northern line. At the next stop I get out, shuffle up the staircase, go into the gents, and step into the right-hand rear stall. I yank *up* on the toilet handle instead of down, and the back wall opens like a big thick door (plumbing and all), ushering me into the vestibule. It's all a bit like a badly funded B-movie remake of some sixties Hollywood spy thriller. A couple of months ago I asked Boris why we bothered with it, but he just chuckled and told me to ask Angleton – meaning, 'Bugger off.'

The wall closes behind me and a hidden solenoid bolt unlocks the stall door: the toilet monster consumes another victim. I put my hand in the ID scanner, collect my badge from the slot next to it, and step across the red line on the threshold. It's another working day at Capital Laundry Services, discreet cleaning agents to the government.

And guess who's in hot water?

First stop: my office. If you can call it an office – it's a sort of niche between a row of lockers and a herd of senile filing cabinets, into which the Facilities gnomes have jammed a plywood desk and a swivel chair with a damaged gas strut. I drop my coat and jacket on the chair and my computer terminal whistles at me: YOU HAVE MAIL. No shit, Sherlock, I *always* have mail. It's an existential thing: if I don't have mail it would mean that something is very wrong with the world, or maybe I've died and gone to bureaucratic hell. (I'm a child of the wired generation, unlike some of the suits hereabouts who have their secretaries print everything out and dictate their replies for an audio-typist to send.) There is also a cold, scummy cup of over-milked coffee on my desk; Marcia's been over-efficient again. A yellow Post-it note curls reproachfully atop one of my keyboards: MEETING 9:30 AM CT ROOM B4. Hell and damnation, why didn't I remember?

I go to meeting room B4.

There's a red light showing so I knock and wave my badge before entering, just in case Security is paying attention. Inside, the air is blue; it looks like Andy's been chain-smoking his foul French fags for the past couple of hours. 'Yo,' I say. 'Everyone here?'

Boris the Mole looks at me stonily. 'You're late.'

Harriet shakes her head. 'Never mind.' She taps her papers into a neat stack. 'Had a good sleep, did we?'

I pull out a chair and slump into it. 'I spent six hours being one with a shrubbery last night. There were three cloudbursts and a rain of small and very confused frogs.'

Andy stubs out his cigarette and sits up. 'Well, now we're here . . .' He looks at Boris enquiringly. Boris nods. I try to keep a straight face: I hate it when the old guard start playing stiff upper lip.

'Jackpot.' Andy grins at me. I nearly have a heart attack on the spot. 'You're coming to the pub tonight, Bob. Drinks on me. That was a straight A for results, C-plus for fieldwork, overall grade B for execution.'

'Uh, I thought I made a mess going in—'

'No. If it hadn't been a semicovert you'd have had to burn your shoes, but apart from that – well. Zero witnesses, you found the target, there's nothing left, and Dr. Denver is about to find himself downsized and in search of a job somewhere less sensitive.' He shakes his head. 'Not a lot more to say, really.'

'But the security guard could have—'

'The security guard was fully aware there was going to be a burglary, Bob. He wasn't going to move an inch, much less see anything untoward or sound the alarm, lest spooks come out of the woodwork and find him crunchy and good with ketchup.'

'It was a set-up?' I say disbelievingly.

Boris nods at me. 'Is a *good* set-up.'

'Was it worth it?' I ask. 'I mean, I just wiped out some poor bastard's last six months of work—'

Boris sighs mournfully and shoves an official memo at me. It's got a red-and-yellow chevron-striped border and the phrase MOST SECRET DESTROY BEFORE READING stamped across its cover. I open it and look at the title page: *Some Notes Toward a Proof of Polynomial Completeness in Hamiltonian Networks*. And a subtitle: *Formal Correctness Report*. One of the departmental theorem-proving oracles has been busy overnight. 'He duplicated the Turing result?'

'Most regrettably,' says Boris.

Harriet nods. 'You want to know if last night was worth it. It was. If you hadn't succeeded, we might have had to take more serious measures. That's always an option, you know, but in general we try to handle such affairs at the lowest possible level.'

I nod and close the folder, shove it back across the table toward Boris. 'What next?'

'Timekeeping,' says Harriet. 'I'm a bit concerned that you weren't available for debriefing on schedule this morning. You really need to do a bit better,' she adds. (Andy, who I think understands how I tick, keeps quiet.)

I glare at her. 'I'd just spent six hours standing in a wet bush, and breaking into someone else's premises. *After* putting in a full day's work in preparation.' I lean forward, getting steamed: 'In case you've forgotten, I was in at eight in the morning yesterday, then Andy asked me to help with this thing at four in the afternoon. Have you ever tried getting a night bus from Croxley to the East End at two in the morning when you're soaked to the bone, it's pouring wet, and the only other people at the bus stop are a mugger and a drunk guy who wants to know if you can put him up for the night? I count that as a twenty hour working day with hardship. Want me to submit an overtime claim?'

'Well, you should have phoned in first,' she says waspishly.

I'm not going to win this one, but I don't think I've lost on points. Anyway, it's not really worth picking a fight with my line manager over trivia. I sit back and yawn, trying not to choke on the cigarette fumes.

'Next on the agenda,' says Andy. 'What to do with Malcolm Denver, Ph.D. Further action is indicated in view of this paper; we can't leave it lying around in public. Cuts too close to the bone. If he goes public and reproduces it we could be facing a Level One reality excursion within weeks. But we can't do the usual brush and clean either, Oversight would have our balls. Ahem.' He glances at Harriet, whose lips are thin and unamused. 'Could have us all cooling our heels for months in a diversity awareness program for the sensitivity-impaired.' He shudders slightly and I notice the red ribbon on his lapel; Andy is too precious by half for this job, although – come to think of it – this isn't exactly the most mainstream posting in the civil service. 'Anyone got any suggestions? Constructive ones, Bob.'

Harriet shakes her head disapprovingly. Boris just sits there, being Boris. (Boris is one of Angleton's sinister gofers; I think in a previous incarnation he used to ice enemies of the state for the Okhrana, or maybe served coffee for Beria. Now he just imitates the Berlin Wall during internal enquiries.) Andy taps his fingers on the desk. 'Why don't we make him a job offer?' I ask. Harriet looks away: she's my line manager – nominally – and she wants to make it clear that this suggestion does not come with her approval. 'It's like—' I shrug, trying to figure out a pitch. 'He's derived the Turing-Lovecraft theorem from first principles. Not many people can do that. So he's bright, that's a given. I think he's still a pure theory geek, hasn't made any kind of connection with the implications of being able to specify correct geometric relations between power nodes – maybe still thinks it's all a big joke. No references to Dee or the others, apart from a couple of minor arcana on his bookshelf. This means he isn't directly dangerous, and we can offer him the opportunity to learn and develop his skills and interests in a new and challenging field – just as long as he's willing to come on the inside. Which would get him covered by Section Three at that point.'

Section Three of the Official Secrets Act (1916) is our principle weapon in the endless war against security leaks. It was passed during a wartime spy scare – a time of deep and extreme paranoia – and it's even more bizarre than most people think. As far as the public knows, the Official Secrets Act only has two sections; that's because Section Three is itself classified *Secret* under the terms of the preceding sections, and merely knowing about Section Three's existence – without having formally signed it – is a criminal offence. Section Three has all kinds of juicy hidden provisions to make life easy for spooks like us; it's a bureaucratic cloaking field. Anything at all can go on behind the shroud of Section Three as if it simply hasn't happened. In American terms, it's a black operation.

'If you section him we have to come up with a job and a budget,' Harriet accuses.

'Yes, but I'm sure he'll be useful.' Andy waves languidly. 'Boris, would you mind asking around your section, see if anyone needs a mathematician or cryptographer or something? I'll write this up and point it at the Board. Harriet, if you can add it to the minutes. Bob, I'd like a word with you after the meeting, about timekeeping.'

Oh shit, I think.

'Anything else? No? Meeting over, folks.'

Once we're alone in the conference room Andy shakes his head. 'That wasn't very clever, Bob, winding Harriet up like that.'

'I know.' I shrug. 'It's just that every time I see her I get this urge to drop salt on her back.'

'Yes, but she's technically your line manager. And I'm not. Which means you are supposed to phone in if you're going to be late on a day when you've got a kickoff meeting, or else she will raise seven shades of low-key shit. And as she will be in the *right*, appeals to matrix management and conflict resolution won't save you. She'll make your annual performance appraisal look like it's the Cultural Revolution and you just declared yourself the reincarnation of Heinrich Himmler. Am I making myself clear?'

I sit down again. 'Yes, four very bureaucratic values of clear.'

He nods. 'I sympathise, Bob, I really do. But Harriet's under a lot of pressure; she's got a lot of projects on her plate and the last thing she needs is to be kept waiting two hours because you couldn't be bothered to leave a message on her voice mail last night.'

Putting it that way, I begin to feel like a shit – even though I can see how I'm being manipulated. 'Okay, I'll try harder in future.'

His face brightens. 'That's what I wanted to hear.'

'Uh-huh. Now I've got a sick Beowulf cluster to resurrect before Friday's batch PGP cluster-fuck kicks off. And then a tarot permutator to calibrate, and a security audit for another of those bloody collecting card games in case a bunch of stoned artists in Austin, Texas, have somehow accidentally produced a great node. Is there anything else?'

'Probably not,' he murmurs, standing. 'But how did you like the opportunity to get out and about a bit?'

'It was wet.' I stand up and stretch. 'Apart from that, well, it made a change. But I might get serious about that overtime claim if it happens too regularly. I wasn't kidding about the frogs.'

'Well, maybe it will and maybe it won't.' He pats me on the shoulder. 'You did all right last night, Bob. And I understand your problem with Harriet. It just so happens that there's a place on a training course open next week; it'll get you out from under her feet and I think you'll enjoy it.'

'A training course.' I look at him. 'What in? Windows NT system administration?'

He shakes his head. 'Computational demonology for dummies.'

'But I already did—'

'I don't expect you to *learn* anything in the course, Bob. It's the other participants I want you to keep an eye on.'

'The others?'

He smiles mirthlessly. 'You *said you* wanted an active service job . . .'

We are not alone. The truth is out there, yadda yadda yadda. That kind of pop-culture paranoia is mostly bunk . . . except there's a worm of truth at the heart of every fictional apple, and while there may be no aliens in the freezer room at Roswell AFB, the world is still full of spooks who will come through your window and trash your hard disk if you discover the wrong mathematical theorem. (Or worse, but that's another kind of problem, one the coworkers in Field Ops get to handle.)

For the most part, the universe really does work the way most of the guys with Ph.D.s after their names think it works. Molecules are made out of atoms which are made out of electrons, neutrons, and protons – of which the latter two are made out of quarks – and quarks are made out of lepto-quarks, and so on. It's turtles all the way down, so to speak. And you can't find the longest common prime factors of a number with many digits in it without either spending several times the life of the entire universe, or using a quantum computer (which is cheating). And there really are *no* signals from sentient organisms locked up in tape racks at Arecibo, and there really are *no* flying saucers in storage at Area 51 (apart from the USAF superblack research projects, which don't count because they run on aviation fuel).

But that isn't the full story.

I've suffered for what I know, so I'm not going to let you off the hook with a simple one-liner. I think you deserve a detailed explanation. Hell, I think *everybody* deserves to know how tenuous the structure of reality is – but I didn't get to make the rules, and it is a Very Bad Idea to violate Laundry security policy. Because Security is staffed by things that you really don't want to get mad at you – in fact, you don't even want them to notice you exist.

Anyway, I've suffered for my knowledge, and here's what I've learned. I could wibble on about Crowley and Dee and mystics down the ages but, basically, most self-styled magicians know shit. The fact of the matter is that most traditional magic doesn't work. In fact, it would all be irrelevant, were it not for the Turing theorem – named after Alan Turing, who you'll have heard of if you know anything about computers.

That kind of magic works. Unfortunately.

You haven't heard of the Turing theorem – at least, not by name – unless you're one of us. Turing never published it; in fact he died very suddenly, not long after revealing its existence to an old wartime friend who he should have known better than to have trusted. This was simultaneously the Laundry's first ever success and greatest ever disaster: to be honest, they overreacted disgracefully and managed to deprive themselves of one of the finest minds at the same time.

Anyway, the theorem has been rediscovered periodically ever since; it has also been suppressed efficiently, if a little bit less violently, because nobody wants it out in the open where Joe Random Cypherpunk can smear it across the Internet.

The theorem is a hack on discrete number theory that simultaneously disproves the Church-Turing hypothesis (wave if you understood that) and worse, permits NP-complete problems to be converted into P-complete ones. This has several consequences, starting with screwing over most cryptography algorithms – translation: *all your bank account are belong to us* – and ending with the ability to computationally generate a Dho-Nha geometry curve in real time.

This latter item is just slightly less dangerous than allowing nerds with laptops to wave a magic wand and turn them into hydrogen bombs at will. Because, you see, everything you know about the way this universe works is correct – except for the little problem that this isn't the only universe we have to worry about. Information can leak between one universe and another. And in a vanishingly small number of the other universes there are things that listen, and talk back – see Al-Hazred, Nietzsche,

Lovecraft, Poe, et cetera. The many-angled ones, as they say, live at the bottom of the Mandelbrot set, except when a suitable incantation in the platonic realm of mathematics – computerised or otherwise – draws them forth. (And you thought running that fractal screen-saver was good for your computer?)

Oh, and did I mention that the inhabitants of those other universes don't play by our rule book?

Just solving certain theorems makes waves in the Platonic over-space. Pump lots of power through a grid tuned carefully in accordance with the right parameters – which fall naturally out of the geometry curve I mentioned, which in turn falls easily out of the Turing theorem – and you can actually amplify these waves, until they rip honking great holes in spacetime and let congruent segments of otherwise-separate universes merge. You really don't want to be standing at ground zero when that happens.

Which is why we have the Laundry . . .

I slink back to my office via the coffee maker from which I remove a mug full of a vile and turgid brew that coats my back teeth in slimy grit. There are three secret memos waiting in the locked pneumatic tube, one of which is about abuse of government-issue toothpaste. There are a hundred and thirty-two email messages waiting for me to read them. And on the other side of the building there's a broken Beowulf cluster that's waiting for me to install a new ethernet hub and bring it back online to rejoin our gang of cryptocrackers. This is my fault for being the departmental computer guy: when the machines break, I wave my dead chicken and write voodoo words on their keyboards until they work again. This means that the people who broke them in the first place keep calling me back in, and blame me whenever they make things go wrong again. So guess what gets my attention first? Yes, you guessed right: it's the institutional cream and off-green wall behind my monitor. I can't even bring myself to read my mail until I've had a good five minutes staring at nothing in particular. I have a bad feeling about today, even though there's nothing obviously catastrophic to lock onto; this is going to be one of those Friday the Thirteenth type occasions, even though it's actually a rainy Wednesday the Seventeenth.

To start with there's a charming piece of email from Mhari, laundered through one of my dead-letter drops. (You'd better not let the Audit Office catch you sending or receiving private email from work, which is why I don't. As I'm the guy who built the departmental firewall, this isn't difficult.) *You slimy scumbag, don't you ever show your nose round my place again.* Oh yes, as if! The last time I was round the flat she's staying in was at the weekend, when she was out, to retrieve my tube of government-issue toothpaste. I somehow resisted the urge to squirt obscene suggestions on the bathroom mirror the way she did when she came round and repo'd my stereo. Maybe this was an oversight on my part.

Next message: a directive on sick leave signed (digitally) by Harriet, pointing out that if more than half an hour's leave is taken a doctor's note must be obtained, preferably in advance. (Why do I feel a headache coming on?)

Thirdly, there's a plea from Fred in Accounting – a loser, basically, who I had the misfortune to smile at last time I was on hell desk duty: 'Help, I can't run my files anymore.' Fred has just about mastered the high art of the on/off switch but is sufficiently proficient with a spreadsheet to endanger your payroll. Last time I got mail from him it turned out he'd reinstalled an earlier version of some critical bits 'n' pieces over his hard disk, trashing everything, and had the effrontery to be mailing virus-infested jokes around the place. (I bounce the plea for help over to the hell desk where the staffer on call will get to grapple with it and curse me vilely for trying to be helpful to Fred.)

I spend a second stretch of five minutes staring at the chipped cream paint on the wall behind my monitor. My head is throbbing now, and because of various Health and Safety directives there isn't so much as an aspirin on the premises. After yesterday's inane fiasco there doesn't seem to be anything I can do here today that conjures up any enthusiasm: I have a horrible gut-deep feeling that if I stay things will only get worse. Besides, I put in two days' worth of overtime yesterday, regs say I'm allowed to take time off in lieu, my self-help book says I should still be grieving for my pet hamster, and the Beowulf cluster can go fuck itself.

I log out of the secure terminal and bunk off home early: your taxes at work.

It's eight in the evening and I still have a headache. Meanwhile, Pinky is down in the cellar, preparing another assault on the laws of nature.

The TV console in the living room of Chateau Cthulhu – the geek house I share with Pinky and Brains, both of whom also work for the Laundry – is basically brain candy, installed by Pinky in a desperate attempt to reduce the incidence of creative psychosis in the household. I think this was during one of his rare fits of sanity. The stack contains a cable decoder, satellite dish, Sony Playstation, and a homemade webTV receiver that Brains threw together during a bored half hour. It hulks in the corner opposite the beige corduroy sofa like a black-brushed postmodern sculpture held together with wiring spaghetti; its purpose is to provide a chillout zone where we can collapse after a hard day's work auditing new age websites in case they've accidentally invented something dangerous. Cogitating for a living can result in serious brain-sprain: if you don't get blitzed on beer and blow or watch trash TV and sing raucously once in a while, you'll end up thinking you're Sonic the Hedgehog and that ancient Mrs. Simpson over the road is Two-Tails. Could be messy, especially if Security is positively vetting you at the time.

I am plugged into the boob tube with a can of beer in one hand and a pizza box in my lap, watching things go fast and explode on the Discovery Channel, when there's a horrible groaning sound from beneath the carpet. At first I pay no attention because the program currently showing is a particularly messy plane-crash docudrama, but when the sound continues for a few seconds I realise that not even Pinky's apocalyptic stereo could generate that kind of volume, and maybe if I don't do something about it I'm going to vanish through the floorboards. So I stand up unsteadily and weave my way into the kitchen. The cellar door is ajar and the light's on and the noise is coming from down below; I grab the fire extinguisher and advance. There's an ominous smell of ozone . . .

Chateau Cthulhu is a mid-Victorian terrace, an anonymous London dormitory unit distinguished mainly by having three cellar rooms and a Laundry residential clearance, meaning that it's probably not bugged by the KGB, CIA, or our enemies in MI6. There is a grand total of four double-bedrooms, each with a lock on the door, plus a shared kitchen, living room, dining room, and bathroom. The plumbing gurgles ominously late at night; the carpet is a peculiarly lurid species of paisley print that was the height of fashion in 1880, and then experienced an undeserved resurrection among cheap-ass landlords during the 1980s.

When we moved in, one of the cellars was full of lumber, one of them contained two rusting bicycle frames and some mummified cat turds, and the third had some burned-out candle stubs and a blue chalk pentacle inscribed on the floor. The omens were good: the house was right at the corner of an equilateral triangle of streets, aligned due east-west, and there were no TV aerials blocking the southern roofline. Brains, pretending to be a God-botherer, managed to negotiate a 10 percent discount in return for exorcising the place after convincing Mr. Hussein that a history of pagan activities could severely impact his revenues on the rental market. (Nonsense, but profitable nonsense.) The former temple is now Pinky's space, and if Mr. Hussein could see it he'd probably have a heart attack. It isn't the dubious wiring or the three six-foot-high racks containing Pinky's 1950s vintage Strowger telephone exchange that make it so alarming: more like the way Pinky replaced the amateurish chalk sketch with a home-made optical bench and properly calibrated beam-splitter rig and five prisms, upgrading the original student séance antics to full-blown functionality.

(Yes, it's a pentacle. Yes, he's using a fifty kilovolt HT power supply and some mucking great capacitors to drive the laser. Yes, that's a flayed goatskin on the coat rack and a half-eaten pizza whirling round at 33 rpm on the Linn Sondek turntable. This is what you get to live with when you share a house with Pinky and the Brain: I *said* it was a geek house, and we all work in the Laundry, so we're talking about geek houses for very esoteric – indeed, occult – values of geek.)

The smell of ozone – and the ominous crackling sound – is emanating from the HT power supply. The groaning/squealing noise is coming from the speakers (black monoliths from the *2001* school of hi-fi engineering). I tiptoe round the far wall from the PSU and pick up the microphone lying in front of the left speaker, then yank on the cord; there's a stunning blast of noise, then the feedback cut out. *Where the hell is Brains?* I look at the PSU. There's a blue-white flickering inside it that gives me a nasty sinking feeling. If this was any other house I'd just go for the distribution board and pull the main circuit breaker, but there are some capacitors next to that thing that are the size of a compact washing machine and I don't fancy trying to safe them in a dark cellar. I heft the extinguisher – a rather illegal halon canister, necessary in this household – and advance. The main cut-off switch is a huge knife switch on the rack above the PSU. There's a wooden chair sitting next to it; I pick it up and, gripping the back, use one leg to nudge the handle.

There's a loud *clunk* and a simultaneous *bang* from the PSU. Oops, I guess I let the magic smoke out. Dumping the chair, I yank the pin from the extinguisher and open fire, remembering to stand well clear of those big capacitors. (You can leave 'em with their terminals exposed and they'll pick up a static charge out of thin air; after half an hour, if you stick a screwdriver blade across them you'd better hope the handle is well-insulated because you're sure as hell going to need a new screwdriver, and if the insulation is defective you'll need a couple of new fingers as well.)

The smoke forms a thin coil in midair, swirling in an unnaturally regular donut below the single swinging light bulb. A faint laughter echoes from the speakers.

'What have you done with him?' I yell, forgetting that the

mike isn't plugged in. The pentacle on the optical bench is powered down and empty, but the jar beside it is labelled *Dust from ye
Tombe of ye Mummy (prop. Winchester Road Crematorium)* and you
don't need to be a necromancer to figure out what that means.

'Done with whom?'

I nearly jump right out of my skin as I turn round. Pinky is
standing in the doorway, holding his jeans up with one hand and
looking annoyed.

'I was having a shit,' he says. 'Who's the fuss about?'

I point at the power supply, wordlessly.

'You didn't—' He stops. Raises his hands and tugs at his thin
hair. 'My capacitors! You bastard!'

'Next time you try to burn the house down, and/or summon
up a nameless monstrosity from the abyss without adequate
shielding, why don't you give me some warning so I can find
another continent to go live on?'

'Those were fifty quid each in Camden Market!' He's leaning
over the PSU anxiously, but not quite anxiously enough to poke
at it without insulated gloves.

'Doesn't matter. First thing I heard was the feedback howl. If
you don't shut the thing down before answering a call of nature,
don't be surprised when Mrs. Nature comes calling on you.'

'Bugger.' He shakes his head. 'Can I borrow your laser
pointer?'

I head back upstairs to carry on watching my plane-crash program. It's at times like this that I think I really need to find a
better class of flatmate — if only the pool of security-cleared
cohabitants was larger.

2: ENQUIRY

IT'S THE AFTERNOON OF DAY TWO OF THE TRAINING course Andy sent me on, and I have just about hit my boredom threshold. Down on the floor of the cramped lecture theatre our teacher is holding forth about the practicalities of summoning and constraining powers from the vasty deeps; you can only absorb so much of this in one sitting, and my mind is a million kilometres away.

'You need to remember that all great circles must be terminated. Dangling links are potent sources of noise in the circuit, and you need to stick a capacitor on the end to drain it and prevent echoes; sort of like a computer's SCSI bus, or a local area network. In the case of the great circuit of Al-Hazred, the terminator was originally a black goat, sacrificed at midnight with a silver knife touched only by virgins, but these days we just use a fifty microfarad capacitor. You, Bob! Are you falling asleep back there? Take some advice: you don't want to do that. Try this and get the termination wrong and you'll be laughing on the other side of your face – because your face will be on the other side of your head. If you still have a head.'

Bloody academic theoreticians ... 'Yes,' I said. I've been over this before with Brains; electrical great circles are a bad thing, best shunned by anyone with easy access to decent quality lasers and a stabilised platform. Electricity, for ages the primary tool of the experimental vitalists, is now pretty much obsolete – but it's so well-understood that these ivory-tower types prefer to use it as a vehicle for their research, rather than trying more modern geometry engines based on light, which doesn't have any of the nasty side effects of electrical invocations. But that's the British school for you. Over in the States, when they're not dangling stupid 'remote viewing' disinformation tricks in front of the press corps the Black Chamber is busy running experiments on the big Nova laser at Los Alamos that everyone thinks is for bomb research. But do we get to play with safe optoisolated geometry engines and invocation clusters here? Do we, fuck: we're stuck with Dr. Volt and his thuggish friend Mr. Amp, and pray we don't get a stray ground loop while the summoning core is present and active.

'Anyway, it's time to break for coffee. After we come back in about fifteen minutes, I'm going to move along a bit; it's time to demonstrate the basics of a constraint invocation. Then this afternoon we'll discuss the consequences of an uncontrolled summoning.' (Uncontrolled summonings are Bad – at best you'll end up with someone going flatline, their brain squatted by an alien entity, and at worst you'll end up with a physical portal leading somewhere else. So don't do that, m'yeah?)

Teacher claps his hands together, brushing invisible chalk dust from them, and I stand up and stretch – then remember to close my file. The one big difference between this training course and a particularly boring stretch at university is that everything we learn here is classified under Section Three; the penalty for letting someone peek in your notebook can be draconian.

There's a waiting room outside, halfway between the lecture theatres, painted institutional cabbage with frumpy modular seating in a particularly violent shade of burnt orange that instantly makes me think of the 1970s. The vending machine belongs in an antique shop; it appears to run on clockwork. We queue up obediently, and there's a shuffle to produce the obligatory twenty-pence pieces. A yellowing dog-eared poster on the wall reminds us that CARELESS TALK COSTS LIVES – it might be indicative of a sardonic institutional sense of humour but I wouldn't bet on it. (Berwick-upon-Tweed was at war with the Tsar's empire until 1992, and it wouldn't surprise me in the slightest to discover that one of the more obscure Whitehall departments – say, the Ministry of Transport's Department of Long-reach Electric Forklift Vehicle Maintenance Inspectorate, Tires Desk – is still locked in a struggle to the death with the Third Reich.)

It is quite in keeping with the character of the Laundry to be aware of the most peculiar anomalies in our diplomatic heritage – the walking ghosts of conflicts past, as it were – and be ready to reactivate them at a moment's notice. That which never lived sleeps on until awakened, and it's not just us citizens of old-fashioned Einsteinian spacetime who make treaties, right?

A fellow trainee shuffles up to me and grins cadaverously. I glance at him and force myself to resist the urge to sidle away: it's Fred from Accounting, the pest who's always breaking his computer and expects me to fix it for him. About fifty-something, with papery dry skin that looks as if a giant spider has sucked all the juice out of him, he's still wearing a suit and tie on the second day of a five-day course – like he's wandered out of the wrong decade. And it looks slept in, if not lived in to the point of being halfway through a second mortgage and a course of damp-proofing. 'Dr. Vohlman seems to have it in for you, eh?'

I sniff, and decide to stop resisting the urge to sidle away. 'Metaphorically or sexually?'

An expression of deep puzzlement flits across Fred's face. 'What's that? Metawatchically? Nah. He's a bad-tempered old bastard, that's all.' He leans closer, conspiratorially: 'This is all beyond me, you know? Dunno why I'm on this junket, our training budget is just way over the top. Got to use the course credits or we lose them next year. Irene's off studying Eunuch device drivers, whatever they are, and I got posted here. Luck of the draw. But it doesn't mean anything to me, if you know what I mean. You look like one of those intellectual types, though. You probably know what's going on. You can tell me . . .'

'Eh?' I try to hide behind my coffee cup and manage to burn

my fingers. While I'm cursing, Fred somehow ends up standing behind my left shoulder.

'See, Torsun in HR told me he was sending me here, to learn to be the departmental system administrator so those people in Support can't pull the wool over our eyes. But his Vohlman-ness keeps cracking these weird jokes about devils and knives and things. Is he one of them satanists we got briefed on four years ago, do you suppose?'

I boggle as discreetly as I can manage. 'I'm not sure you should be in this course. The material gets technical quickly and it can be dangerous if you're not familiar with the appropriate laboratory safety precautions. Are you sure you want to stay here?'

'Sure? I'm sure! 'Course I'm sure. But I ain't too happy with the content. For one thing, where's all the stuff about license terms and support? That comes first. I mean, pacts with the devil is all very well, but I need to know who to phone for real technical support. And has CESG certified all this stuff for use on government networks?'

I sigh. 'Go have a word with Dr. Vohlman,' I suggest, and – a trifle rudely – turn away. I know there's always one person who's in the wrong course, but we're two days in and he still hasn't figured it out – that's got to be some kind of record, hasn't it?

Everyone drinks up and the smokers magically reappear from wherever they vanished to and we troop back into the lecture theatre. Teacher – Dr. Vohlman – has rolled an archaic test bench in; it looks like a couple of Tesla coils fucking a Wheatstone bridge next to what I'll swear is a distributor hub nicked from an old Morris Minor. The wiring on the pentacle is solid silver, tarnished black with age.

'Right, better put your coffee cups down now, because we're going to actually put some of the stuff we were discussing before break into practice.'

Vohlman is all business, attacking his curriculum with the gusto of a born schoolteacher. 'We're going to try a lesser summoning, a type three invocation using these coordinates I've sketched on the blackboard. This should raise a primary manifestation of nameless horror, but it'll be a fairly *tractable* nameless horror as long as we observe sensible precautions. There will be unpleasant visual distortions and some protosapient wittering, but it's no more intelligent than a *News of the World* reporter – not really smart enough to be dangerous. That's not to say that it's safe, though – you can kill yourself quite easily by treating the equipment with disrespect. Just in case you've forgotten, this current is carrying fifteen amps at six hundred volts, and the baseboard is insulated and oriented correctly along a north-south magnetic axis. The geometry we're using for this run is a modified Minkowski space that we can derive by setting pi to four; there's no fractal dimension involved, but things are complicated slightly because the space to which we're mapping this diagram has a luminiferous aether. Gather round, please, you need to be inside the security cordon when I power up the circuit. Manesh, if you could switch on the ABSOLUTELY NO ENTRY sign . . .'

We gather round the test bench. I hover near the back. I've seen similar experiments before: in fact, I've done much more exotic ones in the basement back at Chateau Cthulhu. Compared to the insanely complex summonings Brains assembles inside his laser grid this is introductory level stuff, just an official checkpoint on my personnel record. (Did I tell you about the friend of mine who was turned down for a job as a trainee scientific officer because he was unqualified? His Ph.D. was no good – the job description said 'three GCSE passes' and he'd long since lost all his high school certificates. That's the way the civil service works.)

Still, it's interesting to watch the other students in this course. Babs, blonde bubble-and-squeak with big-framed spectacles, is treating the bench like an unexploded bomb; I think she's new to this and still too much under the influence of *The Exorcist*, probably expects heads to start spinning round and green slime to start spewing at any moment. (Vohlman should have told the students that's what we keep the Ectoplasm Wallahs around for. Impresses the brass no end. But that's another course.) John, Manesh, Dipak, and Mike are behaving just like bored junior technical staff on another week-away-from-the-desk-is-as-good-as-a-holiday training course. Fred from Accounting looks confused, as if he's mislaid his brain, and Callie's found a pressing reason to go powder her nose. Can't say I blame her; this kind of experiment is fun, the same way that demonstrating a thermite reaction in a chemistry lab is fun – it can blow up in your face. I make damn sure that the electrical fire extinguisher is precisely two paces behind me and one pace to my right.

'Okay, everybody pay attention. Don't, whatever happens, touch the grid. Don't, under any circumstances, say anything once I start. Don't, on pain of your life, step outside the red circle on the floor – we're on top of an earthed cage here, but if we go outside it—'

Topology is everything. The idea of a summoning is simple: you create an attractor node at point A. You put the corresponding antinode at point B. You stand in one of 'em, energize the circuit, and something appears at the other. The big 'gotcha' is that a human observer is required – you can't do it by remote control. (Insert some quantum cat mumbo-jumbo about 'collapsing the wave function' and 'Wigner's Friend versus the Animal Liberation Front' here.) Better hope you picked the right circle to stand in, otherwise you're going to learn far more than you ever wanted to know about applied topology – like how the universe looks when you're turned inside-out.

It's not quite as bad as it sounds. For added security, you can superimpose the attractor node and the safety cell, locking in the summoned agency – which means they shouldn't be able to get to us at the antinode. Which is why Herr Doktor Vohlman mit der duelling scars unt ze bad attitude has plonked the test bench right in the middle of the red pentagram painted on the lecture theatre floor and is enjoining us all to stand tight.

Of course, to get to the fire extinguisher I'd have to step out of the circle . . .

'Is this practice approved by the Health and Safety officer?' Fred asks.

'Quiet, please.' Vohlman shuts his eyes, obviously psyching himself up for the activation sequence. 'Power.' He shoves a knife switch over and a light comes on. 'Circuit two.' A button is depressed. 'Is there anybody there?'

Green vapour seems to swirl at the edges of my vision as I focus on the pentagram of silver wire. Lights glow beneath it, set in a baseboard made of timber harvested from a (used) gallows; setup is everything.

'Three.' Vohlman pushes another button, then pulls a twist of paper out of his pocket. Tearing it, he exposes a sterile lancet which he shoves into the ball of his left thumb without hesitation. The hair on the back of my neck is standing on end as he shakes his hand at the attractor and a bead of blood flicks away from it, bounces off the air above one wire, rolls back toward the centre – and hovers a foot above it, vibrating like a liquid ruby beneath the fluorescent lights.

'Is anybody there?' mimics Fred. Abruptly his face crinkles in a grin. 'Good joke! I almost believed it for a minute!' He reaches out toward the drop of blood and I can feel vast forces gathering in the air around us – and all of a sudden I can feel a headache coming on, like the tension before an electrical storm.

'No!' squeaks Babs, realising it's too late to stop him even as she speaks.

I see Vohlman's face. It's a mask of pure terror: he doesn't dare move a muscle to stop Fred because touching Fred will only spread the contagion. Fred is already lost and the last thing you do to someone who's in contact with high tension is grab them to pull them away – that is, if you do it, it's the last thing you'll *ever* do.

Fred stands still, and his jacket sleeve twitches as if his muscles are writhing underneath it. His hand is over the attractor, and the drop of blood begins to drift toward his fingertip. He is still smiling, like a man with his foot clamped to the third rail of the underground before the smoke and sparks appear. He opens his mouth. 'Yes,' he says, in a high, clear voice that is not his own. 'We are here.'

There are luminous worms writhing behind his eyes.

'What did you do next?' Asks Boris.

I lean back and stare up at the slowly roiling smoke-dragons that curl under the fluorescent tubes. It takes me a few seconds to find my voice; my throat is raw, and not from smoke.

'Analysed the situation very fast, the way they train you to: LEAP methodology. Look, evaluate, assign priorities. Fred had grounded the containment field and the level three agency inside it flood-filled him. Level threes aren't sapient but the universe they come from has a much faster timebase than ours; as soon as he crossed the containment they mapped his nervous system and cracked it like a rotten walnut. Full possession in two to five hundred milliseconds.'

'But what did you *do*?' Andy pushes at me.

I swallow. 'Well, I was opposite him, and he'd grounded the containment. At that point neither the attractor or the antinode were up and running, so we were all targets. The obvious priority was to shut down the possession, fast. You do that by physically disabling the possessed before the agency can construct a defence in depth. I'd been worried by the electrics and made sure I knew where the fire extinguisher was, so that was what I grabbed first.'

Boris: 'It was the first thing that come to hand?'

'Yes.'

Andy nods. 'There's going to be a Board of Enquiry,' he says. 'But that's basically what we needed to know. It fits with what we're hearing from the other witnesses.'

'How badly was he hurt?'

Andy looks away. My hands are shaking so much that my coffee cup rattles against its saucer. 'He's dead, Bob. He was dead the moment he crossed the line. You and everybody else there would be dead, too, if you hadn't punched his ticket. You've got one colleague who wasn't there, two who didn't notice what was going on, and five – including the instructor – who swear blind that you saved their lives.' He looks back at me: 'But we have to put you through the enquiry process all the same because it was a fatal incident. He was married with two kids, and there's a pension and other residuals to sort out.'

'I didn't know.' I stop, before I say something silly. Fred was a jerk, but no man is an island. I feel sick, thinking about the consequences of what happened in that room. Maybe if I'd explained things to him during the break, patted him on the back and sent him away to find a course that would use up his departmental training credits harmlessly—

Andy cuts into my introspection: 'Oh, it's a real mess, all right. Always is, when something goes pear-shaped in the line of duty I'll go so far as to say I expect the enquiry to be a formality in this case – you'll probably come out of it with a commendation. But in the meantime, I'm afraid you're going back to your office where Harriet will formally notify you that you're suspended on full pay pending an enquiry and possible disciplinary action. You're going to go home and cool your heels until next week, then we'll try to get it over with as fast as possible.' He leans back from his desk and sighs. 'This sucks, really and truly, but there's no getting around it. So I suggest you treat the suspension as time to chill out and get your head together, get over things – because after the enquiry I expect we'll be resurrecting your application for active duty training and field ops, and looking at it favourably.'

'Huh?' I sit up.

'Ninety percent of active duty consists of desk work. You can do that, even if the hat doesn't fit too well. Another 9 percent is sitting around in bushes while the rain drips down your collar, wondering what the hell you're doing there. I figure you can do that, too. It's the other 1 percent – a few seconds of confused danger – that's hard to get right, and I think you've just demonstrated the capability. To the extent that it's my call, you've got it' – he stands up – 'if you want it.'

I stand up too. 'I'll think about it,' I say, and I walk out the door before I start mouthing obscenities, because I can't get Fred's expression out of my head. I've never seen someone die before. Funny, isn't it? Most of us go through life and never really see someone die, much less die violently. I should be on a high, knowing that I'm going to qualify for field ops, and if this interview had happened yesterday I would be. But now I just want to throw up in a corner.

*

Brains is in the kitchen when I get home attempting to cook an omelette without breaking the eggshell.

It's raining, and my jacket is drenched from the short run between the tube station and the front door; give thanks once more to the invisible boon of contact lenses, without which I would be staring at the world through streak-befuddled spectacles. 'Hi,' says Brains. 'Can you hold this for me?'

He hands me an egg. I stare.

The normally not-so-clean kitchen worktop is gleaming and sterile, as if in preparation for a particularly fussy surgeon. At one side of it sits a syringe and needle preloaded with a grey, opaque liquid – essence of concrete. At the other side of it sits a food processor, its safety shutoff hacked and something that looks worryingly like half an electric motor bolted to the drive shaft that normally turns its blades. I stand there dripping and staring: even for Brains's projects, this is distinctly abnormal.

I hand the egg back. 'I'm not in the mood.'

'C'mon. Just hold it?'

'I mean it. I've just been suspended, pending an enquiry.' I unzip my jacket and let it tumble to the floor. 'Game over, priority interrupt, segmentation fault.'

Brains cocks his head toward one side and stares at me with big bright eyes, like a slightly demented owl. 'Seriously?'

'Yeah.' I hunt around for the coffee jar and begin ladling scoopfuls into the cafetière. 'Water in the kettle?'

'Suspended? On pay? Why?'

In goes the coffee. 'Yes, on pay. I saved six people's lives, plus my own. But I lost the seventh, so there's going to be an enquiry. They say it's a formality, but—' *Click*, the kettle is now on, heating up to a steam explosion.

'Something to do with that training course?'

'Yeah. Fred from Accounting. He grounded a summoning grid—'

'Gene police! You! Out of the pool, now!'

'It's not funny.'

He looks at me again and loses his levity. 'No, Bob, it's not funny. I'm sorry.' He offers me the egg. 'Here, hold this, I implore you.'

I take it and nearly drop it; it's hot, and feels slightly greasy. There's also a faint stench of brimstone. 'What the hell—'

'Just for a moment, I promise you.' He pulls out a roughly made copper coil, the wire wrapped around a plastic pie cutter and hooked up to some gadget or other, and gingerly threads it over the egg, around my wrist and back again. 'There. The egg should now be degaussed.' He puts the coil down and takes the egg from my nerveless hand. 'Observe! The first prototype of the ultimate integral ovine omelette.' He cracks it on the side of the worktop and a yellow, leathery curdled sponge flops out. The smell of brimstone is now pronounced, tickling at my nostrils like the aftereffect of a fireworks show. 'It's still at the development stage – I had to use a syringe on it, but next on the checklist is gel-diffusion electrophoresis using flocculated hemoglobin agglutinates pending in-ovo polymerisation of the rotor elements – so how did your pet luser autodarwinate?'

I pull up a trash can and sit down. Maybe Brains isn't as monumentally self-obsessed as he looks? At least he slipped the question in painlessly enough.

'You know how there's always someone who ends up in the wrong course? It was that dumb accounts clerk I'm always bitching about. He got in the Intro to Occult Computing course by mistake. I shouldn't have been there, anyway, but Harriet managed to convince Andy I needed it; getting her own back for last month, I think.' Harriet has been having problems with her email system and asked my advice; I don't know quite what went wrong, but she ended up blowing five days of the departmental training budget attending a course on sendmail configuration. Took her three weeks to stop twitching every time somebody mentioned rules. 'Well and all, I guess what he did qualifies as a massive self-LART, but . . .'

I realise I'm not talking anymore and shudder convulsively.

'His eyes were full of worms.'

Brains turns, silently, and rummages in the cupboard above

the sink. He pulls down a big bottle labelled DRAIN FLUID, rinses out a couple of chipped cups that are languishing on the draining board, then fills them from the bottle. 'Drink this,' he says.

I drink. It isn't bleach: my eyes don't quite bulge out, my throat doesn't quite catch fire, and most of the liquid doesn't evaporate from the surface of my tongue. 'What the hell is this stuff?'

'Sump degreaser.' He winks at me. 'Stops Pinky dipping his wick in it, right?' I wink back, a bit nonplussed; I do not think that phrase means what Brains thinks that it means, but if I told him I doubt he'd give me any more of this stuff, so I'm not going to enlighten him. Right now I've got a strong urge to get blindingly drunk – which he seems to have sensed. If I'm blind drunk I won't have to think. And not thinking for a while will be a good thing.

'Thank you,' I say, as gravely as I can – it's Brains's secret, after all, and he's confided it in me. I'm obscurely touched, and if I didn't keep seeing Fred grinning at me whenever I closed my eyes it might actually get to me.

Brains peers at me closely. 'I think I know your problem,' he says.

'What's that?'

'You need' – he's already topping up my cup – 'to get pissed. Now.'

'But what about your—' I wave feebly at the worktop.

He shrugs. 'It's an early success; I'll get it working properly later.'

'But you're busy,' I protest, because this whole thing is very un-Brains-like; at his worst he's a borderline autist. To have him paying attention to someone else's emotional upsets is, well, eerie.

'I was only trying to prove that you can make an omelette without breaking eggs. That's just a dumb metaphor or a silly practical experiment; you're real, and a classic example of what it means, too. You're broken, in the course of scrambling a body-snatcher's zero point outbreak, and I figure we need to see if all the king's men can fix you, or at least make you feel better. Then you can help me with my egg-sacting project.'

I do not throw the glass at him. But I make him refill it.

An indeterminate but nonzero number of semifull vodka glasses later, Pinky appears, looking tall and gangly and slightly flustered. He demands to know where the nearest bookshop is.

'Why?'

'For my nephew.' (Pinky has a brother and sister-in-law who live on the other side of London and who have recently spawned.)

'What are you getting him?'

'I'm buying an A to Z and a bible.'

'Why?'

'The A to Z is a christening present and the bible is so I know the way to the church.' Brains groans; I scrabble drunkenly behind the sofa for a sponge bullet for the Nerf gun, but they all seem to have fallen through the wormhole that leads to the planet of lost paper clips, pencils, and irreplaceable but detachable components of weird toys. 'Say, what's going on here?'

'I'm taking a break from my cunning plan to help Bob get drunk, because that's what he needs,' says Brains. 'He needs distracting and I was doing my best until you came in and changed the subject.' He stands up and throws one of the suckers at Pinky, who dodges.

'That's not what I meant; there's a weird smell in the kitchen and something that's, er, squamous and rugose' – a household catch-phrase, and we all have to make the obligatory Cthulhu-waggling-tentacles-on-chin gesture with our hands – 'and yellow tried to eat my shoe. What's up?'

'Yeah.' I struggle to sit up again; one of the straps under the sofa cushions has failed and it's trying to swallow me. 'Just what was that thing in the kitchen?'

Brains stands up: 'Behold' – he hiccups – 'I am in the process of disproving a law of nature; to wit, that it is impossible to make an omelette without breaking eggs! I have a punning clan—'

Pinky throws the (somewhat squashed, but definitely formerly spherical) omelette at his head and he ducks; it hits the video stack and bounces off.

'I have a cunning plan,' Brains continues, 'which if you'll let me finish—'

I nod. Pinky stops looking for things to throw.

'That's better. The question is how to churn up an egg without breaking the shell, then cook it from the inside out, correct? The latter problem was solved by the microwave oven, but we still have to whisk it up properly. This usually means breaking it open, but what I figured out was that if I inject it with magnetised iron filings in a lecithin emulsion, then stick it in a rotating magnetic field, I can churn it up quite effectively. The next step is to do it without breaking the shell at all — immerse the egg in a suspension of some really tiny ferromagnetic particles then use electrophoresis to draw them into it, then figure out some way of making them clump together into long, magnetised chains inside it. With me so far?'

'Mad, *mad* I say!' Pinky is bouncing up and down. 'What are we going to do tonight, Brains?'

'What we do every night, Pinky: try to take over the world!' (Of haute cuisine.)

'But I've got to buy a couple of books before the shops close,' says Pinky, and the spell is broken. 'Hope you feel better, Bob. See you guys later.' And he's gone.

'Well that was useless,' sighs Brains. 'The lad's got no staying power. One of these days he'll settle down and turn all normal.'

I look at my flatmate gloomily and wonder why I put up with this shit. It's a glimpse of my life, resplendent in two-dimensional glory, from an angle that I don't normally catch — and I don't like it. I'm just about to say so when the phone chirrups.

Brains picks it up and all expression drains from his face. 'It's for you,' he says, and hands me the phone.

'Bob?'

My free hand starts to shake because I really don't need to hear this, even though part of me wants to. 'Yes?'

'It's me, Bob. How are you? I heard the news—'

'I feel like shit,' I hear myself saying, even though a small corner of my mind is screaming at me. I close my eyes to shut out the real world. 'It was horrible. How did you hear?'

'Word gets around.' She's being disingenuous, of course. Mhari has more tentacles than a squid, and they're all plugged into the Laundry grapevine. 'Look, are you okay? Is there anything you need?'

I open my eyes. Brains is staring at me blankly, pessimistically. 'I'm getting as drunk as possible,' I say. 'Then I plan to sleep for a week.'

'Oh,' she says in a small voice, sounding about as cute and appealing as she ever did. 'You're in a bad state. May I come round?'

'Yes.' In an abstract sort of way I notice Brains choking on his drain fluid. 'The more the merrier,' I say, hollow-voiced. 'Party on.'

'Party on,' she echoes, and hangs up.

Brains glares at me. 'Have you taken leave of your senses?' he demands.

'Very probably.' I toss back what's left in my cup and reach for the bottle.

'That woman's a psychopath.'

'So I keep telling myself. But after the tearful reconciliation, hot passionate bunny fucks on the bedroom floor, screaming pentacle-throwing tantrum, and final walkout number four, at least she'll give me something concrete and personal to feel *really* depressed about, instead of this gotta-save-'em-all shit I'm kicking my own arse over.'

'Just keep her out of the cellar this time.' He stands up unsteadily. 'Now if you'll excuse me, I've got some omelettes to nuke . . .'

A week later:

'This is an M11/9 machine pistol, manufactured by SW Daniels in the States. In case you hadn't figured it out, it's a gun. Chambered to take 9mm and converted to accept a sten magazine, it has a very high cyclic rate of 1600 rounds per minute, muzzle velocity 350 metres per second, magazine capacity thirty rounds. This cylinder is a two-stage wipeless supressor, *not* what you might have seen in the movies as a 'silencer'; it doesn't silence the gun, but it cuts the noise by about thirty decibels for the first hundred or so rounds you put through it.

'You need to know three things about this machine. One: if someone points one at you, do whatever they tell you, it is not a fashion accessory. Two: if you see one lying around, don't pick it up, unless you know how to carry it safely. You might blow your feet off by accident. Three: if you need one, dial the Laundry switchboard and ask for 1-800-SAS – our lads will be happy to oblige, and they train with these things every day of the week.'

Harry isn't joking. I nod, and jot down some notes, and he sticks the submachine gun back in the rack.

'Now this – tell me about *this*.'

I look at the thing and rattle off automatically: 'Class three Hand of Glory, five charge disposable, mirrored base for coherent emission instead of generalised invisibility . . . doesn't seem to be armed, maximum range line-of-sight, activation by designated power word—' I glance sidelong at him. 'Are you cleared to use these things?'

He puts the Hand of Glory down and picks up the M11/9 carefully. He flicks a switch on its side, looks round to make sure he's clear, points it downrange, and squeezes the trigger. There's a shatteringly loud crackle of gunfire followed by a tinkle of brass on concrete around our feet. 'Your call!' he shouts.

I pick up the hand. It feels cold and waxy, but the activation code is scribed on the sawn-off radius in silver. I step up beside him, point it downrange, focus, and concentrate on the trigger string, knowing that it sometimes takes a few seconds—

WHUMP.

'Very good,' Harry says drily. 'You realise it cost an execution in Shanxi province to make that thing?'

I put it down, feeling queasy. 'I only used one finger. Anyway, I thought our suppliers used orangoutangs. What happened?'

He shrugs. 'Blame the animal rights protesters.'

I'm not back on duty – I'm suspended on full pay. But according to Boris the Mole there's a loophole in our official procedures which means that I'm still eligible for training courses that I was signed up for before being suspended, and it turns out that Andy signed me up for a full package of six weeks of prefield training: some of it down at the village that used to be called Dunwich, and some at our own invisible college in Manchester.

The full package is a course in law and ethics (including International Relations 101: 'Do whatever the nice man with the diplomatic passport tells you to do unless you want to start World War Three by accident.'), the correct use of petty cash receipts, basic tailing and surveillance, timesheets, how to tell when you're being T&S'd, travel authorisation requests, locks and security systems, reconciliation and write-offs, police relations ('Your warrant card will get you out of most sticky situations, if they give you time to show it.'), computer security (roll around the floor, laughing), software purchase orders, basic thaumaturgic security (ditto), and use of weapons (starting with the ironclad rule: 'Don't, unless you have to and you've been trained.'). And so I find myself down on the range with Harry the Horse, a middle-aged guy with an eye patch and thinning white hair who thinks nothing of blowing things away with a submachine gun but seems somewhat startled at my expertise with a HOG-3.

'Right.' Harry ejects the magazine from his gun and places it carefully on the bench. 'I think we'll keep you off the firearms list then, and pencil you in for training to COWEU-2 – certification of weaponry expertise, unconventional, level two. Permission to carry unconventional devices and use them in self-defence when authorised on assignment to hazardous duty. I take it that bullseye wasn't an accident?'

I pick up the hand and remember to disarm it this time. 'Nope. You realise you don't need an anthropoid for this? Ever wondered why there are so many one-legged pigeons in central London?'

Harry shakes his head. 'You young 'uns. Back when I was getting going we used to think the future would be all lasers and food pills and rockets to Mars.'

'It's not that different,' I remonstrate. 'Look, it's a science. You try using a limb from someone who died of motor neurone disease or MS and you'll find out in a hurry! What we're doing is setting up a microgrid that funnels in an information gate from another contiguous continuum. Information gates are, like, easy; with a bit more energy we can crank it open and bring mass through, but that's more hazardous so we don't do it very often. The demonic presences – okay, the extraterrestrial sapient fast-thinkers on the other side – try to grab control over the proprioceptive nerves they can sense the layout of on the other side of the grid. The nerves are dead, like the rest of the hand, but they still act as a useful channel. So the result is an information pulse, raw information down around the Planck level, that shows up to us as a phase-conjugated beam of coherent light—'

I point the hand at the downrange target. Two smoking feet.

'What will you do if you ever have to point that thing at another human being?' Harry asks quietly.

I put it back on the rack hastily. 'I really hope I'm never put in that position,' I say.

'That's not good enough. Say they were holding your wife or kids hostage—'

'The enquiry hasn't been held yet,' I reply. 'So I don't know if I've still got a job. But I hope I never get put in that kind of position again.'

I try to keep my hands from shaking as I padlock the case and reactivate the ward field. Harry looks at me thoughtfully and nods.

'Committee of enquiry will come to order.'

I shuffle the papers in front of me, for no very good reason other than to conceal my nervousness.

It's a small conference room, walled in thick oak panels and carpeted in royal blue. I've just been called in: they're grilling people in order of who was there and who was responsible, and after Vohlman I'm number two. (He was running the course and conducted the summoning; I merely terminated it.) I don't recognise the suits sitting behind the table, but they look senior, in that indefinable way that somehow says, 'I've got my KCMG; how long until you get yours?' The third is a senior mage from the Auditors, which would be enough to make my blood run cold if I were guilty of anything worse than stealing paper clips.

They ask me to stand on the centre of the crest of arms in the carpet: sewn with gold thread, some kind of Latin motto, very nice. I feel the hairs on my arms prickle with static and I know it's live.

'Please state your name and job title.' There's a recorder on the desk and its light is glowing red.

'Bob Howard. Darkside hacker, er, Technical Computing Officer grade 2.'

'Where were you on Thursday the nineteenth of last month?'

'Er, I was attending a training course: Introduction to Applied Occult Computing 104, conducted by Dr. Vohlman.'

The balding man in the middle makes a doodle on his pad then fixes me with a cold stare. 'Your opinion of the course?'

'My – er?' I freeze for a moment; this isn't in the script 'I was bored silly – um, the course was fine, but it was a bit basic. I was only there because Harriet was pissed off at me for coming in late after putting in a twenty-hour shift. Dr. Vohlman did a good job, but really it was insanely basic and I didn't learn anything new and wasn't paying much attention—' *Why am I saying this?*

The man in the middle looks at me again. It's like being under a microscope; I feel the back of my neck burst out in a cold, prickly sweat. 'When you weren't paying attention, what were you doing?' he demands.

'Daydreaming, mostly.' What's going on? I can't seem to stop myself answering everything they ask, however embarrassing. 'I can't sleep in lecture theatres and you can't read a book when there are only eight students. I kept an ear open in case he said something interesting but mostly—'

'Did you bear Frederick Ironsides any ill will?'

My mouth is moving before I can get control: 'Yes. Fred was a fuckwit. He kept asking me stupid questions, was too dumb to learn from his own mistakes, made work for other people to mop up after him, and held a number of opinions too tiresome to list. He shouldn't have been in the course and I told him to tell Dr.

Vohlman, but he didn't listen. Fred was a waste of airspace and one of the most powerful bogon emitters in the Laundry.'

'Bogons?'

'Hypothetical particles of cluelessness. Idiots emit bogons, causing machinery to malfunction in their presence. System administrators absorb bogons, letting the machinery work again. Hacker folklore—'

'Did you kill Frederick Ironsides?'

'Not deliberately – yes – you've got my tongue – no – dammit, he did it himself! Damn fool shorted out the containment wards during a practical so I hit him with the extinguisher, but only after he was possessed. Self-defence. What kind of spell is this?'

'No opinions, Robert, facts only and just the facts, please. Did you hit Frederick Ironsides with the fire extinguisher because you hated him?'

'No, because I was scared shitless that the thing in his head was going to kill us all. I don't hate him – he's just a bore but that isn't a capital offence. Usually.'

The woman on his right makes a note on her pad. My inquisitor nods: I can feel chains of invisible silver holding my tongue still, chains binding me to the star chamber carpet I stand upon. 'Good. Just one more question, then. Of the students on your training course, who least belonged there?'

'Me.' Before I can bite my tongue, the compulsion forces me to finish the sentence: 'I could have been teaching it.'

The sea crashes on the shore endlessly. A grey continuum of churning water that meets the sky halfway to infinity. Shingle crunches as I walk along what passes for a beach here, past the decaying graveyard that topples gently down the slope to the waters below. (Every year the water claims another foot off the headland; Dunwich is slowly sinking beneath the waves, until finally the church bells will toll with the tide.)

Seagulls scream and whirl and snap in the air above me like dervishes.

I came here on foot to get away from the dormitory and the training units and the debriefing offices built from what used to be two rows of ramshackle cottages and a big farmhouse. There are no roads in or out of Dunwich; the Ministry of Defence took over the entire village back in 1940 and redirected the local lanes, erasing it from the map and the collective consciousness of Norfolk as if it never existed. Ramblers are repulsed by the thick hedges that surround us on two sides and the cliff that protects its third flank. When the Laundry inherited Dunwich from MI5, they added subtler wards; anyone approaching cross-country will begin to develop a deep sense of unease a mile or so outside the perimeter. As it is, the only way in or out is by boat – and our watery friends will take care of any unwelcome visitors smaller than a nuclear submarine.

I need space to think. I've got a lot to think about.

The Board of Enquiry found that I was not responsible for the accident. What's more, they approved my transfer to active status, granted my course completion certificate, and blew through the department like a hot desert wind driving stinging sand-grains of truth before it. With their silver-tongue bindings and executive authority the old broom swept clean and left everything behind tidy – if a little shaky, with all the nasty unwashed linen exposed to the cold-eyed view of authority. I would not have liked to answer to their jackal-headed servitors if I were guilty. But, as Andy pointed out, if being a smart-arse was an offence, the Laundry would not exist in the first place.

Mhari moved back into my room after the night of the party and I haven't dared tell her to move back out again. So far she hasn't thrown anything at me or threatened to slash her wrists, in any par-ticular order. (Two months ago, the last time she polled my suicide interrupt queue, I was so pissed off I just said, 'Down, not across,' using a fingernail to demonstrate. That's when she broke the teapot over my head. I should have taken that as a warning sign.)

What I've got to think about now is a lot larger. The business with Fred was a real eye-opener. Do I still want to put my name on the active service list? Join the Dry Cleaners, visit strange countries, meet exotic people, and cast death spells at them? I'm not sure anymore. I *thought* I was sure, but now I know it amounts to shivering in a rainstorm most of the time and having to watch people with worms waggling behind their eyes the rest of it. Is this what I want to do with my life?

Maybe. And then again, maybe not.

There's a large boulder on the shingle ahead of me; beyond it, a decaying upside-down boat marks the no-go border within our security perimeter. This is as far away as I can get without tripping alarms, drawing down security attention, and generally looking stupid in public. I place a hand on the boulder; it's heavily weathered and covered in lichen and barnacles. I sit on it and look back down the beach, back toward Dunwich and the training complex. For a moment, the world looks hideously solid and reliable, almost as if the comforting myths of the nineteenth century were true, and everything runs on clockwork in an orderly, unitary cosmos.

Somewhere down in the village, Dr. Malcolm Denver is undergoing induction briefings, orientation lectures, shoe-size measurements, pension adjustments, and being issued with his departmental toothpaste tube and identification dog tags. He's probably still a bit pissed off, the way I was four years ago when I was pulled in after someone – they never told me who – caught me systematically dumpster-diving through files that were off-limits but inadequately guarded from network infiltration. It was really just a summer vacation job between finishing my CS degree and starting postgrad work: making ends meet doing contract work for the Department of Transport. I smelt a rat in the woodpile and began to dig, never quite suspecting the full magnitude of the rodent whose tail I had grabbed hold of. I was pissed off at first, but over the following four years, spent immersed in the Laundry Basket – our strange collective ghetto of secret knowledge – I acquired the basics of this calling. Thaumaturgy is quite as fascinating as number theory, thank you very much, the hermetic disciplines descended from Trismegistus as engrossing as the sciences he dabbled in. But do I want to dedicate myself to working in a secret field for life?

I can't very well go back to civvy street; they'll let me if I ask nicely, but only as long as I agree to have nothing to do with a wide range of occupations – including everything I can possibly earn a living at. This will cause problems, family problems as well as money problems – mum will probably ignore me and dad will yell about slacking and layabout hippies. Having a son in the civil service suits them down to the ground: they both get to ignore the inconvenient evidence of their mistaken marriage and carry on with their lives, secure in the knowledge that at least they did the parental thing successfully. Meanwhile, I haven't served long enough to earn a pension yet. I suppose I could stagnate in tech support indefinitely, or mutate into management; a generous portion of the Laundry's payroll is devoted to buying the silence of incompetent lambs, manufacturing work for people who need something to fill the time between their first, accidental exposure and final retirement. (There's nothing kindhearted about this; bumping off talkative voices is an expensive, dangerous business with hideous political consequences if you get caught, and it makes for an unpleasant working environment. Paying dead wood to sit at a desk and not rock the boat is comparatively cheap and painless.) But I'd like to think life isn't quite so . . . meaningless.

Seagulls wheel and squawk overhead. There's a faint thud behind me; one of them has dropped something on the beach. I turn round to watch, just in case the bastards are trying to toilet-bomb me. At first glance that's what it looks like: something small, like a starfish, and faintly green. But on closer inspection . . .

I stand up and lean over the thing. Yes, it's starfish-shaped: radial symmetry, five-fold order. Seems to be a fossil, some kind of greenish soapstone. Then I look closer. I know that only two hundred miles away most of the nuclear reactors in Europe are sitting on the Normandy coast, where the prevailing winds would blow a fallout plume out toward us. (And you wonder why the British government insists on keeping its nuclear weapons?) Nevertheless, this is weirder than any radiation mutant has a right to be. Each tentacle tip is slightly truncated; the whole thing looks like a cross-section through a sea cucumber. It must be a representative of an older order, a living fossil left over from some weird family of organisms mostly rendered extinct by the Cambrian biodiversity catastrophe – when the structures that lie buried two kilometres below a nameless British Antarctic Survey base were built.

I stare at the fossil, because it seems like an omen. A thing transported from its natural environment, washed up and left to die on an alien beach beneath the gaze of creatures incomprehensible to it: that's a good metaphor for humanity in this age, the humanity that the Laundry is sworn to defend. Never mind the panoply of state and secrecy, the cold-war trappings of village and security cordon – what it's about, when you get down to it, is this: our appalling vulnerability, collectively, before the onslaught of beings we can barely comprehend. A lesser one, not even one of the great Old Ones, would be enough to devastate a city; we play under the shadow of forces so sinister that a momentary relaxation of vigilance would see all that is human blotted out.

I can go back to London, and they will let me go back to my desk and my stuffy cubicle and my job fixing broken office machines. No recriminations, just a job for life and a pension in thirty years time in return for a promise of silence to the grave. Or I can go back to the office in the village and sign the piece of paper that says they can do whatever they like with me. Unthanked, possibly fatal service, anywhere in the world: called on to do things which may well be repugnant, and which I will never be able to talk about. Maybe no pension at all, just an unmarked grave in some isolated defile on a central Asian plateau, or a sock-shod foot washed up, unaccompanied, on a Pacific beach one morning while the crabs dine heavy. Nobody ever volunteered for field ops because of the pay and conditions. On the other hand . . .

I look at the starfish-thing and see eyes, human eyes, with worms moving inside them, and I realise that there is no choice. Really, there never was a choice.

3: DEFECTOR

THREE MONTHS LATER TO THE NEAREST MINUTE I am loosely attached to the US desk, working on my first field assignment. This would normally be an extremely stressful point in my career, except that this is very much a low-stress training mission, as Santa Cruz is one of the nicest parts of California, and right now having my fingernails pulled out by the Spanish Inquisition would be more pleasant than putting up with Mhari. So I'm making the most of it, sitting in a tacky bar down on a seaside pier, nursing a cold glass of Santa Cruz Brewing Company wheat beer, and watching the pelicans practice their touch-'n'-gos on the railing outside.

It's early summer and the temperature's in the mid-twenties; the beach is covered in babes, boardwalk refugees, and surf nazis. This being Santa Cruz I'm wearing cut-off jeans, a psychedelic T-shirt, and a back-to-front baseball cap but I can't kid myself about passing for a native. I've got the classic geek complexion – one a goth would kill for – and in Santa Cruz even the geeks get out in the sun once in a while. Not to mention wearing more than one earring.

My contact is a guy called Mo. Actually, I'm not sure that isn't a pseudonym. Nobody seems to know very much about the mysterious Mo, except he's an expatriate British academic, and he's having trouble coming home. All of which makes me wonder why the Laundry is involved at all, as opposed to the Consulate in San Francisco.

A bit of background is in order; after all, aren't the UK and the USA allies? Well, yes and no. No two countries have identical interests, and the result is a blurred area where self-interest causes erstwhile allies to act toward one another in a less than friendly manner. Mossad spies on the CIA; in the 1970s, Romania and Bulgaria spied on the Soviet Union. This doesn't mean their leaders aren't slurping each other's cigars, but . . .

In 1945 the UK and the USA signed a joint intelligence-sharing treaty that opened their most secret institutions to mutual inspection and exchange: at the time they were fighting a desperate war against a common enemy. Not many people outside the secret services understand just how close to the abyss we stood, even as late as April 1945: there's nothing like facing a diabolical enemy set on your complete destruction to cement an alliance at the highest level . . . and for the first few postwar years, the UK-USA treaty kept us singing from the same hymn book.

But UK-USA relations deteriorated over the following decade. Partly this was a side effect of the Helsinki Protocol; when even Molotov agreed that occult weapons of the type envisaged by Hitler's Thule Society minions were too deadly to use, a lot of the pressure came off the alliance. When it became apparent that the British intelligence system was riddled with Russian spies, the CIA turned the cold shoulder; thus, a background of shifting superpower politics was established, in which the moth-eaten British lion was unwillingly taught his place in the scheme of things by the new ringmaster, Uncle Sam. I suppose you could blame the Suez crisis and the Turing debacle, or Nixon's paranoia, but in 1958, when the UK offered to extend the 1945 treaty to cover occult intelligence, the US government refused.

My colleagues in GCHQ listen in on domestic US phone calls, compile logs, and pass them across the desk to their NSA liaisons – who are forbidden by charter from spying on domestic US territory. In return, the NSA Echelon listening posts give

GCHQ a plausibly deniable way of monitoring every phone conversation in western Europe – after all, they're not actually
listening; they're just reading transcripts prepared by someone
else, aren't they? But in the twilight world of occult intelligence,
we aren't allowed to cooperate overtly. I don't have a liaison here,
any more than I'd have one in Kabul or Belgrade: I'm technically
an illegal, albeit on a tourist visa. Any nasty reality excursions are
strictly my problem.

On the other hand, the days of midnight insertions – bailing
out of the back door of a bomber by midnight and trying not to
hang your parachute up on the Iron Curtain – are gone for good.
Gone, too, are the days of show trials for captured spies: if I get
caught, the worst I can expect is to be questioned and put on the
first flight home. My way into the country was more prosaic than
a wartime parachute drop, too: I flew in on an American Airlines
MD-11, filled out the visa waiver declaration ('occupation: civil
servant; purpose of visit: work assignment,' and no, I was not a
member of the German Nazi Party between 1933 and 1945), and
entered via the arrival hall at San Francisco Airport.

Which is how I find myself watching the pelicans on the pier at
Santa Cruz, sipping my beer sparingly, waiting for Mo to manifest himself, and trying to figure out just why a British academic
should be having so much trouble coming home as to need our
help – not to mention why the Laundry might be taking him
seriously.

I'm not the only customer in the bar, but I'm the only one
with a beer and a copy (unopened) of *Philosophical Transactions on
Uncertainty Theory* lying in front of me. That's my cover; I'm
meant to be a visiting postgrad student come to talk to the prof
about a possible teaching post. So when Mo walks in he should
have no difficulty identifying me. There are six professors of philosophy at UCSC: one tenured, two assistant, and three visiting. I
wonder which of them he is?

I glance around idly, just in case he's already here. There are two grunge metal skateboard types in the far corner, drinking Bud-Miller-Coors and comparing body piercings; the town's swarming with 'em, nothing to take note of. A gentleman in a plaid shirt, chinos, and short haircut sits on a bar stool on his own, back ramrod-straight, reading the *San Jose Mercury News*. (That dings my suspicion-o-meter because he looks very Company in a casual-Friday kind of way – but if they were tailing me why in hell would they make it so obvious? He might equally well be an affluent local businessman.) A trio of nrrrd grrrlzz with shaven scalps and unicorn forelocks compare disposable tattoos and disappear into the toilet one by one, going in glum and coming out giggly: must be a Bolivian marching powder dispenser or a mendicant sin-eater or something in there. I shake my head and sip my beer, then look up just as a rather amazing babe with classic red hair leans over me.

'Mind if I take this chair?'

'Um—' I'm trying desperately to think of an excuse, because my contact is looking for a single man with a copy of *PTUT* on the table in front of him. But she doesn't give me time:

'You can call me Mo. You would be Bob?'

'Yeah. Have a seat.' I blink rapidly at her, stuck for words. She sits down while I study her.

Mo is striking. She's a good six feet tall, for starters. Strong features, high cheekbones, freckles, hair that looks like you could wrap it in insulation and run the national grid through it. She's got these big dangly silver earrings with glass eyeballs, and she's wearing combat pants, a plain white top, and a jacket that is so artfully casual that it probably costs more than I earn in a month. Oh, and there's a copy of *Philosophical Transactions on Uncertainty Theory* in her left hand, which she puts down on top of mine. I can't estimate her age; early thirties? That would make her a real high-flyer. She catches me staring at her and stares back, challenging.

'Can I buy you a drink?' I ask.

She freezes for a moment then nods, emphatically. 'Pineapple juice.' I wave at the bartender, feeling more than a little flustered. Under her scrutiny I get the feeling that there's something of the

Martian about her: a vast, unsympathetic intelligence from another world. I also get the feeling that she doesn't suffer fools gladly.

'I'm sorry,' I say, 'nobody told me who to expect.' The local businessman looks across from his newspaper expressionlessly: he sees me watching and turns back to the sports pages.

'Not your problem.' She relaxes a little. The bartender appears and takes an order for a pineapple juice and another beer – I can't seem to get used to these undersized pints – and vanishes again.

'I'm interested in a teaching post,' I find myself saying, and hope her contact told her what the cover story is. 'I'm looking for somewhere to continue after my thesis. UCSC has a good reputation, so . . .'

'Uh-huh. Nice climate too.' She nods at the pelicans outside the window. 'Better than Miskatonic.'

'Really? You were there?'

I must have asked too eagerly because she looks at me bleakly and says, 'Yes.' I nearly bite my tongue. (Foreign female professor of philosophy in the snobbish halls of a New England college. Worse: non-WASP, judging from the Irish accent.) 'Some other time. What was the topic of your thesis again?'

Is it my imagination or does she sound half-amused? This isn't part of the script: we're meant to go for a walk and talk about things where we can't be overheard, not ad-lib it in a café. Plus, she thinks I'm from the Foreign Office. What the hell does she expect me to say, early Latin literature? 'It's about' – I mentally cross my fingers – 'a proof of polynomial-time completeness in the traversal of Hamiltonian networks. And its implications.'

She sits up a bit straighter. 'Oh, *right*. That's interesting.'

I shrug. 'It's what I do for a living. Among other things. Where do your research interests lie?'

The businessman stands up, folds his newspaper, and leaves.

'Reasoning under conditions of uncertainty.' She squints at me slightly. 'Not prior probabilities stuff, Bayesian reasoning based on statistics – but reasoning where there are no evidential bases.'

I play dumb: suddenly my heart is hammering between my ribs. 'And is this useful?'

She looks amused. 'It pays the bills.'

'Really?'

The amusement vanishes. 'Eighty percent of the philosophical logic research in this country is paid for by the Pentagon, Bob. If you want to work here you'll need to get your head around that fact.'

'Eighty percent—' I must look dumbfounded, because something goes *click* and she switches out of her half-sardonic *Brief Encounter* mode and into full professorial flow: 'A philosophy professor earns about thirty thousand bucks and costs maybe another five thousand a year in office space and chalk. A marine earns around fifteen thousand bucks and costs maybe another hundred thousand a year in barrack space, ammunition, transport, fuel, weapons, VA expenses, and so on. Supporting all the philosophy departments of the USA costs about as much as funding a single battalion of marines.' She looks wryly amused. 'They're looking for a breakthrough. Knowing how to deconstruct any opponent's ideological infrastructure and derive self-propagating conceptual viruses based on its blind spots, for example. That sort of thing would give them a real strategic edge: their psych-ops people would be able to make enemies surrender without firing a shot, and do so reliably. Cybernetics and game theory won them the Cold War, so paying for philosophers is militarily more sensible than paying for an extra company of marines, don't you think?'

'That's' – I shake my head – 'logical, but weird.' *No weirder than what they pay me to do*.

She snorts. 'It's not exceptional. Did you know that for the past twenty years they've been spending a couple of million a year on research into antimatter weapons?'

'Antimatter?' I shake my head again: I'm going to get a stiff neck at this rate. 'If someone figured out how to make it in bulk they'd be in a position to—'

'Exactly,' she says, and looks at me with a curiously satisfied expression. Why do I have a feeling she's seen right through me?

(Antimatter isn't the most exotic thing DARPA has been

spending research money on by a long way, but it's exotic enough for the average college professor; especially a philosopher who, reading between the lines, has any number of reasons for being cheesed off with the military-academic complex.)

'I'd like to talk about this some more,' I venture, 'but maybe this isn't the right place?' I take a mouthful of beer. 'How about a walk? When do you have to get back to your office?'

'I have a lecture to deliver at nine tomorrow, if that's what you're asking.' She pauses, delicately, tongue slightly extended: 'You're thinking about coming to work here, why don't I show you some of the sights?'

'That would be great.' We finish our drinks and leave the bar – and the bugs, real or imagined – behind.

I can be a good listener when I try. Mo – a diminutive of Dominique, I gather, which is why I couldn't find her on the university's staff roster – is a good talker, or at least she is when she has a lot to unload. Which is why we walk until I have blisters.

Seal Point is a grassy headland that abruptly turns into a cliff, falling straight down to the Pacific breakers. Some lunatics in wet-suits are trying to surf down there; I wouldn't want to underwrite their life insurance policies. About fifty feet away there's a rocky outcrop carpeted in sea lions. Their barking carries faintly over the crash of the surf. 'My mistake was in signing the nondisclosure agreements the university gave me without getting my own lawyer to check them out.' She stares out to sea. 'I thought they were routine academic application agreements, saying basically the faculty would get a cut from any commercial spin-offs from inventions I made while employed by them. I didn't read the small print closely enough.'

'How bad was it?' I ask, shifting from one foot to another.

'I didn't find out until I wanted to go visit my aunt in Aberdeen.' So much for my ear for accents. 'She was sick; they wouldn't give me a visa. Would you believe it, an exit visa from the USA? I was turned back at the security gate.'

'They're usually more worried about people trying to immigrate,' I say. 'Isn't that the case?'

'I'm not a US citizen; I've got British citizenship and a green card residence permit. I just happen to work here because, well, there aren't a lot of research posts in my speciality elsewhere. If I'd stayed with my ex-husband I'd be eligible for Israeli citizenship, too. But they won't let me leave. I didn't realise it would be like this.' She falls silent for a moment; seabirds squawk overhead. 'When the Immigration Service made trouble the Pentagon sorted them out, can you believe it? Told them to get off my case.'

I nod silently: this isn't good news. It means that someone, somewhere, thinks Mo is a strategic asset – *special treatment, kid gloves, do* not *let this one out of your sight*. We do similar things, sometimes: I'm not allowed to go on vacation outside the EU without written permission from my head of department. But that's because I do secret work for the government. Mo is just a professor, isn't she? I wish she'd be a bit more specific, and say which bit of the Pentagon is giving her grief, rather than just using it as a generic category for big government.

'When did the trouble start?' I ask.

She laughs. 'Which trouble?'

Me and my big mouth. 'Uh, the current batch. I'm sorry; nobody briefed me.'

She looks at me oddly. 'Just what kind of Foreign Office employee are you?'

I shrug. 'If you don't ask me any questions, I won't have to tell you any lies. I'm sorry, but I can't discuss my work. Let's just say that when you started complaining someone with a bit more clout than the consulate was listening. They sent me to see if there's anything we can do for you. All right?'

'Bizarre.' She looks askance at me. 'Let's walk.' She turns, and I follow her back toward the road. There's a footpath leading out of town, shaded by trees; we take it. 'The trouble started in Miskatonic,' she says. 'David and I – we're divorced, now – well, it didn't work out. I didn't play the politics right; Miskatonic is really bad for internal backbiting. When it was obvious they weren't going to open the tenure track up any time soon, I got a feeler from someone at UCSC. Nice research grant, an interesting field close to my own, and a promise of the fast track if I got results.'

Tenured professorship is the academic holy grail: a job for life, supposedly to let first-class researchers poke into any corner they feel like, regardless of how popular it is with the administration. Which is, of course, why they're trying to abolish it. 'How did it go?'

'I flew over for the interview. I got the job. Only there was a lot of paper to sign. David is a lawyer, but by then—' She falls silent. I can fill in some of the gaps, I think.

We're walking uphill now, and the path narrows. Dappled patterns of light and shade ripple across the dusty track. It's mid-afternoon and the day is hot and bright. A couple of surf dudes wander past and look at us curiously. 'How did you get into your current field of research?' I ask.

'Oh, it was a natural progression. In Edinburgh I was working on inferential reasoning. When I got the job in Arkham I started out doing more of the same, but the belief systems field has been undersubscribed for years, and it seemed like a good place to stake my claim, especially given the interesting closed archives in their stacks: Arkham has a really unique library, you know? I began publishing papers, and that's about when the shit began happening inside the department. Maybe it was departmental politics, but now I'm beginning to wonder.'

'They've got long tentacles, not to mention other nameless organs. It would help if I could see the documents you signed.'

'They're at the office. I can go in and pick them up later.' We're on a steep slope now, going uphill and I'm breathing hard. Mo has long legs and evidently walks a lot. Exercise or habit?

'Your research,' I say. 'You're certain it's not about any specific military applications?'

I know immediately that I've made a mistake. Mo stops and glares at me. 'I'm a philosopher, with a sideline in folk history,' she hisses angrily. 'What do you take me for?'

'I'm sorry.' I take a step back. 'I've got to make sure. That's all.'

'I shan't be offended then.' I get a creepy feeling that she means exactly what she says. 'No. It's just, I'm certain – no, positive, in the exact meaning of the word – that it's not that. A calculus of belief, a theory for deriving confidence limits in statements of unsubstantiated faith, can't have any military applications, can it?'

'Did you say *faith*?' I ask, hot and cold chills running up and down my spine. 'Specifically, you can analyse the validity of a belief, without—' I stop.

'Let's not get too technical without a whiteboard, hmm?'

'Faith can mean several things, depending on who uses the word,' I say. 'A theologian and a scientist mean different things by it, for example. And "unsubstantiated" has a dismayingly technical ring to it. But let's take a hypothetical example. Suppose I assert that I believe in flying pigs. I haven't seen any, but I have reason to believe that flying peccaries, a related species, exist. You're saying you could place confidence limits on my belief? Quantify the probability of those porcine aviators existing?'

'It works.' She shrugs. 'The numbers are out there. It's a platonic universe; all we can see are the shadows on the wall of the cave, but there are real numbers out there, they have an existence in and of themselves. I just began looking into probabilistic metrics that can be applied to assertions of a theological nature. There are some interesting documents in the Wilmarth folklore collection at Miskatonic . . .'

'Aha.' We round a corner and there's an odd little clearing ahead, ringed with trees, with a hillside rising from the far end. 'So we're back to the old idea of a real universe, and an observable one, and all we know about is what we can observe. So the department of strategic folklore in the Pentagon was concerned about you showing other people where to find their high-altitude hams?'

She stops and looks at me, frankly sizing me up. She comes to some sort of decision because after a moment she answers: 'I think they were more worried about the creatures that cast the shadows on the walls. In particular, the ones that ate the USS

Thresher and a certain Russian *Whisky*-class hunter-killer about thirty years ago . . .'

When I return to my motel room that evening the man in the plaid shirt from the bar is waiting for me. He's got a federal ID card, a warrant, and an attitude problem.

'Sit down, shut up, and listen,' he begins. 'I'm going to say this once, and once only. Then you're going to get the hell out of town because if you're still on this continent in twenty-four hours I'm going to have you arrested.'

I drop my jacket on the back of my chair. 'Who are you and what are you doing here?'

'I said shaddup.' He produces a laminated card and I make a show of looking at it. It says, basically, that someone who may or may not be in front of me works for the Office of Naval Intelligence – assuming I'd know an ONI pass if I tripped over one by accident. I think for a moment that he's unusually trusting for a law enforcement officer – they usually make with the guns before they go in – then I realise why and stifle a shudder. His eyes are dead, and there's a funny-looking scar on his forehead, which means the mind animating the body is probably in a bunker miles away. 'As far as I'm concerned, today you are a tourist. If you're still here tomorrow I will have to investigate the possibility that you are a foreign national engaged in activities detrimental to the security of this nation. But unless you tell me you're working for the Laundry right here and now, I don't have to act on that information until eighteen hundred hours tomorrow. Am I making myself clear?'

'What's the Laundry?' I ask, doing my best to look puzzled.

He snorts. 'Wise guy, huh? Get this through your head – we have wards and sensoids and watchers. We know who you people are, we've got you covered. We know where you live; we know where your dog goes to school. Get it?'

I shrug. 'I think you're making a mistake.'

'Well.' He tries the number four Marine Sergeant glare again, but it bounces off me. 'You're *wrong*. We don't make mistakes. You've just spent the past two hours speaking to a national security asset and we don't like that, Mr. Howard, we don't like it at all. Normally we'd just pull her security clearance and sling her ass on the next flight out, but the piece you've been talking to may be carrying around some items in her head that are not going to be allowed out of this country. Understand? The matter is under review. And if you happen to have overheard anything you shouldn't have, we're not going to let you out either. Luckily for you we happen to know she didn't tell you anything important. Now make yourself a history of not being here, and you'll be all right.'

I sit down and start taking my trainers off. 'Is that all you've got to say?' I ask.

Plaid Shirt snorts again: 'Is that all?' He walks over to the door. 'Yeah buddy, that's all,' he says, and opens it. Then there's a wet slapping sound and he falls over backward, leaking blood onto the carpet from both ears.

I roll sideways, out of the line of sight of the door, and grab for the small monkey's paw I wear on a leather thong round my neck. Electricity jolts the palm of my hand as the ward activates. ('Try not to get yourself killed on friendly territory,' said Andy: Some joke *that* turned out to be!) Plaid Shirt is blocking the suite door from closing and this is one of those California motels where all the doors open off balconies. I steady my nerves, then get myself turned round behind the bathroom sidewall and make a grab for his nearest arm.

They never tell you how heavy a corpse is in training school. I lean forward thoughtlessly to take a two-handed grip under his shoulder and that's when a mule punches my exposed shoulder. I fall over backward, dragging Plaid Shirt behind me, and the door swings shut.

The pool of blood is growing, but I have to be sure; the bullet hole is somewhere above his hairline. I force myself to look closer—

There are faint letters inscribed on his forehead in an ancient alphabet. They glow briefly then fade as I watch.

I do not feel good about sharing a motel room with a ballistically decommissioned intelligence agency spy. Unfortunately there appears to be a lunatic with a rifle waiting for me outside. I have an edgy feeling that the other shoe is about to drop within the next ninety seconds, and if I don't get out of here I'm going to be answering some pointed questions. Of course, I'm not really meant to last that long – or am I? Did they know about the standard-issue ward? Maybe if I'm lucky the ward will keep on working; they don't like taking direct hits, but they lose efficacy bit by bit, not all at once.

There's a loud blat of engine noise from outside the balcony; a motorbike with a blown muffler revs up then shrieks out of the car park on a trail of rubber. I grab my trainers, yank them on (wincing every time I flex my left arm), grab my jacket, wrap a hand around the dry-dusty object in the right front pocket, and yank the door open—

Just in time to see the bike vanishing down the road, and not a single cop in sight.

I duck into the bathroom and run the taps, then thrust my hands under them to rinse the blood away. They're shaking, I notice distantly. After a moment I start thinking very fast; then I dry my hands and go into the bedroom and pick up my mobile phone. The number I want is already programmed in.

'Hello? Winchester Waste Management?'

'Hi, this is Bob H-Howard speaking,' I say. 'I've had a bit of an accident and I could do with some cleaning services.'

'What did you say your address was?' asks the receptionist. I rattle off the hotel address. Then: 'What sort of cleaning do you require?'

'The bedcovers will need changing.' I think for a moment. 'And I cut myself shaving. I'm going to have to go to work now.'

'Okay, our crew will be around shortly.' She hangs up on me.

The coded message I sent translates as follows: 'Warning, my cover is shot. I've got to get out urgently, things are going bad, and under no circumstances should anyone approach me.' *I cut myself shaving:* 'Things turned bloody.' This sort of code, unlike a cypher, is virtually impossible to crack – as long as you never use it twice. With luck it'll take whoever's tapping the line a few minutes to realise that I've pushed the panic button.

I drop the bathroom towels over Plaid Shirt's leaking head, then grab my jacket and flight bag and cautiously nudge the front door open. Nothing nasty happens. I step out onto the balcony, lock the door behind me, and head down to the car park. All thought of getting Mo's travel arrangements in hand is gone: my immediate job is to drive north, drop the rental off at the airport, and bump myself onto the next available flight.

When I zap the car it doesn't explode: the doors unlock and the lights come on. Clutching my lucky monkey's paw I get in, start the engine, and drive away into the night, shaking like a leaf.

'Hello? Who is this?'

'Mo? This is Bob.'

'Bob—'

'Yeah. Look, about this afternoon.'

'It's so good to hear—'

'It was great seeing you too, but that's not what I'm calling about. Something's come up at home and I've got to leave. We'll be reviewing your case notes and seeing what pressure we can—'

'You've got to help me.'

'What? Of course we'll—'

'No, I mean right *now*! They're going to kill me. I'm locked up in here and they didn't search me so they didn't find my phone but—'

CLICK.

'What the fuck?'

I stare at the phone, then hastily switch it off and yank out the battery in case someone's trying to trace my cell.

'What *the fuck*?'

My head whirls. Oh yeah, a redheaded maiden in distress just asked me to rescue her: a chunk of me is cynically thinking that

I must be *really* hard up. There's a pithed spy in my hotel suite and my welcome mat is going to be withdrawn with extreme prejudice when his owners find out about it, just in time to get a cryptic phone call from my target who seems to be in fear for her life. What the – *whatever* – is going on, here?

In the Laundry we supposedly pride ourselves on our procedures. We've got procedures for breaking and entering offices, procedures for reporting a shortage of paper clips, procedures for summoning demons from the vasty deeps, and procedures for writing procedures. We may actually be on track to be the world's first ISO-9000 total-quality-certified intelligence agency. According to our written procedure for dealing with procedural cluster-fucks on foreign assignment, what I should do at this point is fill out Form 1008.7, then drive like a bat out of hell over Highway 17 until it hits the Interstate, then take the turnoff for San Francisco Airport and use my company credit card to buy the first available seat home. Not forgetting to file Form 1018.9 ('expenses unexpectedly incurred in responding to a situation 1008.7 in the line of duty') in time for the end of month accounting cycle.

Except if I do that – and if Mo's abductors are as friendly as my second visitor of the evening – I've just vaped the mission, screwed the pooch, written off the friendly I was supposed to be extracting, and blown my chances of a second date. (And we'll never find out whether the last thought to pass through the mind of the captain of the *Thresher* was, 'It's squamous and rugose,' or simply, 'It's squamous!')

Looking around, I see the parking lot is still empty. So I pull out, and roll through a U-turn across the railway tracks, and back into town. It's time to apply a little thought to the situation.

Mo lives in a rented flat not that far from the university campus. Now that I know her true name it takes me ten minutes with a map and a phone book to find it and drive over. There are no police cars outside and no sign of trouble; just a flat that's showing no lights. I know she's not home but I need something – anything – of hers so I park the car and briskly walk up the path to her front door, and knock as if I expect a welcome, hoping like hell that her abductors haven't left me a nasty surprise.

The screen door is shut but the inner door gapes open. Ten seconds with the blade of a multitool and the screen door's gaping too. The place is a mess – someone tipped over a low table covered in papers, there's a laptop inverted on the floor, and as my eyes become accustomed to the gloom I see a bookcase face down on the carpet in front of a corridor. I step over it, one hand in my pocket, looking for the bedroom.

The bedroom's a mess: maybe someone searched it in a hurry, or maybe she's the nesting kind. There's a pile of clothing by the bed that looks worn, so I bundle a T-shirt into my bag and head back to the car. Skin flakes, that's what I need; I try not to think too hard about what might be happening to her right now.

As I'm going down the path I see someone coming the other way. Middle-aged, male, thickset. 'Howdy,' he says, slightly suspiciously.

'Hi,' I say, 'just dropping by. Mo asked me to water her plants.'

'Oh.' Instant boredom, conjured by her name. 'Well, try not to leave your car there, it's blocking the disabled space.'

'I'll be gone before anyone notices,' I promise, and do my best to do just that.

Parked safely round the corner I pull out the T-shirt. In the dashboard light it looks faded; hopefully that'll do. I reach into my travel bag and pull out my hacked Palm computer, call up a specialised application that will erase itself if I don't enter a valid password within sixty seconds, pop open the expansion slot on its back, and swipe the concealed sensor across the fabric. *Oh great*: The arrow on the screen is pointing right back at me – I must have contaminated that swatch with my own biomagnetic whatever. Swearing, I restart the program and the machine promptly crashes. It takes another three tries before I get an arrow that's pointing somewhere else, and points in the same direction no matter which way I hold the gadget.

The wonders of modern technology.

An hour later I'm lying on my belly in the undergrowth at the edge of a stand of trees. I'm clutching a monkey's paw, a palmtop computer, and a cellphone; my mission, unless I choose to reject it, is to prevent a human sacrifice in the house in front of me – with no backup.

The hiss and crash of Pacific surf drowns out any noise from the road behind me. There's an onshore breeze, and along with the dampness of the ground – it rained earlier – it is making me shiver. The bruise on my left shoulder smarts angrily: I probably won't be able to move it in the morning. (My damn fault for getting in the way of a bullet. The kinetic impact binding worked its intended miracle but I'm not covered anymore.)

There's a truck parked in front of the carport, the house lights are on, and the curtains are drawn. Ten minutes ago a couple of guys came out the front door, took the dirt bike from the garage, drove straight across the lawn and onto the main road without pausing for traffic. I didn't get a good look at them, but an applet on my palmtop is screaming warnings at me: huge, honking great summoning fields are loose in the area, and judging by the subtype it's a gateway invocation that they're planning. They're actually going to try and open a mass-transfer gate to another universe – seriously bad juju. I've no idea who the hell these people are, or why they snatched Mo, but this is not looking good.

A flicker of light from the road; there's the snarl of a two-stroke engine, then the bike is turning back into the carport with its two passengers on board. One of them has a backpack . . . they've picked something up? Something they don't want to store too close to home? I hunker down lower, trying to make myself invisible. Take another reading, like the others I've made around this side of the garden. I think I've got a feel for it; a complex spiral of protection more than two hundred feet across, centred on the house. Major League paranoia, to protect something big that they're planning. This is where they've brought Mo – I wonder why? I sneak closer to a large window at the side, trying to keep the bushes between myself and the road, and hope like hell that there aren't any dogs here.

They've got the curtains drawn but the window itself is open – although there's some kind of bug screen in the way. I can hear voices. I don't recognize the language and they're muffled by the curtain, but there are more than two speakers. One of them laughs, briefly: it's not a pleasant sound. I settle back against the wall and take stock, trying not to breathe too loudly. Item: I'm sure Mo is in here, unless she's in the habit of lending her T-shirts out to strange swarthy men who perform major summoning rituals whenever she's kidnapped by somebody else. Item: they're not with ONI, or the Laundry. In fact, they're presumed hostile until proven otherwise. Item: there are at least four of them – two on the bike, two or more who stayed in here with Mo. I am not a one-man SWAT team and I am not trained in dealing with hostage-rescue situations, and like Harry said, setting out to be a hero without knowing what you're doing is a good way to end up dead. Hmm. What I need right now is a SWAT team, but I don't happen to have one up my sleeve. And aren't SWAT teams supposed to figure out where the hostage is and what's going on before they go storming through the building?

There is, of course, one constructive thing I can do, though it's going to get me yelled at when I go home. I switch my mobile phone back on, then fumble my way through its menus until I find the call log and tell it to dial the last caller. That would be Mo, and if ONI hasn't put a wiretap on her I'm a brass monkey's stepfather. It rings three times before there's an answer and I listen carefully, but there's nothing audible from inside the house.

'Who is this?' It's a man's voice, rather harsh-sounding.

I hold the mouthpiece very close to my lips: 'You're looking for Mo,' I say.

'Who is this?' he repeats.

'A friend. Listen. Where you find this phone you will find a house. There are several perps in the vicinity, at least four in the building. They've kidnapped Mo, they're building a Dho-Nha circle, at least level four, and you will want to take defensive precautions—'

'Stay right there,' says the man on the other end of the phone, so I carefully put it down under the window and scramble round to the back of the house on hands and knees. The front door bangs open. A different voice calls out, 'Is that you, Achmet?'

No answer. I hold my breath, heart pounding in my chest. Footsteps on gravel. 'The American bitch, she is secure.' I back away from the house toward the nearest clump of bushes – the men loom out of the shadows – but the footsteps halt. 'I stay out here. Cigarette.'

Bastard's on a fag break! I glance up at the sky, which is dark as a marketing hack's heart and full of coldly distant stars. *How am I going to get past him?* I grip the monkey's paw in my pocket, carefully withdraw it, and point it at the ground. A red-eyed coal glowers from the doorway, just visible round the side of the house. A distant buzzing bike engine grows louder, heading up the hills far above. Apart from that, the night is silent. *Too* silent, I realise after a minute; that's a road over there – where's the traffic? I begin to edge backward, trying to get farther into the bushes, and that's when everything blanks.

4: THE TRUTH IS
IN HERE

'You don't remember what happened next?'

'Yes, that's what I've been telling you for the past hour.' There's no point getting angry with them; they're just doing their job. I resist the temptation to rub my head, the dressing covering the sore patch behind my right ear. 'All I remember after that is waking up in hospital the next day.'

'Harrumph.' I blink; did I really hear someone say *harrumph*? Yes – it's the guy who looks like something the gravedigger's cat dragged in, Derek something or other. He blinks right back at me with watery eyes. 'According to page four of the medical notes, paragraph six—'

I watch while they all obediently shuffle their notes. Nobody thought to give me a copy, of course, even though they're mine. 'Contusion and hairline fracture on the right occipital hemisphere, some bruising and abrasion consistent with a weighted object.' I turn my head, wincing slightly because of the pain in my neck, and point to the dressing. It's been nearly a week; one thing they don't tell you in the detective potboilers is how bad being whacked on the head with a cosh hurts. No, not a cosh: an Object, Weighted, Black Chamber Field Operatives for the Use of, Complies with US-MIL-STD-534-5801.

'I suppose we can consider this to be substantiated, then,' says the talking corpse. 'Please continue where you left off.'

I sigh. 'I woke up in a hospital room with a needle in my arm and a goon from one of their TLAs baby-sitting me. After about an hour someone who claimed to be running Plaid Shirt turned up and started asking pointed questions. Seems they were already running a stakeout. After the third time that I explained what happened at the motel he agreed that I hadn't waxed their asset and demanded to know why I'd been round at the house. I told him that Mo phoned me and asked for help and it sounded urgent, and after I repeated myself another couple of dozen times he left. The next morning they shipped me to the airport and stuck me on the plane.'

The battle-axe from Accounting who's sitting next to Derek glares at me. '*Business* class,' she hisses. 'I suppose that was your idea of a good ride home?'

Huh? 'That was nothing to do with me,' I protest. 'Did they bill—'

'Yes.' Andy twirls his pen idly as a fly batters itself against the energy-saving lightbulb overhead.

'Uh-oh.' Unsanctioned expenditure isn't quite a hanging offense in the Laundry, but it's definitely up there with insubordination and mutiny. During the Thatcher years they were even supposed to have had paper clip audits, before someone pointed out that the consequences of poor employee morale in this organisation might be a trifle worse than in, say, the Ministry of Agriculture, Fisheries, and Food. 'Not guilty,' I say automatically, before I can stop myself. 'I didn't ask them for that, it happened after the assignment went pear-shaped, and I wasn't conscious at the time.'

'Nobody's accused you of authorising budgetary variances beyond your level of authorisation,' Andy says soothingly. He casts a quelling glance at Derek from Accounting, and then asks: 'What I'd like to know is why you went after her, though. SOP was to leave the area as soon as you were blown. Why did you stick around?'

'Uh—' My lips are dry because I've been expecting this one. 'I was going to leave. I was in the rental car and heading for the road out of town back to the airport, just as soon as I got out of the kill zone. I'd have done it too, except that Mo rang.'

I lick my lips again. 'I was sent to see if I could facilitate an extraction. I figured that meant someone thought Mo was worth extracting. My apologies if that isn't actually the case, but what I heard on the phone sounded like Mo had been abducted, and in the wake of the shooting I figured this was an even worse outcome than a blown mission and withdrawal. So I improvised, went round to her house and used my locator on her.

'I've been thinking about it a lot since then. What I should have done, I mean. I could have found where she was being held then driven back to the motel to find whoever was running that spy. Or something. Or headed for the airport and phoned from the departure lounge. All I can say is I was too involved. Some bastard had just tried to kill me; I mean, ONI was bugging Mo. When I phoned, they had put a diversion on her line, which is how come I was able to tell them where to look. But they probably already *knew*, I mean, when Mo called me on her pocket mobile that would have tipped them off.'

I empty the glass of water down my throat and put it back on the table in front of me.

'Look, I figure ONI or some other TLA outfit – say, the Black Chamber pretending to be ONI investigators – was watching Mo and picked up on me as soon as we made contact. It was a stitch-up. Whoever tried to shoot me and snatch her took them by surprise. That wasn't in the script. I know I should have come home then, but at that point I think everyone was off balance. Who the fuck *were* those loons, anyway? A major summoning in public—'

'You have no need to know,' Derek says snippily. 'Drop it!'

'Okay.' I lean back in my chair, tipping it on two legs; my head aches abominably. 'I get the picture.'

My third interrogator pipes up in a reedy voice: 'This isn't the whole story, is it, Robert?'

I stare at her, annoyed. 'Probably not, no.'

Bridget is a blonde yuppwardly-mobile executive, her sights fixed on the dizzying heights of the cabinet office in seeming ignorance of the bulletproof glass ceiling that hovers over all of us who work in the Laundry. Her main job description seems to be making life shitty for everybody farther down the ladder, principally by way of her number one henchperson, Harriet. She holds forth, strictly for the record: 'I'm unhappy about the way this assignment was set up. This was supposed to be a straightforward meet-and-pitch session, barely one rung up from having our local consul pay a social call. With all due respect, Robert is not a particularly experienced representative and should not have been sent into such a situation without mentoring—'

'It's friendly soil!' Andy interrupts.

'As friendly as it gets without a bilateral arrangement, which is to say, *not* an *active* joint-intelligence-sharing, committee-sanctioned, liaison environment. Foreigners, in other words. Robert was pushed out in the cold without oversight or adequate support from higher management, and when things went off the rails he quite naturally did his best, which wasn't quite good enough.' She smiles dazzlingly at Andy. 'I'd like to minute that he needs additional training before being subjected to solo exercises, and I'd also like to say that I think we need to review the circumstances leading up to this assignment closely in case they are symptomatic of a weakness in our planning and accountability loop.'

Oh great. Andy looks almost as disgusted as I feel. Bridget has just damned us – everyone else, in fact – with faint praise. I did 'as well as could be expected' and need extra supervision before I can be let out of the kindergarten to go pee-pee. Derek and Andy and everyone else involved get to have Bridget poke her long, inquisitive nose into their procedural compliance and see if they're exercising due diligence. As for Bridget, if she turns up anything that even whiffs of negligence she gets to look good to the top brass by cleaning shop, and anyone who disagrees is being 'grossly unprofessional.' Office politics, the Laundry remix.

'My head aches,' I mutter. 'And my body is telling me that it's two in the morning. Do you have any more questions? If you don't mind, I'm going to go home and lie down for a day or two.'

'Take all week,' Andy says dismissively. 'We'll have everything sorted out when you get back.' I stand up fast; in my current state I don't think to ask what strange and perverted definition of 'sorted' he's using.

'I'd like to see a written report of your trip,' Bridget adds before I can close the door behind me. 'Documented in accordance with Operations Manual Four, chapter eleven, section C. No need to hurry, but I want it on my desk by the end of next week.'

Evidence, Written, Bureaucrats for the Malicious Use of. I head for home, anticipating a long hot bath and then eighteen hours in the sack.

Home is much as I left it seven days ago. There's a pile of bills slowly turning brown at the corner propping up one of the kitchen table legs. The bin is overflowing, the kitchen sink likewise, and Pinky hasn't cleaned out his bread-maker since the last time he used it. I look in the fridge and find a limp tea bag and a carton of milk that's good for another day or so before it starts demanding the vote, so I make myself a mug of tea and sit at the kitchen table playing Tetris on my palmtop. Coloured blocks fall like snowflakes in my mind, and I drift for a while. But reality keeps intruding: I've got a week's washing in my suitcase, another week of washing in my room, and while Pinky and the Brain are at work I can get to the washer/dryer. (Assuming nobody's left a dead hamster in it again.)

Deliberately ignoring the bills, I get up and drag my suitcase upstairs. My room is much the way I left it, and I suddenly realise that I hate living this way: hate the secondhand furniture designed by aliens from Planet Landlord, hate sharing my personal space with a couple of hyperintelligent slobs with behavioural problems and explosive hobbies, hate feeling my future possibilities hemmed in by my personal vow of poverty – the signature on my Laundry warrant card. I drag the suitcase into my room through a fog of fatigue and mild despair, then open it and begin to sort everything into piles on the floor.

Something snuffles behind me.

I spin round so fast I nearly levitate, hand fumbling for a

mummified monkey's paw that isn't there — then recognition cuts in and I breathe again. 'You startled me! What are you doing in there?'

Just the top of her head is visible. She blinks at me sleepily. 'What does it look like?'

I consider my next words carefully. 'Sleeping in my bed?'

She pulls down the duvet far enough to yawn, mouth pink and grey in the dim light that filters through the new curtains. 'Yeah. Heard you were due back today so I, mmm, pulled a sickie. Wanted to see you.'

I sit down on the side of the bed. Mhari's hair is mousy-brown with blonde highlights she puts in it every few weeks; it's cut in short flyaway locks that tangle around my fingers when I run my hand over her scalp. 'Really?'

'Yeah, really.' A bare arm reaches out of the bedding, wraps around my waist, and pulls me down. 'Been missing you. Come here.'

I'm meaning to sort my dirty clothing into piles for the washing machine, but instead all my clothing ends up in a heap in the middle of the floor, and I end up in a heap under Mhari, who is naked under the duvet and seemingly intent on giving me a very warm welcome home, if not a rinse and tumble-dry. 'What *is* this?' I try to ask, but she grabs my head and holds my mouth against one generously proportioned nipple. I get the message and shut up. Mhari is in the mood, and this is about the one situation in which our relationship functions smoothly. Besides, it's more than a week since the last time I've seen her, and being ambushed this way is the best thing that's happened to me in quite a while.

About an hour later, fucked-out and completely exhausted — to say nothing of sweaty — we're lying in a tangle on the bed (the duvet seems to have decided to join the washing pile) and she's making buzzing noises in the back of her throat like a cat. 'What brought this on?' I ask.

'I needed you,' she says, with the kind of innocent egotism that a cat could only envy. Grabs at my back: 'Mmm. Hmm. Had a bad week.'

'A bad week?' I'm practising being a good listener; it's usually opening my mouth that gets me into trouble with her.

'First there was a complete mess at the office: Eric was off sick and dropped the ball on a case he was handling and I had to pick up the pieces. Ended up working late three nights running. Then there was a party at Judy's. Judy got me drunk, introduced me to a friend of hers. He turned out to be a real shit, but only after—'

I roll away. 'I wish you wouldn't do this,' I hear myself saying.

'Do what?' She looks at me, hurt.

I sigh. 'Never mind.' Never *fucking* mind, I try not to say. I suddenly feel really dirty. 'I'm going to have a shower, I say, and sit up.

'Bob!'

'Never mind.' I get up, grab a dirty towel from the pile on the floor, and head for the bathroom to wash her off me.

Mhari has a problem: her problem is me. I should just tell her to fuck off and die, sever all links, refuse to talk to her – but she's good company when we're on speaking terms, she can push all my buttons correctly when we're in bed, and she can get right under my skin and leave me feeling about five and a half inches high. My problem is that she wants to trade me in on New Boyfriend, model 2.0, one with a fast car and a Rolex Oyster and prospects. (Warped senses of humour and dead-end Laundry postings are strictly optional.) She's permanently on the rebound, either toward me or away from me – I can't always tell which – and in between she uses me the way a cat uses a scratching post. Partying at Judy's place, for example: Judy is a mindless management functionary bimbo friend of hers who is somehow always impeccably turned out and manages to make me feel like a dirty little schoolboy, although she's far too polite to ever say anything. So when Mhari traps off with some double-glazing salesman she meets via Judy and he turfs her out of his bed the next morning, I'm supposed to be around as a friendly consolation fuck the next day.

My problem is that she doesn't seem to appreciate that I hate being on the receiving end of this. If I try to make a big deal of it she'll accuse me of being jealous and I'll end up feeling obscurely guilty. If I don't make a big deal of it she'll continue to act like I'm some kind of doormat. And who knows? Maybe I'm just being paranoid and she *isn't* looking around for Mr. New Boyfriend. (Yeah, and wild boars have been spotted in the holding pattern over Heathrow with an engine under each wing.)

I haven't had to chase any strangers out of my bed yet, but with Mhari around I keep wondering when it'll happen. The worst of it is, I don't want to just cut things dead; I'd rather she stopped playing games than she stopped seeing me. Perhaps it's self-deception, but I think we could make things work. Maybe.

I'm in the shower cubicle washing my hair when I hear the door open. 'I do not appreciate hearing about your one-night stands,' I say, eyes closed to avoid the sting of shampoo. 'I don't understand why the fuck you hang around me when you're obviously so eager to find someone else. But will you please leave me alone for a bit?'

'Oops, sorry,' says Pinky, and closes the door.

He's waiting on the landing when I finish in the bathroom; we studiously avoid each other's eyes. 'Uh, it's okay to go into your room,' he volunteers. 'She's gone out.'

'Oh good.'

He hurries after me as I head downstairs. 'She asked me to have a word with you,' he calls breathlessly.

'That's fine,' I say distantly. 'Just as long as she isn't asking you to share my bed.'

'She says you need to check out the alt.polyamory FAQ,' he says, and cringes.

I switch the kettle on and sit down. 'Do you really think I have a problem?' I ask. 'Or does *Mhari* have a problem?'

He glances around, trapped. 'You have incompatible lifestyle choices?' he ventures.

The kettle hisses like an angry snake. 'Very good. Incompatible lifestyle choices is such a fucking *civilised* way of putting it.'

'Bob, do you think she might be doing this to get your attention?'

'There are good ways and bad ways to get my attention.

Whacking on my ego with a crowbar will get my attention, sure, but it's not going to leave me well disposed to the messenger.' I pour more hot water into my mug of tea, then stand up and rummage in the cupboard. *Ah, it's right where I left it.* I upend a generous dollop of Wray and Nephew's overproof Jamaican rum into the mug and sniff: brown sugar crossed with white lightning. 'The male ego is a curious thing. It's about the size of a small continent but it's extremely brittle. Drink?'

Pinky sits down opposite me, looking as if he's sharing the kitchen table with an unexploded bomb. 'Why not look on the bright side?' he says, holding out a Coke glass for the rum.

'There's a bright side?'

'She keeps coming back to you,' he says. 'Maybe she's doing it to hurt herself?'

'To—' I bite off the snide reply I was working on. When Mhari gets depressed she gets *depressed*: I've seen the scars. 'I'll have to think about that one,' I say.

'Well, then.' Pinky looks pleased with himself. 'Doesn't that look better? She's doing it because she's depressed and hates herself, not because there's anything wrong with you. It's not a reflection on your virile manhood, you big hunk of beefcake. Go get yourself a one nighter of your own and she'll have to make her mind up what she wants.'

'Is that in the FAQ?' I ask.

'I dunno; I don't pay much attention to breeder reproductive rituals,' he says, fingering his moustache.

'Thank you, Pinky,' I say heavily. He does a little wave and bow, then tips the contents of his glass down his throat. I spend the next minute or two helping save him from choking, and then we have another wee dram. The rest of the afternoon becomes a blur, but when I wake up in bed the next morning I have a stunning hangover, a vague memory of drunkenly talking things over with Mhari for hours on end until it blew up into a flaming row, and I'm on my own.

Situation normal: all fucked up.

*

Two days later, I am booked into an Orientation and Objectivity seminar at the Dustbin. Only God and Bridget – and possibly Boris, though he won't say anything – know *why* I'm booked into an O&O course three days after getting off the plane, but something dire will probably happen if I don't turn up.

The Dustbin isn't part of the Laundry, it's regular civil service, so I try to dig up a shirt that isn't too crumpled, and a tie. I own two ties – a Wile E. Coyote tie, and a Mandelbrot set tie that's particularly effective at inducing migraines – and a sports jacket that's going a bit threadbare at the cuffs. Don't want to look too out of place, do I? Someone might ask questions, and after the *auto-da-fé* I've just been through I do not want anyone mentioning my name in Bridget's vicinity for the next year. I'm halfway to the tube station before I remember that I forgot to shave, and I'm on the train before I notice that I'm wearing odd socks, one brown and one black. But what the hell, I made the effort; if I actually owned a suit I'd be wearing it.

The Dustbin is our name for a large, ornate postmodernist pile on the south bank of the Thames, with green glass curtain walls and a big, airy atrium and potted Swiss cheese plants everywhere there isn't a security camera. The Dustbin is occupied by a bureaucratic organisation famous for its three-hour lunches and impressive history of KGB alumni. This organisation is persistently and mistakenly referred to as MI5 by the popular media. As anyone in the business knows, MI5 was renamed DI5 about thirty years ago; like those Soviet-era maps that misplaced cities by about fifty miles in order to throw American bombers off course, DI5 is helpfully misnamed in order to direct freedom of information requests to the wrong address. (As it happens there is an organisation called MI5; it's in charge of ensuring that municipal waste collection contracts are outsourced to private bidders in a fair and legal manner. So when your Freedom of Information Act writ comes back saying they know nothing about you, they're telling the truth.)

The Dustbin cost approximately two hundred million pounds to construct, has a wonderful view of the Thames and the Houses of Parliament, and is full of rubbish that smells. Whereas we loyal servants of the crown and defenders of the human race against nameless gibbering horrors from beyond spacetime have to labour on in a Victorian rookery of cabbage-coloured plasterboard walls and wheezing steam pipes somewhere in Hackney. That's because the Laundry used to be part of an organisation called SOE – indeed, the Laundry is the sole division of SOE to have survived the bureaucratic postwar bloodletting of 1945 – and the mutual loathing between SIS (aka DI6) and SOE is of legendary proportions.

I turn up at the Dustbin and enter via the tradesman's entrance, a windowless door in a fake-marble tunnel near the waterfront. A secretary who looks like she's made of fine bone china waves me through the biometric scanner, somehow manages to refrain from inhaling in my presence (you'd think I hailed from the Pestilence Division at Porton Down), and finally ushers me into a small cubicle furnished with a hard wooden bench (presumably to make me feel at home). The inner door opens and a big, short-haired guy in a white shirt and black tie clears his throat and says, 'Robert Howard, this way please.' I follow him and he drops one of those silly badge-chains over my head then pushes me through a metal detector and gives me a cursory going over with a wand, airport security style. I grit my teeth. They know exactly who I am and who I work for: they're just doing this to make a point.

He relieves me of my Leatherman multitool, my palmtop computer, my Maglite torch and pocket screwdriver set, the nifty folding keyboard, the MP3 walkman, the mobile phone, and a digital multimeter and patch cable set I'd forgotten about. 'What's all this, then?' he asks.

'Do you guys ever go anywhere without your warrant card and handcuffs? Same difference.'

'I'll give you a receipt for these,' he says disapprovingly, and shoves them in a locker. 'Stand on this side of the red line for now.' I stand. Something about him makes my built-in police detector peg out; Special Branch acting as uniformed commissionaires? *Yeah, right.* 'Present this on your way out to collect your stuff. You may now cross the red line. Follow me, do not, repeat *not*, open any closed doors or enter any areas where a red light is showing, and don't speak to anyone without my say-so.'

I follow my minder through a maze of twisty little cubicle farms, all alike, then up three floors by elevator, then down a corridor where the Swiss cheese plants are turning yellow at the edges from lack of daylight, and finally to the door of what looks like a classroom. 'You can talk now; everyone else in this class is cleared to at least your level,' he says. 'I'll come collect you at fifteen hundred hours. Meanwhile, go anywhere you want on this level — there's a canteen where you'll have lunch, toilet's round that corner there — but don't leave this floor under any circumstances.'

'What if there's a fire?' I ask.

He looks at me witheringly: 'We'd arrest it. I'll see you at three o'clock,' he says. 'And not before.'

I enter the classroom, wondering if teacher is in yet.

'Ah, Bob, nice to see you. Have a seat. Hope you found us okay?'

I get a sinking feeling: it's Nick the Beard. 'I'm fine, Nick,' I say. 'How's Cheltenham?' Nick is some sort of technical officer from CESG, based out at Cheltenham along with the other wire-tap folks. He drops round the Laundry every so often to make sure all our software is licensed and we're only running validated COTS software purchased via approved suppliers. Which is why, whenever we get word that he's about to visit, I have to run around rebooting servers like crazy and loading the padded-cell environments we keep around purely to placate CESG so they don't blacklist our IT processes and get our budget lopped off at the knees. Despite that, Nick is basically okay, which is why I get the sinking feeling; I don't enjoy treating nice guys like they're agents of Satan or Microsoft salesmen.

'They moved me out of the hole on the map two months ago,' he says. 'I'm based here full-time now. Miriam's got a job in the city, so we're thinking of moving. Have you met Sophie? I think she's running this course today.'

'Don't think so. Who else is coming? What do you know

about, um, Sophie? Nobody even showed me a course synopsis; I'm not sure why I'm here.'

'Oh, well then.' He rummages in his brief case and pulls out a sheet of paper, hands it to me: *Orientation and Objectivity 120.4: Overseas Liaison.*

I start reading: *This seminar is intended to provide inductees with the correct frame of mind for conducting negotiations with representatives of allied agencies. Common pitfalls are discussed with a view to inculcating a culture of best practice. A proactive approach to integrating operational agreements with extraterritorial parties is deprecated, and correct protocol for requesting diplomatic assistance is introduced. Status: completion of this seminar and associated coursework is mandatory for foreign postings in Category 2 (nonallied) positions.*

'Ah, really,' I say faintly. 'How interesting.' (Thank you, Bridget.)

'All I wanted was to visit the factory that supplies our PCs out in Taiwan,' Nick mutters darkly. 'All part of our ISO certification cycle, assuring that they're following best industry practices in motherboard assembly and testing . . .'

The door opens. 'Ah, Nick! Nice to see you! How's Miriam?'

It's a new arrival. He's the very image of a schoolteacher: a thin, weedy-looking guy with big horn-rimmed spectacles and thinning hair. Except, when he positively leaps into the room, he gives the impression of being made of springs. Nick obviously knows him: 'She's fine, fine – and how are you yourself? Uh, Bob, have you met Alan?'

'Alan?' I stick out a hand tentatively. 'With what department? If I'm allowed to ask?'

'Umm—' He pumps my hand up and down then looks at me oddly as I nurse my bruised fingertips – he's got a grip like a vice. 'Probably not, but that's okay,' he announces. 'Let's not get carried away, eh!' Over his shoulder to Nick: 'Hillary's fine, but she's having a devil of a time with the guns. We're going to need a new cupboard soon, and the rental in Maastricht is horrible.'

Guns? 'Alan and I belong to the same shooting club,' Nick explains diffidently. 'With all the fuss a few years ago we had to either move our guns out of the country to somewhere where it's legal to own them, or turn them in. Most of us turned ours in and use the club facilities, but Alan's a holdout.'

'Handguns?'

'No, long arms. That's recreational shooting, by the way. I'm just an amateur but Alan takes it a bit more seriously – trained for the Olympics a way back.'

'What's the club?' I ask.

'Damned impudent infringement of our civil rights,' Alan huffs. 'Not trusting their own citizens to own automatic weapons: a bad sign. But we do what we can. Artists' Rifles, by the way. Drop in if you're ever in the neighbourhood, ha ha. So we're just waiting for Sophie now.'

'Could be worse.' Nick ambles over to the table beside the door and prods at what looks like a thermos jug. 'Ah, coffee!' I kick myself mentally for not noticing it first.

'You going anywhere?' asks Alan.

'Just back.' I shrug. 'Didn't even know this course existed.'

'Business or pleasure?'

'Milk or sugar, Alan?'

'Business. I wish it *had* been pleasure. They didn't brief me and nothing was the way I expected it—'

'Ha ha. Milk, no sugar. Typical Laundry turf war, by the sound of it. So your boss's boss's first cousin sent you for remedial classes, stay late after school, dunce cap in the corner, the usual rigmarole?'

'That's about it. Hey, pour me one too?'

'Seen it a dozen times before,' offers Nick. 'Nobody ever thinks to *tell* anyone when they're expected—' I yawn. 'You tired?'

'Still jetlagged, thanks.' I blow on my coffee.

The door opens and a woman in a brown tweed suit – Sophie, I presume – walks in. 'Hello, everybody,' she says. 'Alan, Nick – you must be Bob.' A brief grin. 'Glad you're all here. Today we're going to go over some basic material by way of reminding you of the proper protocol for dealing with foreign agencies while posted abroad on neutral or friendly but not allied territory.' She plonks a bulging briefcase down on the desk at the front of the class-room.

'If I can just confirm – all three of you are due to fly out to California in the next few days, is that right?'

Uh-oh. 'I'm just back,' I say.

'Oh dear. You've done the 120.4 course before, then? This is just a refresher?'

I take a deep breath. 'I can honestly say that the fact that this seminar exists is news to both myself and my immediate super-visors. I think that's why I'm here now.'

'Oh well!' She smiles brightly. 'We'll soon see about that. Just as long as your trip was productive and nothing went wrong! This course is about procedures that should only be necessary in event of an emergency, after all.' She digs into the case and hands us each a hefty wedge of course notes. 'Shall we begin?'

It's been six weeks since I was certified fit active duty, and three weeks since I came back from Santa Cruz in business class with a bandage around my head. Bridget has had her little joke, I've suf-fered through about two weeks of seminars intended to bolt, padlock, and weld shut the stable door in the wake of the equine departure, and I'm slowly going out of my skull with boredom.

For my sins I've been posted to a pokey little office in the Dansey Wing of Service House – little more than a broom closet off a passageway under the eaves, roof wreathed in hissing steam pipes painted black for no obvious reason. There's a valuable antique that Services claims is a computer network server, and when I'm not nursing it from one nervous breakdown to the next I am expected to file endless amounts of paperwork and prepare a daily abstract based on several classified logs and digests that cross my desk. The abstract is forwarded to some senior execu-tives, then shredded by a guy in a blue suit. In between, I'm expected to make the tea. I feel like a twenty-six-year-old office boy. Overqualified, naturally. To add insult to injury, I have a new job title: Junior Private Secretary.

I would, I think, be right out of my skull and halfway down the road by now, chased by men in white coats wielding oversized butterfly nets, were it not for the fact that the word 'secretary' means something very different from its normal usage in the steamy little world of the Laundry. Y'see, before the 1880s, a secretary was a gentleman's assistant: someone who kept the secrets. And there are secrets to be kept, here in the Arcana Analysis Section. In fact, there's a whole bloody wall of filing cabinets full of 'em right behind my cramped secretarial chair. (Some wag has plastered a Post-it note on one of the drawers: THE TRUTH IS IN HERE, SOMEWHERE.) I'm learning things all the time, and apart from the bloody filing work, not to mention the coffee pot from hell and the network server from heck, it's mostly okay. Except for Angleton. Did I mention Angleton?

I'm standing in for Angleton's junior private secretary, who is on sabbatical down at the funny farm or taking a year out doing an MBA or something. And therein lies my problem.

'Mr. Howard!' That's Angleton, calling me into the inner sanctum.

I stick my head round his door. 'Yes, boss?'

'Enter.' I enter. His office is large, but feels cramped; every wall — it's windowless — is shelved floor-to-ceiling in ledgers. They're not books, but microfiche binders: each of them contains as much data as an encyclopaedia. His desk looks merely odd at first sight, an olive-drab monolith bound with metal strips, supporting the TV-sized hood of a fiche reader. It's only when you get close enough to it to see the organlike pedals and the cardhopper on top that, if you're into computational archaeology, you realise that Angleton's desk is an incredibly rare, antique Memex — an information appliance out of 1940s CIA folklore.

Angleton looks up at me as I enter, his face a blue-lit washout of text projected from the Memex screen. He's nearly bald, his chin is two sizes two small for his skull, and his domed scalp gleams like bone. 'Ah, Howard,' he says. 'Did you find the material I requested?'

'Some of it, boss,' I say. 'Just a moment.' I duck out into my office and pick up the hulking dusty tomes that I've carried up from the stacks, two basements and a fifty-metre elevator ride below ground level. 'Here you are. *Wilberforce Tangent* and *Opal Orange*.'

He takes the tomes without comment, opens the first of them, and starts sliding card-index sized chunks of microfilm into the Memex input hopper. 'That will be all, Howard,' he says superciliously, dismissing me.

I grit my teeth and leave Angleton to his microfilm. I once made the mistake of asking why he uses such an antique. He stared at me as if I'd just waved a dead fish under his nose, then said, 'You can't read Van Eck radiation off a microfilm projector.' (Van Eck radiation is the radio noise emitted by a video display; with sophisticated receivers you can pick it up and eavesdrop on a computer from a distance.) Back then I hadn't learned to keep my mouth shut around him: 'Yeah, but what about Tempest shielding?' I asked. That's when he sent me off to the stacks for the first time, and I got lost for two hours on sublevel three before I was rescued by a passing vicar.

I go into my outer office, pull out the file server's administration console, log on, and join the departmental Xtank tournament. Fifteen minutes later Angleton's bell dings; I put my game avatar on autopilot and look in on him.

Angleton positively glowers at me over his spectacles. 'Check these files back into storage, sign off, then come back here,' he says. 'We need to talk.'

I take the tomes and back out of his office. Gulp: he's *noticed* me! Whatever next?

The elevator down to the stacks is about to depart when I stick my foot in the door, holding it. Someone with a whole document trolley has got her back to me. 'Thanks,' I say, turning to punch in my floor as the door closes and we begin our creaky descent into the chalk foundations of London.

'No bother.' I look round and see Dominique with the doctorate from Miskatonic: Mo, whom I last saw stranded in America, phoning me for help on a dark night. She looks surprised to see me. 'Hey! What are you doing here?'

'It's a long story, but to cut it short I was shipped home after you phoned me. Seems those goons who were watching you picked me up. What about you? I thought you were having trouble getting an exit visa?'

'Are you kidding?' She laughs, but doesn't sound very amused. 'I was kidnapped, and when they rescued me I was *deported*! And when I got back here—' Her eyes narrow.

The lift doors open on subbasement two. 'You were conscripted,' I say, sticking my heel in the path of one door. 'Right?'

'If you had anything to do with it—'

I shake my head. 'I'm in more or less the same boat, believe it or not; it's how about two-thirds of us end up here. Look, my *Obergruppenführer* will send his SS hellhounds after me if I'm not back in his office in ten minutes, but if you've got a free lunchtime or evening I could fill you in?'

Her eyes narrow some more. 'I'll bet you'd like that.' *Ouch!* 'Have some good excuses ready, Bob,' she says, rolling her file cart toward me. I notice absently that it's full of *Proceedings of the Scottish Society of Esoteric Antiquaries* from the nineteenth century as I dodge out of the lift.

'No excuses,' I promise, 'only the truth.'

'Hah.' Her smile is unexpected and enigmatic; then the lift doors slide shut, taking her down farther into the bowels of the Stacks.

The Stacks are in what used to be a tube station, built during World War Two as an emergency bunker and never hooked up to the underground railway network. There are six levels rather than the usual three, each level built into the upper or lower half of a cylindrical tube eight metres in diameter and nearly a third of a kilometre long. That makes for about two kilometres of tunnels and about fifty kilometres of shelf space. To make matters worse, lots of the material is stored in the form of microfiche – three by five film cards each holding the equivalent of a hundred pages of text – and some of the more recent stuff is stored on gold CDs (of which the Stacks hold, at a rough guess, some tens of thousands). That all adds up to a *lot* of information.

We don't use the Dewey Decimal Catalogue to locate volumes in here; our requirements are sufficiently specialised that we have to use the system devised by Professor Angell of Brown University and subsequently known as the Codex Mathemagica. I've spent the past few weeks getting my head around the more arcane aspects of a cataloguing system that uses surreal number theory and can cope with the N-dimensional library spaces of Borges. You might think this a deadly boring occupation, but the ever-present danger of getting lost in the stacks keeps you on your toes. Besides which, there are rumours of ape-men living down here; I don't know how the rumours got started, but this place is more than somewhat creepy when you're on your own late at night. There's something weird about the people who work in the stacks, and you get the feeling it could be infectious – in fact, I'm really hoping to be assigned some other duty as soon as possible.

I locate the stack where the *Wilberforce Tangent* and *Opal Orange* files came from and wind the aisles of shelving apart to make way; they are both dead agent files from many years ago, musty with the stench of bureaucratic history. I slide them in, then pause: next to *Opal Orange* there's another file, one with a freshly printed binding titled *Ogre Reality*. The name tickles my silly gland, and in a gross violation of procedure I flip it out of the shelves and check the contents page. It's all paper, at this stage, and as soon as I see the MOST SECRET stamp I move to flip it shut – then pause, my eyeballs registering the words 'Santa Cruz' midway down the first page. I begin speed-reading.

Five minutes later, the small of my back soaked in a cold sweat, I replace the file on the shelf, wind them back together, and head for the lift as fast as my feet will carry me. I don't want Angleton to think I'm late *especially* after reading that file. It seems I'm lucky enough to be alive as it is . . .

'Pay attention to this, Mr. Howard. You are in a privileged position; you have access to information that other people would literally kill for. Because you stumbled into the Laundry through a second-floor window, so to speak, your technical clearance is several levels above that which would be assigned to you if you were a generic entrant. In one respect, that is useful; all organ-isations need junior personnel who have high clearances for certain types of data. On another level, it's a major obstacle.' Angleton points his bony middle finger at me. 'Because you have no *respect*.'

He's obviously seen *The Godfather* one time too many. I find myself waiting for a goon to step out of the shadows and stick a gun in my ear. Maybe he just doesn't like my T-shirt, a picture of a riot cop brandishing a truncheon beneath the caption 'Do not question authority.' I swallow, wondering what's coming up next.

Angleton sighs deeply, then stares at the dark greenish oil painting that hangs on his office wall behind the visitor's hot seat. 'You can fool Andrew Newstrom but you can't fool me,' he says quietly.

'You know Andy?'

'I trained him when he was your age. He has a commitment that is in short supply these days. I know just how devoted to this organisation *you* are. Draftees back in my day used to understand what they'd got themselves into, but you young ones . . .'

'Ask not what you can do for your country, but what your country has ever done for you?' I raise an eyebrow at him.

He snorts. 'I see you understand your deficiencies.'

I shake my head. 'Not me – that's not my problem. I decided I want to make a career here. I know I don't have to – I know what the Laundry's for – but if I just sat around under the cam-eras waiting for my pension I'd get *bored*.'

Those eyes are back on me, trying to drill right through to the back of my head. 'We know that, Howard. If you were simply serving your time you'd be back downstairs, counting hairs on a caterpillar or something until retirement. I've seen your record and I am aware that you are intelligent, ingenious, resourceful, technically adept, and no less brave than average. But that does-n't alter what I've said one bit: you are routinely, grossly insubordinate. You think you have a *right* to know things that people would – and do – kill for. You take shortcuts. You aren't an organisation man and you never will be. If it was up to me you'd be on the outside, and never allowed anywhere near us.'

'But I'm not,' I say. 'Nobody even noticed me until I'd worked out the geometry curve iteration method for invoking Nyarlathotep and nearly wiped out Birmingham by accident. Then they came and offered me a post as Senior Scientific Officer and made it clear that "no" wasn't on the list of acceptable answers. Turns out that nuking Birmingham overrides the positive vetting requirement, so they issued a reliability waiver and you're stuck with me. Shouldn't you be pleased that I've decided to make the best of things and try to be useful?'

Angleton leans forward across the polished top of his Memex desk. With a visible effort he slews the microfiche reader hood around so that I can see the screen, then taps one bony finger on a mechanical keypress. 'Watch and learn.'

The desk whirs and clunks; cams and gears buried deep in it shuffle hypertext links and bring up a new microfilm card. A man's face shows up on the screen. Moustache, sunglasses, cropped hair, forty-something and jowly with it. 'Tariq Nassir al-Tikriti. Remember that last bit. He works for a man who grew up in his home town around the same time, who goes by the name of Saddam Hussein al-Tikriti. Mr. Nassir's job entails arranging for funds to be transferred from the Mukhabarat – Saddam's private Gestapo – to friendly parties for purposes of inconveniencing enemies of the Ba'ath party of Iraq. Friendlies such as Mohammed Kadass, who used to live in Afghanistan before he fell foul of the Taliban.'

'Nice to know they're not all religious fundamentalists,' I say, as the Memex flicks to a shot of a bearded guy wearing a turban-like something on his head. (He's scowling at the camera as if he suspects it of holding Western sympathies.)

'They deported him for excessive zeal,' Angelton says heavily. 'Turns out he was marshalling resources for Yusuf Qaradawi's school. Do I need to draw you a diagram?'

'Guess not. What does Qaradawi teach?'

'Originally management studies and economics, but lately he's added suicide bombing, the necessity for armed struggle preceded by *Da'wa* and military preparation in order to repel the greater *Kufr*, and gauge metrics for rasterdriven generative sepiroth on vector processors. Summoning the lesser shoggothim in other words.'

'Nng,' is all I can say to that. 'What's this got to do with the price of coffee?'

Another photograph clicks up on the screen: this time a gorgeous redhead wearing an academic gown over a posh frock. It takes me a moment to recognise Mo. She looks about ten years younger, and the guy in a tux whose arm she's draped over looks – well, lawyerly seems to fit what she told me about her ex. 'Dr. Dominique O'Brien. I believe you've met?'

I glance up and Angleton is staring at me.

'Do I have your *complete* attention now, Mr. Howard?' he rasps.

'Yeah,' I concede. 'Do you mean the kidnappers in Santa Cruz—'

'Shut up and listen and you may learn something.' He waits for me to shut up, then continues. 'I'm telling you this because you're in it already, you've met the prime candidate. *Now*, when you were sent over there we didn't know what you were dealing with, what Dr. O'Brien was sitting on. The Yanks did, which was why they weren't letting her go, but they seem to have changed their minds in view of the security threat. She's not a US citizen and they've got her research findings; interesting, but nothing fundamentally revolutionary. Furthermore, with enough information about her out in the public domain to attract nuisances like the Izzadin al-Qassem hangers-on who tried to snatch her in Santa Cruz, they don't much want her around anymore. Which is why she's over here, in the Laundry and under wraps. They didn't simply deport her, they asked us to take care of her.'

'If it's not fundamentally revolutionary research, why are we interested in her?' I ask.

Angleton looks at me oddly. 'I'll be the judge of that.' It all clicks into place, suddenly. Suppose you worked out how to build a Teller-Ullam configuration fusion device – a hydrogen bomb. That wouldn't qualify as revolutionary these days, either, but that doesn't mean it's unimportant, does it? I must give some sign of understanding what Angleton's getting at because he nods to himself and continues: 'The Laundry is in the nonproliferation business and Dr. O'Brien has independently rediscovered something rather more fundamental than a technique for landscaping Wolverhampton without first obtaining planning permission. In the States, the Black Chamber took an interest in her – don't ask about where they fit in the American occult intelligence complex, you really don't want to know – but verified that it wasn't anything new. We may not have a bilateral cooperation treaty with them, but once they worked out that all she'd come up with was a variation on the Logic of Thoth there was really no reason to keep her except to prevent her falling into the hands of undesirable persons like our friend Tariq Nassir. It's their damned munitions export regulations again; the contents of her head are classified up there with nerve gas and other things that go bump in the dark. Anyway, once the mess was cleared up' – he glares at me as he hisses the word *mess* – 'they really had no reason not to let her come home. After all, we're the ones who gave them the Logic in the first place, back in the late fifties.'

'Right . . . so that's all there is to it? I *heard* those guys, they were going to open a major gateway and drag her through it—'

Angleton abruptly switches off the Memex and stands up, leaning over the desk at me. 'Official word is that nothing at all like that happened,' he snaps. 'There were no witnesses, no evidence, and nothing happened. Because if anything *did* happen there, that would tend to indicate that the Yanks either fucked up by releasing her, or threw us a live hand grenade, and we know they never fuck up, because our glorious prime minister has his lips firmly wrapped around the presidential cigar in the hope of a renewal of the bilateral trade agreement they're talking about in Washington next month. Do you understand me?'

'Yeah, but—' I stop. 'Ah . . . yes. Official report by Bridget, no?'

For the first time ever Angleton turns an expression on me that might, in a bright light, if you squinted at him, be interpreted as a faint smile. 'I couldn't possibly comment.'

I spin my wheels for a moment. 'Nothing happened,' I say robotically. 'There were no witnesses. If anything happened it would mean we'd been passed a booby prize. It would mean some bunch of terrorists came arbitrarily close to getting their hands on a paranormal H-bomb designer, and someone at ONI figured they could count coup by passing the designer to us for safe keeping, meaning they expect us to fuck up to their political advantage. And that couldn't possibly happen, right?'

'She's in the Library, on secondment to Pure Research for the duration,' Angleton says quite casually. 'You might want to invite the young lady out for dinner. I'd be quite interested in hearing about her research at second hand, from someone who obviously understands so much about predicate calculus. Hmm, five-thirty already. You might want to go now.'

Taking my cue I stand up and head for the door. My hand is outstretched when Angleton adds, tonelessly: 'How many made it back from the raid on Wadi al-Qebir, Mr. Howard?'

I freeze. *Shit.* 'Two,' I hear myself saying, unable to control my traitor larynx: it's another of those auditor compulsion fields. *Bastard's got his office wired like an interrogation suite!*

'Very good, Mr. Howard. They were the ones who didn't try to second-guess their commanding officer. Can I suggest that in future you take a leaf from their book and refrain from poking your nose into things you have been told do not concern you? Or at least learn not to be so predictable about it.'

'Ah—'

'Go away before I mock you,' he says, sounding distantly amused.

I flee, simultaneously embarrassed and relieved.

I find Mo by the simple expedient of remembering that my palmtop is still attuned to her aura; I bounce around the basement levels in the lift, doing a binary search until I zero in on her in one of the reading rooms of the library. She's poring over a fragile illuminated manuscript inscribed with colours that glow brilliantly beneath the hooded spotlight she uses. She seems to be engrossed, so I knock loudly on the door frame and wait.

'Yes? Oh, it's you.'

'It's ten to six,' I say diffidently. 'Another ten minutes and an orangoutang in a blue suit will come round and lock you in for the night. I know some people enjoy that sort of thing, but you didn't strike me as the type. So I was thinking, could you do with a glass of wine and that explanation we were talking about?'

She looks at me deadpan. 'Sounds better than facing the urban gorillas. I've got to get home for nine but I guess I can spare an hour. Do you have anywhere in mind?'

We end up at an earning-facilitated nerd nirvana called Wagamama, just off New Oxford Street: you can't miss it, just look for the queue of fashion victims halfway around the block. Some of them have been waiting so long that the cobwebs have fossilised. My impressions are of a huge stainless steel kitchen and Australian expat waiters on rollerblades beaming infrared orders and wide-eyed smiles at each other from handheld computers as they skate around the refectory tables, where earnest young things in tiny rectangular spectacles discuss Derrida's influence on alcopop marketing via the next big dot-sad IPO, or whatever it is the 'in' herd is obsessing about these days over their gyoza and organic buckwheat ramen. Mo is crammed opposite me at one end of a barrack-room table of bleached pine that looks as if they polish it every night with a microtome blade; our neighbours are giggling over some TV studio deal, and she's looking at me with an analytical expression borrowed from the laboratory razor's owner.

'The food's very good,' I offer defensively.

'It's not that' – she gazes past my shoulder – 'it's the culture. It's very Californian. I wasn't expecting the rot to have reached London yet.'

'We are Bay Aryans from Berkeley: prepare to be reengineered in an attractive range of colour schemes for your safety and comfort!'

'Something like that.' A waitron whizzes past and smart-bombs us both with cans of Kirin that feel as if they've been soaked in liquid nitrogen. Mo picks hers up and winces at me as it bites her fingertips. 'Why do they call it the Laundry?'

'Uh . . .' I think for a moment. 'Back in the Second World War, they were based in a requisitioned Chinese laundry in Soho, I think. They got Dansey House when the Dustbin's new sky-scraper was commissioned.' I pick up my beer carefully, using a mitten improvised from my sleeve, and tip the can into a glass. 'Claude Dansey, he was stuck in charge of SOE. Former SIS dude, didn't get on well with the top nobs – it was all politics; SOE was the cowboy arm of British secret ops during the war. Churchill charged SOE with setting Europe ablaze behind German lines, and that's exactly what they tried to do. Until December 1945, when SIS got their revenge, of course.'

'So the bureaucratic infighting goes that far back?'

'Guess so.' I take a sip of beer. 'But the Laundry survived more or less intact after the rest of SOE was gutted, like the way GCHQ survived even though the Bletchley Park operation was wound up. Only more secretively.' Hmm. This is *not* stuff we should be talking about in public; I pull out my palmtop and tap away at it until a rather useful utility shows up.

'What's that?' she asks interestedly, as the background clatter and racket diminishes to a haze of white noise.

'Laundry-issue palmtop. Looks like an ordinary Palm Pilot, doesn't it? But the secret's in the software and the rather unusual daughterboard soldered inside the case.'

'No, I mean the noise – it isn't just my ears, is it?'

'No, it's magic.'

'Magic! But—' She glares at me. 'You're not kidding, are you? What the hell is going on around here?'

I look at her blankly: 'Nobody told you?'

'*Magic!*' She looks disgusted.

'Well okay, then, it's applied mathematics. I thought you said you're not a Platonist? You should be. These boxes' – I tap the palmtop – 'are the most powerful mathematical tools we've devel-oped. Things were done on an ad-hoc basis until about 1953, when Turing came up with his final theorem; since then, we've been putting magic on a systematic basis, on the QT. Most of it boils down to the application of Kaluza-Klein theory in a Linde universe constrained by an information conservation rule, or so they tell me when I ask. When we carry out a computation it has side effects that leak through some kind of channel underlying the structure of the Cosmos. Out there in the multiverse there are listeners; sometimes we can coerce them into opening gates. Small gates we can transfer minds through, or big gates we can move objects through. Even really huge gates, big enough to take something huge and unpleasant – some of the listeners are *big*. Giants. Sometimes we can invoke local reversals or enhancements of entropy; that's what I'm doing right now with the sound damper field, fuzzing the air around us, which is already pretty random. That's basically the business the Laundry is in.'

'Ah.' She chews her lower lip for a moment, appraising me. 'So that's why you were so interested in me. Say, do you have any references for this work of Turing's? I'd like to read up on it.'

'It's classified, but—'

'Wtyjdfshjwrtha rssradth aeywerg?'

I turn and look at the waitress who's beaming at me inscrutably. ' 'Scuse me.' I tap the 'pause' button on screen. 'What was that again?'

'I said, are you ready to order yet?'

I shrug at Mo, she nods, and we order. The waitron skids off and I tap the 'pause' button again. 'I didn't originally volunteer for the Laundry,' I feel compelled to add. 'They drafted me much the same way they drafted you. On the one hand, it sucks. On the other hand, the alternatives are a whole lot worse.'

She looks angry now. 'What do you mean, worse?'

'Well' – I lean back – 'for starters, your work on probability engineering. You probably thought it was mostly irrelevant, except to theoretical types like Pentagon strategic planners. But if we mix it up with a localised entropy inversion we can make life very hot for whoever or whatever is on the receiving end. I'm not clear on the details, but apparently it's at the root of one particularly

weird directed invocation: if we can set up a gauge field for probability metrics we can tune in on specific EIs fairly—'

'EIs?'

'External Intelligences. What the mediaeval magic types called
demons, gods, spirits, what have you. Sentient aliens, basically,
from those cosmological domains where the anthropic principle
predominates and some sort of sapient creatures have evolved.
Some of them are strongly superhuman, others are dumb as a
stump from our perspective. What counts is that they can be
coerced, sometimes, into doing what people want. Some of them
can also open wormholes – yes, they've got access to negative
matter – and send themselves, or other entities, through. As I
understand it, general indeterminacy theory lets us target them
very accurately: it's the difference between dialling a phone
number at random and using a phone book. I think.'

A crescent-shaped plate of gyoza appears on the table between
us, and for a couple of minutes we're busy eating; then bowls of
soup arrive and I'm busy juggling chopsticks, spoon, and noodles
that are making a bid for freedom.

'So.' She drains her bowl, lays the chopsticks across it, and sits
up to watch me. 'Let's summarise. I've stumbled across a research
field that's about as critical to your – the Laundry – as if I'd been
working on nuclear weapons research without realising it. In this
country, everyone who works on this stuff works for the Laundry,
or not at all. So the Laundry has sucked me in and you're here to
give me an update so I know what I'm swimming in.'

'Other people's dirty underwear, mostly,' I say apologetically.

'Yeah, right. And this concern for keeping me updated was all
your own idea too, huh? Just what the hell was going on in Santa
Cruz? Who were those guys who snatched me, and what were you
doing?'

'I won't say I wasn't asked to have a discreet chat with you.' I
put my spoon down, then turn it over. Then over again. 'Look,
the Laundry is first and foremost a self-perpetuating bureaucracy,
like any other government agency, right? SOP, when shit hits the
fan in the field, is to protect head office by pulling back feelers.'

I turn the spoon over. 'When I got home I was carpeted for going after you – given a going over in front of my boss.'

'You were what?' Her eyes widen. 'I don't remember you—'

I pull a face. 'Standard protocol if something goes down is to get the hell out of town, Mo. But you were obviously in over your head when you rang, so I went round your place and followed you to that safe house they were holding you in. Phoned your mobile, expecting a diversion tap, and the next thing I knew I was sitting up in hospital with a hangover and no alcohol to show for it, being grilled by the Feds. Very clever of me, but at least they pulled us both out alive. Anyway, when I got home it turned out that officially none of that shit happened. You were not abducted by, ahem, Middle Eastern gentlemen who might or might not have been working for a guy called Tariq Nassir, with connections to Yusuf Qaradawi. You were not being kept under surveillance by the Black Chamber. Because if either of those things were true, it would be Bad, and if it was Bad, it would put a black mark on my boss's record book. And she wants her KCMG and DBE so bad you can smell it when she walks in the door.'

Mo is silent for a while. 'I had no idea,' she says presently. There's a slightly wild look in her eyes: 'They were talking about killing me! I heard them!'

'Officially it didn't happen, but unofficially – Bridget isn't the only poker player in the Laundry.' I shrug. 'One of the other players wants to hear your side of the story, off the record.' I glance round. 'This is *not* the place for it. Even with a fuzzbox.'

'I – huh.' She checks her watch. 'An hour to go. Look, Bob. If you've got time to come back to my place for a coffee before I turf you out, we should talk some more.' She looks at me warningly: 'I'm going to have to kick you out at nine-thirty, though. Got a date.'

'Well okay.' I don't think I show any sign of guilty disappointment – or relief that I won't have an opportunity to outscore Mhari at her own game this once. Besides which, I think Mo is too nice to play that kind of dirty trick on. I raise a hand and a waiter zips over, swipes my credit card through her handheld, and wishes me a nice day.

We head over to Mo's place and I get a bit of a surprise; she's renting a flat in a centralish part of Putney, all wine bars and bistros. We catch the tube over and end up walking downstairs from an overhead platform: you know you're entering suburbia when the underground trains poke their noses up into the open air. She walks very fast, forcing me to hurry to keep up. 'Not far,' she remarks, ' just round a couple of corners from the tube stop.'

She marches up a leaf-messed street in near darkness, hemmed in to either side by parked cars, everything washed out by orange sodium lights. I can feel the first chilly fingers of autumn in the air. 'It's up here,' she says, gesturing at a front door set back from the road, with a row of buzzers next to it. 'Just a sec. I'm on the third floor, by the way; I've got the attic.' She fumbles with a key in the lock and the door swings open on a darkened vestibule as the skin on the back of my neck begins to prickle, while the sound goes flat and the light deadens.

'Wait—' I begin to say, and something uncoils from the shadows and lashes out at Mo with a noise like an explosion in a cat factory.

She barely makes a noise as it grabs her with about a dozen tentacles — no suckers here — and yanks her into the darkened vestibule. I scream, 'Shit!' and jump back, then yank at my belt where I happen to have clipped my multitool: the three-inch blade flips out and locks as I fumble around the inside of the door for a light switch, left-handed, holding the knife in front of me.

Now I hear a muffled squeaking noise — Mo is on the floor up against an inner doorway, screaming her head off. What looks like a nest of pythons has wriggled under the woodwork and is trying to drag her in by the neck. But whatever field is damping my hearing is also stifling her cries, and the thing has got her arms and torso. Behind her, the door is bulging; the light from the bulb overhead is attenuated to a dull, candlelike flicker.

I step back, yank out my mobile phone, and hit a quick-dial button, then throw it into the roadway outside. Then I take a deep breath and force myself to go back inside.

'*Get it off me!*' she mouths, thrashing around. I lean over her and try sawing at one of the tentacles. It's dry and leathery and squirms underneath the blade, so I jab the point of the knife into it and force my weight down.

The thing on the other side of the door goes apeshit: a banging and crashing resounds through the floor as if something huge is trying to break down the wall. The tentacles around Mo tighten until her mouth opens and I'm terrified she's going to turn blue. Something black begins to ooze out around my knife so I concentrate on ramming the thing down against the floor and slicing from side to side. It feels as if I'm trying to skewer a rubber band big enough to power a wind-up freight locomotive.

Mo thrashes around until her back is against the door; her eyes roll and I give a desperate yank on the tentacle with my free hand. The pain is indescribable: it feels like I've just grabbed hold of a mass of razor blades. Something black and oily is squirting out around the knife blade and I try to keep my hand out of it. How long is it going to take Capital Laundry Services to answer the sodding phone and get a Plumber out here? Too fucking long – a quarter of an hour at least. Maybe I can do something else—

A steel vice closes around my left ankle and yanks my shin against the doorframe so hard I scream and drop the knife. Another one wraps around my waist like an animated hawser and constricts violently. Mo valiantly lends a hand and succeeds in elbowing me under the chin: I see stars for a second or two and fumble around with a left hand that feels like a lump of raw meat for that dropped multitool. There's got to be a better way. If I've remembered my Gadget Man cigarette lighter . . . I reach into my pocket and, instead, find my palmtop. Illumination dawns.

The light of its display is a mycoid green glow in the darkness. A thousand miles away something is roaring at me. Icons shimmer, hovering above the screen. I thumb one of them, an ear with a red line through it, smearing blood across the glass as I cut in the anti-sound field and pray that it works.

5: OGRE REALITY

I WAKE UP TO DISCOVER MY BACK FEELS AS IF the All Blacks have been performing a victory dance on it, my ankle's been turned on a lathe, and my left hand worked over with a steak tenderiser. I open my eyes; I'm lying on the floor, legs stretched out, and Mo is leaning over me. 'Are you all right?' she asks, in a ragged voice.

'Death shouldn't hurt like this,' I croak. I blink painfully and wonder what the hell happened to her shirt – it looks as if it's been used as a nest by a family of hungry ferrets. 'It had you for longer—'

'Once you began hacking at it,' she begins, then pauses to clear her throat. 'It let go. Think you can stand up? You turned that gadget on and the thing just *vanished*. Whipped back under the door and sort of faded out. Turned translucent and – went away.'

I look round. I'm lying in a sticky black puddle of something that isn't blood, thankfully – or, at least, not human blood. The light is normal for a dingy vestibule with an energy-saver bulb, and the tentacles have gone from the walls. 'My phone,' I say, pushing my back up against the wall. 'I threw it out—'

Mo heaves herself upright and staggers to the front door, bends down and picks something up delicately. 'You mean this?'

She drops it beside me, in about three separate pieces.

'Fuck. That was meant to call the Plumbers.'

'Come upstairs, you'd better explain.' She pauses. 'If you think it's safe?'

I try to laugh but a vicious stabbing pain in my ribs stops me. 'I don't think that thing will be coming back any time soon: I fuzzed its eigenvector but good.'

She unlocks the inner door and we stumble up three flights of stairs, then she opens another door and I somehow end up slumped across another overstuffed sofa from the Planet of the Landlords, gasping with pain. She double-locks and deadbolts the door then flops into an armchair opposite me. 'What the hell was that?' she asks, rubbing her throat.

'That was what we call in the trade an Unscheduled Reality Excursion, usually abbreviated to "Oh fuck."'

'Yes, but—'

'What I said earlier? We live in an Everett-Wheeler cosmology, all possible parallel universes coexisting. That thing was an agent someone summoned from elsewhere to, um—'

'Fuck with our metabolic viability,' she suggests.

'Yeah, that.' I pause and take stock of my ribs, ankle, and general frame of mind. My hands are shaking slightly and I feel clammy and cold with the aftershock, but not entirely out of control. Good. 'You mentioned something about coffee.' I lever myself upright. 'If you tell me where it is . . .'

'Kitchen's over there.' I realise there's a breakfast bar and a cramped cooking niche behind me. I shamble over, fumble for the light switches, check there's water in the kettle, and begin scooping instant out of the first available jar. Mo continues: 'My neck hurts. Do you have lots of, uh, reality excursions in this line of work?'

'That's the first I've ever had follow me home,' I say truthfully. Fred the Accountant doesn't count.

'Well I am glad to hear that.' Mo stands up and goes somewhere else – bathroom, at a guess; I need the caffeine so badly that I don't really notice. While the kettle boils I root out a couple of mugs and some milk, and when I turn round she's back in the armchair wearing a clean T-shirt. I fill the mugs. 'Milk, no sugar. Bathroom's behind you on the left,' she adds, noncommittally.

One splash of water on my face later I'm back on the sofa with a mug of coffee, beginning to feel a bit more human – Neanderthal, maybe.

'What was that thing doing here?' she asks me.

'I don't know, and I'm not sure I want to know.'

'Really?' She glares at me. 'Trouble has a bad habit of following you around. First time I meet you, an hour later some Middle Eastern thugs stick me in the trunk of their car, drive me halfway round Santa Cruz, lock me in a cupboard, and gear up to sacrifice me. Second time I meet you, an hour later some random bad dream with too many tentacles ambushes me in my front hall.' She pauses for a thoughtful moment. 'Now granted, you seem to turn up in time to stop them, but, on the balance of prior probabilities, there appears to be a statistical correlation between you appearing in my life and horrible things happening. What's *your* excuse?'

I shrug painfully. 'What can I say? There seems to be a positive correlation in my life between people telling me to talk to you and horrible things happening to me. I mean, it's not as if I make a habit of letting random nightmares with too many tentacles come along on a date, is it? Parenthetically speaking,' I add hastily.

'Huh. Well then. Got any ideas as to why this is happening, Mr. Spy Guy?'

'I am *not* a spy,' I say, nettled, 'and the answer—' is right in front of my pointy nose if I'd bloody well focus on it, I suddenly realise.

'Yes?' she prompts, noticing my pause.

'Those guys who officially didn't abduct you.' I take a sip of coffee and wince; I'm not used to the instant stuff she uses. 'And who weren't officially talking about sacrificing you. I want you to tell me everything you didn't officially tell anyone who debriefed you. Like the whole truth.'

'What makes you think I didn't tell—' She stops.

'Because you were afraid nobody would believe you. Because you were afraid they'd think you were a nut. Because there were no witnesses and nobody wanted to believe anything had happened to you in the first place because they'd have had to fill in too many forms in triplicate and that would be bad. Because you didn't owe the bastards anything for fucking up your life, if you'll excuse my French.' I wave a hand in the general direction of the doorway. 'I believe you. I know something really stinks around here. If I can figure out what it is, stopping it features high on my list of priorities. Is that enough for you?'

Mo grimaces, a strikingly ugly expression. 'What's to say?'

'Lots. Your call: if you won't tell me what happened, I can't try and sort things out for you.'

She sips her coffee as it cools. 'After we met, I went home thinking everything was going to be okay. You, or the Foreign Office, or whoever, would sort things out so I could come home. It was all just a mix-up, right? I'd get my visa sorted out and be allowed to go back home without any more problems.'

Another mouthful of coffee. 'I walked back to my condo. That's one of the things I liked about UCSC: the town's small enough you can walk anywhere. You don't have to drive as long as you don't mind getting to SF being a royal pain. I was turning over a problem I'm working on, a way to integrate my probability formalism with Dempster-Shaffer logic. Anyhow, I stopped off at a convenience store to buy some stuff I was running out of and who should I run into but David? At least, I *thought* it was David.' She frowns. 'I thought he was out east, and I really didn't want to see him anyway – I mean, I'm over him. He's history.'

'What makes you think it wasn't your ex-husband?' I ask.

'Nothing, at the time. He just turned round from the counter and smiled at me and said, 'Can I give you a lift home?' and I sort of . . .' she trails off.

'It offered you a lift home,' I echo.

'What do you mean, *it*?'

I close my eyes. 'You got yourself into some really smelly shit there. Say some son of a bitch wants to abduct somebody. They have to get a victim profile, samples from the victim – it's not simple, not just messing around with hair or fingernail clippings for the DNA – but suppose they get it. Then they invoke, um, generate a vector field oriented on the victim's—'

'Yeah, yeah, I'll take that bit on trust.'

'Okay then. I'll give you some references tomorrow. Basically it's what used to be called an incubus: a demon lover. Something the victim won't resist because they don't *want* to resist. It's not actually a demon; it's just a hallucination, like a website gener- ated by customer relationship management software from hell.'

'A lure?'

'Yes, that's it exactly. A lure.' I placed my unfinished mug down between my feet.

She shudders, looks worried. 'Maybe I wasn't over him as thor- oughly as I wanted to be.'

'I know the feeling,' I say, thinking of Mhari.

She shakes herself. 'Anyway. Next thing I know I'm sitting in the back of a Lincoln and some guy I don't know who's wearing a Nehru suit and a beard is sticking a pistol in my side. And he says something like, 'American bitch, you have been selected for a great honour.' And I say, "I'm not American," and he just sneers.'

Her hand is shaking so badly that coffee slops on the floor.

'He just—'

'It doesn't matter, what happens next?' I ask, trying to get her over the emotional hump. Over there they hold grudges for a long time. Some of the Pathans are probably still plotting their revenge for Lord Elphinstone's expedition.

'We drive around for a bit and head out of town, northbound on Highway 1, then the car pulls up to this house and the driver opens the door and they push me in through a side door into the house. The driver's wearing that long, baggy shirt and trousers you see on TV, and a scarf around his head, and he's got a beard, too. They push me through the kitchen and into a closet with a light then shut the door, and I hear them chain the door handles together. Someone else comes in and they talk for a bit, then I hear a door slam. That's when I pulled out my mobile phone and called you.'

'You overheard them talking. What about?'

'I – wasn't concentrating much. Tell the truth' – she puts the cup down on the floor; its saucer is swimming in coffee – 'I was afraid they were going to rape me. *Really* afraid; I mean, this was kidnapping, what would you expect? When they didn't, when they were talking, it was almost worse. Does that make any kind of sense? The waiting. But he – the one I didn't see – he had a deep voice, some accent – sounded German to me. Thick, gravelly, lots of sibilants. Had to keep repeating himself to the others, the Middle Eastern men. 'The Opener of the Ways requires the wisdom,' he kept saying. 'It needs information.' I think one of the Middle Eastern guys was objecting because after a bit there was a noise like—' She pauses, and swallows. 'Like downstairs. And I didn't hear him again.'

I shake my head. 'This isn't making any sense so far—' Hastily: 'No, I'm not saying you're wrong, I just can't figure out how it fits together. That's *my* problem, not yours.'

I drain my coffee and wince as it hits my stomach and sits there, burning like a lump of molten lead. 'Sounds like they were talking about a blood sacrifice. That's the Sacrifice of Knowledge rite. Middle Eastern guys. An incubus. German accent. You're sure it was German?'

'Yes,' she says gloomily. 'At least, I think it was German; Middle European for sure.'

'That really *is* odd.' Which distracts me and catapults my train of thought right into terra incognita because there are *no* usual suspects in the occult field in Germany; the Abwehr's Rosenberg Gruppe and any survivors of the Thule Gesellschaft were 'shot trying to escape' by late June 1945. The camp guards were mostly executed or pulled long prison sentences, the higher-ups responsible for the Ahnenerbe-SS were executed, the whole country turned into a DMZ as far as the occult is concerned. After the Third Reich's answer to the Manhattan Project came so close to completion, that was about the one thing that Truman and Stalin and Churchill all saw eye-to-eye on – and the current government shows no desire to go back down that route of blood and madness.

'He went on a bit,' Mo adds unexpectedly.

'Really? What about?'

'He wanted to go home, to take help home, something like that. I think.'

I sit up, wince as my ribs remind me not to move too fast. 'Help. Did he say what kind?'

Mo frowns again. Her thick, dark eyebrows almost join in the middle, looming like thunderclouds. 'He went on about the Opener of the Ways a bit more. Oddly, as if he was talking about me. Said that help for the struggle against the Dar-al-Harb would wait until the ceremony of, uh, "Unbinding the roots of Ig-drazl"? Then he would "Open the bridge and bring the ice giants through." He was very emphatic about the bridge, the bridge to living space. That was his term for it: *living space*. Does that make any sense?'

'It makes an *oh-shit* kind of sense.' I watch as she picks up her mug and rolls it round between her hands. 'Was that all?'

'All? Yes. I waited until I heard them go out, then I phoned you. I obviously got things wrong, though, because the next thing I knew they yanked open the door and the one with the gun grabbed the phone and stamped on it. He was *angry*, but the other – with the accent—' She judders to a stop.

'Can you describe him?'

She swallows. 'That's the crazy thing. From the voice I kind of expected Arnie Schwarzenegger in *The Terminator*, except he *wasn't*. There were just these four Middle Eastern guys, and one of them had – I can't, uh, can't remember his face. Just those eyes. They seemed to glow, sort of greenish. Like marbles. Like there was something luminous and wormy behind his face. He – the one with the eyes and this weird German accent – he was *angry* and yelled at me and I was so afraid, but they just smashed my phone then shut the door on me again. Chained the door shut and overturned a table or something against it. And I – hell.' She finishes her coffee. 'That was about the worst hour of my life.' Pause.

'It could have been worse.' Pause. 'They could have.' Pause. 'You might not have answered.' Pause. 'They might not have found me.'

'All in a day's work,' I say with forced lightheartedness, which has nothing to do with the way I feel. 'When the cops brought you out, did you see anything?'

'I wasn't paying much attention,' she says shakily. 'There were gunshots, though. Then what looked like a whole SWAT team kicked the cupboard door in and pointed their toys at me. You ever had two guys point assault rifles at your head, so close you can see the grooves on the inside of the barrels? You just lie there very still and try very hard not to look threatening.' Pause. 'Anyway, one of the agents in charge figured out I was the hostage in about three seconds flat and they led me out through the front. There was blood everywhere and two bodies, but not the guy with the weird eyes. I'd recognize him. Thing is, there were strange symbols all over the wall; it was whitewashed and it looked like they'd been painting on it in thick black paint, or blood, or something. A low table under it, with a trashed laptop and some other stuff. Candlesticks, an arc-welding power supply. It was weird, I guess you'd know how weird it looked. Then they drove me away.'

My bad feeling is getting worse. In fact, it's not setting off alarm bells in my head anymore: it's sounding the Three Minute Warning. 'Mind if I use your phone?' I ask, carefully nonchalant. 'I think we still need the Plumbers.'

Due to the miracles of matrix management Bridget is my head of department and writes my personal efficiency assessments, and Harriet is her left hand of darkness and handles administrative issues like training; but since I moved to active service, Andy is now my line manager with overall responsibility for my effectiveness and work assignment, and Angleton is just the guy I'm acting as temporary private secretary for. I decide to start at the bottom of the seniority queue, consign Harriet to the pits of operational ineffectiveness – I mean, this is a woman who would give you a written reprimand for wasting departmental funds if you used silver bullets on a werewolf – and conclude that my best chance of survival is to throw myself on Andy's mercy.

Which means I nobble him absolutely as soon as I can, first thing in the morning.

'Mind if I have a word?' I ask, sticking my head around his door without asking – the red light is off.

Andy is slumped behind his desk, nursing his starter-motor coffee mug. He raises an eyebrow at me. 'You look—' He stabs a finger at his keyboard, raises another eyebrow at his email. 'Oh. So it was *you* who called the Plumbers out last night.'

I sit down in the chair opposite his desk without asking permission. 'Angleton told me to pump Mo after work' – I see his expression – 'for information, dammit!'

Andy hides behind his coffee. 'Do go on,' he says warmly, 'this is the best entertainment I'm going to get all morning.'

'Then you must be hard up. We ate out, then went back to her place for some more sensitive discussions about the, uh, non-events last month. Something was waiting for us in the lobby.'

'Something.' He looks sceptical. 'And you called out the Plumbers for that?'

I yawn: it's been a long night. 'It tried to rip her fucking head off and I've got a cracked rib to show for it. If you'd read that goddamn report you'd see what forensics found in the carpet; they're never going to get the ichor stains out—'

'I'll read it.' He puts his coffee mug down. 'First, give me the basics. How did you deal with it?'

I produce the wreckage of my Laundry-issue palmtop. 'I'll be needing a new PDA, this one's fucked. Mind you, it's not as fucked as the malevolent mollusc from Mars that jumped us; I bumped the fuzz diffuser up to full power and piped the entire entropy pool into it over wide-spectrum infrared. It decided it didn't like that and discorporated instead of sticking around to finish the job, otherwise you'd be spending this morning watching them hoover me off the walls and ceiling.'

I take as deep a breath as the strapping around my ribs will permit. 'Anyway, afterward I got the whole story out of Mo. The bits she was afraid of telling anyone for fear they wouldn't believe her. And that's why I called the Plumbers. See, the Yank field group who rescued her didn't tell us what the hell was going on. The leader was some Arab guy with a German accent, talking about help for the struggle with the Dar-al-Harb once the roots of Yggdrasil are unbound. Only they didn't get him – or she didn't see his body. Boss, do we have anything on German terror groups using Beckenstein-Skinner actor theory to possess their victims? Hell, anything about any German terror groups more recent than the Ahnenerbe using occult techniques?'

Andy looks at me with a stony expression. 'Wait here. Do *not* move.' He pushes the DNI button (turning on the red warning light outside the door – WARNING: CLASSIFIED ACTIVITIES: DO NOT INTRUDE) then stands up and hurries out.

I sit there and let my eyes roam around Andy's cubbyhole. The contents are prosaic: one institutional desk (scratched), one swivel chair (used), two armless visitor chairs (ditto), one bookcase, and a classified document safe (basically a steel cabinet with lockable metal doors on it). His PC is five years old and running a password-locked screensaver, and his desk is clear – no papers lying around. In fact, if it wasn't for the classified document safe and the lack of papers it could be a low-level manager's office in any cash-pinched business in corporate Britain.

I'm leaning back in my chair and inspecting the flecks of institutional paint smeared on the frosted glass in the high window when the door opens again. Andy enters, closely followed by Derek and – shock, horrors – Angleton. I'm surrounded! 'Here he is,' says Andy.

Angleton claims Andy's chair behind the desk – the privilege of the senior inquisitor – and Andy sits down next to me, while Derek stands at parade rest in front of the door, as if to stop me escaping. He's got some kind of box like a small briefcase, which he parks on the floor next to his feet.

'Speak,' says Angleton.

'I did as you told me. Mo and I were talking. I kept it to non-classified while we were in public; I convinced her I needed to hear the full story, not just the official version, so we went back to her place. We were jumped in the hallway. Afterward, she told me enough that I thought there was a clear and present danger to her life. Did Andy tell you—'

Angleton snaps his fingers at Derek. Derek, who is not my idea of an obedient flunky, nevertheless obediently passes him the briefcase, which he opens on the desk. It turns out to contain a small mechanical typewriter with a couple of sheets of paper already wound around the roller. He laboriously taps out a sentence, then turns the typewriter toward me: it says SECRET OGRE CARNATE GECKO, and I get an abrupt sinking feeling in my stomach.

'Before you leave this office you will write down everything you remember about last night,' he says tersely. 'You will not leave this office until you have finished and signed off on the report. One of us will stay with you until the job is done, and countersign that this is a true transcript and that there were no uncleared witnesses. Once you leave this office you will not see this document again. You will not, repeat *not*, discuss last night's events with anyone other than the participants and the people in this room without first obtaining written permission from one of us. Do you understand?'

'Uh, yeah. You're classifying everything under OGRE CARNATE GECKO and I'm not to discuss it with anyone who isn't cleared. Can I ask why the typewriter? I could email—'

Angleton looks at me witheringly: 'Van Eck Radiation.' He snaps his fingers. *But we're in the Laundry*, I protest silently, *the whole building is Tempest-shielded*. 'Start typing, Bob.'

I start typing. 'Where's the delete key on this – oh.'

'You're typing on carbon paper. In triplicate. Once you finish, we burn the carbons. And the typewriter ribbon.'

'You could have offered a quill pen: that'd be more secure, wouldn't it?' I peck away at the keyboard in a purposeful manner. After a minute or two Angleton silently rises and ghosts out of the room. I peck on, occasionally swearing as I catch a fingernail under a key or jam a bunch of letters together. Finally I'm done: one page of single-spaced, densely printed text, detailing the events of last night. I sign each copy and present them to Andy, who countersigns, then carefully inserts them into a striped-cover folder and passes it to Derek, who writes out receipts for them and hands a copy to each of us. He leaves without a word.

Andy walks round the desk, stretches, then looks at me. 'What am I going to do with you?'

'Huh? What's wrong?'

Andy looks morose. 'If I'd known you'd show such a well-developed talent for raking up the mud . . .'

'Comes of my hacking hobby before I came to the attention of . . . look. I called the Plumbers because I had reason to be afraid that Mo — Professor O'Brien — was in serious danger. Would you rather I hadn't?'

'No.' He sighs. For a moment he looks old. 'You did the right thing. It's just that the Plumbing budget is chargeable to departmental accounts. That leaves us open to some rather nasty maneuvering if the usual suspects decide it's an opportunity to extend their little empires. I'm wondering how the hell we're going to spin it past Harriet.'

'Why don't you just tell — oh.'

'Yes.' He nods at me. 'You're beginning to catch on. Now run along and get back to work. I'm sure your in-tray is overflowing.'

I'm working my way through that overcrowded in-tray late in the afternoon when Harriet stalks in without knocking. (Actually, I'm up to my eyeballs in a clipping from the *Santa Cruz County Sentinel*. It makes for fascinating reading: TWO DEAD IN MURDER, SUICIDE. Two unidentified males, one believed to be a Saudi Arabian national, found dead in a house out toward Davenport. Police investigating weird occult symbols smeared on the walls in blood. Drugs suspected.) 'Ah, Bob,' she coos with malevolent solicitude. 'Just the person I was looking for!'

Oh shit. 'What can I do for you?' I ask.

She leans over my desk. 'I understand you called out the

Plumbers last night,' she says. 'I happen to know that you're currently assigned to Angleton as JPS, which is a nonoperational role and therefore doesn't give you release authority for wet-and-dry issues. You are no doubt aware that cleanup funds are allocated on a per-department basis, and require prior authorisation from your head of department, in writing. You didn't obtain authorisation from Bridget, and funnily enough, you didn't approach me for a release either.' She smiles with chilly insouciance. 'Would you like to explain yourself?'

'I can't,' I say.

'I – *see*.' Harriet looms over me, visibly working on her anger. 'You realise that last night you cost our working budget more than seven *thousand* pounds? That's going to have to be justified, Mr. Howard, and *you* are going to justify it to the Audit Commission when they come round next month. Let's see' – she flips through what looks for all the world like a commercial invoice – 'cleaning up Professor O'Brien's front door, sweeping her apartment for listeners and actors, *rehousing* Professor O'Brien in a secure apartment, armed escort, medical expenses. What on earth have you been up to?'

'I can't tell you,' I say.

'You're going to tell me. That's an order, by the way,' she says in conversational tones. 'You're going to tell me in writing *exactly* what happened there last night, and explain why I shouldn't take the expenses out of your pay packet—'

'Harriet.'

We both look round. Angleton's door is ajar; I wonder how long he's been standing there.

'You don't have clearance,' he says. 'Let it drop. *That's* an order.'

The door shuts. Harriet stands there for a moment, her jaw working soundlessly as if she's forgotten how to speak. I commit the spectacle to memory for future enjoyment. 'Don't think this is the last you'll hear of this,' she snaps at me as she leaves, slamming the door.

TWO DEAD IN MURDER, SUICIDE. Hmm. Ahnenerbe.

Thule Gesellschaft. Incubi. German accents. Opener of the Ways. Double-hmm. I pull my terminal closer; it's only got access to low-classification and public sources, but it's time to do some serious data mining. I wonder . . . just what have Yusuf Qaradawi's friends and the Mukhabarat got to do with the last and most secret nightmares of the Third Reich?

The next day I go into the office and find Nick waiting for me at my desk like an overexcited trainee schoolmaster. This is an unscheduled intrusion in my plans, which mostly revolve around applying some security patches to the departmental file server and digging out the maintenance schematics to Angleton's antique Memex.

'Come along now! I've got something to show you,' he says, in a tone that makes it clear I don't have any choice. He leads me up a staircase carpeted in a thick bottle-green pile that I haven't seen before, then along a corridor with dark, oak-panelled walls like a provincial gentlemen's club from the 1930s, except that gentlemen's clubs don't come with closed circuit TV cameras and combination locks on the doors.

'What *is* this place?' I ask.

'Used to be the director's manor,' he explains. 'When we had a director.' When we had a director: I don't ask. He stops at a thick oak door and punches some digits into the lock, then opens it. 'After you,' he says.

There's a conference table and a modern – by Laundry standards – laptop set up at one end of it. A whole shitload of electronics racked up on shelves behind, along with some thick leather-bound books and a bunch of stuff like silver pencils, jars of mouldy dust, and what looks for all the world like a polygraph. As I go in I notice that the doorframe is unusually thick and there are no outside windows. 'Is this shielded?' I ask.

Nick nods jerkily. 'Well spotted, that man! Now sit down,' he suggests.

I sit. The top shelf of the equipment rack is dominated by a glass bell jar with a human skull in it; I grin back at it. '"Alas, poor Yorick."'

'Carry on like you have been and maybe your head will fetch up in there one day,' Nick says, grinning. 'Ah.' The door opens. 'Andy.'

'Why am I here?' I ask. 'All this cloak and dagger shit is—'

Andy drops a fat lever-arch file on the table in front of me. 'Read and enjoy,' he says dryly. 'One day you, too, can have the fun of maintaining this manual.'

I open the cover to be confronted by a sheet which basically says I can be arrested for so much as thinking about disclosing the contents of the next page. I flip to page two and read a paragraph that essentially says 'Abandon hope all ye who enter here,' so I turn *that* one over and get to the title page: FIELD OPERATIONS MANUAL FOR COUNTER-OCCULT OPERATIONS. Below it, in small print: *Approved by Departmental Quality Assurance Team* and then *Complies with BS5750 standard for total quality management*. I shudder. 'Since when have we been into mummification?' I ask.

'Embalming—' Andy frowns for a moment. 'Oh, you mean total quality—' He stops and clears his throat. 'One of these days your sense of humour is going to get you into trouble, Bob.'

'Thanks for the advance warning.' I look at the manual gloomily. 'Let me guess. I'm to do as we discussed earlier – by the book. *This* book, right? Why wasn't I issued it before Santa Cruz?'

Andy pulls out the chair beside me and flops down in it. 'Because that wasn't officially an operation,' he says in tones of sweet reason. 'That was an informal information-gathering exercise involving a nonclassified source. Operations require sign-off at director level. Informal information-gathering exercises don't.'

I put the folder down on the table. 'Does Bridget have anything to do with this?'

'Tangentially.'

Nick sniffs, loudly, from his post by the door. 'Arse-covering, boy. *That* was meant to be a risk-free chat. *This* is about what you do when you're ordered to stick your head in the lion's mouth. Or up its arse to inspect the hemorrhoids.'

I look round at him. 'You're planning on sending me on an op?' I ask. 'Happy joy. Not.'

Andy glances at Nick. 'He's beginning to get it,' he comments.

'Are you planning on involving Professor O'Brien in this?' I ask. 'I mean, it seems to me that she's the one under threat. Isn't she?'

'Well.' Andy glances at Nick, then back at me. 'You're on active service, so you need to know this stuff inside out and upside down. But you're right, the specific reason for this session is what happened the other night. I can't confirm or deny the identities of anyone else involved, though.'

'Then I've got a problem,' I tell him. 'I don't know if I should bring it up right now, but if I sit on it and I'm wrong . . . well, way I see it is, Mo is the one who's under threat and in need of protection. Right? I mean, *I* can cope with being drooled over by things with more tentacles than brains, but it's not exactly part of her job description, is it? You're supposed to be responsible for her safety. If you've got me going over rules of engagement, and she's involved, then when the shooting starts—'

Andy is nodding. It's a bad sign when your boss starts nodding at you before you finish each sentence.

'As a matter of fact I agree with your concerns completely,' he says. 'And yes, I agree we've got a problem. But it's not quite what you think it is.' He leans forward and makes a steeple out of his fingers, elbows together on the table. The steeple leans sideways at an architecturally unsound angle. 'We can probably keep her safe indefinitely, as long as she's locked down under a protection program and resident in one of our secure accommodation units. That's not in question; if nobody can see or track her, they can't attack her – although I'm not sure about the inability to track given that they must have obtained samples in order to spring that incubus on her last month. What concerns me is that such a posture is essentially defensive. We don't know for sure just what we're defending *against*, Bob, and that's bad.'

Andy takes a deep breath, but Nick jumps in before he can continue: 'We've dealt with Iraqi spies before, boy. This doesn't smell like them.'

'Uh.' I pause, unsure what to say. 'What do you mean?'

He means that the Mukhabarat simply don't have the technology to summon an incubus. Nor do they generally manage incarnations that leave Precambrian slime all over the carpet; about all they're up to is interrogation and compulsion of Watchers and a little bit of judicious torture. No real control of phase-space geometry, no Enochian deep grammar parse-tree generators – at least none that we've seen the source code to. So we can't make any assumptions about the attacks on Mo. Someone tried to grab her for whatever purpose. By now, they must know we're onto them. The next logical step is for them to pull back and switch track to whatever they were working on in the first place – which is extremely dangerous for us because if they were trying to snatch her, they were probably working on weapons of mass destruction. We badly need to get them out in the open and our only bait is Professor O'Brien. But if she knows she's bait, she'll keep looking round for sharks – which will tip them off. So we're assigning you to shadow her, Bob. You keep an eye on her. We'll keep eye on you. When they bite, we'll reel them in. You don't need to know how, or when, but you'll do well to read this manual so you know how we set up this kind of situation. Clear?'

I crane my neck round at Nick, whose expression is uncharacteristically flat: he stares right through me with eyes like gunsights. 'I don't like it. I *really* don't like it.'

'You don't have to,' Andy says flatly. 'We're *telling* you what to do. Your job is – I shouldn't be telling you this, it should be Angleton, this afternoon, but what the hell – you're going to be assigned to shadow Mo. We'll do the rest. All I want to hear from you now is that you're going to do as you're told.'

I tense. 'Is that an order?'

'It is now,' says Nick.

When I get home after receiving my mission orders and pre-emptive chewing-out from Angleton I find my key doesn't turn in the lock. It's dark and it's raining so I lean on the doorbell continuously until the door swings open. Pinky stands behind it, one hand on the latch. 'What took you so long?' I ask him.

He steps back. 'These are yours, I believe,' he says, handing me a bunch of shiny new keys. He clanks as he walks; he's wearing black combat boots, matching trousers, what looks like a leather vest, and enough chains to stock a medium-sized prison. 'I'm off clubbing tonight.'

'Why the new keys?' I close the door and shake my hair, shrug off my coat, and try to find room to hang it in the hall.

'They changed the locks today,' he says conversationally, 'departmental orders, apparently.' There's a new mat inside the front door, and when I look closely I see silvery lettering in a very small font stitched into its edges. 'They came and swept the house for listeners and actors then renewed the wards on all the windows, the doors, the air vents – even the chimney. Any idea why?'

'Yeah,' I grunt. I head for the kitchen, squeezing past someone's battered suitcases that are parked in the hall.

'We've got a new flatmate, too,' he adds. 'Oh, Mhari's fucked off again, but this time she says she's moving into House Orange for good.'

'Ah-hum.' *Twist the knife in the wound, why don't you?* I inspect the kettle, then poke around inside my cupboard to see if there's any food more substantial than a pot noodle.

'You'll probably like the new flatmate, though,' Pinky continues. 'She's helping Brains with his omelettes in the front cellar – he's using high-intensity ultrasound, this time.'

I find a pot noodle and a desiccated supermarket pizza base. There's cheese and tomato paste in the fridge, and a pork sausage I can chop up to go on top of it, so I turn the grill on. 'Any newspapers?' I ask.

'Newspapers? Why?'

'I have to book a flight. I'm taking a week's leave next Monday, and it's already Wednesday.'

'Going anywhere interesting?'

'Amsterdam.'

'Cool!' There's a pair of fur-lined handcuffs on the bread board; Pinky picks them up and eyes them critically, then starts polishing them on a square of kitchen roll. 'Party on?'

'I have some research to do at the Oostindischehuis. And in the basement of the Rijksmuseum.'

'Research.' He rolls his eyes and tucks the handcuffs into a belt clip. 'What a *boring* use for a holiday in Amsterdam!'

I chop bits of pork sausage up and sprinkle them over my garbage pizza, oblivious. The cellar door swings open. 'Did somebody mention Amsterdam – hey, what are *you* doing here?'

I drop my knife. 'Mo? What are *you*—'

'Bob? Hey, have you guys met?'

' 'Scuse me, would you mind moving? I need to get through—'

With four people in the kitchen it's distinctly cosy, not to say crowded. I move my pizza up under the grill and switch the kettle on again. 'Who put you up here?' I ask Mo.

'The Plumbers – they said this was a secure apartment,' she says, rubbing the side of her nose. She peers at me suspiciously. 'What's going on?'

'It *is* a secure apartment,' I say slowly. 'It's on the Laundry list.'

'Bob's girlfriend just moved out for the fourth time,' Pinky explains helpfully. 'They must have thought the spare room needed filling.'

'Oh, this is too much.' Mo pulls out a chair and sits down with her back against the wall, arms crossed defensively.

'Guys?' I ask. 'Could you take it outside?'

'Certainly,' Brains sniffs, and disappears back into the cellar.

Pinky smiles. 'I knew you'd hit it off!' he says, then ducks out of the room hastily.

A minute later the front door slams. Mo fixes me with a magistrate's stare. 'You live here? With those two?'

'Yeah.' I inspect the grill. 'They're mostly harmless, when they're not trying to take over the world each night.'

'Trying to—' She stops. 'That one. Uh, Pinky? He's out clubbing?'

'Yes, but he never brings any rough trade home,' I explain. 'He and Brains have been together for, oh, as long as I've known them.'

'*Oh.*' I see the light bulb go on above her head: some people are a bit slow on the uptake about Pinky and Brains.

'Brains doesn't get out a lot. Pinky is a party animal, a bit of rubber, a bit of leather. Every few weeks, whenever the moon is in the right phase, hairs burst from the palms of his hands and he turns into a wild bear with a compulsion to terrorise Soho. Brains doesn't seem to notice. They're like an old married couple. Once a year Pinky drags Brains out to Pride so he can maintain his security clearance.'

'I *see.*' She relaxes a little but looks puzzled. 'I thought the secret services sacked you for being homosexual?'

'They used to, said it made you a security risk. Which was silly, because it was the practice of firing homosexuals that made them vulnerable to blackmail in the first place. So these days they just insist on openness – the theory is you can only be blackmailed if you're hiding something. Which is why the Brain gets the day off for Gay Pride to maintain his security clearance.'

'Ah – I give up.' She smiles. The smile fades fast. 'I've still got to move my stuff in. They're packing up the flat and I didn't have much anyway, most of my furniture is in a shipping container somewhere on the Atlantic . . . Why Amsterdam, Bob?'

I prod at the pizza, which is beginning to melt on top as the grill strains to heat it up. 'I've been doing a bit of digging.' I wince: my rib stabs at me. 'Things you said last night. Oh, has anyone said anything to you?'

'No.' She looks puzzled.

'Well, don't be surprised if in the next couple of days Andy or Derek drops by and gets you to sign a piece of paper saying that you'll cut your own throat before talking to anyone without clearance. That's what they did to me; they're taking it seriously.'

'Well *that's* a relief,' she says with heavy irony. 'Did you learn anything?'

The pizza is bubbling away on top; I turn the grill down so that it can heat right through. 'Coffee?'

'Tea, if you've got it.'

'Okay. Um, I did some reading. Did you know that what you overheard is completely impossible? As in, it can't happen because it's not allowed?'

'It's not – hang on.' She glares at me. 'If you're pulling my leg—'

'Would I do a thing like that?' I must look the image of hurt innocence because she chuckles wickedly.

'I wouldn't put anything past you, Bob. Okay, what do you mean by "it's not allowed"? As your professor I am ordering you to tell me everything.'

'Uh, isn't it my job to say, "Tell me, professor"?'

She waves it off: 'Nah, that would be a cliché. So tell me. What the fornicating hell is happening? Why does someone or something try to render me metabolically incompetent whenever I meet you?'

'Well, it goes back to around 1919,' I say, dropping tea bags into a chipped pot. 'That was when the Thule Gessellschaft was founded in Munich by Baron von Sebottendorff. The Thule Society were basically mystical whack-jobs, but they had a lot of clout; in particular they were heavily into Masonic symbolism and a load of post-Theosophical guff about how the only true humans were the Aryan race, and the rest – the *Mindwertigen*, "inferior beings" – were sapping their strength and purity and precious bodily fluids. All of this wouldn't have mattered much except a bunch of these goons were mixed up in Bavarian street politics, the Freikorps and so on. They sort of cross-fertilised with a small outfit called the NSDAP, whose leader was a former NCO and agent provocateur sent by the Landswehr to keep an eye on far-right movements. He picked up a lot of ideas from the Thule Society and when he got where he wanted he told the head of his personal bodyguard – a guy called Heinrich Himmler, another occult obsessive – to put Walter Darre, one of Alfred Rosenberg's protégés, in charge of the Ahnenerbe Society.

Ahnenerbe was originally independent, but rapidly turned into a branch of the SS after 1934; a sort of occult R&D department cum training college. Meanwhile the Gestapo orchestrated a pretty severe crackdown on all nonparty occultists in the Third Reich; Adolf wanted a monopoly on esoteric power, and he got it.'

I switch off the grill. 'All this would have amounted to exactly zip except that some nameless spark in the Ahnenerbe research arm unearthed David Hilbert's unpublished Last Question. And from there to the Wannsee Conference was just a short step.'

'Hilbert, Wannsee – you've lost me. What did the calculus of variations have to do with Wannsee, wherever that is?'

'Wrong question, right Hilbert; it's not one of the Twenty-Three Questions on unsolved problems in mathematics, it's something he did later. Thing is, Hilbert was experimenting with some very odd ideas toward the end, before he died in 1943. He'd more or less pioneered functional analysis, he came up with Hilbert Space – obviously – and he was working toward a 'proof theory' in the mid-thirties, a theory for formally proving the correctness of theorems. Yeah, I know, Gödel holed that one under the waterline in 1931. Anyhow, you know Hilbert's published work dropped off sharply in the 1930s and he didn't publish *anything* in the 1940s? And yes, he'd read Turing's doctoral thesis. Do I need to draw you a diagram? No? Good.

'Now, Wannsee . . . that was the conference in late 1941 that set the Final Solution in motion. Before then, it was mostly an alfresco atrocity – *Einsatzgruppen,* mobile murder units, running around behind the front line machine-gunning people. It was the Ahnenerbe-SS, with the Numerical Analysis Department founded on the back of that unpublished work by Hilbert – he pointedly refused to cooperate any further once he realised what was going on, by the way – which provided the seed for the Wannsee Invocation. The Wannsee Conference was attended by delegates from about twenty different Nazi organisations and ministries. It set up the organisation of the Final Solution. The Ahnenerbe ran it behind the scenes, using Karl Adolf

Eichmann – at the time, head of Section IV B4 of the Reich Main Security Office – as organisational head, a kind of Nazi equivalent of General Leslie Groves. In the USA, General Groves was a Corps of Engineers officer; he organised the massive logistical and infrastructure mobilisation needed to build the Manhattan Project. In Vienna, Eichmann, an SS *Obersturmbannführer*, was in charge of providing raw material for the largest necromantic invocation in human history.

'The goal of what the Ahnenerbe called Project Jotunheim, and what everyone else called the Wannsee Invocation, was what we'd today designate the opening of a class four gate – a large, bidirectional bridge to another universe where the commutative operation, opening gates back to our own, is substantially easier. A bridge big enough to take tanks, bombers, U-boats. Can you spell "counter-strike"? We're not sure quite what their constraint requirements were, or what the Wannsee Invocation was intended to accomplish, but they'd have been pretty drastic; Wannsee cost the Nazi state a greater proportion of its wealth than the Manhattan Project cost the US, and would have had similar or bigger military implications if they'd succeeded. Of course, their spell was grotesquely unoptimised; you could probably do it with a budget of a million pounds for equipment and only use a couple of sacrifices if you had a proper understanding of the theory. They tried to do a brute-force attack on the problem, and failed – especially when the Allies got wind of it and bombed the crap out of the big soul-capacitors at Peenumënde. But that's not the point. They failed, and those deaths, all ten million or so of the people they murdered in the extermination camps that fed the death spell, didn't suffice to pull their heads out of the noose.'

Mo shivers. 'That's *horrible*.' She stands up and walks over to inspect the tea. 'Hmm, needs more milk.' She leans against the counter next to me. 'I can't believe Hilbert would have cooperated with the Nazis willingly on that kind of project.'

'He didn't. And when the Allies found out, they, um, demilitarised Germany with extreme prejudice. In the occult field, anyway. None of the Ahnenerbe-SS researchers from the

Numerical Analysis Division survived; if the SOE death squads didn't get them, it was the OSS or the NKVD. That's what the Helsinki Protocol was about: *nobody* wanted to see systematic mass murder of civilians adopted as a technique in strategic warfare, especially given some of the more unpleasant and extreme effects the weapon Ahnenerbe-SS were working on could give rise to. Like collapsing the false vacuum or letting vastly superhuman alien intelligences gain access to our universe. This stuff made atom bombs and ballistic missiles look harmless.'

'Oh.' She pauses. 'Which is why what happened to me is impossible, right? I think I begin to see. Curiouser and curiouser . . .'

'I'm going to Amsterdam next Monday, soon as I've booked a flight,' I say slowly. 'Want to come along?'

I feel like a real shit. Andy told me I would, and Angleton ground the message home; but it doesn't help any as I tell her half the reasons why I'm going to Amsterdam – the half she's cleared for.

'The Rijksmuseum has an interesting basement,' I say lightly. 'It's off-limits to civ – to people who don't have need-to-know on the Helsinki Protocols. Thing is, Holland is part of the EUIN-TEL agreement, a treaty group that provides for joint suppression operations directed against paranormal threats. I'm not allowed to visit the USA on business without a specific invitation, but Amsterdam is home territory. As long as it's official and I've established a liaison relationship I can call for backup and expect to get it. And if I want to examine the basement library, well, it's the best collated set of Ahnenerbe-SS memorabilia and records this side of Yad Vashem.'

'So if you get a hankering to go look at some old masters and disappear through a side door for a couple of hours—'

'Exactly.'

'Bullshit, Bob.' She frowns at me, eyebrows furrowing. 'You've just been lecturing me about the history of this bunch of Nazi necromancers. You obviously think there's some connection with the Middle Eastern guys in Santa Cruz, the one with the weird eyes and the German accent. Your flatmates have just been telling me how safe this house is, and how all the wards have just been updated. If you're afraid of something, why not just sit tight at home?'

I shrug. 'Well, leaving aside that the bastards seem to want you for something – I'm not sure. Look, there's some other stuff I'm not allowed to talk about, but right now Amsterdam looks like the right place to be, if I want to find these idiots before they try and kidnap you again.'

I pull the grill tray out and slide my garbage pizza onto a plate. 'Slice of pizza?'

'Yes, thank you.'

I cut the thing in two pieces and slide one onto another plate, pass it to her. 'Look, there's a connection between those goons who kidnapped you in Santa Cruz and something my boss has been keeping an eye on for a couple of years. It turns out that they're connected to the Mukhabarat, the Iraqi secret police; there's a proliferation spin on the whole thing, rogue state trying to get its hands on weapons forbidden by treaty. Right?' She nods, mouth too full to reply. 'From that perspective, kidnapping you makes perfect sense. What I don't understand is the sacrifice bit. Or the attempt to kill you. It just doesn't make sense if it's simply a Mukhabarat technology transfer deal. Those guys are vicious but they're not idiots.'

I take a deep breath. 'No, the trouble you've got is something related to the Ahnenerbe-SS's legacy. Which is deep, dark shit. I wouldn't put it beyond Saddam Hussein to be dealing in such things – the Ba'ath party of Iraq explicitly modelled their security apparatus on the Third Reich, and they've got a real down on Jews – but it puzzles me. I mean, the possessed guy you saw who wasn't in the flat when the Black Chamber SWAT team stormed it – was he something to do with the Mukhabarat or one of their proxies summoning up some psychotic Nazi death magic or something? If so, the question is who they are, and the answer may be buried in the Rijksmuseum basement. Oh, and there's one other thing.'

'Oh? What would that be?'

I can't look her in the eye; I just can't. 'My boss says he'd value your insight. On an informal basis.'

Which is only half the truth. What I *really* want to say to her is: *It's you they're after. As long as you're here in a Laundry safe house they can't get to you. But if we trail you in front of them, in the middle of a city that happens to be the Mukhabarat's headquarters for Western Europe, we might be able to draw them out. Get them to try again, under the guns of a friendly team. Be our tethered goat, Mo?* But I'm chicken. I don't have the guts to ask her to bait my hook. I hold my tongue and I feel about six inches tall, and in my imagination I can see Andy and Derek nodding silent approval, and it still doesn't help. 'Given enough pairs of eyes, all problems are transparent,' I say, falling back to platitudes. 'Besides, it's a great city. We could maybe study etchings together, or something.'

'You need to work on your pickup lines,' Mo observes, yanking a particularly limp segment of pizza base loose and holding it up. 'But for the sake of argument, consider me charmed. How much will this trip cost?'

'Ah, now that's the good bit.' I drain my mug and push it away from me. 'There aren't many perks that come from working for the Laundry, but one of them is that it happens to be possible to get a cheap travel pass. Special arrangement with BA, apparently. All we have to pay is the airport tax and our hotel bill. Know any decent B&Bs out there?'

6: THE ATROCITY ARCHIVES

THREE DAYS FLICK BY LIKE MICROFICHE CARDS through the input hopper of Angleton's Memex. Mo has settled into the vacant room on the second floor of our safe house like a long-term resident; as a not very senior academic, her Ph.D. years not long behind her, she probably spent years in flat-shares like this. I focus on my day-to-day work, fixing broken network servers, running a security audit of some service department's kit (two illicit copies of Minesweeper and one MP3 music jukebox to eliminate), and spending the afternoons up in the secure office in the executive suite, learning the bible of field operations by heart. I try not to think about what I'm getting Mo into. In fact, I try not to see her at all, spending long hours into the evening poring over arcane regulations and petty incantations for coordinating joint task-force operations. I feel more than a little bit guilty, even though I'm only obeying orders, and consequently I feel a little bit depressed.

At least Mhari doesn't try to get in touch.

The Sunday before we're due to leave I have to stay home because I need to pack my bags. I'm dithering over a stack of T-shirts and an electric toothbrush when someone knocks on my bedroom door. 'Bob?'

I open it. 'Mo.'

She steps inside, hesitant, eyes scanning. My room often has that effect on people. It's not the usual single male scattering of clothes on every available surface – aggravated by my packing – so much as the groaning, double-stacked bookcase and the stuff on the walls. Not many guys have anatomically correct life-sized plastic skeletons hanging from a wall bracket. Or a desk made out of Lego bricks, with the bits of three half-vivisected computers humming and chattering to each other on top of it.

'Are you packing?' she asks, smiling brightly at me; she's dressed up for a night out with some lucky bastard, and here's me wondering when I last changed my T-shirt and looking forward to a close encounter with a slice of toast and a tin of baked beans. But the embarrassment only lasts for a moment, until her wandering gaze settles in the direction of the bookcase. Then: 'Is that a copy of Knuth?' She homes in on the top shelf. 'Hang on – volume *four*? But he only finished the first three volumes in that series! Volume four's been overdue for the past twenty years!'

'Yup.' I nod, smugly. Whoever she's dating won't have anything like *that* on his shelves. 'We – or the Black Chamber – have a little agreement with him; he doesn't publish volume four of *The Art of Computer Programming*, and they don't render him metabolically challenged. At least, he doesn't publish it to the public; it's the one with the Turing Theorem in it. Phase Conjugate Grammars for Extra-dimensional Summoning. This is a very limited edition – numbered and classified.'

'That's—' She frowns. 'May I borrow it? To read?'

'You're on the inside now; just don't leave it on the bus.'

She pulls the book down, shoves a bundle of crumpled jeans to one side of my bed to make room, and perches on the end of it. Mo in dress-up mode turns out to be a grownup designer version of hippie crossed with Goth: black velvet skirt, silver bangles, ethnic top. Not quite self-consciously pre-Raphaelite, but nearly. Right now she's destroying the effect completely by being 100 percent focussed on the tome. 'Wow.' Her eyes are alight. 'I just wanted to see if you were, like, getting ready? Only now I don't want to go; I'm going to be up all night!'

'Just remember we need to be out the door by seven o'clock,'

I remind her. 'Allow two hours for getting to Luton and check in . . .'

'I'll sleep on the plane.' She closes the book and puts it down, but keeps one hand on the cover, protectively close. 'I haven't seen you around much, Bob. Been busy?'

'More than you can imagine,' I say. Setting up scanners that will slurp through the Laundry's UPI and Reuters news feeds and page me if anything interesting comes up while I'm away. Reading the manual for field operations. Avoiding my guilty conscience . . . 'How about you?'

She pulls a face. 'There's so *much* stuff buried in the stacks, it's unbelievable. I've been spending all my time reading, getting indigestion along the way. It's just such a waste – all that stuff, locked up behind the Official Secrets Act!'

'Yeah, well.' It's my turn to pull a face now. 'In principle, I kind of agree with you. In practice . . . how to put it? This stuff has repercussions. The many-angled ones live at the bottom of the Mandelbrot set; play around with it for too long and horrible things can happen to you.' I shrug. 'And you know what students are like.'

'Yes, well.' She stands up, straightening her skirt with one hand and holding the book with the other. 'I suppose you've got more experience of that than I have. But, well.' She pauses, and gives a little half-smile: 'I was wondering if, if you'd eaten yet?'

Ah. Suddenly I figure it out: I'm *so* thick. 'Give me half an hour?' I ask. *Where the hell did I leave that shirt?* 'Anywhere in particular take your fancy?'

'There's a little bistro on the high street that I was meaning to check out. If you're ready in half an hour?'

'Downstairs,' I say firmly. 'Half an hour!' She slips out of my room and I waste half a minute drooling at the back of the door before I snap out of it and go in search of something to wear that doesn't look too shop-soiled. The sudden realisation that Mo might actually enjoy my company is a better antidepressant than anything I could get on a prescription.

* * *

I'm brought to my senses by the shrill of my alarm clock: it's eight in the morning, the sky's still dark outside, my head aches, and I'm feeling inexplicably happy for someone who this afternoon will be baiting the trap for an unknown enemy.

I pull on my clothes, grab my bags, head downstairs still yawning vigorously. Mo is in the kitchen, red-eyed and nursing a mug of coffee; there's a huge, travel-stained backpack in the hall. 'Been up all night with the book?' I ask. She was thinking about it all through what was otherwise a really enjoyable quiet night out.

'Here. Help yourself.' She points to the cafetière. She yawns. 'This is *all* your fault.' I glance at her in time to catch a brief grin. 'Ready to go?'

'After this.' I pour a mug, add milk, shudder, yawn again, and begin to work on it. 'Somehow I'm not hungry this morning.'

'I think that place goes on the visit-again list,' she agrees. 'I must try the couscous next time . . .' She mounts another attack on her mug and I decide that she's just as attractive wearing jeans and sweat shirt and no warpaint first thing in the morning as in the evening. I'll pass on the red eyes, though. 'Got your passport?'

'Yeah. And the tickets. Shall we go?'

'Lead on.'

Some hours later we've emerged from Arrivals at Schiphol, caught the train to the Centraal Station, grappled with the trams, and checked into a cutesy family-run hotel with a theme of hot and cold running philosophers – Hegel on the breakfast room place mats, Mo in the Plato room on the top floor, and myself relegated to the Kant basement. By early afternoon we're walking in the Vondelpark, between the dark green grass and the overcast grey sky; a cool wind is blowing in off the channel and for the first time I'm able to get the traffic fumes out of my lungs. And we're out of sight of Nick and Alan who, until the hotel, tailed us all the way from the safe house to the airport and then onto our flight – I suppose they're part of the surveillance team. It's bad practice to acknowledge their presence and they made no attempt to talk to me; as far as I can tell, Mo doesn't suspect anything.

'So where is this museum then?' asks Mo.

'Right there.' I point. At one end of the park, a neoclassical lump of stonework rears itself pompously toward the sky. 'Let's check in and get our restricted area passes validated, huh? Give it an hour or so and we can try and find somewhere to eat.'

'Only a couple of hours?'

'Everywhere closes early in Amsterdam, except the bars and coffee shops,' I explain. 'But don't go in a coffee shop and order a coffee or they'll laugh at you. What we call a café is an *Eethuis*, and what they call a café we call a pub. Got it?'

'Clear as mud.' She shakes her head. 'Good thing for me everyone seems to speak English.'

'It's a common affliction.' I pause. 'Just don't let it make you feel too secure. This isn't a safe house.'

We walk past a verdigris-covered statue while she considers this. 'You have another agenda for coming here,' she says finally.

My guts feel cold. 'Yes,' I admit. I've been dreading this moment.

'Well.' Unexpectedly she reaches out and takes my hand. 'I assume you're prepared for the shit to hit the fan, right?'

'All feco-ventilatory intersections are covered. They assure me.'

'*They*.' She shrugs, uncomfortably. 'This was their idea?'

I glance round, keeping a vague eye on the other wanderers in the park; a couple of elderly pensioner types, a kid on a skateboard, that's about it. Of course that doesn't mean we aren't being tailed – a raven that's had its central nervous system hijacked by a demonic imperative, a micro-UAV cruising silent a hundred metres overhead with cameras focussed – but at least you can do something about human tradecraft, as opposed to the esoteric or electronic kinds.

'They're not keen on letting whoever's tracking you get a chance to say "third time lucky,"' I try to explain. 'This is a setup. We're on friendly territory and if anyone tries to grab you, I'm not the only one on your case.'

'That's nice to know.' I look at her sharply but she's got her innocent face on, the absent-minded professor musing over a theorem rather than focussing on the world, the flesh, and the devils of Interpol's most-wanted list.

'You never did tell me about the *Thresher*,' I comment as we cross the road to the museum.

'Oh, what? The submarine? I didn't think you were interested.'

'Huh.' I lead her along the side of the building instead of climbing the steps, and I keep an eye open for the side entrance I'm looking for. 'Of course I'm interested.'

'I was kidding, you know.' She flashes me a grin. 'Wanted to see if it would make you pull your finger out. You spooks are just *so focussed*.'

There's a blank door set between two monolithic granite slabs that form one flank of the museum; I rap on it thrice and it opens inward automatically. (There's a camera in the ceiling of this entrance tunnel: unwanted visitors will not be made welcome.) 'What *is* this?' Mo asks, 'Hey, that's the first secret door I've seen!'

'Nah, it's just the service entrance,' I say. The door closes behind us and I lead her forward, round a bend, and up to the security desk. 'Howard and O'Brien from the Laundry,' I say, placing my hand on the counter.

The booth is empty, but there are two badges waiting on the counter and the door ahead of us opens anyway. 'Welcome to the Archive,' says a speaker behind the counter. 'Please take your ID badges and wear them at all times except when visiting the public galleries.'

I take them and pass one to Mo. She inspects it dubiously. 'Is this solid silver? What's the language? This isn't Dutch.'

'It probably came from Indonesia. Don't ask, just wear it.' I pin mine on my belt, under the hem of my T-shirt – it doesn't need to be visible to human guards, after all. 'Coming?'

'Yeah.'

The cellars under the Rijksmuseum remind me of an upmarket version of the Stacks at Dansey House – huge tunnels, whitewashed and air-conditioned, chock-full of shelves. There's a difference: almost all the contents at Dansey House are files. Here there are boxes, plastic or wooden, full of evidence, left over from the trials that followed a time of infinite horrors.

The Ahnenerbe-SS collection is in a subbasement guarded by locked steel doors; one of the curators – a civilian in jeans and sweater – takes us down there. 'Don't you be staying too long,' she advises us. 'This place, it gives me creeps; you not sleeping well tonight, yah?'

'We'll be all right,' I reassure her. The Ahnenerbe collection has about the strongest set of guards and wards imaginable – nobody involved in looking after it wants to worry about lunatics and neo-Nazis getting their hands on some of the powerfully charged relics stored here.

'You say.' She looks at me blackly, then one eyebrow twitches. 'Sweet dreams.'

'Just what are we looking for?' asks Mo.

'Well, to start with—' I clap my hands. We're facing a corridor with numbered storage rooms off to either side. It's well lit and empty, like a laboratory where everyone has just nipped out for afternoon tea. 'The symbols painted on the walls of the apartment in Santa Cruz,' I say. 'Think you'd recognise them if you saw them again?'

'Recognise? I, uh . . . maybe,' she says slowly. 'I wouldn't like to say for sure. I was half out of my head and I didn't get a real good look at them.'

'That's more than I got, and the Black Chamber didn't send us any postcards,' I say. 'Which is why we've come here. Think of it as a photo-fit session for necromancy.' I read the plaque on the nearest door, then push it open. The lights come on automatically, and I freeze. It's a good thing the lights are bright, because the contents of the room, seen in shadow, would be heart-stopping. As it is, they're merely heart-breaking.

There's a white cast-iron table, a thing of curves and scrollwork, just inside the doorway. Three chairs sit around it, delicate-looking white assemblies of struts and curved sections. I blink, for there's something odd about them, something that reminds me of the art of Giger, the film set *of Alien*. And then I realise what I'm looking at: the backs of the chairs are vertebrae, wired together. The chairs are made of scrimshaw, carved from the thigh bones of the dead; the decorative scrollwork of the table is a rack of human ribs. The table-top itself is made of polished, interlocking shoulder blades. And as for the cigarette lighter—

'I think I'm going to be sick,' whispers Mo. She looks distinctly pale.

'Toilet's down the corridor,' I bite out, gritting my teeth while she hurries away, retching. I take in the rest of the room. *They're right*, I think in some quiet, rational recess of my mind, *some things you just can't tell the public about*. The Holocaust, even seen at arm's length through newsreel footage, was bad enough to brand the collective unconscious of the West with a scar of indelible evil, madness on an inconceivable scale. Hideous enough that some people seek to deny it ever happened. But *this*, this isn't something you can even begin to describe: this is the dark nightmare of a diseased mind.

There were medical laboratories attached to the death camp at Birkenau. Some of their tools are stored here. There were other, darker, laboratories behind the medical unit, and their tools are stored here, too, those that have not been destroyed in accordance with the requirements of disarmament treaties.

Next to the charnel house garden furniture sits a large rack of electronics, connected to a throne of timber with metal straps at ankle and wrist – an electric chair; the Ahnenerbe experimented with the destruction of human souls, seeking a way to sear through the Cartesian bottleneck and exterminate not only the bodies of their victims, but the informational echoes of their consciousness. Only the difficulty of extinguishing souls on a mass production basis kept it from featuring prominently in their schemes.

Beyond the soul-eater there's a classical mediaeval iron maiden, except that the torturers of the Thirty Years War didn't get to play with aluminium alloy and hydraulic rams. There are other machines, all designed to maim and kill with a maximum of agony: one of them, a bizarre cross between a printing press and a rack made of glass, seems to have materialised from a nightmare of Kafka's.

They were trying to generate pain, I realize. They weren't simply killing their victims but deliberately *hurting* them in the process, hurting them as badly as the human body could stand, squeezing the pain out of them like an evil seepage of blood, hurting them again and again until all the pain had been extracted—

I'm sitting down but I don't remember how I got here. I feel dizzy; Mo is standing over me. 'Bob?' I close my eyes and try to control my breathing. 'Bob?'

'I need a minute,' I hear myself saying.

The room reeks of old, dead terror – and a brooding malevolence, as if the instruments of torture are merely biding their time. *Just you wait*, they're saying. I shudder, open my eyes, and try to stand up.

'This was what the . . . the Ahnenerbe used?' asks Mo. She sounds hoarse.

I nod, not trusting my voice. It's a moment before I can speak. 'The secret complex. Behind the medical block at Birkenau, where they experimented with pain. Algemancy. They took Zuse's Z-2 computer, you know? It was supposed to have been bombed by the Allies, in Berlin. That was what Zuse himself was told, he was away at the time. But they took it . . .' I swallow. 'It's in the next room.'

'A computer? I didn't know they had them.'

'Only just; Konrad Zuse built his first programmable computer in 1940. He independently invented the things: after the war he founded Zuse Computer Company, which was taken over by Siemens in the early sixties. He wasn't a bad man; when he didn't cooperate they stole his machine, demolished the house where he had built it, and claimed the destruction was an Allied bomb. The cabbalistic iterations, you see – they rebuilt it at Sobibor camp, using circuits soldered with gold extracted from the teeth of their victims.' I stand up and head for the door. 'I'll show you, but that's not really why we're . . . hell. I'll show you.'

The next room in the Atrocity Archive contains the remains of the Z-2. Old nineteen-inch equipment racks tower ceiling-high; there are mounds of vacuum tubes visible through gaps in the front panels, dials and gauges to monitor power consumption, and plugboards to load programs into the beast. All very quaint, until you see the printer that lurks in the shadowy recess at the back of the room. 'Here they ran the phase-state calculations that dictated the killing schedule, opening and closing circuits in time to the ebb and flow of murder. They even generated the railway timetables with this computer, synchronising deliveries of victims to the maw of the machine.' I walk toward the printer, look round to see Mo waiting behind me. 'This printer.' It's a plotter, motors dragging a Ouija-board pen across a sheet of – it would have been parchment, but not from a cow or a sheep. I swallow bile. 'They used it to inscribe the geometry curves that were to open the way of Dho-Na. All very, very advanced: this was the first real use of computers in magic, you know.'

Mo backs away from the machines. Her face is a white mask under the overhead strip lighting. 'Why are you showing me this?'

'The patterns are in the next room.' I follow her out into the corridor and take her by the elbow, gently steering toward the third chamber – where the real Archive begins. It's a plain-looking room, full of the sort of file drawers you find in architects' offices – very shallow, very wide, designed to hold huge, flat blueprints. I pull the top drawer of the nearest cabinet out and show her. 'Look. Seen anything like this before?' It's very fine parchment inscribed with what looks like a collision between a mandala, a pentagram, and a circuit diagram, drawn in bluish ink. At the front and left, a neat box-out in engineering script details the content of the blueprint. If I didn't know what it was meant to be, or what the parchment was made of, I'd think it was quite pretty. I take care not to touch the thing.

'It's – yes.' She traces one of the curves with a fingertip, carefully holding it an inch above the inscription. 'No, it wasn't this one. But it's similar.'

'There are several thousand more like this in here,' I say, studying her expression. 'I'd like to see if we can identify the one you saw on the wall?' She nods, uneasily. 'We don't have to do it right now,' I admit. 'If you would rather we took a breather there's a café upstairs where we can have a cup of coffee and relax a bit first—'

'No.' She pauses for a moment. 'Let's get it over and done with.' She glances over her shoulder and shudders slightly. 'I don't want to stay down here any longer than I have to.'

About two hours later, while Mo is halfway through the contents of drawer number fifty-two, my pager goes off. I scrabble at the waistband of my jeans in a momentary panic then pull the thing out. One of the newsgreppers I left running on the network servers back home has paged me: in its constant trawl through the wire feeds it s come across something interesting. KILLING IN ROTTERDAM, it says, followed by a reference number.

'Got to go upstairs,' I say, 'think you'll be okay here for twenty minutes?'

Mo looks at me with eyes like bruises. 'I'll take you up on that coffee break if you don't mind.'

'Not at all. Not having much luck?'

'Nothing so far.' She yawns, catches herself, and shakes her head. 'My attention span is going. Oh God, coffee. I never realised it was possible to be horrified and bored out of your skin at the same time.'

I refrain from calling her on the unintentional pun; instead I make a note of where she's got up to – at this rate we could be here for another week, unless we get lucky – and slide the drawer shut. 'Okay. Time out.'

The coffee shop is upstairs, attached to the museum shop; it's all whitewash and neat little tables and there's a stand with patisseries on it next to the counter. All very *gezelig*. A row of cheap PCs along one wall offer Internet access for the compulsives who can't kick their habit for a day of high culture. I home in on one and begin the tedious process of logging into one of the Laundry's servers by way of three firewalls, two passwords, an encrypted tunnel, and an S/Key challenge. At the end of the day I'm onto a machine that isn't exactly trusted – the Laundry will not allow classified servers to be connected on the net, by any arrangement of wires or wishful thinking – but that happens to run my news trawler. Which, after all, is fishing in the shallow waters of Reuters and UPI, rather than the oceanic chasm of state secrets.

So what made my pager go off? While Mo is drinking a mug full of mocha and contemplating the museum's catalogue of forthcoming attractions, I find myself reading an interesting article from the AP wire service. DOUBLE KILLING IN ROTTERDAM (AP): Two bodies discovered near a burned-out shipping container in the port appear to be victims of a brutal gangland-style slaying. Blood daubed on the container, victims – ah, a correlation with a restricted information source, something sucked out of the Police National Computer and not available in the usual wire service bulletin. One victim is a known neo-Nazi, the other an Iraqi national, both shot with the same gun. *Is that all?* I wonder, and go clickety-click, sending out a brief email asking where was the shipping container sent from and where was it bound for because you never know . . .

I shake my head. The article dinged my search filter's 'phone home' bell by accumulating little keyword matches until it passed a threshold, not because it's obviously important. But something nags at the back of my mind: there's seawater nearby, graffiti in blood on the wall, an Iraqi connection. *Why Rotterdam?* Well, it's one of the main container-port gateways into Europe, that's for starters. For seconds, it's less than fifty kilometres away.

There's no other real news. I log out and leave the terminal; time to drink a coffee and get back to work.

Three hours later: 'Found it,' she says.

I look up from the report I'm reading. 'Are you sure?'

'Certain.' I stand up and walk over. She's leaning over an open drawer and her arms are tense as wires. I think she'd be shaking if she wasn't holding herself still and stiff. I look over her shoulder. The drawing is a geometry curve all right. Actually, I've seen ones like this before. The aborted summoning Dr. Vohlman demonstrated in front of the class that day – was it only a few weeks ago? – looked quite similar. But that one was designed to open a constrained information channel to one of the infernal realms. I can't quite see where this one is directed, at least not without taking it home and studying it with the aid of a protractor and a calculator, but a quick glance tells me it's more than a simple speakerphone to hell.

Here we see a differential that declares a function of tau, the rate of change of time with distance along one of the Planck dimensions. *There* we see an admonition that this circuit is not to be completed without a cage around it. (A good thing the notation we use, and that of the Ahnenerbe, is derived from the same source, or I wouldn't be able to figure it out.) *This* formula looks surprisingly modern, it's some sort of curve through the complex number plane – each point along it is a different Julia set. And *that* is where the human sacrifice is wired into the diagram by its eyeballs while still alive, for maximum bandwidth—

I blank for a second, flashing on the evil elegance of the design. 'Are you *sure* this is it?' I mumble.

'Of course I'm sure!' Mo snaps at me. 'Do you think I'd—' She stops. Takes a deep breath. Mutters something quietly to herself, then: 'What is it?'

'I'm not 100 percent certain,' I say, carefully placing the notepad I was reading from down on my chair and moving to one side so I can inspect the diagram from a different angle, 'but it looks like a resonator map. A circuit designed to tune in on another universe. This one is similar to our own, in fact it's astonishingly close by; the energy barrier you have to tunnel through to reach it is high enough that nothing less than a human sacrifice will do.'

'Human sacrifice?'

'It doesn't take much energy to talk to a demon,' I explain. 'They're pretty much waiting to hear from us, at least the ones people mostly want to talk to. But they come from a long way away – from universes with a very weak affinity to our own. Information leakage doesn't imply an energy change in our own world; it's concealed in the random noise. But if we try to talk to a universe close to home there's a huge potential energy barrier to overcome – this sort of prevents causality violations. The whole thing is mediated by intelligence – observers are required to collapse the wave function – which is where the sacrifice comes in: we're eliminating an observer. Done correctly, this lets us talk to a universe that isn't so much next door as lying adjacent to our own, separated by a gap less than the Planck length.'

'Oh.' She points at the map. 'So this thing . . . it's a very precise transformation through the Mandelbrot set. Which you guys have used as a map onto a Linde continuum, right? Why don't they just set up an n-dimensional homogeneous matrix transformation? It's so much more intuitively obvious.'

'Uh—' She manages to surprise me at the damnedest times. 'I don't know. Have to read up on it, I guess.'

'Well.' She pauses for an instant and looks very slightly disappointed, as if her star pupil has just failed a verbal test. 'This is very like what I saw. Got any suggestions for what to do next, wise guy?'

'Yes. There's a photocopier upstairs. Let's call the curator and run off a copy or two. Then we can get someone back home to compare it to the photographs of the shipping container at that murder site in Rotterdam. If they're similar we have a connection.'

Our hotel has a bijou bar and a breakfast room, but no restaurant; so it seems natural that after running off our copies we should go home, head for our respective rooms, freshen up, and head out on the town to find somewhere to eat. (And maybe share a drink or two. Those hours in the basement of horrors are going to give me bad dreams tonight, and I'd be surprised if Mo is any better.) I spend half an hour soaking in the bathtub with a copy of *Surreal Calculus and the Navigation of Everett-Wheeler Continua* – hoping to brush up on my dinner-table patter – then dry myself, pull on a clean pair of chinos and an open-necked shirt, and head upstairs.

Mo is waiting at the bar with a cup of coffee and a copy of the *Herald Tribune*. She's wearing the same evening-out-on-the-town outfit as last time. She folds the newspaper and nods at me. 'Want to try that Indonesian place we passed?' I ask her.

'Why not.' She finishes the coffee quickly. 'Is it raining outside?'

'Wasn't last time I looked.'

She stands up gracefully and pulls her coat on. 'Let's go.'

The nights are drawing in, and the evening air is cool and damp. I'm still self-conscious about navigating around the roads – not only do they run on the wrong side, but they've got separate bike lanes everywhere, and, to make matters worse, separate tram lanes that sometimes don't go in the same direction as the rest of the traffic. It makes crossing the road an exercise in head-twitching, and I nearly get mown down by a girl on a bicycle riding without lights in the dusk – but we make it to the tram stop more or less intact, and Mo doesn't laugh at me out loud. 'Do you always jerk around like that?'

'Only when I'm trying to avoid the feral man-eating mopeds. Is this tram – ah.' Two stops later we get off and head for that Indonesian place we passed earlier. They have a vacant table, and we have a meal.

I turn on my new palmtop's antisound and Mo talks to me over her satay: 'Was that what you were hoping to find at the museum?'

I dribble peanut sauce over a skewer before replying. 'It was what I was hoping *not* to find, really.' She has her back to the plateglass window and I have a decent view of the main road behind her shoulder. Which is important, and I keep glancing that way because I am on edge – our friendly neighbourhood abductors seem to go to work at dusk, and when all's said and done this is a stakeout and Mo is the goat. I look back at her. She's very decorative, for a goat: most goats don't wear ethnic tops, large silver earrings, and friendly expressions. 'On the other hand, at least we know we're dealing with something profoundly unpleasant. Which means that *Carnate Gecko* gets something solid to chew on and we've got a lead to follow up.'

'Assuming it doesn't follow *us* up instead.' Her expression clouds over in an instant: 'Tell me the truth, Bob?'

My mouth turns dry: this is a moment I've been dreading even more than the discovery in the basement. 'What?'

'Why are they after me?'

Oh, *that* truth. I manage to breathe again. 'Your . . . research. And the stuff you were really working on in the States.'

'You know about that.' She looks tense and I suddenly wonder, *How many secrets are we keeping from each other?*

'Angleton told me about it. Black Chamber notified us when they deported you. Don't look so startled. About the restricted theoretical work on probability manipulation − lucky vectors, fate quantisation? It's all classified, but it's not − no, what I mean to say is, they don't like us running around on their turf, but information sharing goes on at different levels.'

I point my skewer at her and dissemble creatively. 'That stuff is fairly serious juju in our field. The Pentagon plays with it. We've got it. A couple of other countries have occult operations groups who make use of destiny entanglement fields. But the likes of Yusuf Qaradawi can't get his hands on it without a hell of a lot of reverse engineering, any more than the provisional IRA ever got their hands on cruise missile technology. The difference is, to build a cruise missile takes a ton of aerospace engineers, an advanced electronics industry, and factories. Whereas to build a scalar field that can locally boost probability coefficients attached to a Wigner's Friend observer − say, to allow a suicide bomber to walk right through a ring of bodyguards as if they aren't there − takes a couple of theoreticians and one or two field ops. Occult weapons are so much more *portable* that you can think in terms of stealing the infrastructure − if you've got people who can understand it. As most nongovernmental activist groups rely on cannon fodder so dumb they have 'mom' and 'dad' tattooed on their knuckles so the cops know who they belong to, that isn't usually much of a threat.'

'But.' She raises her last satay and swallows the skewered morsel. 'This time there is.' I see motion outside the window: see a familiar face, little more than a pale blur in the darkness, glance inside as it walks past.

'Evidently,' I mumble, feeling guilty.

'So your bosses decided to trail me in public and see what they picked up while trying to identify the group by way of the museum basement,' she adds briskly. 'How many people are watching us, Bob?'

'At least one right now,' I say, heart bouncing around my rib cage. 'That I know of, I mean. This is supposed to be a full top-and-tail job, guards outside the hotel and round the clock watch on your movements. Same as most politicians at risk of assassination get. Not that we're expecting any suicide bombers,' I add hastily.

She smiles at me warmly: 'I'm *so* pleased to know that. It really makes me feel secure.'

I wince. 'Can you suggest any alternatives?' I ask.

'Not from your boss's – what's his name? Angleton? His point of view. No, I don't suppose there is.' A waiter appears silently and removes our plates. She looks at me with an expression that I can't read. 'Why are *you* here, Bob?'

'Uh . . .' I pause to get my thoughts in order. 'Because it's my mess. I got roped in because I didn't follow procedures and hang you out to dry in California, and then I was there when things turned nasty, and this whole mess is classified up to stupid levels because there's a turf war going on between project management and operational executive—'

'That's not what I meant.' She's silent for a moment. Then: 'Why did you break the rules in Santa Cruz? Not that I object, but . . .'

'Because' – I inspect my wineglass – 'I like you. I don't think leaving people I like in the shit is a good way to behave. And, frankly, I don't have a very professional attitude to my work. Not the way the spooks think I should.'

She leans forward. 'Do you have a more professional attitude to your work now?'

I swallow. 'No, not really.'

Something – a foot – rubs up and down my ankle and I nearly jump out of my skin. 'Good.' She smiles in a way that turns my stomach to jelly, and the waiter arrives with a precariously balanced pile of dishes before I can say anything and risk embarrassing myself. We just stare at each other until he's gone, and she adds: 'I hate it when people let their professionalism get in the way of real life.'

We eat, and we talk about people and things, not necessarily in complimentary terms. Mo explains what it's like to be married to a New York lawyer and I commiserate, and she asks me what it's like to live with a manic-depressive psycho bitch from hell, and evidently she's been talking to Pinky and Brains about things because I find myself describing my relationship with Mhari with sufficient detachment that it might as well be over – ancient history. And she nods and asks if running into Mhari in Accounts and Payroll isn't embarrassing and this leads to a long discourse on how working for the Laundry is about as embarrassing as things can get: from the paper clip audits to the crazy internal billing system, and about how I hoped that getting into field ops would get me out from under Bridget's thumb, but no such luck. And Mo explains about tenure track backbiting politics in small American university departments, and about why you can kiss your career goodbye if you publish too much – as well as too little – and about the different ways in which a dual-income no-kiddies couple can self-destruct so messily that I'm left thinking maybe Mhari isn't that unusual after all.

We end up walking back to the hotel arm in arm, and under a broken streetlamp she stops, wraps her arms around me, and kisses me for what feels like half an hour. Then she rests her chin on my shoulder, beside my ear. 'This is so good,' she whispers. 'If only we weren't being followed.'

I tense. 'We're—'

'I don't like being watched,' she says, and we let go of each other simultaneously.

'Me neither.' I glance round and see a lone guy on the street behind us looking in the window of a closed shop, and all the romance flees the evening like gas from a punctured balloon. 'Shit.'

'Let's just . . . go back. Hole up and wait for morning.' I guess.

We start moving again and she takes my hand. 'Great evening out. Try it again some time?'

I smile back at her, feeling both regret and optimism. 'Yeah.'

'*Without* the audience.'

We reach the hotel, share a last drink, and head for our separate rooms.

I dream of wires, dark landscape, cold mud. Something screams in the distance; lumpy shapes strung up on barbed wire stretched before the fortress. The screams get louder and there's a rumbling and crashing and somewhere in the process I become aware that I'm not dreaming – someone is screaming, while I lie in bed halfway between sleeping and waking.

I'm on my feet almost before I realise I'm awake. I grab a T-shirt and leans, somehow slide my feet into both legs simultaneously and I'm out the door within ten seconds. The corridor is silent and dim, the only lighting coming from the overhead emergency strips; it's narrow, too, and by night the pastel-painted walls form a claustrophobic collage of grey-on-black shadows. Silence – then another scream, muffled, coming from upstairs. It's definitely human and it doesn't sound like anything you'd expect to hear from a hotel room at night. I pause for a moment, feeling silly as I consider that particular possibility – then duck back into my room and grab the multitool and the palmtop I've left atop the dresser. *Now* I head for the staircase.

Another scream and I take the steps two at a time. A door opens behind me, a tousled head poking out and mumbling, 'I'm trying to sleep . . .'

The hair on my arms stands on end. The stair rail is glowing a faint, eerie blue; sparks sting my bare feet as I climb, and the handle of the fire door at the top of the stairs gives me a nasty shock. Air sighs past me, a thin breeze blowing along the corridor where blue flickering outlines the door frames in darkness. Another scream and this time a thudding noise, then a muffled crash; I hear a door slam somewhere below me, then the shattering whine of a fire alarm going off.

Mo is in the Plato suite. That's where the screams are coming from, where the wind blows – I hit the door with my shoulder as hard as I can, and bounce.

'What is going on?'

I glance round. A middle-aged woman, thin-faced and worried. 'Fire alarm!' I yell. 'I heard screaming in here. Can you get help?'

She steps forward, waving a big bunch of keys: she must be the concierge. 'Allow me.' She turns the door handle and the key, and the door slams open inward as a gust of wind grabs us both and tries to yank us into the room. I grab her arm and brace my feet against the doorframe. Now there's a scream right in my ear, but she grabs my wrist with another hand and I wrestle her back into the corridor. A howling gale is blowing through the doorway, as if someone's punched a hole in the universe. I risk a glance round it and see—

A hotel bedroom in chaos and disarray – wardrobe tumbled on the floor, bedclothes strewn everywhere – all the hallmarks of a fight, or a burglary, or something. But where in my room there's another door and then a cramped bathroom, here there's a *hole*. A hole with lights on the other side of it that cast sharp shadows across the damaged furniture. Stars, harsh and bright against the darkness of a flat, alien landscape shrouded in twilight.

I pull my head back and gasp into the woman's ear: 'Get everybody out of here! Tell them it's a fire! I'll get help!' She's half doubled-over from the wind but she nods and stumbles toward the staircase. I turn to follow, shocked, half-dazed. *Where the hell have the watchers gone? We're supposed to be under surveillance, dammit!* I look back toward the bedroom for a final glance through that opening that shouldn't be there. The wind batters at my back, a gale howling past my ears. The opening is the size of a large pair of doors, ragged bits of lath and wallpaper showing where the small gate ripped through the wall. Beyond it, rolling ground, deep cold; a valley with a still lake beneath the icy, unwinking stars that form no constellations I can recognize. Something dim frosts the sky; at first I think it's a cloud, but then I recognise the swirl – the arms of a giant spiral galaxy raised above a dim land-scape not of this world.

I'm freezing, the wind is trying to rip me through the doorway and carry me into the alien landscape – and there's no sign of Mo, nor of her abductor. She's in there somewhere, that's for sure. Whoever, whatever opened it was waiting for her to go to bed when we came back to the hotel. They left fragments of their geometry inscribed in bloody runes on the walls and floor. They'll have planned this, taken her for their own purposes—

A hand grabs my arm. I jerk round: it's Alan, looking just as much like a schoolteacher as ever, wearing an expression that says the headmaster is angry. His other hand is wrapped around the grips of a very large pistol. He bends close and yells, 'Let's get the fuck out of here!'

No argument. He pulls me toward the fire door and we make our way down the stairs, shocked and frostbitten. The wind quietens behind us as we rush down to the ground floor, all the way to the bar where Angleton is waiting to be briefed.

7: BAD MOON
RISING

THE EMERGENCY GATHERS PACE OVER THE NEXT three hours.

When I glance out the front door I see a fire-control truck – a big lorry with a control room mounted on its load bed – squatting in the middle of the street outside the hotel, blue lights strobing against the darkness; a couple of pumps are drawn up on either side, and a gaggle of police vans are parked round the corner. Cops are busy buzzing around, evacuating everyone on the block from hotel and dwelling alike. The cover story is that there's a gas leak. The pump engines are real enough, but the control vehicle has nothing to do with the fire brigade: Angleton had it shipped to Holland before Mo and I arrived, just in case. It belongs to OCCULUS – Occult Control Coordination Unit Liaison, Unconventional Situations – the NATO occult equivalent of a NEST, or Nuclear Emergency Search Team. But while NEST operatives are really only trained to look for terrorist nukes, OCCULUS has to be ready for Armageddon in a variety of guises. I only just found out about OCCULUS and I really don't know whether or not I want to punch Angleton or just be grateful for his foresight.

There's rack after rack of specialised communication equipment in the back of the truck, and a scarier bunch of paramilitaries than I've ever seen outside of a movie. They're poking around the hotel right now – sending in robots with cameras, installing sensors on the way up the staircase – laying the groundwork for whatever comes next.

Alan leads me into the bar, where Angleton is waiting. Angleton has dark hollows under his eyes; his tie is loose and his collar unbuttoned. He's scribbling notes on a yellow pad in between snapping instructions on a mobile phone that's just about glued to his ear. 'Sit down,' he gestures as he listens to someone at the other end.

'We ought to pull back to the amber zone,' Alan says. 'There's structural damage.'

'Later.' Angleton waves him off and goes back to talking on the phone. 'No, there's no need to go to Rung Four yet, but I want the backup wagon on twenty-four by seven alert, and we'll need Plumbers crawling over everything. And Baggers, but especially Plumbers. Tell Bridget to fuck off.' He glances at me. 'Grab a drink from the bar and get ready to tell me everything.' Back to the phone: 'I'll expect hourly updates.' He puts the phone down and turns to me. 'Now. Tell me exactly what happened.'

'I don't *know* what happened,' I say. 'I went to bed. Next thing, I hear screams and wake up—' I clench my fists to stop my hands shaking.

'Fast forward. What did you find in her room?' Angleton leans forward intently.

'How did you know . . . . hell. I got up there, heard whistling like wind. So I tried to break the door down. Then the concierge showed up, unlocked the door, and nearly got sucked in; I grabbed her and sent her back down. There's a gate in there, class four at least – it's about two-plus metres in diameter, runs straight through the wall, and it's stable. Furniture was thrown around as if there was a fight, but there's a big wind blowing. On the other side of the gate there's no atmosphere to speak of.'

'No atmosphere.' Angleton nods and makes a note as two firemen – I think they're firemen – enter the bar and begin setting up something that looks like a rack of industrial scaffolding in the middle of the room. 'The source of the wind?'

'I think so. It was bloody cold, which suggests expansion into vacuum.' I shiver and glance up; above our heads the whistle of wind through rubble continues unabated. 'She wasn't there,' I add. 'I think they took her.'

Angleton's lips quirk. 'That is not an unreasonable deduction.' His expression hardens. 'Describe the other side of the gate.'

'Twilight, a shallow valley. I couldn't see the ground very clearly; it sloped down to a distant lake, or something that looked like one. The stars were very clear, not twinkling at all, and I could see they weren't familiar. There was a huge galaxy covering, uh, about a third of the sky.'

Alan sticks a glass between my fingers: I take an experimental swallow. Orange juice spiked with something stronger. I continue: 'No air on the other side. Alien starscape. But there *are* stars, and at least one planet; that means it's pretty damn close to us, it's not one of those universes where the ratio of the strong nuclear force to the electromagnetic force prevents fusion.' I shiver. 'Whoever they are, they've got her and they've got an open mass-transfer gate. What do we do now?'

Alan silently leaves the room. Angleton looks at me oddly. 'That's a very good question. Do you have any ideas to contribute?' he asks.

I swallow. 'I have one idea. It's the Ahnenerbe, isn't it? That's the connection. The Middle Eastern guy, the one with the luminous eyes that she described – it's a possession. Something left over from the war, an Ahnenerbe revenant of some kind, possessing the leader of a Mukhabarat strike cell in California. And now they've snatched Mo.'

He closes his eyes. 'Your email this afternoon. You are *sure* she positively identified the scan you sent me from California? You'd bet your life on it?'

'Pretty sure.' I nod. 'Was it—'

'We found the same pattern in Rotterdam.' He sighs and opens his eyes again. 'The very same; my compliments on your search criteria. Was there something similar in her room?'

'I honestly can't say; it was dark, I was trying not to be dragged in by the wind, and the gate had instantiated in the middle of it. I don't think so, but if you can get a photograph from up there I can confirm——'

'In progress.'

Alan comes back in; he's wearing a bright orange overall and carrying a bulky box, some kind of sensor gear. 'You'll have to move now,' he tells Angleton. 'The top floor's in danger of collapsing. Hole up in the van and stay out of the way; we need to sweep the block for werewolves.'

'Were——'

I must look surprised because Alan barks a brief laugh at me. 'Leftovers from the authors of this incursion, old boy, not hairy-palmed wolf-men with a silver allergy. Come on, shift yourself.'

'Shift——' I find myself on my feet, Angleton holding my elbow in a vicelike grip.

'Come now, Mr. Howard. This is no time to lose your self-control.' He steers me out into the street (barefoot, the tarmac under my toes makes me wince) and then up the steps into the OCCU-LUS command vehicle. A guard waves us in, insect-eyed in respirator. 'A spare overall for Mr. Howard here,' Angleton calls, and a minute later I'm loaded down with enough survival gear to equip a small polar expedition, from the y-fronts out.

'You're going to send people in to try and close the gate,' I predict in the general direction of the back of Angleton's head as he dials a phone number. 'I want to go with them.'

'Don't be silly, boy. What do you think you can achieve?'

'I can try to rescue her,' I say.

There's a burst of static from farther up the compartment and one of the men in black (black turtleneck, black fatigues, black face-paint, and MP-10 slung over his chair) turns and calls out: 'Message for the captain!' Alan mutters a curse and squeezes past me. I begin pulling on a sock. There are one-way windows along one side of the cabin and outside in the road I see some kind of large truck squeezing past us.

'I'm serious,' I tell Angleton. 'I know what's going on here, or most of it. Or I can guess. Werewolves, he said. Holdovers from the Reich, huh? And the Mukhabarat connection. That gate doesn't go into the dark anthropic zone; it stops short, somewhere where humans can exist. Really *evil* humans, whoever survived from the Ahnenerbe-SS after the war was lost.' I begin to wriggle into the bottom half of my survival suit shell. 'I've been studying Sheet 45075 from Birkenau, you know. If it's the same one they used over there, I can shut it down safely – without a massive discharge when it arcs to ground.'

He's on the phone again. 'Very good, any survivors? Two, you say, and three sacrifices? That's excellent. Have you identified—'

I tap him on the shoulder. 'Mo told me what she was researching on the Black Chamber contract,' I say. 'You really don't want them to get their hands on it.'

Angleton's head whips round. 'One minute, boy.' Back to the phone: 'Get them to sing. I don't care how you do it; by dawn I want to know who they thought they were summoning.' He puts the phone down and glares at me. 'Tell me.'

'Probability manipulation,' I say.

'Close, but not close enough,' Angleton says coldly. He stands up, leaving the armless chair swinging – in the confined space of the truck this is not a good idea. 'You got some of it right and the rest wrong. And what makes you think I can afford to risk you? This is an OCCULUS job now: straight in, find out what's there, plant demolition charges, straight out.'

'Demolition charges.' I look past his shoulder. The door opens and a familiar face is coming in. Odd, I'd never imagined what Derek the Accountant would look like in battle dress. (Worried, mostly.)

'The commander's due in half an hour,' Derek says by way of introduction. 'What's the goat doing here?'

'Enough.' Angleton waves me to follow as he heads for the door. I slide my feet into moon boots, follow him without bothering to fasten the straps. I hurry down the steps into a flashing hell of red and blue lights; Dutch police escorting sleepy hotel guests and residents to safety, firemen gearing up with breathing apparatus in the road. Angleton pulls me aside. 'Interrupt if you see Captain Barnes—'

'Who?'

'Alan Barnes,' he says impatiently. 'Listen.' He fixes me with a beady stare: 'This is not a game. There's a very good chance that Dr. O'Brien is already dead – in case you hadn't noticed, there's no air on the other side of that gate, and unless her abductors wanted her alive they won't have bothered with niceties like a respirator for her. That lack of air is one of the reasons we must close it as fast as possible, the other being to stop the people who opened it from making use of it as a stable egress portal.'

'You say *people*,' I mutter. 'Who? The Ahnenerbe-SS?'

'I hope so,' he replies grimly. 'Anything else would be infinitely worse. At the end of the war, Himmler ordered a number of so-called werewolf units to continue the struggle. We've never been able to track down the Ahnenerbe's final redoubt, but the suspicion that it lies on the other side of a gate goes back a long way – you've read OGRE REALITY, you can imagine why the Mukhabarat might want to get in touch with them.'

'So the other side of that gate is' – my mind races – 'a holdout from the Third Reich, a colony intended to keep the dark flame burning and exact revenge on the enemies of Nazism in due course . . . One that's had fifty years to fester and grow on an alien world . . . But they lost the coordinates for the return journey, didn't they? Something went wrong and they were trapped there until—' I stop and stare at Angleton. 'You *hope* that's what's on the other side of the gate?'

He nods. 'The alternatives are all much worse.'

On further thought I have to admit he's right: a colony of leftover Nazi necromancers and their SS bodyguards are trivially dangerous compared to things like the one that took over Fred the Accountant. And *they* are small beer by the standards of the sea of universes, where malignant intelligences wait only for an invitation to surge through a knothole in the platonic realm and infect our minds.

'How are you going to deal with them?' I ask. Angleton leads me around the truck; I can get a good view of the big low-loader that squeezed past us, and there's some sort of tracked vehicle sitting on its load bed. There's a crane, too. I peer closer, but the cordon of cops around it bars my view. 'How the hell are you going to get that through a third-floor window?' I ask.

Angleton shrugs. 'I'm sure the hotel owners will file a claim on their building insurance.' He looks at me. 'Alan's men are professionals, Robert. They're not used to being slowed down by civilians like you – or me. What can you do that they can't?'

I lick my lips. 'Can they open a temporary gate back home if the door there slams shut behind them? Can they safely disarm a live geometry node?'

'They're the Artists' Rifles,' Angleton says witheringly. 'They're the bloody SAS, boy, 21st Battalion Territorial Army; what did you think they were, a gun club? Who else do you think we'd trust with a hydrogen bomb wired up to a dead man's handle?'

I stare at the low-loader and realise that the cops around it are all carrying HK-4s and facing outward. 'I can provide you with a different kind of insurance policy. Give me the charts and I'll see they make it back alive – with Mo, if I have any say in the matter. Plus, aren't you just a little *curious* about what the Ahnenerbe might have been doing with a Z-2 and its descendants for the past fifty years?'

'Do you want me to strangle him now, or wait till he's finished annoying you?' asks Alan, who has sneaked up behind me so quietly I never even noticed. Needless to say I almost jump out of my skin.

'Leave him be.' Angleton almost looks amused. 'He's still young enough to think he's immortal – and he's cleared for active. All waivers signed, next of kin on file, carries an organ donor card, that sort of thing. Can you use him?'

I have to turn my head to keep both of them in view: Angleton, the old, dried-up ghost of intelligence spooks past, and Alan – Captain Barnes, that is – schoolmasterly and intense. 'That depends,' Alan tells Angleton. Then he focuses on me.

'Bob, you can come along on this trip on one condition. The condition is that if you get any of my men killed by arsing around, I will personally shoot you. Do you understand and agree?'

Somehow I manage to nod, although my mouth's gone very dry all of a sudden. 'Yup, got it. No arsing around.'

'Well, that's all right then!' He claps his hands together briskly, then softens very slightly. 'As long as you do what you're told, you'll pass. I'm going to give you to Blevins and Pike; they'll look after you. I know what your specialities are: weird alien runes, ancient Nazi computers, esoteric rocket science, that sort of thing. Boffin city. If we run into anything like that I'll let you know. What's your weapons clearance, if any?'

'I'm certified to level two, unconventional.' I frown. 'What else do you need?'

'Ever used scuba gear?'

'Er, yes.' I neglect to add that it was on a holiday package deal, an afternoon of training followed by supervised swimming near a coral reef, with instructors and guides on hand.

'Okay, then I'll leave Pike to check you out on the vacuum gear. You'll be issued with a weapon; you are not, repeat *not*, to use it under any circumstances while any soldiers are left alive unless you are explicitly ordered to. Got that?'

'Find Pike. Learn how to use vacuum gear. Do not use weapon without orders.'

'That'll do.' Alan glances at Angleton. 'He'll make a good Norwegian Blue, don't you think?'

Angleton raises an eyebrow. 'Bet you he'll be "pining for the fiords" within hours.'

'Hah! Hah!' Alan doesn't bray: his laughter is oddly fractured, as if it's escaping from a broken muffler. Loss of control, that's what it is. He's thin, wiry, intense, and looks like the kind of schoolmaster who's spent years slitting throats in strange countries, and took to teaching as a way of passing on his knowledge. A weird breed, not uncommon in the British public schools, who recycle their own graduate cannon fodder to train the next generation in an ethos of military service. And whose mannerisms are aped lower down the academic ladder. Artists' Rifles indeed!

I try telling myself that Mo will be all right, that they wouldn't have bothered abducting her if they didn't want her alive, but it's no good: whenever I get some idle time my brain keeps looping on the fact that someone I feel strongly about has been snatched and may already be dead. Luckily I don't have much time to obsess because Alan immediately drags me back inside the OCCULUS control truck and throws me to Sergeant Martin Pike, who takes one look at me, mutters something about the blessings of Loki, and starts grilling me about nitrogen narcosis, the bends, partial pressure of oxygen, and all sorts of other annoying things I haven't studied since school. Pike is a sergeant. He's also a Ph.D. in mechanical engineering and designs things that go fast and explode, when he isn't being a weekend soldier in a special unit hung off the SAS. He's met people like me before and knows how to deal with them.

A second – and then a third – fire-control truck has drawn up outside the evacuated hotel and we're in the back of vehicle number two, which seems to be a mobile armoury. I'm stripping off the survival gear and struggling into something like a bastard cross between a body stocking and a piece of bondage rubberwear from hell – low pressure survival gear, Pike tells me – a lycra and silk contraption that seems to consist mostly of straps and is designed to do the same job as a space suit in terms of holding me together and helping me breathe.

'Vacuum isn't as hostile as you probably imagine if you've read too much bad science fiction,' he says while I'm grunting and wheezing over the upper half of the suit. 'But you'd have real fun breathing without a decent gas seal around your regulator, and without this suit and pressurized goggles you'll end up half-blind and covered in blood blisters within ten or twenty minutes. The real problems are heat dissipation – there's no air around you to keep you cool by convection and insulated from the ground, which is going to be *fucking* cold – and maintaining your breathing. Cooling we can deal with – this cloth is porous, you start sweating and the sweat will evaporate and keep you cool, and there's a drinking bottle in your helmet. Don't let it run dry, because running one of these suits is a bit like running a noddy suit in the Iraqi desert – you will sweat like hell, you will drink a pint of water and electrolytes every hour, and if you forget to do that you will keel over from heat stroke. Turn round, now.' I turn round and he starts tightening straps all the way up my back as if I'm wearing a corset. 'These are to keep your rib cage under a bit of elastic tension, help you breathe out.'

'What if I need to take a piss?' I ask.

He chuckles. 'Go ahead. There's enough adsorbent padding that you probably won't freeze your wedding tackle off.'

Trussed up in the pressure suit, I feel like a fifties comic-book hero who's blundered through a fetish movie's wardrobe. Pike passes me a bunch of elbow and knee protectors, a tough overall, and a pair of massively padded moon boots. Somehow I struggle into them. Then he comes up with a lightweight backpack frame with air tanks and – 'A rebreather? Isn't that dangerous?' I ask.

'Yup. We aren't NASA and we can't waste five hours depressurising you down to run on pure oxygen. 'Sides, you're not wearing a hard-shell suit. You're going to breathe a seventy/thirty nitrogen-oxygen mix; we scrub the carbon dioxide out with these lithium hydroxide canisters and recycle the nitrogen, adding oxygen to order.'

'Uh-huh. How do I change tanks?'

'On your own? You don't – there's a trick to it and we don't have time to teach you. You cut over from tank one to tank two with the regulator valve here, then you ask me to change tanks for you. If someone wants you to change their tank, which they won't unless things go pear-shaped in a big way, you do it like this—' He demonstrates on an unmounted backpack and I try to keep track of it. Then he shows me the helmet and the chest-mounted monitors that keep track of my gas supply, temperature, and so on. Finally he seems satisfied. 'Well, if you remember all that you're not going to die by accident – at least not immediately. Still happy?'

'Um.' I think about it. 'It'll have to do. What about radio?'

'Don't worry about it – it's automatic.' He flicks a switch or two on my chest panel, evidently making sure of that. 'You're on the general channel – everyone will be able to hear you unless they explicitly shut you out. Now . . .' He picks up a gadget that looks like a pair of underwater digital video cameras strapped with gaffer tape to either side of a black box gizmo of some kind. 'Have you ever seen one of these before?'

I peer closely, then unclip the lid on the box and look inside. 'I didn't know they'd successfully weaponised that.'

He looks surprised. 'Can you tell me what it is and how it works?'

'Can I – yeah, I've seen this arrangement before but only in the lab. This chip *here is* a small custom-built ASIC processor that emulates a neural network that was first identified in the *cingulate gyrus* of a medusa. Turns out you can find the same pathways in a basilisk, but . . . well. There's a load of image processing stuff on the front end, behind those video cameras. Now, I would guess that the two cameras are the optical component of this gadget: we're performing some sort of wave superposition on the target, so . . .'

'Fine, fine.' He passes me a somewhat shop-soiled video camera manual. 'Give this a read. And this.' He hands me a bundle of typed pages with bright red SECRET headers, then passes me the lash-up. I look it over dubiously: there's an arrow on top of the neural network box with the caption THIS SIDE TOWARD ENEMY, and a flat-panel camcorder viewfinder on the back so you can pretend it's just a computer game you're playing with while you kill people.

What this gadget does violates the second law of thermodynamics: nobody's quite sure why it's so specific, but the medusa effect seems to be some kind of observationally mediated quantum tunnelling process. It turns out that something like 0.01 percent of all the atomic nuclei of carbon in the target zone acquire eight extra protons and a balancing number of neutrons, turning 'em into highly electronegative silicon ions. A roughly balancing proportion of carbon nuclei just seem to vanish, wrecking whatever bonds they were part of.

'How much damage can this thing do to a person?' I ask.

'How much damage will a stubby shotgun do?' Pike responds. 'Enough. Silicon-hydrogen bonds aren't stable. Don't point it at anyone and don't switch it on and most of all don't hit the OBSERVE button unless I tell you to. Which I won't, unless you are very, very unlucky. Or unless you decide to blow your feet off by accident, which is your own lookout.'

'Understood.' I switch off the viewfinder and power down both cameras then gingerly put the gadget down. 'You aren't expecting trouble by any chance?'

Pike stares at me. 'No, it's my job to see that you don't get into trouble,' he says. I take a second to recognise the expression: he's wondering if I'm going to be a liability.

'Tell me what to do and I'll do it,' I say. 'You're the expert on this.'

'Am I?' He looks sceptical. 'You're the occult specialist, you tell me what we're up against.' He bends down, picks up a rebreather regulator, begins stripping off the insulation panels in an absent-minded sort of way. 'I mean it. What are you expecting to find on the other side of this gate?'

Something clicks in my mind: 'You've gone through gates before, right?'

He glances at me. 'Maybe. Maybe not.' I realise that he isn't looking at the rebreather as he strips it: he's got it down to a set of motions he can run through in total darkness. Then it hits me: I'm going to be hopelessly dependent on these guys for just about everything more challenging than breathing. Liability, me? Maybe I don't know what I'm getting myself into after all. But it's a bit late to back out now.

'Well.' I lick my suddenly dry lips. 'This one, we *hope* the only things waiting for us are a bunch of superannuated Nazis who've kidnapped one of our scientists. Trouble is, this bunch sent someone through to California, and London, and maybe to Rotterdam, who isn't too superannuated to be banging heads. So I'll take a rain check on the predictions, if you don't mind — expect the worst and hope you're disappointed.'

'Indeed.' His tone is dry as he adds, 'I love these bastard colostomy-fucking reconnaissance jobs, I really do.'

The force me to catch a couple or three hours sleep by sticking a needle full of phenobarbitone into my left arm and making me count backward from ten. I never make it past five; then there's a pain in my other arm and Pike is shaking my shoulder. 'Wake up,' he says. 'Briefing in five minutes, action in half an hour.'

'Euurgh,' I say, or something equally coherent. He passes me a mug full of something that might be mislabelled as coffee and I sit up and try to drink it while he disposes of the used antidote syrette. I have a vague memory of dreams: eyes with luminous worms swimming in them, eyes like a friendly death staring at me across an electro-dynamic summoning trap. I shudder as a little rat-faced guy sits down opposite me and opens up a zippered and incongruously expensive-looking golf bag.

Pike takes it upon himself to introduce us. 'Bob, this is Lance-Corporal Blevins. Roland, this is Bob Howard, a Laundry necromancer.'

Rat-face looks at me and grins, baring unfeasibly large and yellow incisors. 'Pleased ter meet yer,' he says, pulling an iron out of his golf bag — one with telescopic sights and thick foam insulation over most of the visible surfaces. Vacuum-adapted, I realise: these guys *have* been exploring gates before. 'Allus nice ter 'ave a bit of animal with us.'

'Animal?'

'Magic,' Pike explains. 'Listen, you stay close to me or Roland unless I tell you otherwise. He's the squadron backup: what this means is, he'll either be in the rear or deployed to cover a quick in-and-out. He'll park you somewhere safe and keep an eyeball on you if I'm too busy to nursemaid. '

'Diamond geezer, mate,' Blevins says, winking horribly, then he pulls out a bunch of jeweller's screwdrivers and goes to work on his gun, fiddling with the sights.

What I think is, *You guys really know how to make someone feel wanted*, but I end up saying nothing because, once I get my ego out of the way, Pike is right. I am not a soldier, I know nothing about what to do and what not to do, and I'm not even in good physical condition. Fundamentally, I guess I am a liability to these guys, except for my specialist expertise. It's not a very pleasant thought, but they're not going out of their way to rub it in, so the least I can do is be polite. And hope Mo is all right.

'Wot you fink I should load up on?' Roland asks. 'I got silver bullets in seven point sixty-two, but they tend to tumble in low pressure regimes like wot's on the other side of this gate—'

'Briefing first,' Pike says. 'Let's go.'

The hotel bar is barely recognisable. Scaffolding and jacks in every corner support a protective raft just under the ceiling; there's a nest of wiring and monitors on the bar top, and some sort of stair-climbing robot camera waiting just inside the doorway. Alan – Captain Barnes – is waiting next to a woman who's sort of slumped all over the robot's control panel, muttering to it and twiddling a circuit tester in a meaningful way. A dozen other men in pressure suits and camouflage overalls are leaning against the walls or sitting down: half of them have backpacks and full face-covering helmets to hand, but there's a surprising shortage of guns and I'm the only one in the room without a notepad – until I pull out my palmtop, which I've been carrying in a pocket more or less continuously since I was ejected from my bedroom.

There's not much idle chatter: the mood in the room is pretty sombre, and Alan gets down to business at once, like a headmaster conducting a staff meeting. 'The situation we're facing is an open gate, class four, with unknown – but undesirable – parties on the other side. They've snatched one of our scientists. A secondary mission goal is to get her back alive. But the primary goal is to identify the parties responsible and, if they are who we think they are, neutralise them and then withdraw, ensuring the gate closes behind us. Let me stress that we are not 100 percent certain who we're up against, so identification and threat characterisation are our first tasks. This isn't as clear-cut a job as we'd like, so I want you all to focus on it and give it a bit of thought. First, the situation. Derek?'

Derek from the Laundry, Derek the dried-up old accountancy clerk, stands up and delivers a terse, comprehensive sitrep as if he's done it a thousand times before. Who'd have thought it? 'Ahnenerbe werewolf colony left over from Himmler's last stand.' Mumble. 'Mukhabarat.' Cough. 'Republican guard.' Mutter. 'Kidnapped scientist.' Mumble. I don't need to take notes; near as I can tell I've heard it all before. Glancing round I try to catch Angleton's eye – just in time to see him slipping out the back. Then Derek finishes. 'Back to you, Captain.'

'Our mission is to take a look on the other side of the hill,' says Alan. 'Bringing back kidnapped scientists and neutralising undesirables are tactical tasks, but our number one strategic priority is to do a full threat evaluation and ensure word gets back home. So, step one is to send through a crawler and make sure there isn't a welcome party waiting for us on the other side. If it's clear, we insert. Step two' – he pauses – 'we secure the other side, emplace the demolition package in case things go to pieces on us, then improvise depending on what we find.' He grins, briefly. 'I love surprises. Don't you?'

Well, yes, otherwise I'd never have volunteered for active duty in the first place. Which is why, half an hour later, I find myself standing on a purple-painted hotel staircase beneath a portrait of Martin Heidegger, breathing through an oxygen mask and waiting to follow a dumpy little tracked robot, half a platoon of territorial SAS, and an armed hydrogen bomb through a rip in the spacetime continuum.

Blurred shadows dance across the video screen, grey and black textures like ripped velvet laid over volcanic ash. On the floor in front of my feet the coil of cable unspools, snaking into darkness. Hutter, the equipment tech with the control panel, is hunched over it like a video game addict, twitching her joystick with gloved hands. I lean over behind Alan, who has the ringside view; I have to lean because the backpack is a solid mass, thirty kilograms pushing me forward if I even think about relaxing.

'One metre forward; now pan left.'

The screen jerks. There's a thin wail as air vents through the doorframe and the cable reels out, then the scenery on screen begins to rotate. We see more blurred grey rubble, then a view that swoops away, down to a distant sea. As the camera pans round further the back of the robot comes into view, trailing a white umbilical back into the incongruous side of a wall. There isn't enough light to examine the wall, or enough scan lines: it's a night-vision camera, but we're operating in starlight. The camera continues to rotate until it's pointing back to its original bearing. There is no sign of life.

'Looks clear,' someone whispers in my ear, voice tinny and half-masked by static.

'If you want to go first, feel free to volunteer,' Alan says dryly. 'Mary. See any hot spots?'

'Nothing,' the tech reports.

'Okay. Bearing zero six zero, forward ten or until you see anything, then halt and report.'

She follows through and the little robot lurches forward into the grey and black landscape on the other side of the gate. 'Ambient air pressure, ten pascals. Ambient temperature – thermocouple gives an error, FLIR is flat lined, but that backup sensor is claiming somewhere between forty-five and sixty Kelvin. Gravimetric – it's Earthlike. Uh, I'm worried about the power, boss. Battery load is normal, but we're losing power like crazy – I think it's in danger of freezing solid. We never designed a robot to do this kind of environment – it's colder than summer on Pluto.'

Someone whistles tunelessly until Pike tells them to shut up.

'How does this affect our environment model?' Alan asks aloud. 'The suits are only certified down to a hundred and twenty Kelvin.'

Someone else clears their throat. 'Donaldson here. I think we should be okay, sir. We're only going to be in contact with the ground via the feet, and we've got plenty of insulation – and heating – there. No air means no convective loss, and we're not going to radiate any faster just because ambient is cooler. Our regulators use a countercurrent loop to warm incoming air from whatever we breathe out, so they're not in danger of icing up. The real risk is that we're going to be more visible on infrared, and if we get into a firefight and have to take cover we are going to get frostbitten so fast it isn't funny. That lake is probably liquid nitrogen – don't walk on any shiny blue ice, it'll be frozen oxygen and the heat from your feet will flash-boil it. Oh, and it's dia-magnetic: your compasses won't work.'

'Thank you for that reminder, Jimmy,' says Alan. 'Any more compelling insights into why the laws of physics are not our friends?'

The camera pans round: same landscape, but now we see the gate framed by a low mound of dirt heaped up on one side, and a broken-down wall on the other. The lake is clearer, and some sort of rectilinear structure is just visible over the crest of the ridge.

'I don't understand the temperature,' Donaldson says pen-sively. 'There's something about it I can't quite put my finger on.'

'Well, you're going to get a chance to put your finger on it quite soon. Mary, still no hot spots? Good. Alpha team – ready, insert.'

On the other side of the doorway three guys wearing dark, insulated suits and backpacks quickly duck through the open gate and are gone from our universe. The robot's camera, point-ing backward, catches them for posterity: ghosts leaping over it and passing out of view to either side.

'Chaitin: clear, over.'

'Smith: nothing in view. Over.'

'Hammer: clear, over.'

The camera pans round and takes in three shapes hunched low behind the bluff, one of them pointing a stubby pipe back past the robot.

'Don, if you'd be so good as to take a look round the rear of the gate. Mike, Bravo team insert.'

Three anonymous bulky figures push past behind me, through the pressure doors erected in front of the hotel room: a gust of wind howls past my helmet as they enter the gate. The camera pans—

'Chaitin: nothing behind the gate. Landscape is clear, rising to hills in the middle distance. I see some kind of geometric inscription on the ground and one, no, two bodies. Male, naked, gutted with a sharp implement. They look to be frozen – handcuffed behind their backs.'

My heart flops over and I begin to breathe again, ashamed but relieved that neither of them is Mo. 'Howard here: that'll be the human sacrifices they used to open the gate,' I say. 'Is there a kind of metal tripod nearby with an upturned dish on top?'

'Chaitin: nope, somebody's cleaned up around here.'

'Bloody typical,' somebody mutters out of turn.

'Charlie, insert,' says Andy. He taps me on the arm: 'C'mon, Bob. Time to party.'

Ahead of us, Pike picks up the controls on something that looks like an electric street cleaner – the kind of wheeled cart you walk behind – and drives it forward toward the doors. It nudges through and the gale almost sucks me forward; I follow in his wake, trying not to think about the cart's payload. You can make a critical mass out of about six kilos of plutonium, but you need various other bits and pieces to make a bomb; while they've been fitted inside an eight-inch artillery shell before now, nobody has yet built a nuke that you can carry easily – especially when you're wearing a thirty-kilo life-support backpack.

Mist spurts out around me as I walk through the gate, and suddenly the ground under my feet isn't carpet anymore: it's crumbly, crunchy, like a hard frosted snowfall over gravel. I hear a faint buzz as heat exchangers switch on in my helmet, using the warmth of my breath to heat the air I'm breathing in. My skin prickles, abruptly feeling tight, my suit seems to contract all around me, and I emit an enormous and embarrassing fart.

External air pressure: zero. Temperature: low enough to freeze oxygen. Jesus, it *is* springtime on Pluto.

Pike drives his gadget forward about five metres, halfway to the parked robot, then stops and begins unreeling a spool of cable from on top of it. He almost backs into me before I get out of his way. 'Bob, take this.' He hands me some kind of joystick-like gadget with a trigger built into it, plugged into the wire.

'What is it?' I ask, thumbing my intercom to his channel.

'Dead man's handle. We use two of them to detonate while we're out of range of the permissive action link signal – this side of the gate. Go on, pull the trigger, I've got the other one. It's perfectly safe to let go of one trigger at a time, it only goes bang if both triggers are released for ten seconds at the same time.'

'Gee, thanks. How long did you say this wire is?'

I lumber in a circle, taking care not to let the wire get twisted around my feet as I take in the view. The gate is inscribed in a low wall; our footsteps have obscured the transient map in front of it, but behind the wall that supports the aperture the pattern is more or less intact (along with the two victims who were sacrificed to open it). The ground is crunchy, like loose soil after a heavy frost. Behind us and to the left and right it slopes up toward a low ridge; in front, the ground slopes down and broadens out into a valley. The stars overhead are unwinking, dimensionless points of light in a harsh vacuum. They look reddish, demonic eyes staring down at me; a universe of red dwarves, long after the sun has burned down.

Alpha and Bravo teams have fanned out ahead and behind the wall, advancing in a curious duck-walking crouch from cover to cover. I spot a lump sticking out of the ground about five metres away, and plod over to inspect it. It's a tree stump, shattered half a metre above the ground and hard as ice. I reach out to touch it and a thin mist bursts from the wood – I yank my fingers back before the stream of gas can chill them into frostbite. Wood crumbles and falls away from the stump, shattered by the warmth. I shudder inside my layers of compression fabric and insulation, and fart again.

There are boot imprints in the ground behind the gate, and they don't look like ours.

'Howard, get back to the gate. Don't tangle up the wire you're holding.'

'Understood.' I stomp back toward the gate, collecting loops of wire from the handle (which I have carefully avoided arming).

'Give.' An anonymous, bulky figure holds out a hand: above the visor I see the name BLEVINS. I pass Roland the trigger and he attaches it to his chest with a Velcro pad, then heads for the low rise behind the gate.

'Howard, Barnes here. I'm on the rise behind you, twenty metres upslope. Come tell me what you think of this.' A *click* as he hops frequency, to check on everybody else in turn.

I come up beside him on the rise and find him hefting a heavily insulated camera in front of his faceplate. Someone – Sergeant Howe, I think – is crouching farther up the slope with some kind of shotgun or grenade launcher in his arms. 'Come on and look at this,' Alan says; he sounds mildly amused as he waves me forward. 'Keep your head low and no sudden movements. That's far enough, Bob.'

I can just peep over the ridge, which falls away abruptly in front of me. More dead tree stumps; the ground beneath me, the crunching – now I can see that it's grass, freeze-dried and mummified beneath a layer of carbon dioxide frost. Hills or low mounds of some kind rise in the near distance, and then—

'Disneyland?' I hear myself saying.

Alan laughs quietly. 'Not Disneyland. Think Mad King Ludwig's last commission, as executed by Buckminster Fuller.' Cheesecake crenellations, battlements with machicolations, moat and drawbridge and turrets. Spiky pointed roofs on the towers – like the police stations in West Belfast, designed to deflect incoming mortar fire. Arrow slots filled with mirror glass half a metre thick. Radomes and antenna masts in the courtyard where you'd expect armoured knights to mount up.

'I didn't know the RUC were Cthulhu-worshippers.'

'They're not, laddie,' says Howe, and I flush. 'Check out the slope up to that moat. Probably got rammed earth behind those walls, but they're not really expecting direct artillery fire. Intruders on foot, rockets, I don't know what — but not tanks or direct fire.'

'They won,' Alan says distantly. 'This isn't a fortification. Bob, I should apologise: it *is* a police station.' Light glistens on the Gestapo battlements as I try to understand what he means.

'What happened to them?' I ask.

'Look,' says Howe, pointing off to the left. I follow his direction and get my first inkling of just how far beyond our experience this world is. From up here the moon is visible, gibbous and close to the horizon; but the familiar man-in-the-moon pattern of marias and seas has been erased, replaced by a shadow-scribed visage carved across the entire lunar surface in runes ten kilometres deep. It's astonishing to behold, a miracle testimonial to one man's vanity on a scale that makes Mount Rushmore or the pyramids look like a child's sandcastle. And from the small tuft of moustache to the keynote cowlick of hair, the face is instantly recognisable.

From a quarter of a million miles away, Hitler's image stares at me across a land given over to ice and shadow. And I know the Ahnenerbe can't be far away.

8: STORMING MOUNT IMPOSSIBLE

THE ARTISTS' RIFLES STORM THE AHNENERBE'S secret fortress with speed and élan, moderated only by tactical caution and a degree of perplexity that deepens as they determine that the castle is, in fact, unoccupied.

First in is the little reconnaissance robot, portaged into position and released by a couple of tense soldiers half a kilometre away from the rest of the expedition. As it rolls onto the flat killing apron around the redoubt, Bravo team moves like ghosts through the petrified forest on the other side of the castle. Everybody is tense: nobody talks on radio while their line of sight is on the castle, and nobody wants to be visible, either – on infrared against this chill landscape, a human being will stand out like a magnesium flare.

The robot rolls out onto the killing apron in front of the castle, little puffs of snow fountaining up behind its treads. At this point if anyone is guarding it we'd expect to see fireworks, but nothing happens: nobody shoots, nothing lights up. I hunch over behind Hutter's shoulder, watching the video feed via the secure fibre-optic cable. The castle is dark, except for a central building that glows red hot, two hundred and fifty degrees hotter than the ambient temperature. It silhouettes the battlements, towers, and radomes nicely.

Alan circles a hand above his head twice, and a long way away a sleeping dragon erupts. A dot of light sizzles across the frozen landscape on a jet of flame and slams into the outer door of the gatehouse: lumps of stone and metal tumble silently through the empty vacuum above it. Things begin to happen very quickly as Alpha team lays down fire on the gatehouse and Bravo team skids out across the ice behind the castle and makes for the forbiddingly high walls. A chain of fireworks erupts from the ground and bursts over the battlements in front of them, then—

Nothing. Nothing but silence and the jerky movements of Alan's men. They reach the foot of the wall and swarm up it as if they aren't wearing heavy backpacks, while a second Dragon launcher pops a rocket off at the front of the castle and someone – Sergeant Howe, I think – beats the courtyard with machine-gun fire that makes small mushroom clouds of white vapour burst from the ground. And there's *still* no answering fire.

'Alpha secure,' someone grunts in my headphones. Then: 'Bravo secure. Cease fire, cease fire, we've got an empty venue.'

'Empty? Confirm.' It's Alan's voice. He doesn't sound perturbed, but—

'Alpha here, the place is *empty*,' insists whoever's using that call sign. 'As in abandoned.'

'Bravo confirms, Mike here. There's a dead truck in the courtyard but no sign of life up here. Dunno about the central target, but if they've retreated in there they aren't coming out. They wouldn't have heard us, anyway.' He sounds nervous, breathy.

'Mike, keep under cover, don't assume anything. Hammer, close in fast and secure the gatehouse. Chaitin, lay on the central blockhouse but hold fire on my word. Charlie team move in.'

Alan stands up and runs forward, crouching close to the ground; across the landscape I can see the others moving toward the castle's shattered gates – popping up and lunging forward for a few seconds then diving flat to the ground, ready to fire.

Still nothing happens. *What's going on?* I wonder. Only one way to find out: I stand up and jog forward heavily, feeling the backpack ramming my feet down onto the frozen ground. The empty killing apron is about a hundred metres wide and I feel really naked as I step out onto it, out of the cover of the petrified forest. But there's no sign of life in the castle. Nothing at all untoward happens as I trot forward and, panting, heave myself into the shadow of the gatehouse.

It looms overhead, a grey mound of concrete or stone in the darkness; a narrow window, dark as the crypt, overlooks the entranceway. The gates are solid slabs of wood bound in metal, but they lean drunkenly away from the huge hole that the Dragon blew between them. I pause, and someone whacks me in the back: 'Howard, get *down*!'

I get down and feel icy cold through the thick padding on my knees and elbows. There's some radio chatter: terse announcements as each team makes its way through a series of checkpoints. 'Chaitin, keep the blockhouse covered. Hutter, any signs of life?'

'Hutter: nothing, boss. Blockhouse is warm, but nothing's moving outside it. Uh, correction. I have a temperature fix on the courtyard; it's a couple of degrees warmer than outside. Probably heat from the blockhouse.' The blockhouse is glowing brightly on infrared, a surer sign of life than anything else we've seen.

I edge through the tunnel under the walls – rammed earth overhead, frozen like cement – and peer round the corner at the blockhouse. The name doesn't do it justice; it's the central building in the complex and it's built like a small castle. Windows, high up, big dome erupting from the roof, small doors shut tight against the chill. Some kind of small vehicle, like a weird cross between a tank and a motorbike, is parked against the wall, dusty with a sprinkling that isn't snow.

'Cool, I always wanted a Kettenkrad,' someone remarks on the common channel.

'Morris, shut the fuck up; the cylinder heads are probably vacuum welded anyway. Chaitin, check out the doors. Scary Spice, cover with the M40.'

Someone who doesn't look at all like one of the Spice Girls moves up beside me and levels something that looks like a drainpipe fucking a submachine gun at the blockhouse. Someone else, anonymous in winter camouflaged pressure gear, jogs forward and then dashes at the door. Bazooka man whacks me on the shoulder to get my attention: 'Get back!' he hisses.

'Okay, I'm back,' I say. Funnily enough I don't feel afraid at all, which surprises me. 'Say, are you sure this isn't Castle Wolfenstein?'

'Fuckin' dinna say that else ye can live with the fuckin' consequences,' someone rumbles in my ears. Soldier #1 raises something that looks like a plumber's caulking gun and squirts white paste around the frame of the blockhouse door. Still no sign of a welcoming committee. I glance up at the hostile red stars above the battlements and wonder why I can't see very many of them. A thought strikes me just as the guy with the plumber's mate sticks a timer into the goop and bounds back our way then crouches: 'Cover!' The ground bounces and smoke and gas puffs out from the edges of the door – the gunk is a high-brisance explosive and it cuts through the reinforced steel door like a blowtorch through butter. r see the door getting bigger and beginning to squash vertically – then it slams past us and the escaping gush of air bowls me right over and nearly rolls me along the frigid ground.

'*Jesus*,' someone says, and I turn round to see where the door landed behind me. Something is *wrong* my nerves are screaming – where the hell are the Ahnenerbe? *There should be people here*, that's what's wrong.

Scary Spice has his grenade launcher levelled on the chamber behind the door, but the air flow has stopped and when Chaitin tosses in a flare it lights up a bare, empty room the size of a garage, with sealed doors to either side. 'Spooky,' I remark. 'Looks empty. Anyone home?'

The SAS aren't waiting around to find out; the whole of Bravo team piles into the empty vestibule in a hurry and Chaitin moves forward. More chatter: 'Airlocks, this is a fucking death trap get us in *get us in* . . .'

'Castle fucking Wolfenstein, eh?' Alan remarks in my ear, and according to my chest panel he's on a private channel. I join him.

'Why isn't anybody here?' I ask.

'Who the fuck knows? Let's just get inside, fast. You got any ideas?'

'Yeah. If you depressurize this building and Mo's inside you'll have lost us our best clue yet.'

'If I *don't* depressurize that building and some fucking Nazi revenant ices my people I'll have lost more than just our best clue.' Someone taps me on the shoulder and I jump, then turn far enough to recognise Alan. 'Remember that,' he says.

'We're here for information first—' I say, but he's cut over to another channel already so I don't know if he hears me. In any case, he taps me on the shoulder again and waves me toward the vestibule. Where Bravo team has sprung a door with a big locking wheel, hopped through, and the wheel is now spinning behind them. Airlock door, at a guess.

'Bravo, Mike here, we have atmosphere – half a kilopascal at only twenty below freezing. Pressure's coming up: lock safety is tripped. Everything here looks to be in working order, but dusty as hell. We're ready to go through on your word.'

I follow Alan and Alpha squad into the vestibule. Scary Spice is busy laying strips of some kind of explosive gunk all around the airlock door, while one of the other soldiers lines up on it with a heavily insulated light machine gun. I flick to the main channel and listen to the crackly chatter; something seems to be wrong with my radio because I'm picking up a lot of noise. Noise—

'Howard here, anybody else picking up a lot of radio hash?'

'Hutter here, who was that? Repeat please, I'm reading you strength three and dropping.'

'Hutter, Bob, cut the chatter and use your squelch. We've got a job to do here.' Alan sounds distinctly preoccupied; I decide interrupting is a bad idea and focus instead on my suit radio in case there's a problem with it. A minute of fiddling tells me that there isn't. It's a really cute UHF set, able to hop around about a zillion sidebands at high speed – analogue, not digital, but the pinnacle of that particular technology. If it's picking up hash then the hash is spread far and wide.

I walk back to the vestibule entrance and look up at the sky.

The stars are really prominent; the smoky red whirlpool of the galaxy stares down at me like a malignant red eye, startlingly visible against the night. I hunt around for the moon but it's out of direct sight, casting knife-edged black shadows across the pale blue snowscape. I blink, wishing I could rub my eyes. *Blue?* I must be seeing things. Or maybe the optical filters on my helmet are buggering my colour sensitivity – I've had it happen with computer screens before now.

I turn back to face the interior and someone is waving me forward; the airlock door gapes open. 'Howard, Hutter, Scary, your cycle.' I move forward carefully. The concrete floor is chipped and scarred, stained with old grease marks. I look round: something large is inching toward the gates – Pike, and the cart with the H-bomb. 'I'll follow you through with the charge,' Alan adds. I step through into the airlock room, boggling at the array of pipework on view – it's like something out of a war movie, the interior of a beached U-boat, all plumbing and dials and big spinner wheels. Hutter pushes the door closed behind us and cranks a handle. The airlock is narrow, and dark except for our helmet lamps; I shudder, and try not to think about what would happen if the door jams. On my other side Scary Spice yanks a valve-lever in the opposite door, and there's a thin hissing as fog spills into the room from vents along the floor. A needle in my suit's chest instrument panel quivers and begins to move – air pressure. After a few more seconds I feel my suit going limp and clammy around me, and hear a distinct *clank* as the hissing stops.

'Going through,' says Scary Spice, and he spins the locking wheel on the inner door and pushes it open.

I'm not sure what I am expecting to see; Castle Wolfenstein is a definite maybe, and I was subjected to the usual run of second-rate war movies during my misspent childhood, but the last thing on my list would have been a kennel full of freeze-dried Rottweilers. Someone has powered up an overhead light bulb which is swinging crazily at the end of its cord, casting wild shadows across the emaciated-looking corpses of a dozen huge dogs. Next to the airlock is a table, and behind it a wall of lockers; ahead of us, a wooden door leading onto a corridor. The light doesn't reach far into those shadows. Hutter prods me in the back and as I step forward something crunches under my boot heel, leaving a nasty brownish stain on the floor. 'Yuck.' I look round.

'You can switch your transmitter off,' says Hutter, 'we've got air.' She fiddles with her suit panel: 'Looks breathable, too, but don't take my word for it.'

'Quiet.' Scary Spice looks round. 'Mike?'

'Mike here.' My radio isn't crackling as much now we're indoors. 'No signs of life so far – lots of dusty offices, dead dogs. We've swept the ground floor and it looks as if there's nobody home.' He sounds as puzzled as I feel. Where the hell *are* the bad guys?

'Roger that, Hutter and yon boffin are with me in the guard-house. We're waiting on reinforcements.'

I hear a squeal of metal and look round; Hutter is closing the airlock door again, and it sounds like it hasn't been oiled for fifty years.

'Uh, we have bodies.' I jump; it's a different voice, worryingly shaky. Chaitin? 'I'm in the third door along on corridor B, left wing, and it isn't pretty.'

'Barnes here. Chaitin, sitrep.' Alan sounds purposeful.

'They're – looks like a mess room, boss. It's hard to tell, temperature's subzero so everything's frozen but there's a lot of blood. Bodies. They're wearing – yeah, SS uniforms, I'm vague on the unit insignia but it's definitely them. Looks like they shot themselves. Each other. O Jesus, excuse me sir, need a moment.'

'Take ten, Greg. What's so bad? Talk to me.'

'Must be, uh, at least twenty of them, sir. Freeze-dried, like the doggies: they're kind of mummified. Can't have happened recently. There's a pile against one wall and a bunch around this table, and – one of them is still holding a pistol. Dead as they come. There's some papers on the table.'

'Papers. What can you tell me?'

'Not much sir, I don't speak German and that's what they look to be in.'

Someone swears creatively. After a moment I realise that it's Chaitin.

'*Status*, Chaitin!'

'Just trod in—' More swearing. 'Sorry, sir.' Sound of heavy breathing. 'It's safe but, but anyone who comes here better have a strong stomach. Looks like some kind of black magic—'

Hutter taps me on the shoulder and motions me forward: 'Howard coming through. Don't touch anything.'

The building is a twilight nightmare of narrow corridors, dust and debris, too narrow to turn round in easily with the bulky suit backpacks. Scary Spice leads me through a series of rooms and a mess hall, low benches parked to either side of a wooden table in front of a counter on which sit pans that have tarnished with age. Then we're into a big central hall with a staircase leading up and down, and another corridor, this one with gaping doors – and Chaitin waiting outside the third door with someone else inside.

The scene is pretty much what Chaitin described: table, filing cabinets, pile of withered mummies in grey and black uniforms, black-brown stains across half of them. But the wall behind the door—

'Howard here: I've seen these before,' I transmit. 'Ahnenerbe-issue algemancy inductance rig. There should be – ah.' A rack of stoppered glass bottles gleams from below the thing like a glass printing press with chromed steel teeth. There's a wizened eyeless horror trapped in it, his jaws agape in a perpetual silent scream, straining at manacles drawn tight by dehydrating muscle tissue. I carefully pay no attention to it: throwing up inside a pressure suit would be unwise. Bulldog clips and batteries and a nineteen-inch-wide rack – where's the trough? Answer: below the blood gutters.

'One last summoning, by the look of it, before they all died. Or shot themselves.' I trace a finger along the boundary channel of the arcane machine, careful not to touch it: they probably filled the channel with liquid mercury – a conductor – but it's long since evaporated. If it was a possession, that tends to spread by touch, or along electrical conductors. (Visuals, too, although that usually takes serious computer graphics work to arrange.) I turn away from the poor bastard impaled on the torture machine and look at the table. The papers there are brittle with age: I turn one page over, feeling the binder crackling, and see a Ptath transform's eye-warping geometries. 'They were summoning something,' I say. 'I'm not sure what, but it was definitely a possessive invocation.' For some reason I have an unaccountable sense of wrongness about the scene. What have I missed?

The mummy with the pistol in its hand seems to be grinning at me.

I flick my radio off and rely on plain old-fashioned speech to keep my words local: 'Chaitin,' I say slowly, 'that corpse. The one with the gun. Did he shoot everyone else here – or could it have been someone else? Was he defending himself?'

The big guy looks puzzled. 'I don't see—' He pauses, then sidles round the table until he's as close to the corpse as he can get. 'Uh-huh,' he says. 'Maybe there was someone else here, but he sure looks as if he shot himself. That's funny—'

My radio drowns him out. 'Barnes to all: we've found Professor O'Brien. Howard, get your arse downstairs to basement level two, we're going to need your expertise to get her out. Everyone else, eyes up: we have at least one bad guy unaccounted for.'

My skin crawls for a moment: What the hell can be wrong with Mo if they need me to help rescue her? Then I notice Chaitin watching me. 'Take care,' he says gruffly. 'You know how to use that thing?'

'This?' I clumsily pat the basilisk gun hanging from my chest pack. 'Sure. Listen, don't touch that machine. I mean, like really *don't touch* it. I think it's dead but you know what they say about unexploded bombs, okay?'

'Go on.' He waves me past him at the door and I go out to find Scary Spice crouched in the corridor, eyes swivelling like a chameleon on cocaine.

'Let's go.' We head for the stairs, and I can't shed the nagging feeling that I've missed something critically important: that we're being sucked into a giant cobweb of darkness and chilly lies, doing exactly what the monster at its centre wants us to do – all because I've misinterpreted one of the signs around me.

The basement level is colder than the surface rooms and passages. I find Sergeant Pike there, helmet undogged, breath steaming and sparkling in the light of a paraffin lamp someone has coaxed into oily, lambent life. 'What kept you?' he asks.

I shrug. 'Where is she and how is she?'

He points at the nearer of two corridor entrances; this one is lit by a chain of bioluminescent disposables, so that a ghastly chain of green candlelight marks the route. My stomach feels suddenly hollow. 'She's conscious but nobody's touching her till you've given the okay,' he says.

Oh great. I follow the chain of ghost lights to the open door—

The door may be wide open but there's no mistaking it for anything other than a cell. Someone's stuck another lantern on the floor, just so I can see what else is inside. The room is almost completely occupied by some kind of summoning rig – not a torture machine like the one upstairs, but something not that far away from it. There's a wooden framework like a four-poster bed, with elaborate pulleys at each corner. Mo is spread-eagled on her back, naked, tied to the uprights, but the effect is just about anything other than kinky-sexy – especially when I see what's suspended above her by way of more pulleys and the same steel cables that loop through her manacles. Each of the uprights is capped by a Tesla coil, there's some kind of bug-fuck generator rig in the corner, and half the guts of an old radar station's HF output stage arranged around the perimeter of a crazy pentacle surrounding the procrustean contraption. It's like a bizarre cross between an electric chair and a rack.

Her eyes are closed. I think she's unconscious. I can't help myself: I fumble with the locking ring on my helmet then raise my visor and take a breath. It's cold in here – it's been about eight hours since she was abducted, so if she's been there that long she's probably halfway to hypothermia already.

I shuffle closer, careful not to cross the solder-dribbled circuit inscribed on the stone floor. 'Mo?'

She twitches. 'Bob? Bob! Get me out of here!' She's hoarse and there's an edge of panic in her voice.

I take a shuddering, icy breath. 'That's exactly what I'm going to do. Only question is *how*.' I glance around. 'Anyone there?' I call.

'Be with you in a sec,' replies Hutter from outside the door. 'Waiting for the boss.'

I go fumbling in my padded pocket for the PDA, because before I go anywhere near that bed I want to take some readings. 'Talk to me, Mo. What happened? Who put you here?'

'Oh, God, he's out there—'

She just about goes into spasm, straining at the cables in panic. 'Stop that!' I shout, on edge and jittery myself. 'Mo stop *moving*, that thing could cut loose any moment!'

She stops moving so suddenly that the bed-rack-summoning-bench shakes. 'What did you say?' she asks out of one corner of her mouth.

I squat, trying to see the base of the frame she's lying on. 'That thing. I'm going to untie you just as soon as I've checked that it isn't wired. Dead man's handle. Looks like a Vohlman-Knuth configuration – powered down right now but stick some current through those inductors and it could turn very nasty indeed.' I've tapped up an interesting diagnostic program on the palmtop and the Hall-effect sensor embedded in the machine is giving back some even more interesting readings. Interesting, in the sense of the Chinese proverb – 'May you live in interesting times.' – or more likely die in them. 'You use it for necromantic summonings. Demons, they used to call them: now they're primary manifestations, probably 'cause that doesn't frighten the management. Who put you on it?'

'This skinny guy, with a suntan and a German accent—'

'From Santa Cruz?'

'No, I'd never seen him before.'

'Shit. Did he have any friends? Or do anything to set up that rack over there?'

I inspect the top of the framework. The chandelier-thing hangs from the roof of the execution machine like a bizarre, three-dimensional guillotine blade: cut any of the ropes holding Mo to the bed and it will fall. I'm not sure what it's made of – glass and bits of human bone seem to figure in the design, but so do colour-coded wires and gears – but the effect will be about as final as flicking the switch on a frog in a liquidiser. Trouble is, I'm not sure the damned thing won't fall anyway, if someone switches on the device.

'No,' Mo says, but she sounds doubtful.

I'm checking around the foot of the necromantic bed now, and it's a good thing the instrument's got a log display: lots of *very* bad shit has gone down here, ghosts howling in the wires, information destroyed and funnelled out of our spacetime through weirdly tangled geometries of silver wire and the hair of hanged women. Bastards. I really ought to keep Mo talking.

'I was asleep,' she says. 'I remember a dream – howling air, very cold, being carried somewhere, unable to move. Like being paralysed, scary as hell and I couldn't breathe. Then I woke up down here. *He* was leaning over me. My head aches like the mother of all hangovers. What happened?'

'Did he say anything?' I ask. 'Make any adjustments?'

'He said I'd served my purpose and this would be my final contribution. His eyes, they were *really* weird. Luminous. What do you mean, make adjust—' She tries to raise her head and the bed creaks. There's an ominous buzzing sound from the control panel at the far side of the room and a red light comes on.

'Oh shit,' I say, as the door opens and two soldiers in vacuum gear come in and the lights flicker. I see the chandelier-like thing above Mo sway on its ropes, hear the bedframe creak. As she gathers breath to scream I clumsily jump onto the bed and brace myself on hands and knees above her. 'Someone cut the fucking cables, pull her out, and *cut the fucking wires*!' I yell. I'm kneeling on one of them when the descending mass of obsidian and bone and wire lands on my backpack with a crunch – and I discover the hard way that the thing is electrified, and Mo is wired to earth.

My head is spinning, I feel nauseous, and my right knee feels like it's on fire. *What am I doing—*

'Bob, we're going to pull it off you now. Can you hear me?'

Yeah, I can hear you. I want to throw up. I grunt something. The crushing weight on my back begins to lift. I blink stupidly at the wooden slats in front of me, then someone grabs my arm and tries to pull me sideways. Their touch hurts; someone, maybe me, screams, and someone else yells 'Medic!'

Seconds or minutes later I realise that I'm lying on my back and someone is pounding on my chest. I blink and try to grunt something. 'Can you hear me?' they say.

'Yeah – *oof*.'

The pounding stops for a moment and I force myself to breathe deeply. I know I should be lying on something, but what? I open my eyes properly. 'Oh, that wasn't good. My knee—'

Alan leans over my field of view; people are bustling about behind him. 'What was that all about?' he asks.

'Is Mo—'

'I'm all right, Bob.' Her voice comes from right behind me. I start, and it feels like someone's clubbed me behind the ear again – my head is about to split open. 'That – thing—' her voice is shaky.

'It's an altar,' I say tiredly. 'Should have recognised the design sooner. Alan, the bad guy is loose here. Somewhere. Mo was bait for a trap.'

'Explain,' Alan says, almost absent-mindedly. I roll my head round and see that Mo is sitting with her back to the wall, legs stretched out in front of her; someone's given her one of the red survival suits, no good in vacuum but enough to keep her warm, and she's got a silver foil blanket stretched around her shoulders. Behind her, the altar is a splintered wreck.

'It's not so hard to open a gate and bring an information entity through, especially if you've got a body ready and waiting for it at the other end, right? Physical gates are harder, and the bigger you want 'em, the more energy or life you have to expend to stabilize it. Anyway, this is an altar; there are a couple like it in the basement of that museum we came to visit. You put the sacrifice on the altar, wire it to an invocation grid, and kill the victim – that's what the chandelier was for – channelling what comes back out. Only this one – the guards and wards around the altar are buggered. They'd offer no protection at all once the summoning was manifest, and the thing would take over anyone it could come into contact with. Transfer by electrical conduction, that's how a lot of these things spread.'

'So you tried to shield her with your body,' says Alan, 'How touching!'

'Huh.' I cough and wince at the answering pain in my head. 'Not really; I figured the scaffold wouldn't be able to cut through my air tanks. And if it killed her we'd all be dead, anyway.'

'What was it set up to summon?' Mo asks. Her voice still hoarse.

'I don't know.' I frown. 'Nothing friendly, that's for sure. But then, this isn't the Ahnenerbe, is it? Even though they built this place, they've been dead for a long time. Suicide, by the look of it. This bastard's some kind of possessor entity – jumps from body to body. It's been shadowing you from the States, but when it got you all it did was use you as raw material in a summoning sacrifice. Doesn't make sense, does it? If it wanted you so bad, why not just walk up to you, shake hands, and move into your head?'

'It doesn't matter right now.' Alan stands. 'We're leaving soon. According to Roland the gate's shrinking; we've got about four hours to pull out, and your mystery kidnapper hasn't tried to make a break for it. What we're going to do is put a guard on the gate, get the hell out of here, and leave the demo charge ticking. He won't be able to sneak back around us, and the gadget will toast what's left of this place.'

'Uh-huh. How's my tankage?'

'Dented, and your suit front panel is blown – it took the brunt of the charge, otherwise you'd be a crispy critter right now. Look, I'm going to get things organised in person, seeing all our radios are flaking out.' Alan looks round. 'Hutter, get these people sorted out and ready to pull back; I want them both mobile within the hour, we've got a lot of shit to move out of here.' He glances down at me and winks. 'You've done well.'

Over the course of the next fifteen minutes I recover enough to sit up against the wall, and Mo just about manages to stop shivering. She leans against me. 'Thank you,' she says quietly. 'That went *way* beyond—'

Hutter and Chaitin bang in through the door, heaving a couple of bulky kit-bags full of assorted gear: vacuum support underwear, heated outer suit, a new regulator and air tank for my framework, a new backpack and helmet for Mo. 'Look at the lovebirds,' Chaitin says, apparently amused by us. 'On your feet, pretties, got to get you ready to move and ain't nobody going to carry you.'

While Hutter is getting Mo into her pressure gear I stumble around the wreckage of the procrustean bed and hunt for my palmtop – dropped when I had to leap for her life. I find it lying on the concrete floor, evidently kicked into a corner of the room, but it's undamaged, which is a big relief. I pick it up and check the thaum level absently, and freeze: something is really *not* right around here. Following the display I trail around the walls until I find an inexplicably high reading in front of that rack of high tension switchgear. *Something* is happening here: local entropy is sky-high as if information is being destroyed by irreversible computation in the vicinity. But the rack is switched off. I pocket the small computer and give the rack an experimental yank; I'm nearly knocked off my feet when it slides toward me.

'Hey!' Chaitin is right behind me, shoving me out of the way and pointing his gun into the dark cavity behind the rack.

'Don't,' I say tersely. 'Look.' I switch on my suit headlamp, and promptly wish I hadn't.

'Oh Jesus.' Chaitin lowers his gun but doesn't look away. The room behind the instrument rack is another cell: it must have been undisturbed for a long time, but it's so cold that most of the body parts are still recognisable. There's a butcher's shop miasma hanging over it, not decay, exactly, but the smell of death. Enough spare parts for Dr. Frankenstein to make a dozen monsters lie heaped in the room, piled in brown-iced drifts in the corners. 'Shut the fucking door,' he says distantly, and steps out of my way.

'Anyone got a hacksaw?' I ask.

'You can't be serious—' Chaitin pushes up his visor and stares at me. 'Why?'

'I want to take samples from the top few bodies,' I say slowly. 'I think they may be something to do with the Mukhabarat's Santa Cruz operation.'

'You're nuts,' he says.

'Maybe, but don't you want to know who these people were?'

'No fucking way, mate,' he says. Then he breathes deeply. 'Look, I was in Bosnia, y'know, the mass graves?' He glances down and scuffs the floor. 'Spent a couple of weeks guarding the forensics guys one summer. The worst thing about those pits, you scrubbed like crazy but in the end you had to throw your boots away. Once that smell gets into the leather it won't leave.' He looks away. 'You're fucking out of your skull if you think I'm going to help you take trophies.'

'So just get me an axe,' I snap irritably. (Then I wince again and wish I hadn't.) He looks at me oddly for a moment, as if trying to make his mind up whether or not to get physical, then turns and stomps off.

When Chaitin returns he's carrying a fireman's axe and an empty kit-bag. He leaves me alone for ten minutes while I discover just how difficult it is to chop through the wrist bones of a corpse that's been frozen for days or months. I find that I'm angry, very angry indeed – so angry, in fact, that the job doesn't upset me. I want to find the bastard who did this and give him a taste of his own medicine, and if chopping off dead hands is the price then it's a price I'm happy to pay – with interest.

But why do I still feel as if I'm missing something obvious? Like, maybe, what the demon – dybbuk, possessor, whatever-you-call-it – lured us here for?

9: BLACK SUN

WHEN I COME OUT OF THE CELLAR CLUTCHING MY
grisly handbag, Hutter and Mo are gone. Chaitin is stooging
around, shuffling from foot to foot as he waits for me. 'Let's go,'
he says, so I heft the bag at him.

'Got it.' We head back up the corridor past the glow-tubes and
I glance over my shoulder just once, breath steaming in the frigid
air. Then I lower my visor and lock it in place, check my regulator, and listen to the hiss of cool air through my helmet. 'Where
is everybody?'

'Boss man's up top arming the gadget; your squeeze is on her
way back to the gateway.'

'Great,' I say, and I mean it. This place is getting to me; I
almost want to dance a little jig at the thought of blowing it to
atoms. 'Did anybody find any documentation?'

'Documentation? Tons of it. These guys were Germans, dude.
You ever worked with the fucking Wehrmacht, you'd be able to
tell a story about documentation, too.'

'Huh.' We hit the bottom of the stairs. Scary Spice is waiting
for us.

'Go on up,' he says to Chaitin. He stops me: 'You, wait.' He
twists a dial on my chest pack: 'Hear me?'

'Yeah,' I say, 'loud and clear. Has anyone seen any sign of the
bastard who kidnapped Mo?'

'The target, you mean?' Scary hefts his heavily insulated gun and for a moment I'm glad I can't see through his face mask. 'Naah, but you're going up the stairs right now and I'm following you, and if you see anyone behind me yell like hell.'

'That,' I say fervently, 'is fine by me.' Already the shadows are lengthening as the glow-tubes slowly burn out.

There's crosstalk and terse chatter all over the radio channel Scary has tuned me to; I get the impression of three teams retreating to prearranged positions, keeping their eyes peeled for company. Some evil bastard demon has been here in the past couple of hours, wearing a stolen body: Can't we move faster? Evidently not. 'Timer set to seven thousand seconds by my mark,' Alan cuts in on the common channel. 'This is your hundred and ten minute warning, folks. I've pulled the spoiler chain and the initiator is now live; anyone still here in two hours better have some factor one-billion sunblock. Sound off by name.'

Everyone seems to be accounted for, except the three outside. 'Okay, pull out in LIFO order. Scary, Chaitin, make sure Howard's in tow and cycle when ready.'

'Right, boss.' Chaitin. 'C'mon, you, let's go.'

'Okay.' I wait while Chaitin cycles through the airlock into the garage, then open the door and squeeze into the cramped closet-like space. 'I'm on tank one, everything working.'

'It better be. Okay, cycle yourself through.'

I wait for a tense two minutes while the air hisses out of a tiny tube and I feel the pressure suit tightening around me. Oddly, I begin to feel warmer once I'm in partial vacuum; the chilly air in the redoubt was sapping my body heat. Presently the outer door swings open. 'Move, move!'

I walk out into the garage, open doors gaping at the ink-black sky, then out into the courtyard in front of the building. Chaitin's waiting there. Someone's parked that electric trolley next to the wall, but the little half-track thing with a motorcycle's front wheel is missing. 'Someone taking souvenirs?' I ask.

A burst of static that I just about decode as 'What?' tells me that the interference is worse than before; I glance up and see red stars, a dull red swirl of galaxy overhead . . . a distinct pink tinge to the moon, in fact.

I point at where the Kettenkrad was parked. 'There, it's gone,' I say. 'Who took it?'

Chaitin shrugs. I look round. 'Go there.' He points at the main gatehouse. I start walking. The moonlight is dim, rosy: either I'm reeling lightheaded or . . . or what?

It's about a kilometre to the wall where our unseen enemy opened the gate to Amsterdam, and with no sign of him in the vicinity I have time to do a little bit of thinking. Looking straight up I see only darkness; the visible stars mostly stretched in a wide belt above the horizon, the moon an evil-faced icon staring down at us. The power to suck all the life and heat out of a planet like this – it's horrifying. While a sacrificial murder will get you a hot-line to a demon capable of possessing you, or a window to some universe so alien you can't comprehend its physical laws, it takes a lot of power to open a physical gate to another version of the Earth. Shadow Earths interfere with each other, and it's very difficult to generate congruence. But whatever happened here . . .

I try to picture what might have happened. I can only come up with two scenarios:

Scenario one. An Ahnenerbe detachment in Germany, some time in April of 1945. They know they're losing, but defeat is not an acceptable option to them. They quickly gather all the supplies they can: foodstuffs, machine tools, seeds, fuel. Using a handful of captured enemy POWs, a gate is opened to somewhere cold and airless where they can wait out the hue and cry before making a break for home.

Nope, that doesn't work. How'd they build this fortress? Or mess with the moon?

Scenario two. A divergent history; a different branch of our own universe, so close to our own timeline that the energy it takes to open a full bridge between the two realities approximates the mass-energy of the universe itself. The point of departure, the fork in the river of time, is an invocation the Ahnenerbe attempted late in the war – but not too late. It's an act of necromancy so bloody that the priests of Xipe Totec would have cringed in horror, so gruesome that Himmler would have protested. They opened a gateway. We thought it was just a tactical move, a way to move men and materials about without being vulnerable to Allied attack – shunt them into another world, travel across it bypassing their enemies, then open a gateway back to our own continuum. But what if they were doing something more ambitious? What if they were trying to open a channel to one of the nameless places where the infovores dwell: beings of near-infinite cold, living in the darkened ghosts of expanded universes that have succumbed to the ancient forces of proton decay and black hole evaporation? Invoking Godlike powers to hold their enemies at bay, the forces of the Red Army and the Western Allies are held in check . . .

What happened next?

Pacing through the petrified forest I can see it as clearly as a television documentary. A wind of desolation and pain screams out of the heart of Europe, hurling bombers from the skies like dandelion seeds. A darkness rises in the west, a maelstrom that sucks Zhukov's divisions in like splinters of a shattered mast sent flying in a hurricane. The SS necromancers are exultant: their demons harrow the Earth in stolen bodies, scouring it clean of enemy forces, eating the souls of the *untermenschen* and spitting up their bones. Snow falls early *fimbulwinter* sets in, for the ice giants of legend have returned to do the bidding of the thousand-year Reich, and the Fuhrer's every dream shall be made real. A pale sun that warms nothing gazes down across a wilderness of ice and fire, ravaged by the triumph of the will.

They only realise how badly they'd miscalculated some months later as the daylight hours shorten, and shorten further – until the equinox passes, the temperature continues to fall as the sunlight dims, and the giants cease to do their bidding.

Götterdämmerung has come for the victorious Third Reich . . .

Up the low rise with the wall on the other side, I turn round and look back at the redoubt, at the last island of warmth in a cold world that's been sucked dry. I contemplate it for a minute or so. 'Had a thought,' I say aloud, and get a burst of static in return.

I look round. Chaitin is standing farther up the hillside; he waves at me. More static. 'You there?' I ask, fiddling with my radio controls. 'Can you hear me?'

He walks toward me, brandishing something. I focus on a coil of cable with a plug on the end, but as he approaches the static begins to clear up. He pokes it at my chest pack but I bat his hand away. 'Speak,' he says roughly.

I take a deep breath: 'I need to make some measurements. There is something very, very wrong with this whole picture, you know? Why is it so cold? Why are our suit radios all malfunctioning? What killed everyone in that bunker? Seems to me that Alan needs to know. Hell! I need to know – it's important.'

Through his suit helmet Chaitin's expression is unreadable. 'Explain.'

I shiver with a sudden realisation. 'Look, they summoned something that hunkered down and sucked all the fucking energy out of this universe, and if Alan sets off an H-bomb – what do you think is going to happen?'

'Talk more.' Chaitin offers me the cable again.

I point to my damaged chest pack, then point my finger straight up. 'Look, the stars are all reddish, and they're too far apart. That's number one. Red shift means they're all flying away from each other like crazy! That, or the energy in the light they're emitting is being sapped by something. I figure that effect is also what's screwing with our radios: in this universe the Planck constant is changing. Number two, the sun – the sun's gone out. It went out a few decades ago, that's why the temperature's down to forty absolute and dropping; the only thing keeping the Earth above cosmic background temperature is the fact that it's a honking great reservoir of hot rocks, with enough thorium and uranium mixed in that decay heat will keep it simmering for billions of years. But that's losing energy faster than it should, too, because something here is distorting the laws of physics. Third:

for all we know all the other suns have gone out, too – the light we see from the stars is fossil radiation, it's been travelling for years, centuries.'

I take a deep breath and shift my feet. Chaitin isn't saying anything; he's just looking around, looking for signs in the sky or the earth. 'Something is eating energy, and information,' I say. 'Our primary objective – in coming here – is to find out what's going on and report back. I'm saying we haven't found out yet, and what the captain doesn't know can hurt us all.'

Chaitin turns back to face me.

'It makes sense, doesn't it?' I say. 'Like, it all hangs together?'

He holds up a torch to illuminate his face through his visor. He's grinning at me with a face I haven't seen before: 'Sehr gut,' he says, then he drops the torch, releases the catches, and lifts his helmet off. Luminous worms of light writhe soundlessly behind his eyelids, twisting in the empty space of his skull, just like the thing that took Fred from Accounting. The out-gassing air from his suit wreathes him in vapour as he leans toward me, grabbing, trying to make a close flesh-to-flesh contact seeing as his commscable gambit has failed. Just one moment of electrical conduction—

The thing that occupies Chaitin's skin and bone is not very intelligent: it's forgotten that I'm wearing a suit, too and that these suits are designed to take a fair bit of abuse. Still, it's pretty freaky. I drop my sack and hop backward, nearly going arse-over-ears as gravity seems to suck at my backpack. The possessed body scrabbles toward me and I can see, very clearly, a trickle of blood bubbling from his nose as I fumble for the basilisk gun at my waist, grab onto it with both hands, and punch both red buttons with my thumbs. For a panicky moment I think that it's dead, batteries drained by the chilling cold out here – then all hell breaks loose.

Roughly one in a thousand carbon nuclei in the body that used to belong to Chaitin spontaneously acquire an extra eight protons and seven or eight neutrons. The mass deficit is bad enough – there's about as much energy coming out of nowhere as a small nuke would put out – but I'll leave that to the cosmologists. What's bad is that each of those nuclei is missing a whopping eight electrons, so it forms a wildly unstable carbosilicate intermediary that promptly grabs a shitload of charge out of the nearest electron donor molecules. Then it destabilizes for real, but in the process it's set off a cascade of tiny little acid/base reactions throughout the surrounding hot chemical soup that used to be a human body. Chaitin's body turns red, the kind of dull red of an electric heating element – then it *steams*, bits of his kit melting as his skin turns black and splits open. He begins to topple toward me and I yell and jump away. When he hits the ground he shatters, like a statue made of hot glass.

The next thing I know I'm on my knees on the frozen ground, breathing deeply and trying desperately to tell my stomach to be still. I can't afford to throw up because if I vomit in my face mask I will die, and then I won't be able to tell Alan what kind of mistake he'll be making if he sets off the demolition charge.

This whole world has been turned into a mousetrap: a body-snatching demon, patient and prepared, waiting for us little furry folk with beady black eyes to stick our curious noses inside.

I pick myself up, watching the steamy vapour pour from the ground around the molten depressions my kneepads melted in the permafrost as I take more deep, laborious breaths. Static ebbs and flows in my ears like bacon frying, the distorted sidebands of a transmission counting down the minutes to the artificial sunrise. I try not to look at what's left of Chaitin.

They summoned an infovore: something that eats energy and minds. A thing – I don't know what sort – from a dead cosmos, one where the stars had long since guttered into darkness and evaporated on a cold wind of decaying protons, the black holes dwindling into superstring-sized knots on a gust of Hawking radiation. A vast, ancient, slow thinker that wanted access to the hot core of a youthful universe, one mere billions of years from the Big Bang, poised for a hundred trillion years of profligate star-burning before the long slide into the abyss.

On my feet now, I check my air supply: good for two and a

quarter hours. That will see me through – the bomb's going to blow in just over an hour. I look round, trying to work out which way to go. Thoughts are clamouring in my head, divergent priorities—

The thing was hungry. First it did what it was invited to do, sucked the minds and life from the Ahnenerbe's enemies, occupied their bodies, and learned how to pass for human. Then it pulled more of itself through the gate than they'd expected. It's big – far too big to fit through a man-sized gate – but it had access to all the energy it wanted, and all the minds to sacrifice, more than enough power to force it wide open and squirm through into this new, rich cosmos.

The monster they summoned gave the Ahnenerbe more than they asked for. As well as damping the fusion phoenix at the heart of every star, it started to drain energy directly out of space-time, messing with the Planck constant, feeding on the false vacuum of space itself. Light stretched, grew redder; the gravitational constant became a variable, dropping like a barometer before a storm. Fusion processes in the sun guttered and died, neutrons and protons remaining stubbornly monogamous. The solar neutrino flux disappeared first, though it would take centuries for the sun itself to show signs of cooling, for the radiation-impeded gravitational collapse to a white dwarf core to resume. Meanwhile, the universe began to expand again, prematurely ageing by aeons in a matter of years.

Back to the here-and-now. Here I am with a corpse. And a gun. And the corpse manifestly killed using the gun in my hands. *Shit.* I twiddle the squelch on my radio but get nothing but loud hissing and incoherent bursts of static. What am I going to tell Alan – 'Look, I know I appear to have shot one of your men, but you've got to abort the mission'?

I glance up at the sky. It's night, but maybe the sun would be visible if I knew where to look. Visible – and shrunken, farther away than it is back home, for as the creature sucks energy out of spacetime, space itself is getting bigger, and emptier. Losing energy. *Find Alan. Stop the bomb. Get everybody out fast.* It took a lot of energy for the thing to fully open the gate to its original home and bring itself through to this shattered Earth; energy that is no longer available in this drained husk of a universe, energy that it needs if it's to move on to pastures new. About all it's capable of on its own right now was to listen for an invitation – from the terror cell in Santa Cruz – and answer their call. What will it do if we dump more energy into it? Open a gate back to its original home? Expand the gate to *our* Earth? There's a worst-possible-case scenario here that I don't even want to think about – I'm going to have nightmares about it for years, *if* I have any years ahead of me to have nightmares in.

Having dragged its huge, cold presence through to squat in the ruins of the victorious Reich, it settled down to wait: patient, for it has waited for an infinity of infinities already, waiting for a hot, fast thinker to open the gate to the next universe. Focussed in one place, it will be able to move far faster this time – no need for a sacrifice of millions to get its attention. Once invited – by the clever stupidity of a terrorist cell, perhaps – it can take possession of a body and, using what it has learned of the nature of humanity from the Ahnenerbe-SS, manipulate those around it. The possessed, its agent on the other side of that first gate, must arrange to open a connection, then find an energy source to crack it wide open, big enough to admit the rest of the eater. Opening a gate wide enough for a human body, with an agent at both ends, would take about as much energy as it had left – the lives of all the remaining Ahnenerbe-SS survivors in this world, hoarded against such an eventual need. But to open a gate so that it can admit an ice giant – a being big enough to carve monuments on the moon and suck dry a universe – will take much more energy: energy gained from either a major act of necromancy or a singularly powerful local source.

I look around. I'm at the foot of a hill; on the other side of it there's a wall, and a couple of pathetic corpses, and half a platoon of SAS specialists. Behind me there's a petrified forest and a castle of shadows, populated with nightmares. (Oh, and a hydrogen bomb that's going to go off in about seventy minutes.) Where is everybody? Strung out between the castle and the gate, that's where.

Got to tell Alan not to set off the bomb. I pick up my sack of hands and stagger downhill toward the skeletal trees, feet and ankles tensed with that walking on glass sensation you get when you're afraid there's nothing but black ice underfoot, one hand clutching the basilisk gun at arm's reach. Branches claw at me in the twilight, making me flinch inside my helmet; they snap and tinkle against my visor, rigid bundles of mummified twigs with all the heat sucked out of them. *If there's more than one of the body snatchers here . . .*

I skid and go down on one thigh, hard. Something crunches underfoot, like twigs snapping. I lever myself upright, rub my leg and wince, breath loud in my ears. Looking down I see a hump of frozen brown, a small rabbit or a rat or something else that's been dead for years. *Dead.* I stoop and pick up my bag of severed hands, tagged for identification at a later date. *Wouldn't this be a good time to think about precautions?* In case there are other demons stalking this frozen plain in stolen bodies?

Well, yes. I cast a glance in the direction of the redoubt, racking my brains for a half-forgotten lecture on occult stealth technologies.

Fifteen minutes later – ten precious minutes of which expire in a feverish rush of poking clumsily at a severed ulna and radius with my multitool and a roll of duct tape – I'm standing in the middle of the dead ground in front of the redoubt. Things have clearly gone very pear-shaped indeed. I clutch the talisman like a drowning man and try to figure out what to do now.

(The talisman glows dimly, an eerie blue light chewing away at the fingertips. To get it lit, I used the basilisk gun on a tree stump and thrust it against the glowing coals. The deep incisions in the palm are the red of firelight reflected in freshly spilt blood. I grip the grisly artifact by its exposed wrist bones and hope like hell that it performs as advertised. See, if you stick a phase-conjugate mirror on the base of a Hand of Glory you can make it spit light; but that's a modern perversion of its original function . . .)

Overhead, the stars are going out one by one. The moon is a blood-soaked red disk; shadows are creeping across the landscape, settling across the hills I can glimpse through my night-vision goggles. And something like a fire is burning on the roofline above the last redoubt of the Ahnenerbe-SS: What's going on?

I try the radio again. 'Howard to anyone, anyone still out there, please respond.' The hissing, frying interference crashes in on my ears, obscuring any answer. I stumble forward on the icy ground just as something that might once have been human dashes around the side of the building, heading in the direction of the gate. It doesn't see me, but someone inside sees it: sparks blossom on the cold ground behind it, and I see brief muzzle flashes coming from a window-slit on the second floor. It was one of ours originally, but no human being can sprint around a building with their helmet off and backpack missing in a *fimbulwinter* cold enough to freeze liquid oxygen.

The possessed soldier raises something blocky to its shoulder and sprays cartridge cases all over the night. Maybe one or two of the bullets come close to the upstairs window, but if so they don't stop whoever's upstairs from catching it with their next burst: for a moment it capers across the ice, then it flops down and lies still. 'Shit,' I mutter, and find myself stumbling into a clumsy trot toward the gaping garage door with its welcoming airlock.

Nobody shoots at me; the talisman is doing its job, fogging the senses of anyone who can see me. I skid to a halt just outside, a nasty suspicion blossoming in my mind, and very carefully inspect the threshold. Yup, there it is: a black box taped to the wall, thin wire stretched taut across the threshold at knee level. Some wag has stencilled THIS SIDE TOWARD LIFE INSURANCE CLAIMANT on its case. I very carefully step over the tripwire then try the radio again. 'Howard to anyone. What's going on? Who's shooting?'

A crackling whine flattens the answer, but at least this time there *is* one: 'Howard! What's your condition? Report.' I try to remember who it is, those clipped tones: Sergeant Howe.

'I'm in the garage with a Hand of Glory,' I say. I swallow. 'It got Chaitin while I wasn't watching him, but I got away – shot it while it was trying to assimilate me. A demon, that is. They take possession if they can touch you – it takes skin-to-skin or electrical contact. There was more than one out here but I'm not sure any are still up. I improvised a stealth talisman to get me back in here; you've got to put me through to Alan, *immediately*.'

'Wait right there.' He sounds tense. 'You in the garage?'

I try to nod, then answer: 'Yeah, I'm in the garage – I spotted the spring surprise in time. Look, this is urgent; we've got to disable the demo gadget before we get out of here. If it blows—'

The outer airlock door edges open. 'Get your ass in the airlock *now*, Howard. Close and lock the door. When it cycles, put anything you're carrying down and raise your arms. When the door opens, don't move until I say so. Don't even *breathe* until I say so. Got it?'

'Got it,' I say, and open the airlock door. I freeze – then carefully put the Hand of Glory down outside the lock, power down the basilisk gun and isolate the charge circuit, drop the sack of severed hands, and make sure my palmtop is asleep before I look inside the chamber again. I swallow. There's a green spheroid taped to the inner door, a fine wire stretching from one end to the rubberised gasket that seals the lock. Below it, there's another gadget: a thaumometer, a sensor that monitors spatiotemporal disturbances indicative of occult activity. That, too, has a wire vanishing inside the gasket. I swallow again. 'I'm stepping inside the lock now,' I say. My legs don't want to move. 'I'm closing the outer door.'

I tell myself I know Alan, and he's not going to do anything stupid. I tell myself that Sergeant Howe is a professional. Locking myself in a room the size of a shower cubicle with a live hand grenade on the end of a string still gives me the cold shudders.

Air hisses through vents and I raise my arms, stiffly forcing the suit to comply. At the last moment I think to turn and make sure that I'm leaning against the side of the lock, not facing the inner door. Then the door clicks – audible, there must be air pressure inside – and swings open. Someone is kneeling outside, pointing a gun at me from behind a body that's sprawled on the floor right in front of the lock.

'Bob.' It's Alan. 'If that's you, I want you to tell me who else was in the classroom with us.'

Phew. 'It was taught by Sophie, and we were in it with Nick from CESG.'

'That's good. And you're still wearing your helmet. That's good, too. Now I want you to turn around slowly, keeping your hands up – that's right. Now, I want you to slowly raise your visor. Hold it – keep your hands still.' The guy with the gun keeps it levelled on my face. Mo was right: I never realised you could see the grooves – lands – of a rifle barrel at three metres; it looks huge, large enough to drive a freight train down.

Something jabs at my left leg and I nearly stumble, then: 'He's clean,' announces someone who was right next to me all the time – I never noticed – and I lower my arms. The guy who's been keeping me covered points his gun at the floor, and suddenly I'm breathing normally again.

'Where's Alan?' I ask. 'What's been happening here?'

'I was hoping you could tell me,' Alan says in my left ear. I look round and he grins tensely. The grin doesn't reach his eyes, which are the colour of liquid oxygen and just as warm. 'Tell me *exactly* what happened to you when you went outside. Tell it like your life depends on it.'

'Uh, okay.' I shuffle away from the lock door and someone – Scary Spice? – swings it shut again.

I spill the beans, including the way Chaitin jumped me. I figure they already know that something's taking over brains and bodies wherever possible. My eyes keep being drawn back to the floor. It's Donaldson, the guy who was speculating about meteorology earlier. He doesn't look real, somehow, as if he ought to get up and walk away in a minute or two, peel off the rubber gore applied by the special effects people and have a laugh with us over a pint. 'I figure the whole thing is a trap,' I finish. 'We were lured here deliberately. Only one of the possessors came through to our world, and it could only control one body at a time, but there may be more here. They're working for, or are part of, something that's not human, but that's had years to study us – to study the survivors from the Ahnenerbe-SS. It took over some useful idiots who tried to summon it from our side in order to use it for a terrorist incident; then it stalked us, kidnapped Mo as bait. It did that because it wants us to provide a power source that'll allow it to expand the gate and push its main body through into our universe. It's a lot bigger than the possessors we've seen so far – it's, like, it's achieved a limited beachhead but it needs to grab an entire harbour from the defenders – us – before it can land the main body of its forces.'

'Right.' Alan looks pensive. 'And how do you think it's going to do this?'

'The demolition gadget. What yield have you set it to?' I ask.

Howe raises an eyebrow. 'Tell him,' says Alan.

'It's a selective yield gadget,' says Howe. 'We can set it to anything from fifteen kilotons to a quarter of a megaton – it's a mechanical process, screw jacks adjust the gap between the fusion sparkplug and the initiator charge so that we get more or less fusion output. Right now it's at the upper end of the yield curve, dialled all the way up to city-buster size. What's this got to do with anything?'

'Well.' I lick my lips; it's really cold in here now and my breath is steaming. 'To open a gate big enough to bring through a large creature like whatever ate this universe takes a whole lot of entropy. The Ahnenerbe did it in this universe by ritually murdering roughly ten million people: information destruction increases entropy. But you can do it in other ways – an H-bomb is a really great entropy *and* energy generator, it minimizes the information content of *lots* of stuff.' They look blank: I glare at them. 'Look, it's the intersection between thermodynamics and information theory, right? Information content is inversely proportional to entropy, entropy is a measure of how well randomized a system is – that's one of the core assumptions of magic, right? That you can transfer energy between universes via the platonic realm of ordered information – mathematics. I think what this monster has been doing all along was raising enough hell via its minor agents to provoke a response – one in which we'd lash out, giving it all the juice it needs to expand the gate. As it is, the minor gate it yanked Mo through is shrinking; I figure that was all it could manage. It's drained so much energy from this universe already that it had to wait for precisely the right moment before it dared open that one; this place is falling apart, and there may not be enough power for the monster to open even one more minor gate. Have you noticed how the stars are going out and we're getting radio interference? I think what we're seeing is fossil starlight – what's left of this universe may only be a bit larger than the solar system, and it's shrinking at close to light-speed. Give it another few hours and it'll collapse like a soap bubble, taking the ice giant with it. Unless we feed it, or them, or whatever the hell it is, enough energy to shore open the gate to our own world and expand it until they can squeeze through.'

'Ah.' Alan looks as if he's just swallowed something unpleasant. 'So. It's your considered opinion that our best course of action would be to disable the bomb and retire, hmm?'

'That's about the size of it,' I agree. 'Where did you plant the gadget anyway?'

'Downstairs; but that's a bit of a sore point,' Alan comments airily. 'The bomb's armed and we've switched over from manual detonation control via the dead man's handle to the internal timer. But there's a catch. You see, Her Majesty's Government doesn't *really* like the idea of leaving armed hydrogen bombs lying around the place without proper supervision. PAL control is fine, and so is a detonation wire and dead man's handle, but these things are designed in case they might get overrun, and we wouldn't want to hand an H-bomb on a plate to some random troublemaker, what?'

Alan begins to pace. Alan pacing, that's a bad sign. 'Once

we've inserted the initiator, dialled a yield, armed the detonators, punched in the permissive action codes, set the timer, *then* removed the control wires, nothing's going to stop it. Can't even open it up: someone messes with the tamper piece, it calls 'tilt' and the game's over. Y'see, we might be a Soviet Guards Motor Rifle formation that's just captured the bridge it's strapped to. Or a bunch of uglies from the backwoods behind the Khyber Pass. So, as you can understand, even conceding that letting it blow here and now might be a very bad idea, it's going to go. Unless you fancy trying your hand at dissecting a booby-trapped, ticking H-bomb, and I don't recall seeing UXB training on your résumé.

He glances at his watch. 'Only another fifty-seven minutes to go, lad. We can probably make it to the gate if we leave in less than half an hour, as long as there aren't too many of the blighters left outside – so I'd hurry up if I was you.'

'Could we take it with us?' I ask.

He barks a short laugh. 'What, you think they'd thank us for dragging a live quarter-megaton bomb back into one of the most densely populated cities in Europe?'

'They can't stop it then?'

'Take an act of God to stop it now,' Howe says with gloomy satisfaction. 'Take an act of God to get us all out of here alive, too. Bet you're wishing you hadn't come back!'

I lick my lips, but my tongue seems to have turned to dry leather. Leathery, like one of Brains's weirdly scrambled-in-its-own-shell eggs. Which reminds me: suddenly what I have to do comes crystal clear. 'I think I know how to get your people out regardless of whether there are any revenants outside,' I say. 'Same way I got in here without anyone spotting me. As for the bomb – what if just a bit of the implosion charge goes off prematurely? Say, at one end of it?'

Alan looks at me oddly. 'How are you going to do that?'

'Never mind. What happens *if*? If, if. Way I remember it, all nuclear weapons these days use a core of plutonium and a set of shaped charges that interlock around it. When they go off, they have to be really precisely timed or the core doesn't implode properly, and if it doesn't implode it doesn't reach critical mass, and if it doesn't go supercritical it doesn't go bang. Right?' I'm almost bouncing up and down. 'There's some stuff I need just outside the airlock – a bag of severed hands, a basilisk gun. I've got the rest of the kit here. How many of us are there upstairs, roundabout, who need to walk out? The sack has enough samples cut from execution victims to make Hands of Glory for everyone – walk right past the lurkers in the forest. *If* someone goes and gets them right now. As for the bomb . . .'

I'm still thinking about the bomb as Sergeant Howe wordlessly ducks into the airlock and I hear the hiss of depressurisation. Ticking, ticking. The bomb's booby-trapped. I need to figure out a way of reaching through the case, reaching past the wires and the polystyrene foam spacers around the plutonium rod, past the surrounding parcels of lithium deuteride wrapped in depleted uranium, through the steel casing of the A-bomb trigger—

Alan is standing in front of me, leaning in my face. 'Bob.'

'Yeah.' *The basilisk gun is the solution. I think . . .*

'Hand of Glory. Tell me what the hell I need to know.'

'A Hand of Glory is fabricated from the hand and wrist of someone who has been wrongly executed. A fairly simple circuit is inscribed around the radius and ulna and the fingertips are ignited. What it does is a limited invocation that results in the bearer becoming invisible. In effect. There are variations, like the inversion laser – stick a phase-conjugate mirror on the base and it makes a serious mess of whatever the hand's pointed at – but the original use of the hand is as a disintermediating tool for observer/subject interactions. Or so Eugene Wigner insisted. How many people have you got?'

The airlock door is cycling: Alan crouches, gun levelled on the door. He waves me off to one side impatiently.

It's Howe. No luminous worms behind his face plate; he hefts a lumpy, misshapen sack and my basilisk gun as he steps through the door.

'Seven, plus yourself. You were saying?' Alan asks.

'Give me.' I take the sack. *It's like peeling potatoes*, I tell myself, *just like peeling potatoes*. 'Anyone got a roll of duct tape? And a pen? Great, now clear the fuck away and give me room to breathe.' Just like peeling potatoes, strange vegetables that grow in a soil of horror, watered with blood. A lot of the original bits of folklore surrounding the Hand of Glory are just that. You don't need a candle made of human fat, horse dung, and suchlike, with a wick made of the hair of a hanged man. You don't need fingers from the fetus of a hanged pregnant woman, amputated stealthily at midnight. All you need is a bunch of hands, some wire or solder, a pen, a digital-analogue converter, a couple of programs I carry on my palmtop, and a strong stomach. Well, I can fake the stomach: just tell myself I'm peeling spuds, sticking bits of wire in Mr. Potato Head, triggering ghost echoes in a decaying neural network, feeding something arcane. Howe pushes in and insists on copying what I do; it's annoying at first, but monkey-see monkey-do gets results and between us we make short work of the sack. A couple of the hands are washouts but in twenty minutes flat I've got a shrunken bag and a row of ghastly trophies arranged on the guardroom table.

'Here,' I say. Scary Spice — who has been shuffling nervously and keeping one eye on the airlock door — jumps.

'What's up?'

Howe watches with silent interest.

I hold up a hand. 'Look.' Thank Cthulhu for pocket soldering irons: the fingertips ignite neatly, that crypt-glow dancing around them.

Scary Spice looks confused. 'Where are you? What's up?' His eyeballs are sliding around like greased marbles; he instinctively raises his gun.

'Safe that!' snaps Howe. He winks in my general direction.

'Hold out your left hand, Scary,' I say.

'Okay.' He shuts his eyes; I shove the stump of the hand into his glove. 'What the fuck *is* this?'

I blink and try to focus on him, but he's slipping away. It's weird; I try to track him but my eyes refuse to lock on. 'What you're holding is called a Hand of Glory. While you're holding it, nobody can see you – it works on the possessors outside, too, or I wouldn't be here.'

'Uh, yeah. How long's it good for?'

'How the fuck should I know?' I reply. I glance at Howe.

'Put it down *now*,' he says. A hand appears on the table and I find I can focus on Scary again. Howe glances at me. 'This is a bloody miracle,' he says morosely. 'Pity we didn't have it a couple of years ago in Azerbaijan.' He keys his mike: 'Howe to all, we've got a ticket home. Alpha, Bravo, Charlie, everyone downstairs *now*. Captain, you're going to want to see this too.'

It's like being at school again, sitting one fucking exam after another, sure that if you don't finish the question in the set time it's going to screw your life. *This* exam, the fail grade is anything short of 100 percent and you get the certificate, with no appeal possible, milliseconds after you put your pen down.

I'm crouching in the basement with Alan and a thing that looks like a steel dustbin on a handcart, if steel dustbins came painted green and neatly labelled THIS WAY UP AND DO NOT DROP. I will confess that I'm sweating like a pig, even in the frigid air of the redoubt, because we are now down to about fifteen minutes and if this fails we won't have time to reach the gate.

'Take five,' says Alan. 'You're doing really well, Bob. I mean that. You're doing *really* well.'

'I bet you say that to all the boys,' I mutter, turning the badly photocopied page of arming instructions – the pamphlet that comes with the bomb has a blue cardboard cover, like a school exercise book that's been classified top secret by mistake.

'No, really.' Alan leans back against the wall. 'They got away, Bob. Everyone but us. Maybe you don't think that's a big deal, but they do; they'll remember it for the rest of their lives, and even if we don't follow them they'll be drinking a toast to your memory for a long time to come.'

'That's reassuring.' I flip another page. I didn't know H-bombs came with user manuals and cutaway diagrams, exploded views of the initiator core. 'Look, this is where the pit goes, right?' I point at the page and then at a spot about five centimetres above the base of the dustbin.

'No.' Alan moves my hand right up to the top of the bomb casing. 'You've got it upside down.'

'Well, that's a relief,' I say lightly.

'At least, I *think* it's upside down,' he says in a worried tone of voice.

'Uh-huh.' I move my finger over the diagram. 'Now *this* is where the detonation controller goes, right?'

'Yes, that's right,' he says, much more reassuringly. I give the green dustbin a hard glance.

Atom bombs aren't that complicated. Back in the late 1970s an American high school physics teacher got together with his class. They designed and built an A-bomb. The US Navy thanked them, trucked it away, added the necessary plutonium, and detonated it down on the test range. The hard bit about building an A-bomb is the plutonium, which takes a specialised nuclear reactor and a chemical reprocessing plant to manufacture and which tends to be kept behind high barbed-wire fences patrolled by guys with guns.

However, atom bombs do have one interesting trait: they go 'bang' when you squeeze a sphere of plutonium using precisely detonated explosive lenses. *Conventional* explosives. And if those lenses don't detonate in exactly the right sequence, if you scramble them, you may get a fizzle, but you don't get a firework. It's like an egg, with a yolk (the A-bomb detonator) and a white (the fusion spark plug and other bang-amplifying widgets) inside it.

So here I am, sitting next to a rogue H-bomb with fourteen minutes to run on its clock; and when Alan passes me a magic marker I draw a big fat X on its casing, because I intend to do to this bomb exactly what Brains did to his eggs – scramble it without breaking the shell.

'How many lenses in this model?'

'Twenty. Dodecahedral layout, triangular sections. Each of 'em is a slab of RDX with a concave centre and a berylide-alloy facing pointing inward.'

'Gotcha.' More chalk marks. RDX is mondo nasty high explosive; its detonation speed is measured in kilometres per second. When they blow, those explosive lenses will punch the beryllium-alloy sheet inward onto a suspended sphere of plutonium about the size of a large grapefruit or a small melon. If you blow them all within a microsecond or so, the shock wave closes around the metallic core like a giant fist, and squeezes. If they go off asymmetrically, instead of squeezing the plutonium until it goes bang, they squirt it harmlessly out the side. Well, harmlessly unless you're standing nearby. A slug of white-hot supercritical plutonium barreling out of a ruptured bomb casing at several hundred metres per second is not exactly fun for all the family. 'That puts the top half of the hemisphere about – here.'

'Very good. What now?'

'Fetch a chair and some books or boxes or something.' I pick up the basilisk gun and begin fiddling with it. 'I need to align this on the hemisphere and tape it in position.'

When the beryllium-alloy sphere assembles it squishes the plutonium pit inward. Plutonium is about twice as dense as lead, and fairly soft; it's a metal, warm to the touch from alpha particle decay, and it exhibits some of the weirdest heavy-metal chemistry known to science. It exists in half a dozen crystalline forms between zero and one hundred Celsius; what it gets up to inside an imploding nuclear core is anybody's guess.

'Chair.'

'Duct tape.'

'What next?'

'Get me a cordless drill, a half-inch bit, and a pair of scissors.'

At the core of the grapefruit there's a hollow space, and inside the hollow there's a pea-sized lump of weirdly shaped metal alloy, the design of which is a closely guarded secret. When the molten-hot compressed plutonium hits it, it vomits neutrons. And the neutrons in turn start a cascade reaction inside the plutonium;

every time a plutonium nucleus is hit by a neutron it wobbles like jelly, splits in two, and emits a bunch more neutrons and a blast of gamma radiation. This happens in a unit of time called a 'shake' – about a tenth of a thousandth of a millionth of a second – and every plutonium nucleus in the core will have been blasted into fragments within fifty shakes of the core shockwave hitting the initiator and triggering that initial neutron burst. (*If* it collapses symmetrically.) And maybe a few milliseconds later the devil will be free to dance in our universe.

Twelve minutes to go. I position the chair in front of the bomb. The back of the chair is made of plywood – a real win – so I drill holes in it at the right separation, then get Alan to hold the basilisk box while I chop strips of duct tape off the reel and bind it to the chair immediately in front of the X where I think the explosive lenses lie.

'Bingo.' One chair. One basilisk gun – a box with a camcorder to either side – taped to the back of the chair. One ticking hydrogen bomb. The back of my neck itches, as if already feeling the flash of X-rays ripped from the bleeding plasma of the bomb's casing when the pit disassembles in a few scant shakes of Teller's alarm clock. 'I'm powering up the gun now.' The gun's sensors face the bomb through the holes I've drilled in the chair's back. I switch it on and watch the charge indicator. Damn, the cold doesn't seem to have done the batteries any good. It's still live, but close to the red RECHARGE zone.

'Okay,' I say, leaning back. 'One more thing to do: we have to trip the observe button.'

'Yes, that seems obvious,' says Alan. 'Um, mind me asking why?'

'Not at all.' I close my eyes, feeling as if I've just run a marathon. 'The basilisk spontaneously causes about 1 percent of the carbon nuclei in the target in front of it to tunnel into silicon. With one hell of an energy release at the same time, of course.'

'But plutonium isn't carbon—'

'No, but the explosive lenses are made of RDX, which is a polynitrated aromatic hydrocarbon compound. You turn 1 percent of the RDX charge into silicon and it will go bang very enthusiastically indeed. If we offset it to one side like *this*' – I nudge the chair a couple of centimeters – 'one side of the A-bomb's explosive lenses predetonate, totally out of sequence, causing a fizzle. Imagine a giant's fist, squeezing the plutonium core; now imagine he's left his thumb off the top. Molten plutonium squirts out instead of compressing around the initiator and going bang. You get a messy neutron pulse but no supercriticality excursion. Maybe explosive disassembly of the case, and a mess of radiation, but no mushroom cloud.'

Alan glances at his watch. 'Nine minutes. You'd better be going.'

'Nine – what do you mean?'

He looks at me tiredly. 'Laddie, unless there's a timer on this basilisk gadget, *someone* has to stay here and pull the trigger. You're a civilian, but I signed up for the Queen's shilling.'

'Bullshit!' I glare at him. 'You've got a wife and kids. If anyone's disposable around here it's me.'

'Firstly, I seem to remember you saying you'd do whatever I said before you came along on this road trip. Secondly, you understand what's going on: you're too bloody important to leave behind. And thirdly, it's my job,' he says heavily. 'I'm a soldier. I'm paid to catch bullets, or neutrons. You're not. So unless you've got some kind of magic remote controller for—'

I blink rapidly. 'Let me look at it again,' I say.

The basilisk gun is a bunch of customised IC circuits bolted to a pair of digital camcorders. I lean closer. The good news is they have fast interfaces. The bad news—

Shit. No infrared. The TV remote control program on my palmtop won't work. I straighten up. 'No,' I say.

'Get the hell out of here then,' says Alan. 'You've got six minutes. I'm going to wait sixty seconds after you leave the room, then hit the button.' He sounds very calm. 'Go on, now. Unless you think losing two lives is better than losing one.'

Shit. I punch the door frame twice, oblivious to the pain in my wrist.

'Go!' he yells.

Upstairs, I pause in the guardroom, about to ignite one of the two Hands of Glory that are waiting for me on the table. I wonder if I'm far enough away from the bomb. (That American scientist – Harry Dagnian, wasn't it? – who did something similar by accident in the Manhattan Project: dropped a neutron reflector on top of a weapon core during an experiment. He died a couple days later, but a guard just ten feet away wasn't affected.) There's a muffled thud that I feel through the soles of my boots; a split second later I hear a noise like a door slamming.

I hear my pulse racing erratically. I hear it, therefore I am still alive. I heard the explosion, therefore the bomb fizzled. There will be no nuclear fireball to energize the conquest dreams of the ancient evil that lurks in this pocket universe. All I have to do is pick up the Hand and walk back to the slowly evaporating gate before it closes . . .

A minute passes. Then I put down the Hand of Glory and wait for another minute. It's no good. My feet carry me back inside and I fasten down my faceplate, switching to my canned air supply as I head down the corridor that leads to the staircase.

At the top of the stairs I key my microphone. 'Alan? Are you there?'

A momentary pause, then: 'Right you are.' He chuckles hoarsely. 'Always knew I'd die in my own bed, laddie.' Another pause. 'Make sure you're buttoned up before you come downstairs. This isn't a sight most people ever get to see.'

10: INQUEST

Three days later I am back in London. Most of the intervening time seems to be spent in interview rooms, doing debriefs and going over every last aspect of events. When I'm not talking myself hoarse I am fed institutional food and sleep in a spartan institutional bed. Officer's Mess or something. The flight back to London is an anticlimax, and I go straight from the airport to Alan's hospital bed.

It's in a closed bay off a ward devoted to tropical diseases in one of the big London teaching hospitals. There's a staff nurse on the desk out in front, and a police officer on the door. 'Hi,' I say. 'I'm here to see Alan Barnes.'

The nurse barely looks up. 'No visitors for Mr. Barnes.' He goes back to studying someone else's medication chart.

I lean on the front of the nursing station. 'Look,' I say. 'Personal friend *and* coworker. It's visiting hours. Please.'

This time the nurse looks at me. 'You really don't want to see him,' he says. The cop straightens up and takes notice of me for the first time.

I pull my warrant card. 'How is he?' I ask.

The nurse exhales sharply. 'He's stable for now but we may have to move him to the ICU at short notice; it isn't pretty.' He glances at the cop. 'We can arrange to call you if there's any change.'

I glance at the officer of the law, who is inspecting my warrant card as if it's the clue to a particularly nasty murder: 'Are you going to let me in or not?'

The cop looks at me sharply. 'You can go in, Mr. Howard.' She opens the door and steps inside first, not bothering to give me back the card.

'No more than five minutes!' calls the nurse.

It's a small room with no window; fluorescent lights and a trolley bed surrounded by machines that have far too many dials and knobs for comfort. A trolley beside the bed is draining bags of transparent fluid into the arm of the bed's occupant by way of a vicious-looking cannula. The bed's occupant is reclining on a mound of pillows; his eyelids flicker open as I come in. He smiles. 'Bob.'

'I came as soon as they let me go,' I say. I reach into my inner pocket for the card, barely noticing the policewoman behind me tense; when she sees the envelope she relaxes again. 'How are you feeling?'

'Like shit.' He grins cadaverously. 'Like the world's worst-ever case of Montezuma's revenge. Have you been all right, lad?'

'Can't complain much. They haven't given me a chance to talk to Mo, and I spent the first day back being prodded by the witch doctors – I think they liked the colour of my bile or something.' I'm babbling. *Get a grip.* 'Guess there was enough concrete between you and me. Have they let you talk to, uh, Hillary? Is the food okay?'

'Food—' He turns his head to look at the cannula in his arm. His skin is brown and ulcerated and seems to be hanging loose, patchy white flakes falling from the underlying reddish tissue. 'Seem to be eating through a hose these days, Bob.' He closes his eyes. 'Not seen Hillary. Shit, I'm tired. Feverish, too, some of the time.' His eyes open again. 'You'll tell her?'

'Tell her what, Alan?'

'Just tell her.'

The policewoman clears her throat behind me. 'Yeah, I'll tell her,' I say. Alan doesn't give any sign of showing that he's heard me; he just nodded right off, like an eighty-year-old on Valium. I open the envelope and put the card in it on his bedside table, where he'll see it when he wakes up. If. He always knew he'd die in his own bed. *Tell Hillary?*

I turn and walk through the door, blind to the world. The cop follows me out, shutting it carefully. 'Do you know who did that to him, Mr. Howard?' she asks quietly.

I stop. Clench my fists behind my back. 'Sort of,' I say quietly. 'They won't be doing it to anyone else, if that's what you're asking. If you'll give me back my card now, I have to go in to the office and make sure someone's told his wife where he is. I take it you'll let her in?'

She glances at the nurse. 'Up to him.' She nods at me, then some misplaced piece of Metropolitan Police customer relations training kicks in on autopilot: 'Have a nice day, now.'

I check into the Laundry via the back door. It's three in the afternoon and a light rain is falling: mild breeze from the southeast, cloud cover at 90 percent, a beautiful match for my mood. I head for my cubicle and find it unchanged from when I was last here, more than a week ago: there s a coffee cup containing some amazingly dead dregs, a pile of unread unclassified memos, and a bunch of yellowing Post-it notes saying SEE ME plastered all over my terminal and keyboard.

I drop into the chair in front of the terminal and poke listlessly at the decaying hayrick of email that's cluttering up my user account. Oddly, there doesn't seem to be a lot from more than one day into the trip. That's kind of strange: I should be deluged with stupid nonsense from HR, requests for software upgrades from the losers in Accounting, and peremptory reports for the GDP of Outer Mongolia in 1928 from Angleton – well, not the latter.

I kick back for a moment and stare at the ceiling. There are a couple of coffee-coloured stains up there, relics of who-knows-what mishap, deep in the Precambrian era of Laundry history. Rorschach-like, they call up the texture of Alan's skin: brown, loose, looking burned from the inside out. I glance away. For a moment even the fossil Post-it notes are preferable to thinking about what I have to do next.

Then the door opens. 'Robert!' I look round. It's Harriet, and I know something's wrong because Bridget is lurking behind her, face a contemplative middle-management mask, and she's clutching a bunch of blue-covered files. 'Where've you been hiding? We've been looking for you for days.'

'I don't know if you're cleared,' I respond wearily. I think I can see what's coming.

'Would you please come with us?' says Bridget, voicing the order as a request. 'We have some things to talk about.'

Harriet backs out of the cramped doorway and I haul myself upright and let them march me down the corridor and up the stairs to a vacant conference room, all dusty pine veneer and dead flies trapped between perpetually closed Venetian blinds. 'Have a seat.' There are four chairs at the table, and as I glance round I notice that we seem to have picked up an escort: Eric the Ancient Security Officer, a dried-up prune of a former RAF sergeant whose job is to lock doors, confiscate papers left lying on unoccupied desks, and generally make a pestilential nuisance of himself – a sinecure for the irreformably officious.

'What's this about?' I place both hands palms-down on the table.

'It's about several things, as a matter of fact,' begins Harriet. 'Your controller and I have been worried for some months now about your timekeeping.' She plonks a thin blue file down on the table. 'We note that you're seldom in the department before 10 A.M., and your observance of core hours falls short of the standard expected of an employee.'

Bridget picks up the tag-team prosecution: 'Now, we understand that you're used to working occasional off-shift hours, being called out on those odd occasions when there's a problem with one of the servers. But you haven't been filling out variance form R-70 each time you've put in these hours, and without an audit trail I'm afraid we can't automatically accept requests for time off

in lieu. According to our records you've been taking off an average of two unscheduled days per month – which could get us,
your supervisors, into serious trouble if Audit Bureau were to get
interested.'

Harriet clears her throat. 'Simply put, we can't cover for you
anymore. *In* fact—'

Bridget is shaking her head. 'This latest escapade is unaccept-
able, too. You've absented yourself from work for five consecutive
working days without following either the approved sick/leave-
of-absence procedure or applying to your department head for a
holiday variance or even compassionate leave. This sort of thing
is not only antisocial – think of the additional work you've made
for everybody else who's been covering your absence! – but it's a
gross violation of procedures.' She pronounces the last phrase
with the sort of distaste usually reserved by the tabloid press for
ministers caught soliciting on Hampstead Heath. 'We simply
cannot overlook this.'

Harriet nods. 'And then there's what Eric found in your mail-
box.'

By this time my neck is aching as I try to keep my eyes on all
three of them at the same time. *What the hell's going on?* Harriet
and Bridget administering a procedural mugging is all very well,
and I'm damned if I'll let them plant a written warning on my
personnel file without an appeal. But Eric's the departmental
security officer. What's he in here for?

'Very bad indeed, young fellow,' he quavers. And now Bridget
barely tries to conceal a triumphant, somewhat feral grin as she
plants a raw printout of an email message on the tabletop.
'Subject: Some Notes Toward a Proof of Polynomial
Completeness in Hamiltonian Networks.' My mind goes blank
for a moment, then I remember the black-bag job, Croxley
Industrial Estate, the hum of servers at midnight and security
guards hiding under their desks. And my stomach goes icy cold.

'What's this about?' asks Bridget.

'I think you've got some explaining to do,' opines Eric, peer-
ing at me with watery blue eyes like an elderly vulture

contemplating a wildebeest that's just made the terminal mistake of drinking from a poisoned watering hole.

My stomach feels like ice, but the sense of gathering outrage at the back of my head is like a red-hot band. As I see them watching me with varied degrees of expectancy I feel a flash of raw anger: I press my hands down on the tabletop because I really feel like punching somebody in the face, and that wouldn't be the right way to handle this situation.

'You have no need to know,' I say as firmly as possible.

Harriet's smile slips first. 'I'm your team leader,' she says sternly. 'You aren't in a position to tell me what I need to know.'

'*Fuck* that.' I stand up. 'Minute this, if you're going to start writing it down: I want it noted that I deny all accusations, that my actions are justified. I am not going to be party to a procedural lynch mob held on spurious grounds. You don't have need to know and I don't have permission to tell you. If you want to take this further I insist that you take it up with Angleton.'

'Angleton—' Now Bridget's smile has slipped, too. Eric is blinking rapidly, confused. I pick on him.

'Let's put this on Angleton's desk,' I say soothingly. 'He'll know what to do with it.'

'If you say so—' Eric looks uncertain. He's been around so long that he doesn't have to imagine the reasons behind Angleton's mystique: he *knows*. He almost looks afraid.

'Come on.'

I grab the papers off the table, yank the door open and march out. Behind me, Bridget protests: 'You can't!'

'I bloody can,' I snarl over my shoulder, speeding up to a trot as I head for his basement lair. 'You bloody see if I can!' I've got a fistful of accusations and a startled Harriet flapping after me: that's all I need. Fucking departmental politics, see where it gets you.

Angleton's outer vestibule; the door gapes open. I barge right in, startling the spotty young geek who's threading microfilm between the Memex's rollers. 'Boss!' I call.

The inner door swings open. 'Howard. We were just discussing you. Enter.'

I slide to a halt on the green carpet, in front of the great olive-coloured metal desk. I hold up the papers. 'Bridget and Harriet,' I say. 'Oh, and Eric.'

Andy leans against the wall next to Angleton's desk and whistles quietly. 'You sure know how to make friends and influence people.'

'Silence, please.' Angleton leans forward, 'Ms. Brody. May I ask what you're trying to pin on our young friend here?'

Bridget parks herself on the other side of the desk from Angleton, and leans over him. 'Violation of departmental procedures. Security breaches. Misuse of Internet access. Poor timekeeping. Absence without official leave. Breach of protocol and abusive behaviour toward a superior amounting to gross misconduct.'

'I . . . see.' Angleton's voice is cold enough to freeze liquid hydrogen.

Out of the corner of my eye I find Andy trying to catch my eye. He seems to be twitching his cheek in Morse code – telling me to keep my mouth shut.

'He's a loose cannon,' Bridget insists, in a Thatcheresque tone of total conviction. 'He's a menace. Can't even fill out a time sheet accurately.'

'Ms. Brody.' Angleton leans back, looking up at Bridget across the expanse of his desk. *That's odd, why is he relaxing?* I wonder.

He holds something up. 'You appear to have overlooked something.' The thing in his hand is small and walnut coloured: a tuft of hair sticks out of one end of it, bristly and dry. Bridget inhales sharply. 'Howard works for me now. He's on your budget allocation, I agree, but he works for *me*, and you will henceforth confine your relationship with him to issuing monthly payslips and ensuring that his office is not accidentally re-allocated, unless you wish to wind up emulating the fate of your illustrious predecessor.' He jiggles the thing in his hand.

Bridget's eyes are fixed on the thing. She swallows. 'You wouldn't.'

'My dear, I assure you that I am an equal-opportunity executioner. Eric!' The elderly security officer shuffles forward. 'Please remove Ms. Brody from my office before she makes me say something I might regret.'

'You *bastard*,' she snarls, as Eric places a hand on her shoulder and urges her away from the room. 'Just because you think you can go outside channels and talk to the director, don't let that fool you—'

The door shuts behind her. Angleton puts the wizened thing down on his blotter. 'Do you think I'm bluffing, Robert?' he asks me, his tone deceptively mild.

I swallow. 'Uh-uh. No way. Never.'

'Good.' He smiles at the shrunken head before him. 'Something the pen-pushers never seem to get straight: don't threaten, don't bluff. Isn't that right, Wallace?'

The shrunken head seems to nod, or maybe it's just my imagination. I take a deep breath. 'Actually, I was meaning to see you. It's about Alan.'

Angleton nods. 'He took five hundred rems, boy. They tell me that ten years ago that would probably have been fatal.'

'Has anyone told Hillary yet?'

Andy coughs. 'I'm going round there in a couple of hours.' My expression must be sceptical because he adds, 'Who do you think was best man at their wedding?'

'Oh. Okay.' I feel an enormous letdown, as if some tension I'd barely been aware of has been released. 'Well, then. That's the main thing.'

'Not really.'

I glance back at Angleton. 'There's more?'

'Bad timekeeping.' He looks contemplative. 'So you visited Alan first off, then came in to work. I'd say you've done a full day's work today already, Howard. Better go home before you're too late.'

'Home?' Then I realise. 'How long has she been back?'

'Two days.' His cheek twitches. 'Better hope she isn't angry with you.'

* * *

As I stick the key in the front door lock, I look up at the roofline – both infinitely familiar and strangely alien. *I've only been away one week*, I tell myself. *What can have changed?*

The front hall is full of petite tank tracks. They're about twenty centimetres wide, covered in dried-up mud, and they run past the hulking Victorian coat rack and the living room door to stop just short of the kitchen. I stumble between them as I close the outer and inner doors, try to find somewhere to stow my bag that isn't covered in leftovers from the retreat from Moscow, and remove my coat.

There's most of an engine block on the kitchen table. Whoever put it there for dissection had the good sense to spread a couple of copies of the *Independent* under it; a headline peeps out from under one oily corner: AMSTERDAM HOTEL GAS BLAST KILLS FOUR. Yeah, right. Depression crashes down on me like a black tide: I suddenly feel very ancient, old beyond my years' span in centuries. The kitchen sink is full of unwashed dishes; I turn on the hot tap and swirl it around in search of a mug that's more or less cleanable, then go rummage in my cupboard for some tea bags.

A new crop of bills has sprouted in the fertile soil of the cork notice board. I'll have to read them sooner or later – later will do.

There's a small pile of letters with my name on them in the usual place – half of them look to be junk mail, judging by the glossy envelopes. And there's no water in the kettle. I fill it, then sit down next to the engine block and wait for enlightenment to spring on me. I am, I realise, tired; also depressed, lonely, and afraid. Until a couple of months ago I never saw anyone die; for the past couple of nights I haven't been able to dream about anything else. It's exhausting, physically and emotionally. One of the doctors said something about stress disorders but I wasn't listening properly at the time. I wonder if the engine block belongs to Pinky or Brains: I've got a mind to give them a chewing out over it when they come home. It's antisocial as hell – what if someone wanted to eat lunch in here?

The kettle boils, then clicks off. I sit in silence for a moment, feeling a chill in the air, then stand up to pour a mug of tea.

'Make one for me, too?'

I nearly scald myself but control the kettle in time. 'I didn't hear you come in.'

'That's okay.' She moves a chair behind me. 'I didn't hear you come in, either. Been back long?'

'Back in the country?' I'm rummaging in the sink for another mug as my mouth freewheels without human intervention, seemingly autonomous, as if it isn't a part of me. 'Only since this morning. I had to visit Alan in hospital first, then I went in to work for a couple of hours. Been in meetings. They've kept me in meetings ever since . . .'

'Did they tell you not to talk about it – to anybody?' she asks. I detect a note of strain in her voice.

'Not . . . exactly.' I rinse the mug, drop a tea bag in it, pour on hot water, put it down, and turn round to face her. Mo looks the way I feel: hair askew, clothes slept-in, eyes haunted. 'I can talk to you about it, if you like. You're cleared for this by default.' I drag another chair out from the table. She drops into it without asking. 'Did they tell you what was going on?'

'I—' she shakes her head. 'Tethered goat.' She sounds faintly disgusted, but her face is a mask. 'Is it over?'

I sit down next to her. 'Yes. Definitely and forever. It's not going to happen again.' I can see her relaxing. 'Is that what you wanted to hear?'

She looks at me sharply. 'As long as it's the truth.'

'It is.' I look at the engine block gloomily. 'Whose is this?'

She sighs. 'I think it belongs to Brains. He brought it home yesterday; I don't know where he got it from.'

'I'm going to have words with him.'

'Won't be necessary; he said he's going to take it away when he moves out.'

'What?'

I must look puzzled, because she frowns: 'I forgot. Pinky and Brains are moving out. By the end of the week. I only found out yesterday, when I got back.'

'Oh great.' I glance at the collection of papers, pinned like butterflies to the corkboard: there's nothing like a change of flat-mates to induce feelings of fear and loathing over the phone bill. 'That's kind of short notice.'

'I think it's been brewing for some time,' she says quietly. 'He said something about your attitude . . .' She trails off. 'Hard to live with, so they're going to leave you to your cosy domesticity, unquote.' Her eyes sparkle for a moment, angry and hard. 'Know any sensitivity training camps with watchtowers and armed guards? I think he could do with an enforced vacation.'

'Him and my line manager, both. At least, my old manager.' The mugs of tea have been brewing long enough; I fish the bags out and add milk. 'Here. You didn't tell me what else you've been doing.'

'Doing?' She stares at me. 'I've been passed around in a pres-surised plastic sack by a bunch of soldiers, poked and prodded by doctors, grilled by security officers, and packed off home like a naughty little girl. I haven't exactly done much *doing*, if you follow. In fact—' She shakes her head in disgust. 'Forget it.'

'I can't.' I can't meet her eyes, either. I'm staring at a cooling mug of tea, and all I can see are worms of pale light, writhing slowly. 'I think this was important, Mo. To people other than us, people who'll sleep better at night now.'

'Why. Me.' She's gritting her teeth; platitudes won't work.

'Because you were there,' I say tiredly. 'Because someone in your town was trying to carry out a petty act of terrorism, and summoned up an ancient evil they couldn't control. Because you were close and were thinking the unthinkable on a regular, pro-fessional basis. A mind is a dangerous thing to taste, and sometimes – only sometimes – things come out of the woodwork that like the flavour of our thoughts. This particular thing was relying on our stupidity, or on our failure to recognise what it was, and used you as bait to sucker us in. We thought *we* were using *you* as bait, but all the time it was playing us like a fish on a line. In the end, at least five people died because of that mis-take, and another is in hospital right now and maybe isn't going to make it.'

'Thanks.' Her tone of voice is like granite. 'Whose mistake was it?'

'Committee decision.' I put my mug down and look at her. 'If we hadn't come after you, those other guys would still be alive. So I guess, from a purely utilitarian point of view everyone in the Laundry fucked up, all the way down the line, from start to finish. I shouldn't have come after you in Santa Cruz: end of story.'

'Is that what you really think?' she asks, wonderingly.

I shake my head. 'Sometimes we make mistakes for all the right reasons. If Angleton had run this according to the book, by our wonderful ISO-9000-compliant recipe for intelligence operations in the occult sphere, you'd be dead – and the ice giant would still have come through. We'd *all* have been dead, soon enough.'

'Angleton broke the rules? I didn't think he was the type. Dried-up old bureaucrat.'

'A vintage that sometimes isn't what it seems.'

She stands up. 'Why were *you* there?' she asks.

I shrug. 'Did you expect me to leave you?'

She looks at me for a moment that feels like eternity. 'I didn't know you long enough to guess the answer to that, before. Funny what a crisis teaches you about other people.' She holds out a hand. 'Brains probably isn't going to get back until seven and I need to go back to my flat in half an hour; give me a hand moving this thing off the table?' She gestures at the engine block.

'Guess so. Um, what are you planning on doing, if I may be so bold?'

'Doing?' She pauses with one hand on the Kettenkrad engine block: 'I'm moving the rest of my stuff into Brains's room once he's gone. You didn't think you could get rid of me that easily, did you?' She grins, suddenly. 'Want to help me pack?'

THE CONCRETE JUNGLE

THE CONCRETE JUNGLE

THE DEATH RATTLE OF A MORTALLY WOUNDED
telephone is a horrible thing to hear at four o'clock on a Tuesday
morning. It's even worse when you're sleeping the sleep that follows a pitcher of iced margueritas in the basement of the Dog's
Bollocks, with a chaser of nachos and a tequila slammer or three
for dessert. I come to, sitting upright, bare-ass naked in the
middle of the wooden floor, clutching the receiver with one hand
and my head with the other — purely to prevent it from exploding, you understand — and moaning quietly. 'Who is it?' I croak
into the microphone.

'Bob, get your ass down to the office right away. This line isn't
secure.' I recognize that voice: I have nightmares about it. That's
because I work for its owner.

'Whoa, I was asleep, boss. Can't it' — I gulp and look at the
alarm clock — 'wait until morning?'

'No. I'm calling a code blue.'

'Jesus.' The band of demons stomping around my skull strike
up an encore with drums. 'Okay, boss. Ready to leave in ten minutes. Can I bill a taxi fare?'

'No, it can't wait. I'll have a car pick you up.' He cuts the call,
and *that* is when I start to get frightened because even Angleton,
who occupies a lair deep in the bowels of the Laundry's Arcana
Analysis Section — but does something far scarier than that ano-
dyne title might suggest — is liable to think twice before
authorising a car to pull in an employee at zero-dark o'clock.

I manage to pull on a sweater and jeans, tie my shoelaces, and
get my ass downstairs just before the blue and red strobes light
up the window above the front door. On the way out I grab my

emergency bag – an overnighter full of stuff that Andy suggested I should keep ready 'just in case' – and slam and lock the door and turn around in time to find the cop waiting for me. 'Are you Bob Howard?'

'Yeah, that's me.' I show him my card.

'If you'll come with me, sir.'

Lucky me: I get to wake up on my way in to work four hours early, in the front passenger seat of a police car with strobes flashing and the driver doing his best to scare me into catatonia. Lucky London: the streets are nearly empty at this time of night, so we zip around the feral taxis and somnolent cleaning trucks without pause. A journey that would normally take an hour and a half takes fifteen minutes. (Of course, it comes at a price: Accounting exists in a state of perpetual warfare with the rest of the civil service over internal billing, and the Metropolitan Police charge for their services as a taxi firm at a level that would make you think they provided limousines with wet bars. But Angleton has declared a code blue, so . . .)

The dingy-looking warehouse in a side street, adjoining a closed former primary school, doesn't look too promising – but the door opens before I can raise a hand to knock on it. The grinning sallow face of Fred from Accounting looms out of the darkness in front of me and I recoil before I realise that it's all right – Fred's been dead for more than a year, which is why he's on the night shift. This isn't going to degenerate into plaintive requests for me to fix his spreadsheet. 'Fred, I'm here to see Angleton,' I say very clearly, then I whisper a special password to stop him from eating me. Fred retreats back to his security cubbyhole or coffin or whatever it is you call it, and I cross the threshold of the Laundry. It's dark – to save light bulbs, and damn the health and safety regs – but some kind soul has left a mouldering cardboard box of hand torches on the front desk. I pull the door shut behind me, pick up a torch, and head for Angleton's office.

As I get to the top of the stairs I see that the lights are on in the corridor we call Mahogany Row. If the boss is running a crisis team then that's where I'll find him. So I divert into executive territory until I see a door with a red light glowing above it. There's a note taped to the door handle: BOB HOWARD ACCESS PERMITTED. So I 'access permitted' and walk right in.

As soon as the door opens Angleton looks up from the map spread across the boardroom table. The room smells of stale coffee, cheap cigarettes, and fear. 'You're late,' he says sharply.

'Late,' I echo, dumping my emergency bag under the fire extinguisher and leaning on the door. ' 'Lo, Andy, Boris. Boss, I don't think the cop was taking his time. Any faster and he'd be billing you for brown stain removal from the upholstery.' I yawn. 'What's the picture?'

'Milton Keynes,' says Andy.

'Are sending you there to investigate,' explains Boris.

'With extreme prejudice,' Angleton one-ups them.

'Milton Keynes?'

It must be something in my expression; Andy turns away hastily and pours me a cup of Laundry coffee while Boris pretends it's none of his business. Angleton just looks as if he's bitten something unpleasant, which is par for the course.

'We have a problem,' Angleton explains, gesturing at the map. 'There are too many concrete cows.'

'Concrete cows.' I pull out a chair and flop down into it heavily, then rub my eyes. 'This isn't a dream is it, by any chance? No? Shit.'

Boris glowers at me: 'Not a joke.' He rolls his eyes toward Angleton. 'Boss?'

'It's no joke, Bob,' says Angleton. His normally skeletal features are even more drawn than usual, and there are dark hollows under his eyes. He looks as if he's been up all night. Angleton glances at Andy: 'Has he been keeping his weapons certification up-to-date?'

'I practice three times a week,' I butt in, before Andy can get started on the intimate details of my personal file. 'Why?'

'Go down to the armoury right now, with Andy. Andy, self-defense kit for one, sign it out for him. Bob, don't shoot unless it's you or them.' Angleton shoves a stack of papers and a pen across the table at me. 'Sign the top and pass it back — you now have GAME ANDES REDSHIFT clearance. The files below are part of GAR — you're to keep them on your person at all times until you get back here, then check them in via Morag's office; you'll answer to the auditors if they go missing or get copied.'

'Huh?'

I obviously still look confused because Angleton cracks an expression so frightening that it must be a smile and adds, 'Shut your mouth, you're drooling on your collar. Now, go with Andy, check out your hot kit, let Andy set you up with a chopper, and *read* those papers. When you get to Milton Keynes, do what comes naturally. If you don't find anything, come back and tell me and we'll take things from there.'

'But what am I looking for?' I gulp down half my coffee in one go; it tastes of ashes, stale cigarette ends, and tinned instant left over from the Retreat from Moscow. 'Dammit, what do you expect me to find?'

'I don't expect anything,' says Angleton. 'Just go.'

'Come on,' says Andy, opening the door, 'you can leave the papers here for now.'

I follow him into the corridor, along to the darkened stairwell at the end, and down four flights of stairs into the basement. 'Just what the fuck *is* this?' I demand, as Andy produces a key and unlocks the steel-barred gate in front of the security tunnel.

'It's GAME ANDES REDSHIFT, kid,' he says over his shoulder. I follow him into the security zone and the gate clanks shut behind me. Another key, another steel door — this time the outer vestibule of the armoury. 'Listen, don't go too hard on Angleton, he knows what he's doing. If you go in with preconceptions about what you'll find and it turns out to be GAME ANDES RED-SHIFT, you'll probably get yourself killed. But I reckon there's only about a 10 percent chance it's the real thing — more likely it's a drunken student prank.'

He uses another key, and a secret word that my ears refuse to hear, to open the inner armoury door. I follow Andy inside. One wall is racked with guns, another is walled with ammunition lockers, and the opposite wall is racked with more esoteric items. It's this that he turns to.

'A prank,' I echo, and yawn, against my better judgement. 'Jesus, it's half past four in the morning and you got me out of bed because of a student prank?'

'Listen.' Andy stops and glares at me, irritated. 'Remember how you came aboard? That was *me* getting out of bed at four in the morning because of a student prank.'

'Oh,' is all I can say to him. *Sorry* springs to mind, but is probably inadequate; as they later pointed out to me, applied computational demonology and built-up areas don't mix very well. I thought I was just generating weird new fractals; *they* knew I was dangerously close to landscaping Wolverhampton with alien nightmares. 'What kind of students?' I ask.

'Architecture or alchemy. Nuclear physics for an outside straight.' Another word of command and Andy opens the sliding glass case in front of some gruesome relics that positively throb with power. 'Come on. Which of these would you like?'

'I think I'll take this one, thanks.' I reach in and carefully pick up a silver locket on a chain; there's a yellow-and-black thaumaturgy hazard trefoil on a label dangling from it, and NO PULL ribbons attached to the clasp.

'Good choice.' Andy watches me in silence as I add a Hand of Glory to my collection, and then a second, protective amulet. 'That all?' he asks.

'That's all,' I say, and he nods and shuts the cupboard, then renews the seal on it.

'Sure?' he asks.

I look at him. Andy is a slightly built, forty-something guy; thin, wispy hair, tweed sports jacket with leather patches at the elbows, and a perpetually worried expression. Looking at him you'd think he was an Open University lecturer, not a managerial-level spook from the Laundry's active service division. But that goes for all of them, doesn't it? Angleton looks more like a Texan oil-company executive with tuberculosis than the legendary and terrifying head of the Counter-Possession Unit. And me, I look like a refugee from CodeCon or a dot-com startup's engineering department. Which just goes to show that appearances and a euro will get you a cup of coffee. 'What does this code blue look like to you?' I ask.

He sighs tiredly, then yawns. 'Damn, it's infectious,' he mutters. 'Listen, if I tell you what it looks like to me, Angleton will have my head for a doorknob. Let's just say, *read* those files on the way over, okay? Keep your eyes open, count the concrete cows, then come back safe.'

'Count the cows. Come back safe. Check.' I sign the clipboard, pick up my arsenal, and he opens the armoury door. 'How am I getting there?'

Andy cracks a lopsided grin. 'By police helicopter. This is a code blue, remember?'

I go up to the committee room, collect the papers, and then it's down to the front door, where the same police patrol car is waiting for me. More brown-pants motoring – this time the traffic is a little thicker, dawn is only an hour and a half away – and we end up in the north-east suburbs, following the roads to Lippitts Hill where the Police ASU keep their choppers. There's no messing around with check in and departure lounges; we drive round to a gate at one side of the complex, show our warrant cards, and my chauffeur takes me right out onto the heliport and parks next to the ready room, then hands me over to the flight crew before I realise what's happening.

'You're Bob Howard?' asks the copilot. 'Up here, hop in.' He helps me into the back seat of the Twin Squirrel, sorts me out with the seat belt, then hands me a bulky headset and plugs it in. 'We'll be there in half an hour,' he says. 'You just relax, try to get some sleep.' He grins sardonically then shuts the door on me and climbs in up front.

Funny. I've never been in a helicopter before. It's not quite as loud as I'd expected, especially with the headset on, but as I've been led to expect something like being rolled down a hill in an oil drum while maniacs whack on the sides with baseball bats, that isn't saying much. *Get some sleep* indeed; instead I bury my nose in the so-secret reports on GAME ANDES REDSHIFT and try not to upchuck as the predawn London landscape corkscrews around outside the huge glass windscreen and then starts to unroll beneath us.

REPORT 1: Sunday September 4th, 1892
CLASSIFIED MOST SECRET, Imperial War Ministry, September 11th, 1914
RECLASSIFIED TOP SECRET GAME ANDES, Ministry of War, July 2nd, 1940
RECLASSIFIED TOP SECRET REDSHIFT, Ministry of Defense, August 13th, 1988

My dearest Nellie,

In the week since I last wrote to you, I have to confess that I have become a different man. Experiences such as the ordeal I have just undergone must surely come but once in a lifetime; for if more often, how might man survive them? I have gazed upon the gorgon and lived to tell the tale, for which I am profoundly grateful (and I hasten to explain myself before you worry for my safety), although only the guiding hand of some angel of grace can account for my being in a position to put ink to paper with these words.

I was at dinner alone with the Mehtar last Tuesday evening – Mr. Robertson being laid up, and Lieutenant Bruce off to Gilgut to procure supplies for his secret expedition to Lhasa – when we were interrupted most rudely at our repast. 'Holiness!' The runner, quite breathless with fear, threw himself upon his knees in front of us. 'Your brother . . .! Please hasten, I implore you!'

His excellency Nizam ul Mulk looked at me with that

wicked expression of his: he bears little affection for his brutish hulk of a brother, and with good reason. Where the Mehtar is a man of refined, albeit questionable sensibilities, his brother is an uneducated coarse hill-man, one step removed from banditry. Chittral can very well do without his kind. 'What has happened to my beloved brother?' asked ul Mulk.

At this point the runner lapsed into a gabble that I could barely understand. With patience the Mehtar drew him out – then frowned. Turning to me, he said, 'We have a – I know not the word for it in English, excuse please. It is a monster of the caves and passes who preys upon my people. My brother has gone to hunt it, but it appears to have got the better of him.'

'A mountain lion?' I said, misunderstanding.

'No.' He looked at me oddly. 'May I enquire of you, Captain, whether Her Majesty's government tolerates monsters within her empire?'

'Of course not!'

'Then you will not object to joining me in the hunt?'

I could feel a trap closing on me, but could not for the life of me see what it might be. 'Certainly,' I said. 'By Jove, old chap, we'll have this monster's head mounted on your trophy room wall before the week is out!'

'I think not,' Nizam said coolly. 'We burn such things here, to drive out the evil spirit that gave rise to them. Bring you your *mirror*, tomorrow?'

'My—' Then I realised what he was talking about, and what deadly jeopardy I had placed my life in, for the honour of Her Majesty's government in Chittral: he was talking about a Medusa. And although it quite unmans me to confess it, I was afraid.

The next day, in my cramped, windowless hut, I rose with the dawn and dressed for the hunt. I armed myself, then told Sergeant Singh to ready a squad of troopers for the hunt.

'What is the quarry, sahib?' he asked.

'The beast that no man sees,' I said, and the normally imperturbable trooper flinched.

'The men won't like that, sir,' he said.

'They'll like it even less if I hear any words from them,' I said. You have to be firm with colonial troops: they have only as much backbone as their commanding officer.

'I'll tell them that, sahib,' he said and, saluting, went to ready our forces.

The Mehtar's men gathered outside; an unruly bunch of hillmen, armed as one might expect with a mix of flint-locks and bows. They were spirited, like children, excitable and bickering; hardly a match for the order of my troopers and I. We showed them how it was done! Together with the Mehtar at our head, kestrel on his wrist, we rode out into the cold bright dawn and the steep-sided mountain valley.

We rode for the entire morning and most of the afternoon, climbing up the sides of a steep pass and then between two towering peaks clad in gleaming white snow. The mood of the party was uncommonly quiet, a sense of apprehensive fortitude settling over the normally ebullient Chittrali warriors. We came at last to a mean-spirited hamlet of tumbledown shacks, where a handful of scrawny goats grazed the scrubby bushes; the hetman of the village came to meet us, and with quavering voice directed us to our destination.

'It lies thuswise,' remarked my translator, adding: 'The old fool, he say it is a ghost-bedevilled valley, by God! He say his son go in there two, three days ago, not come out. Then the Mehtar – blessed be he – his brother follow with his soldiers. And that two days ago.'

'Hah. Well,' I said, 'tell him the great white empress sent me here with these fine troops he sees, and the Mehtar himself and his nobles, and *we* aren't feeding any monster!'

The translator jabbered at the hetman for a while, and he

looked stricken. Then Nizam beckoned me over. 'Easy, old fellow,' he said.

'As you say, your excellency.'

He rode forward, beckoning me alongside. I felt the need to explain myself further: 'I do not believe one gorgon will do for us. In fact, I do believe we will do for it!'

'It is not that which concerns me,' said the ruler of the small mountain kingdom. 'But go easy on the hetman. The monster was his wife.'

We rode the rest of the way in reflective silence, to the valley where the monster had built her retreat, the only noises the sighing of wind, the thudding of hooves, and the jingling of our kits. 'There is a cave halfway up the wall of the valley, here,' said the messenger who had summoned us. 'She lives there, coming out at times to drink and forage for food. The villagers left her meals at first, but in her madness she slew one of them, and then they stopped.'

Such tragic neglect is unknown in England, where the poor victims of this most hideous ailment are confined in mazed bedlams upon their diagnosis, blindfolded lest they kill those who nurse them. But what more can one expect of the half-civilized children of the valley kingdoms, here on the top of the world?

The execution – for want of a better word – proceeded about as well as such an event can, which is to say that it was harrowing and not by any means enjoyable in the way that hunting game can be. At the entrance to the small canyon where the woman had made her lair, we paused. I detailed Sergeant Singh to ready a squad of rifles; their guns loaded, they took up positions in the rocks, ready to beat back the monster should she try to rush us.

Having thus prepared our position, I dismounted and, joining the Mehtar, steeled myself to enter the valley of death.

I am sure you have read lurid tales of the appalling scenes in which gorgons are found; charnel houses strewn

with calcined bodies, bones protruding in attitudes of
agony from the walls as the madmen and madwomen who
slew them gibber and howl among their victims. These
tales are, I am thankful to say, constructed out of whole
cloth by the fevered imaginations of the degenerate scrib-
blers who write for the penny dreadfuls. What we found
was both less – and much worse – than that.

We found a rubble-strewn valley; in one side of it a cave,
barely more than a cleft in the rock face, with a tumbledown awning stretched across its entrance. An old woman
sat under the awning, eyes closed, humming to herself in an
odd singsong. The remains of a fire lay in front of her, logs
burned down to white-caked ashes; she seemed to be
crying, tears trickling down her sunken, wrinkled cheeks.

The Mehtar gestured me to silence, then, in what I only
later recognized as a supremely brave gesture, strode up to
the fire. 'Good evening to you, my aunt, and it would please
me that you keep your eyes closed, lest my guards be forced
to slay you of an instant,' he said.

The woman kept up her low, keening croon – like a wail
of grief from one who has cried until her throat is raw and
will make no more noise. But her eyes remained obediently
shut. The Mehtar crouched down in front of her.

'Do you know who I am?' he asked gently.

The crooning stopped. 'You are the royal one,' she said,
her voice a cracked whisper. 'They told me you would
come.'

'Indeed I have,' he said, a compassionate tone in his
voice. With one hand he waved me closer. 'It is very sad,
what you have become.'

'It *hurts*.' She wailed quietly, startling the soldiers so
that one of them half-rose to his feet. I signalled him back
down urgently as I approached behind her. 'I wanted to see
my son one more time . . .'

'It is all right, aunt,' he said quietly. 'You'll see him soon
enough.' He held out a hand to me; I held out the leather

bag and he removed the mirror. 'Be at peace, aunt. An end to pain is in sight.' He held the mirror at arms length in front of his face, above the fire before her: 'Open your eyes when you are ready for it.'

She sobbed once, then opened her eyes.

I didn't know what to expect, dear Nellie, but it was not this: somebody's aged mother, crawling away from her home to die with a stabbing pain in her head, surrounded by misery and loneliness. As it is, her monarch spared her the final pain, for as soon as she looked into the mirror she *changed*. The story that the gorgon kills those who see her by virtue of her ugliness is untrue; she was merely an old woman – the evil was something in her gaze, something to do with the act of perception.

As soon as her eyes opened – they were bright blue, for a moment – she changed. Her skin puffed up and her hair went to dust, as if in a terrible heat. My skin prickled; it was as if I had placed my face in the open door of a furnace. Can you imagine what it would be like if a body were to be heated in an instant to the temperature of a blast furnace? For that is what it was like. I will not describe this horror in any detail, for it is not fit material for discussion. When the wave of heat cleared, her body toppled forward atop the fire – and rolled apart, yet more calcined logs amidst the embers.

The Mehtar stood, and mopped his brow. 'Summon your men, Francis,' he said, 'they must build a cairn here.'

'A cairn?' I echoed blankly.

'For my brother.' He gestured impatiently at the fire into which the unfortunate woman had tumbled. 'Who else do you think this could have been?'

A cairn was built, and we camped overnight in the village. I must confess that both the Mehtar and I have been awfully sick since then, with an abnormal rapidity that came on since the confrontation. Our men carried us back home, and that is where you find me now, lying abed as I

write this account of one of the most horrible incidents I
have ever witnessed on the frontier.

I remain your obedient and loving servant,

Capt. Francis Younghusband

As I finish reading the typescript of Captain Younghusband's
report, my headset buzzes nastily and crackles. 'Coming up on
Milton Keynes in a couple minutes, Mr. Howard. Any idea where
you want to be put down? If you don't have anywhere specific in
mind we'll ask for a slot at the police pad.'

Somewhere specific . . .? I shove the unaccountably top-secret
papers down into one side of my bag and rummage around for
one of the gadgets I took from the armoury. 'The concrete cows,'
I say. 'I need to take a look at them as soon as possible. They're in
Bancroft Park, according to this map. Just off Monk's Way, follow
the A422 in until it turns into the H3 near the city centre. Any
chance we can fly over them?'

'Hold on a moment.'

The helicopter banks alarmingly and the landscape tilts
around us. We're shooting over a dark landscape, trees and neat,
orderly fields, and the occasional clump of suburban paradise
whisking past beneath us – then we're over a dual carriageway,
almost empty at this time of night, and we bank again and turn
to follow it. From an altitude of about a thousand feet it looks
like an incredibly detailed toy, right down to the finger-sized
trucks crawling along it.

'Right, that's it,' says the copilot. 'Anything else we can do for
you?'

'Yeah,' I say. 'You've got infrared gear, haven't you? I'm looking for an extra cow. A hot one. I mean, hot like it's been cooked,
not hot as in body temperature.'

'Gotcha, we're looking for a barbecue.' He leans sideways and
fiddles with the controls below a fun-looking monitor. 'Here.
Ever used one of these before?'

'What is it, FLIR?'

'Got it in one. That joystick's the pan, this knob is zoom, you use this one to control the gain, it's on a stabilised platform; give us a yell if you see anything. Clear?'

'I think so.' The joystick works as promised and I zoom in on a trail of ghostly hot spots, pan behind them to pick up the brilliant glare of a predawn jogger, lit up like a light bulb – the dots are fading footprints on the cold ground. 'Yeah.' We're making about forty miles per hour along the road, sneaking in like a thief in the night, and I zoom out to take in as much of the side view as possible. After a minute or so I see the park ahead, off the side of a roundabout. 'Eyes up, front: Can you hover over that roundabout?'

'Sure. Hold on.' The engine note changes and my stomach lurches, but the FLIR pod stays locked on target. I can see the cows now, grey shapes against the cold ground – a herd of concrete animals created in 1978 by a visiting artist. There should be eight of them, life-sized Friesians peacefully grazing in a field attached to the park. But something's wrong, and it's not hard to see what.

'Barbecue at six o'clock low,' says the copilot. 'You want to go down and bring us back a take-away, or what?'

'Stay up,' I say edgily, slewing the camera pod around. 'I want to make sure it's safe first . . .'

REPORT 2: Wednesday March 4th, 1914
CLASSIFIED MOST SECRET, Imperial War Ministry,
September 11th, 1914
RECLASSIFIED TOP SECRET GAME ANDES, Ministry
of War, July 2nd, 1940
RECLASSIFIED TOP SECRET REDSHIFT, Ministry of
Defense, August 13th, 1988

Dear Albert,

Today we performed Young's double-slit experiment upon Subject C, our medusa. The results are unequivocal;

the Medusa effect is both a particle *and* a wave. If de Broglie is right . . .

But I am getting ahead of myself.

Ernest has been pushing for results with characteristic vim and vigor and Mathiesson, our analytical chemist, has been driven to his wits' end by the New Zealander's questions. He nearly came to blows with Dr. Jamieson who insisted that the welfare of his patient – as he calls Subject C – comes before any question of getting to the bottom of this infuriating and perplexing anomaly.

Subject C is an unmarried woman, aged 27, of medium height with brown hair and blue eyes. Until four months ago, she was healthy and engaged as household maid to an eminent KC whose name you would probably recognize. Four months ago she underwent a series of seizures; her employers being generous, she was taken to the Royal Free Infirmary where she described having a series of blinding headaches going back eighteen months or so. Dr. Willard examined her using one of the latest Roentgen machines, and determined that she appeared to have the makings of a tumour upon her brain. Naturally this placed her under Notification, subject to the Monster Control Act (1864); she was taken to the isolation ward at St. Bartholomew's in London where, three weeks, six migraines, and two seizures later, she experienced her first Grand Morte fit. Upon receiving confirmation that she was suffering from acute gorgonism, Dr. Rutherford asked me to proceed as agreed upon; and so I arranged for the Home Office to be contacted by way of the Dean.

While Mr. McKenna was at first unenthusiastic about the prospect of a gorgon running about the streets of Manchester, our reassurances ultimately proved acceptable and he directed that Subject C be released into our custody on her own cognizance. She was in a state of entirely understandable distress when she arrived, but once the situation was explained she agreed to cooperate fully in return for a settlement which will be made upon her next of kin. As she is young and healthy, she may survive for several months, if not a year, in her current condition: this offers an unparallelled research opportunity. We are currently keeping her in the old Leprosarium, the windows of which have been bricked up. A security labyrinth has been installed, the garden wall raised by five feet so that she can take in the air without endangering passersby, and we have arranged a set of signals whereby she can don occlusive blindfolds before receiving visitors. Experiments upon patients with acute gorgonism always carry an element of danger, but in this case I believe our precautions will suffice until her final deterioration begins.

Lest you ask why we don't employ a common basilisk or cockatrice instead, I hasten to explain that we do; the pathology is identical in whichever species, but a human source is far more amenable to control than any wild animal. Using Subject C we can perform repeatable experiments at will, and obtain verbal confirmation that she has performed our requests. I hardly need to remind you that the historical use of gorgonism, for example by Danton's Committee for Public Safety during the French revolution, was hardly conducted as a scientific study of the phenomenon. This time, we will make progress!

Once Subject C was comfortable, Dr. Rutherford arranged a series of seminars. The New Zealander is of the opinion that the effect is probably mediated by some electromagnetic phenomenon, of a type unknown to other areas of science. He is consequently soliciting new designs for experiments intended to demonstrate the scope and nature of the gorgon effect. We know from the history of Mademoiselle Marianne's grisly collaboration with Robespierre that the victim must be visible to the gorgon, but need not be directly perceived; reflection works, as does trivial refraction, and the effect is transmitted through glass thin enough to see through, but the gorgon cannot work in darkness or thick smoke. Nobody has demonstrated a physical mechanism for gorgonism that doesn't involve an unfortunate creature afflicted with the characteristic tumours. Blinding a gorgon appears to control the effect, as does a sufficient visual distortion. So why does Ernest insist on treating a clearly biological phenomenon as one of the greatest mysteries in physics today?

'My dear fellow,' he explained to me the first time I asked, 'how did Madame Curie infer the existence of radioactivity in radium-bearing ores? How did Wilhelm Roentgen recognize X-rays for what they were? Neither of those forms of radiation arose within our current understanding of magnetism, electricity, or light. They had to be something else. Now, our children of Medusa apparently need to behold a victim in order to injure them – but how is the effect transmitted? We know, unlike the ancient Greeks, that our eyes work by focussing ambient light on a membrane at their rear. They used to think that the gorgons shone forth beams of balefire, as if to set in stone whatever they alighted on. But we know that cannot be true. What we face is nothing less than a wholly new phenomenon. Granted, the gorgon effect only changes whatever the medusoid can see directly, but we know the light reflected from those bodies isn't responsible. And Lavoisier's calorimetric experiments – before he met his unfortunate end before the looking glass of l'Executrice – proved that actual atomic transmutation is going on! So what on earth mediates the effect? How can the act of observation, performed by an unfortunate afflicted with gorgonism, transform the nuclear structure?'

(By nuclear structure he is of course referring to the core of the atom, as deduced by our experiments last year.)

Then he explained how he was going to seat a gorgon on one side of a very large device he calls a cloud chamber, with big magnetic coils positioned above and below it, to see if there is some other physical phenomenon at work.

I can now reveal the effects of our team's experimentation. Subject C is cooperating in a most professional manner, but despite Ernest's greatest efforts the cloud chamber bore no fruit – she can sit with her face pressed up against the glass window on one side, and blow a chicken's egg to flinders of red-hot pumice on the target stand, but no ionization trail appears in the saturated vapour of the chamber. Or rather, I should say no direct trail appears. We had more success when we attempted to replicate other basic experiments. It seems that the gorgon effect is a continuously variable function of the illumination of the target, with a sharply defined lower cut-off and an upper limit! By interposing smoked glass filters we have calibrated the efficiency with which Subject C transmutes the carbon nuclei of a target into silicon, quite accurately. Some of the new electrostatic counters I've been working on have proven fruitful: secondary radiation, including gamma rays and possibly an elusive neutral particle, are given off by the target, and indeed our cloud chamber has produced an excellent picture of radiation given off by the target.

Having confirmed the calorimetric and optical properties of the effect, we next performed the double-slit experiment upon a row of targets (in this case, using wooden combs). A wall with two thin slits is interposed between the targets and our subject, whose gaze was split in two using a binocular arrangement of prisms. A lamp positioned between the two slits, on the far side of the wall from our subject, illuminates the targets: as the level of illumination increases, a pattern of alternating gorgonism was produced! This exactly follows the constructive reinforcement and destruction of waves Professor Young demonstrated with his examination of light corpuscles, as we are now supposed to call them. We conclude that gorgonism is a wave effect of some sort – and the act of observation is intimately involved, although on first acquaintance this is such a strange conclusion that some of us were inclined to reject it out of hand.

We will of course be publishing our full findings in due course; I take pleasure in attaching a draft of our paper for your interest. In any case, you must be wondering by now just what the central finding is. This is not in our paper yet, because Dr. Rutherford is inclined to seek a possible explanation before publishing; but I regret to say that our most precise calorimetric analyses suggest that your theory of mass/energy conservation is being violated — not on the order of ounces of weight, but by enough to detect. Carbon atoms are being transformed into silicon ions with an astoundingly high electropositivity, which can be accounted for if we assume that the effect is creating nuclear mass from somewhere. Perhaps you, or your new colleagues at the Prussian Academy, can shed some light on the issue? We are most perplexed, because if we accept this result we are forced to accept the creation of new mass *ab initio*, or treat it as an experimental invalidation of your general theory of relativity.

Your good friend,

Hans Geiger

A portrait of the agent as a (confused) young man:

Picture me, standing in the predawn chill in a badly mown field, yellowing parched grass up to the ankles. There's a wooden fence behind me, a road on the other side of it with the usual traffic cams and streetlights, and a helicopter in police markings parked like a gigantic cyborg beetle in the middle of the roundabout, bulging with muscular-looking sensors and nitesun floodlights and making a racket like an explosion in a noise factory. Before me there's a field full of concrete cows, grazing safely and placidly in the shadow of some low trees which are barely visible in the overspill from the streetlights. Long shadows stretch out from the fence, darkness exploding toward the ominous lump at the far end of the paddock. It's autumn, and dawn isn't due for another thirty minutes. I lift my modified camcorder and zoom in on it, thumbing the record button.

The lump looks a little like a cow that's lying down. I glance over my shoulder at the chopper, which is beginning to spool up for takeoff; I'm pretty sure I'm safe here but I can't quite suppress a cold shudder. On the other side of the field—

'Datum point: Bob Howard, Bancroft Park, Milton Keynes, time is zero seven fourteen on the morning of Tuesday the eighteenth. I have counted the cows and there are nine of them. One is prone, far end of paddock, GPS coordinates to follow. Preliminary surveillance indicated no human presence within a quarter kilometre and residual thermal yield is below two hundred Celsius, so I infer that it is safe to approach the target.'

One unwilling foot goes down in front of another. I keep an eye on my dosimeter, just in case: there's not going to be much secondary radiation hereabouts, but you can never tell. The first of the cows looms up at me out of the darkness. She's painted black and white, and this close up there's no mistaking her for a sculpture. I pat her on the nose. 'Stay cool, Daisy.' I should be safely tucked up in bed with Mo – but she's away on a two-week training seminar at Dunwich and Angleton got a bee in his bonnet and called a code blue emergency. The cuffs of my jeans are damp with dew, and it's cold. I reach the next cow, pause, and lean on its rump for a zoom shot of the target.

'Ground zero, range twenty metres. Subject is bovine, down, clearly terminal. Length is roughly three metres, breed . . . unidentifiable. The grass around it is charred but there's no sign of secondary combustion.' I dry-swallow. 'Thermal bloom from abdomen.' There's a huge rip in its belly where the boiling intestinal fluids exploded, and the contents are probably still glowing red-hot inside.

I approach the object. It's clearly the remains of a cow; equally clearly it has met a most unpleasant end. The dosimeter says it's safe – most of the radiation effects from this sort of thing are prompt, there are minimal secondary products, luckily – but the ground underneath is scorched and the hide has blackened and charred to a gritty, ashlike consistency. There's a smell like roast beef hanging in the air, with an unpleasant undertang of something else. I fumble in my shoulder bag and pull out a thermal probe, then, steeling myself, shove the sharp end in through the rip in the abdomen. I nearly burn my hand on the side as I do so – it's like standing too close to an open oven.

'Core temperature two six six, two six seven . . . stable. Taking core samples for isotope ratio checks.' I pull out a sample tube and a sharp probe and dig around in the thing's guts, trying to tease a chunk of ashy, charred meat loose. I feel queasy: I like a well-cooked steak as much as the next guy, but there's something deeply wrong about this whole scene. I try not to notice the exploded eyeballs or the ruptured tongue bursting through the blackened lips. This job is quite gross enough as it is without adding my own dry heaves to the mess.

Samples safely bottled for analysis, I back away and walk in a wide circle around the body, recording it from all angles. An open gate at the far end of the field and a trail of Impressions in the ground completes the picture. 'Hypothesis: open gate. Someone let Daisy in, walked her to this position near the herd, then backed off. Daisy was then illuminated and exposed to a class three or better basilisk, whether animate or simulated. We need a plausible disinformation pitch, forensics workover of the paddock gate and fence – check for exit signs and footprints – and some way of identifying Daisy to see which herd she came from. If any livestock is reported missing over the next few days that would be a useful indicator. Meanwhile, core temperature is down to under five hundred Celsius. That suggests the incident happened at least a few hours ago – it takes a while for something the size of a cow to cool down that far. Since the basilisk has obviously left the area and there's not a lot more I can do, I'm now going to call in the cleaners. End.'

I switch off the camcorder, slide it into my pocket, and take a deep breath. The next bit promises to be even less pleasant than sticking a thermocouple in the cow's arse to see how long ago it was irradiated. I pull out my mobile phone and dial 999. 'Operator? Police despatch, please. Police despatch? This is Mike Tango Five, repeat, Mike Tango Five. Is Inspector Sullivan available? I have an urgent call for him . . .'

REPORT 3: Friday October 9th, 1942
CLASSIFIED TOP SECRET GAME ANDES, Ministry of War, October 9th, 1942
RECLASSIFIED TOP SECRET REDSHIFT, Ministry of Defense, August 13th, 1988

ACTION THIS DAY:
Three reports have reached SOE Department Two, office 337/42, shedding new light on the recent activities of Dr. Ing Professor Gustaf Von Schachter in conjunction with RSHA Amt. 3 and the inmates of the Holy Nativity Hospital for the Incurably Insane.

Our first report ref. 531/892-(i) concerns the cessation of action by a detached unit of RSHA Amt. 3 Group 4 charged with termination of imbeciles and mental defectives in Frankfurt as part of the Reich's ongoing eugenics program. An agent in place (code: GREEN PIGEON) overheard two soldiers discussing the cessation of euthanasia operations in the clinic in negative terms. Herr Von Schachter had, as of 24/8/42, acquired a Führer Special Order signed either by Hitler or Bormann. This was understood by the soldiers to charge him with the authority to requisition any military resources not concerned with direct security of the Reich or suppression of resistance, and to override orders with the effective authority of an *obergruppenführer*. This mandate runs in conjunction with his existing authority from Dr. Wolfram Sievers, who is believed to be operating the Institute for Military Scientific Research at the University of Strasbourg and the processing centre at Natzweiler concentration camp.

Our second report ref. 539/504-(i) concerns prescriptions dispensed by a pharmacy in Frankfurt for an unnamed doctor from the Holy Nativity Hospital. The pharmaceutical assistant at this dispensary is a sympathiser operated by BLUE PARTRIDGE and is considered trustworthy. The prescriptions requisitioned were unusual in that they consisted of bolus preparations for intrathecal (base of cranium) injection, containing colchicine, an extract of catharanthides, and morphine. Our informant opined that this is a highly irregular preparation which might be utilized in the treatment of certain brain tumours, but which is likely to cause excruciating pain and neurological side effects (ref. GAME ANDES) associated with induction of gorgonism in latent individuals suffering an astrocytoma in the cingulate gyrus.

Our final report ref. 539/504-(ii) comes from the same informant and confirms ominous preparatory activities in the Holy Nativity Hospital grounds. The hospital is now under guard by soldiers of Einsatzgruppen 4. Windows have been whitewashed, *mirrors* are being removed (our emphasis) or replaced with one-way observation glass, and lights in the solitary cells rewired for external control from behind two doors. Most of the patients have disappeared, believed removed by Group 4 soldiers, and rumours are circulating of a new area of disturbed earth in the countryside nearby. Those patients who remain are under close guard.

Conclusion: The preparation referenced in 539/504-(i) has been referred to Special Projects Group ANDES, who have verified against records of the suppressed Geiger Committee that Von Schachter is experimenting with drugs similar to the catastrophic Cambridge IV preparation. Given his associate Sievers's influence in the Ahnenerbe-SS, and the previous use of the Holy Nativity Hospital for the Incurably Insane as a secondary centre for the paliative care of patients suffering seizures and other neuraesthenic symptoms, it is believed likely that Von Schachter intends to induce and control gorgonism for military purposes in explicit violation of the provisions for the total suppression of stoner weapons laid out in Secret Codicil IV to the Hague Convention (1919).

Policy Recommendation: This matter should be escalated to JIC as critical with input from SOE on the feasibility of a targeted raid on the installation. If allowed to proceed, Von Schachter's program shows significant potential for development into one of the rumoured *Vertlesgunswaffen* programs for deployment against civilian populations in free areas. A number of contingency plans for the deployment of gorgonism on a mass observation basis have existed in a MOW file since the early 1920s and we must now consider the prospects for such weapons to be deployed against us. We consider essential an immediate strike against the most advanced development centres, coupled with a strong reminder through diplomatic back channels that failure to comply with all clauses (secret and overt) of the Hague Convention *will* result in an allied retaliatory deployment of poison gas against German civilian targets. We cannot run the risk of class IV basilisks being deployed in conjunction with strategic air power . . .

By the time I roll into the office, four hours late and yawning with sleep deprivation, Harriet is hopping around the common room as if her feet are on fire, angrier than I've ever seen her before. Unfortunately, according to the matrix management system we operate she's my boss for 30 percent of the time during which I'm a technical support engineer. (For the other 70 percent I report to Angleton and I can't really tell you *what* I am except that it involves being yanked out of bed at zero four hundred hours to answer code blue alerts.)

Harriet is a back-office suit: mousy and skinny, forty-something, and dried up from spending all those years devising forms in triplicate with which to terrorize field agents. People like Harriet aren't supposed to get excited about anything. The effect is disconcerting, like opening a tomb and finding a break-dancing mummy.

'Robert! Where on earth have you been? What kind of time do you call this? McLuhan's been waiting on you – you were supposed to be here for the licence policy management committee meeting two hours ago!'

I yawn and sling my jacket over the coat rack next to the 'C' department coffee station. 'Been called out,' I mumble. 'Code blue alert. Just got back from Milton Keynes.'

'Code blue?' she asks, alert for a slip. 'Who signed off on it?'

'Angleton.' I hunt around for my mug in the cupboard over the sink, the one with the poster on the front that says CURIOUS EYES COST LIVES. The coffee machine is mostly empty, full of black tarry stuff alarmingly similar to the toxic waste they make roads out of. I hold it under the tap and rinse. 'His budget, don't worry about it. Only he pulled me out of bed at four in the morning and sent me off to' – I put the jug down to refill the coffee filter – 'never mind. It's cleared.'

Harriet looks as if she's bitten into a biscuit and found half a beetle inside. I'm pretty sure that it's not anything special; she and her boss Bridget simply have no higher goal in life than trying to cut everyone else down so they can look them in the eye. Although, to be fair, they've been acting more cagy than usual lately, hiding out in meetings with strange suits from other departments. It's probably just part of their ongoing game of Bureaucracy, whose goal is the highest stakes of all – a fully vested Civil Service pension and early retirement. 'What was it about?' she demands.

'Do you have GAME ANDES REDSHIFT clearance?' I ask. 'If not, I can't tell you.'

'But you were in Milton Keynes,' she jabs. 'You told me that.'

'Did I?' I roll my eyes. 'Well, maybe, and maybe not. I couldn't possibly comment.'

'What's so interesting about Milton Keynes?' she continues.

'Not much.' I shrug. 'It's made of concrete and it's very, very boring.'

She relaxes almost imperceptibly. 'Make sure you get all the paperwork filed and billed to the right account,' she tells me.

'I will have before I leave this afternoon at two,' I reply, rubbing in the fact that I'm on flexitime; Angleton's a much more alarming, but also understanding, manager to work for. Due to the curse of matrix management I can't weasel out completely from under Bridget's bony thumb, but I must confess I get a kick out of having my other boss pull rank on her. 'What was this meeting about?' I ask slyly, hoping she'll rise to it.

'You should know, you're the administrator who set up the mailing list,' she throws right back at me. *Oops*. 'Mr. McLuhan's here to help us. He's from Q Division, to help us prepare for our Business Software Alliance audit.'

'Our—' I stop dead and turn to face her, the coffee machine gurgling at my back. 'Our audit with *who*?'

'The Business Software Alliance,' she says smugly. 'CESG outsourced our COTS application infrastructure five months ago contingent on us following official best practices for ensuring quality and value in enterprise resource management. As you were *too busy* to look after things, Bridget asked Q Division to help out. Mr. McLuhan is helping us sort out our licencing arrangements in line with guidelines from Procurement. He says he's able to run a full BSA-certified audit on our systems and help us get our books in order.'

'Oh,' I say, very calmly, and turn around, mouthing the follow-on *shit* silently in the direction of the now-burbling percollator. 'Have you ever been through a BSA audit before, Harriet?' I ask curiously as I scrub my mug clean, inside and out.

'No, but they're here to help us audit our—'

'They're funded by the big desktop software companies,' I say, as calmly as I can. 'They do that because they view the BSA as a *profit centre*. That's because the BSA or their subcontractors – and that's what Q Division will be acting as, they get paid for running an audit if they find anything out of order – come in, do an audit, look for *anything* that isn't currently licensed – say, those old machines in D3 that are still running Windows 3.1 and Office 4, or the Linux servers behind Eric's desk that keep the departmental file servers running, not to mention the FreeBSD box running the Daemonic Countermeasures Suite in Security – and demand an upgrade to the latest version under threat of lawsuit. Inviting them in is like throwing open the doors and inviting the Drugs Squad round for a spliff.'

'They said they could track down all our installed software and offer us a discount for volume licensing!'

'And how precisely do you think they'll do that?' I turn round and stare at her. 'They're going to want to install snooping software on our LAN, and then read through its take. I take a deep breath. 'You're going to have to get him to Sign the Official Secrets Act so that I can formally notify him that if he thinks he's going to do that I'm going to have him sectioned. Part Three. Why do you *think* we're still running old copies of windows on the network? Because we can't afford to replace them?'

'He's already signed Section Three. And anyway, you said you didn't have time,' she snaps waspishly. 'I asked you five weeks ago, on Friday! But you were too busy playing secret agents with your friends downstairs to notice anything as important as an upcoming audit. This wouldn't have been necessary if you had time!'

'Crap. Listen, we're running those old junkers because they're so old and rubbish that they can't catch half the proxy Internet worms and macro viruses that are doing the rounds these days. BSA will insist we replace them with stonking new workstations running Windows XP and Office XP and dialing into the Internet every six seconds to snitch on whatever we're doing with them. Do you *really* think Mahogany Row is going to clear that sort of security risk?'

That's a bluff – Mahogany Row retired from this universe back when software still meant silk unmentionables – but she isn't likely to know that, merely that I get invited up there these days. (Nearer my brain-eating God to thee . . .)

'As for the time thing, get me a hardware budget and a tech assistant who's vetted for level five Laundry IT operations and I'll get it seen to. It'll only cost you sixty thousand pounds or so in the first year, plus a salary thereafter.' Finally, *finally,* I get to pull the jug out of the coffee machine and pour myself a mug of wake-up. 'That's better.'

She glances at her watch. 'Are you going to come along to the meeting and help explain this to everybody then?' she asks in a tone that could cut glass.

'No.' I add cow juice from the fridge that wheezes asthmatic-ally below the worktop. 'It's a public/private partnership fuck-up, film at eleven. Bridget stuck her foot in it out of her own free will: if she wants me to pull it out for her she can damn well ask. Besides, I've got a code blue report meeting with Angelton and Boris and Andy and that trumps administrative make-work any day of the week.'

'Bastard,' she hisses.

'Pleased to be of service.' I pull a face as she marches out the room and slams the door. 'Angleton. Code blue. Jesus.' All of a sudden I remember the modified camcorder in my jacket pocket. 'Shit, I'm running late . . .'

REPORT 4: Tuesday June 6th, 1989
CLASSIFIED TOP SECRET GAME ANDES REDSHIFT,
Ministry of Defense, June 6th, 1989

ABSTRACT: Recent research in neuroanatomy has charac-terised the nature of the stellate ganglial networks responsible for gorgonism in patients with advanced astro-cytoma affecting the cingulate gyrus. Tests combining the 'map of medusa' layout with appropriate video preprocess-ing inputs have demonstrated the feasibility of mechanical induction of the medusa effect.

Progress in the emulation of dynamically reconfigurable hidden-layer neural networks using FPGA (fully program-mable gate array) technology, combined with real-time digital video signal processing from binocular high-resolution video cameras, is likely within the next five years to allow us to download a 'medusa mode' into suitably prepared surveillance CCTV cameras, allowing realtime digital video monitoring networks to achieve a true line-of-sight look-to-kill capability. Extensive safety protocols are discussed which must be implemented before this technology can be deployed nationally, in order to minimize the risk of misactivation.

Projected deployment of CCTV monitoring in public places is estimated to result in over one million cameras *in situ* in British mainland cities by 1999. Coverage will be complete by 2004–06. Anticipated developments in Internetworking and improvements in online computing bandwidth suggest for the first time the capacity of achieving a total coverage defense-in-depth against any conceivable insurgency. The implications of this project are discussed, along with its possible efficacy in mitigating the consequences of CASE NIGHTMARE GREEN in September 2007.

. . .

Speaking of Mahogany Row, Angleton's picked the boardroom with the teak desk and the original bakelite desk fittings, and frosted windows onto the corridor, as the venue for my debriefing. He's sitting behind the desk tapping his bony fingers, with Andy looking anxious and Boris imperturbable when I walk in and flip the red MEETING light on.

'Home movies.' I flip the tape on the desktop. 'What I saw on my holiday.' I put my coffee mug down on one of the disquietingly soft leather mats before I yawn, just in case I spill it. 'Sorry, been up for hours. What do you want to know?'

'How long had it been dead?' asks Andy.

I think for a moment. 'I'm not sure – have to call Pathology if you want a hard answer, I'm afraid, but clearly for some time when I found it after zero seven hundred. It had cooled to barely oven temperature.'

Angleton is watching me like I'm a bug under a microscope. It's not a fun sensation. 'Did you read the files?' he asks.

'Yes.' Before I came up here I locked them in my office safe in case a busy little Tom, Dick, or Harriet decided to do some snooping. 'I'm really going to sleep well tonight.'

'The basilisk is found.' Boris said.

'Um, no,' I admit. 'It's still in the wild. But Mike Williams said he'd let me know if they run across it. He's cleared for OSA-III, he's our liaison in—'

'How many traffic cameras overlooked the roundabout?' Angleton asks almost casually.

'Oh—' I sit down hard. 'Oh shit. *Shit.*' I feel shaky, very shaky, guts doing the tango and icy chills running down the small of my back as I realise what he's trying to tell me without saying it out loud, on the record.

'That's why I sent you,' he murmurs, waving Andy out of the room on some prearranged errand. A moment later Boris follows him. 'You're not supposed to get yourself killed, Bob. It looks bad on your record.'

'Oh shit,' I repeat, needle stuck, sample echoing, as I realise how close to dying I may have been. And the crew of that chopper, and everyone else who's been there since, and—

'Half an hour ago someone vandalized the number seventeen traffic camera overlooking Monk's Road roundabout three: put a .223 bullet through the CCD enclosure. Drink your coffee, there's a good boy, do try not to spill it everywhere. '

'One of ours.' It comes out as a statement.

'Of course.' Angleton taps the file sitting on the desk in front of him – I recognize it by the dog-ear on the second page, I put it in my office safe only ten minutes ago – and looks at me with those scary grey eyes of his. 'So. The public at large being safe for the moment, tell me what you can deduce.'

'Uh.' I lick my lips, which have gone as dry as old boot leather. 'Some time last night somebody let a cow into the park and used

THE CONCRETE JUNGLE 247

it for target practice. I don't know much about the network topology of the MK road traffic-control cams, but my possible suspects are, in order: someone with a very peculiar brain tumour, someone with a stolen stoner weapon – like the one I qualified for under OGRE REALITY – or someone with access to whatever GAME ANDES REDSHIFT gave birth to. And, going from the questions you're asking, if it's GAME ANDES REDSHIFT it's unauthorised.'

He nods, very slightly.

'We're in deep shit then,' I say brightly and throw back the last mouthful of coffee, spoiling the effect slightly by nearly coughing my guts up immediately afterward.

'Without a depth-gauge,' he adds drily, and waits for my coughing fit to subside. 'I've sent Andrew and Mr. B down to the stacks to pull out another file for you to read. Eyes only in front of witnesses, no note-taking, escort required. While they're signing it out I'd like you to write down in your own words everything that happened to you this morning so far. It'll go in a sealed file along with your video evidence as a deposition in case the worst happens.'

'Oh shit.' I'm getting tired of saying this. 'It's internal?' He nods.

'CPU business?'

He nods again, then pushes the antique portable manual typewriter toward me. 'Start typing.'

'Okay.' I pick up three sheets of paper and some carbons and begin aligning their edges. 'Consider me typing already.'

REPORT 5: Monday December 10th, 2001
CLASSIFIED TOP SECRET GAME ANDES REDSHIFT,
Ministry of Defense, December 10th, 2001
CLASSIFIED TOP SECRET MAGINOT BLUE STARS,
Ministry of Defense, December 10th, 2001

Abstract: This document describes progress to date in establishing a defensive network capable of repelling wide-scale incursions by reconfiguring the national closed-circuit television surveillance network as a software-controlled look-to-kill multiheaded basilisk. To prevent accidental premature deployment or deliberate exploitation, the SCORPION STARE software is not actually loaded into the camera firmware. Instead, reprogrammable FPGA chips are integrated into all cameras and can be loaded with SCORPION STARE by authorised MAGINOT BLUE STARS users whenever necessary.

. . .

Preamble: It has been said that the US Strategic Defense Initiative Organisation's proposed active ABM defense network will require the most complex software ever developed, characterised by a complexity metric of > 100 MLOC and heavily criticized by various organisations (see footnotes [1][2][4]) as unworkable and likely to contain in excess of a thousand severity-1 bugs at initial deployment. Nevertheless, the architectural requirements of MAGINOT BLUE STARS dwarf those of the SDIO infrastructure. To provide coverage of 95 percent of the UK population we require a total of 8 million digitally networked CCTV cameras (terminals). Terminals in built-up areas may be connected via the public switched telephone network using SDSL/VHDSL, but outlying systems may use mesh network routing over 802.1 la to ensure that rural areas do not provide a pool of infectious carriers for demonic possession. TCP/IP Quality of Service issues are discussed below, along with a concrete requirement for IPv6 routing and infrastructure that must be installed and supported by all Internet Service Providers no later than 2004.

There are more than ninety different CCTV architectures currently on sale in the UK, many of which are imported and cannot be fitted with FPGAs suitable for running the SCORPION STARE basilisk neural network prior to installation. Data Disclosure Orders served under the terms of the Regulation of Investigatory Powers Act

(2001) serve to gain access to camera firmware, but in many regions upgrades to Level 1 MAGINOT BLUE STARS compliance is behind schedule due to noncompliance by local police forces with what are seen as unreasonable Home Office requests. Unless we can achieve a 340 percent compliance improvement by 2004, we will fail to achieve the target saturation prior to September 2007, when CASE NIGHTMARE GREEN is due.

. . .

Installation has currently been completed only in limited areas; notably Inner London ('Ring of Steel' for counter-terrorism surveillance) and Milton Keynes (advanced next-generation MAN with total traffic management solution in place). Deployment is proceeding in order of population density and potential for catastrophic demonic takeover and exponential burn through built-up areas . . .

. . .

Recommendation: One avenue for ensuring that all civilian CCTV equipment is SCORPION STARE compatible by 2006 is to exploit an initiative of the US National Security Agency for our own ends. In a bill ostensibly sponsored by Hollywood and music industry associations (MPAA and RIAA: see also CDBTPA), the NSA is ostensibly attempting to legislate support for Digital Rights Management in all electronic equipment sold to the public. The implementation details are not currently accessible to us, but we believe this is a stalking-horse for requiring chip manufacturers to incorporate on-die FPGAs in the one million gate range, reconfigurable in software, initially laid out as DRM circuitry but reprogrammable in support of their nascent War on Un-Americanism.

If such integrated FPGAs are mandated, commercial pressures will force Far Eastern vendors to comply with regulation and we will be able to mandate incorporation of SCORPION STARE Level Two into all digital consumer electronic cameras and commercial CCTV equipment under cover of complying with our copyright protection obligations in accordance with the WIPO treaty. A suitable pretext for the rapid phased obsolescence of all Level Zero and Level One cameras can then be engineered by, for example, discrediting witness evidence from older installations in an ongoing criminal investigation.

If we pursue this plan, by late 2006 any two adjacent public CCTV terminals – or private camcorders equipped with a digital video link – will be reprogrammable by any authenticated MAGINOT BLUE STARS superuser to permit the operator to turn them into a SCORPION STARE basilisk weapon. We remain convinced that this is the best defensive posture to adopt in order to minimize casualties when the Great Old Ones return from beyond the stars to eat our brains.

'So, what this boils down to is a Strategic Defense Initiative against an invasion by alien mind-suckers from beyond space-time, who are expected to arrive in bulk at a set date. Am I on message so far?' I asked.

'Very approximately, yes,' said Andy.

'Okay. To deal with the perceived alien mind-sucker threat, some nameless genius has worked out that the CCTV cameras dotting our green and pleasant land can be networked together, their inputs fed into a software emulation of a basilisk's brain, and turned into some kind of omnipresent look-to-kill death net. Even though we don't really know how the medusa effect works, other than that it relies on some kind of weird observationally mediated quantum-tunneling effect, collapse of the wave function, yadda yadda, that makes about 1 percent of the carbon nuclei in the target body automagically turn into silicon with no apparent net energy input. That right?'

'Have a cigar, Sherlock.'

'Sorry, I only smoke when you plug me into the national grid. Shit. Okay, so it hasn't occurred to anyone that the mass-energy of those silicon nuclei has to come *from* somewhere, somewhere else, somewhere in the Dungeon Dimensions . . . damn. But that's not the point, is it?'

'Indeed not. When are you going to get to it?'

'As soon as my hands stop shaking. Let's see. Rather than do this openly and risk frightening the sheeple by stationing a death ray on every street corner, our lords and masters decided they'd do it bottom-up, by legislating that all public cameras be net-worked, and having back doors installed in them to allow the hunter-killer basilisk brain emulators to be uploaded when the time comes. Which, let's face it, makes excellent fiscal strength in this age of outsourcing, public-private partnerships, service char-ters, and the like. I mean, you can't get business insurance if you don't install antitheft cameras, someone's got to watch them so you might as well outsource the service to a security company with a network operations centre, and the brain-dead music industry copyright nazis are campaigning for a law to make it mandatory to install secret government spookware in every Walkman – or camera – to prevent home taping from killing Michael Jackson. Absolutely brilliant.'

'It is elegant, isn't it? Much more subtle than honking great ballistic missile submarines. We've come a long way since the Cold War.'

'Yeah. Except you're *also* telling me that some script kiddie has rooted you and dialed in a strike on Milton Keynes. Probably in the mistaken belief that they think they're playing MISSILE COMMAND.'

'No comment.'

'Jesus Fucking Christ riding into town on top of a pickup truck full of DLT backup tapes – what kind of idiot do you take me for? Listen, the ball has gone *up*. Someone uploaded the SCORPION STARE code to a bunch of traffic cams off Monk's Road round-about and turned Daisy into six hundred pounds of boiled beef on the bone *à la* basilisk, and all you can say is *no comment*?'

'Listen, Bob, I think you're taking this all too personally. I can't comment on the Monk's Road incident because you're offi-cially the tag-team investigative lead and I'm here to provide backup and support, not to second-guess you. I'm trying to be helpful, okay?'

'Sorry, sorry. I'm just a bit upset.'

'Yes, well, if it's any consolation that goes for me, too, and for Angleton believe it or not, but "upset" and fifty pence will buy you a cup of coffee and what we really need is to finger the means, motive, and murderer of Daisy the Cow in time to close the stable door. Oh, and we can rule out external penetration – the network loop to Monk's Road is on a private backbone intranet that's fire-walled up to the eyeballs. Does that make it easier for you?'

'No shit! Listen, I happen to agree with you in principle, but I am *still* upset, Andy, and I want to tell you – no shit. Look, this is so not-sensible that I know I'm way the hell too late but I think the whole MAGINOT BLUE STARS idea is fucking insane, I mean, like, bull-goose, barking-at-the-moon, hairs-on-the-palm-of-your-hands crazy. Like atomic landmines buried under every street corner! Didn't they know that the only unhackable computer is one that's running a secure operating system, welded inside a steel safe, buried under a ton of concrete at the bottom of a coal mine guarded by the SAS and a couple of armoured divisions, and *switched off*? What did they think they were *doing*?'

'Defending us against CASE NIGHTMARE GREEN, Bob. Which I'll have you know is why the Russians are so dead keen to get Energiya flying again so they can launch their Polyus orbital battle stations, and why the Americans are getting so upset about the Rune of Al-Sabbah that they're trying to build censorware into every analogue-to-digital converter on the planet.'

'Do I have CASE NIGHTMARE GREEN clearance? Or do I just have to take it on trust?'

'Take it on trust for now, I'll try and get you cleared later in the week. Sorry about that, but this truly . . . look, in this instance the ends justify the means. Take it from me. Okay?'

'Shit. I need another – no, I've already had too much coffee. So, what am I supposed to do?'

'Well, the good news is we've narrowed it down a bit. You will be pleased to know that we just ordered the West Yorkshire Met's computer crime squad to go in with hobnailed boots and take down the entire MK traffic camera network and opcentre. Official reason is a suspicion of time bombs installed by a disgruntled former employee – who is innocent, incidentally – but it lets us turn it into a Computer Misuse case and send in a reasonably clueful team. They're about to officially call for backup from CESG, who are going to second them a purported spook from GCHQ, and that spook is going to be you. I want you to crawl all over that camera network and figure out how SCORPION STARE might have got onto it. Which is going to be easier than you think because SCORPION STARE isn't exactly open source and there are only two authorised development teams working on it on the planet that we know of, or at least in this country. One of them is – surprise – based in Milton Keynes, and as of right this minute you have clearance to stamp all over their turf and play the Gestapo officer with our top boffin labs. Which is a power I trust you will not abuse without good reason.'

'Oh great, I always fancied myself in a long, black leather trench coat. What will Mo think?'

'She'll think you look the part when you're angry. Are you up for it?'

'How the fuck could I say no, when you put it that way?'

'I'm glad you understand. Now, have you got any other questions for me before we wrap this up and send the tape to the auditors?'

'Uh, yeah. One question. Why me?'

'Why – well! Hmm. I suppose because you're already on the inside, Bob. And you've got a pretty unique skill mix. Something you overlook is that we don't have many field qualified agents, and most of those we have are old school two-fisted shoot-from-the-hip-with-a-rune-of-destruction field necromancers; they don't understand these modern Babbage engine Internet contraptions like you do. And you've already got experience with basilisk weapons, or did you think we issued those things like toothpaste tubes? So rather than find someone who doesn't know as much,

you just happened to be the man on the spot who knew enough
and was thought . . . appropriate.'

'Gee, thanks. I'll sleep a lot better tonight knowing that you
couldn't find anyone better suited to the job. Really scraping the
barrel, aren't we?'

'If only you knew . . . if only you knew.'

The next morning they put me on the train to Cheltenham –
second class of course – to visit a large office site, which appears
as a blank spot on all maps of the area, just in case the Russians
haven't noticed the farm growing satellite dishes out back. I
spend a very uncomfortable half hour being checked through
security by a couple of Rottweilers in blue suits who work on the
assumption that anyone who is not known to be a Communist
infiltrator from North Korea is a dangerously unclassified security
risk. They search me and make me pee in a cup and leave my
palmtop at the site security office, but for some reason they don't
ask me to surrender the small leather bag containing a mummified pigeon's foot that I wear on a silver chain round my neck
when I explain that it's on account of my religion. The idiots.

It is windy and rainy outside so I have no objection to being
ushered into an air-conditioned meeting room on the third floor
of an outlying wing, being offered institutional beige coffee the
same colour as the office carpet, and spending the next four hours
in a meeting with Kevin, Robin, Jane, and Phil, who explain to
me in turn what a senior operations officer from GCHQ detached
for field duty is expected to do in the way of maintaining security,
calling on backup, reporting problems, and filling out the two
hundred and seventeen different forms that senior operations officers are apparently employed to spend their time filling out. The
Laundry may have a bureaucracy surfeit and a craze for ISO-9000
certification, but GCHQ is even worse, with some bizarre spatch-
cock version of BS5720 quality assurance applied to all their
procedures in an attempt to ensure that the Home Office minister can account for all available paper clips in near real-time if

challenged in the House by Her Majesty's loyal opposition. On the other hand, they've got a bigger budget than us and all they have to worry about is having to read other people's email, instead of having their souls sucked out by tentacular horrors from beyond the universe.

'Oh, and you really ought to wear a tie when you're representing us in public,' Phil says apologetically at the end of his spiel.

'And get a haircut,' Jane adds with a smile.

Bastards.

The Human Resources imps billet me in a bed and breakfast run by a genteel pair of elderly High Tory sociopaths, a Mr. and Mrs. MacBride. He's bald, loafs around in slippers, and reads the *Telegraph* while muttering darkly about the need for capital punishment as a solution to the problem of bogus asylum seekers; she wears heavy horn-rimmed glasses and the hairdo that time forgot. The corridors are wallpapered with an exquisitely disgusting floral print and the whole place smells of mothballs, the only symptom of the twenty-first century being a cheap and nasty webcam on the hall staircase. I try not to shudder as I slouch upstairs to my room and barricade the door before settling down for the evening phone call to Mo and a game of Civ on my palmtop (which I rescued from Security on my way out). 'It could be worse,' Mo consoles me, 'at least *your* landlord doesn't have gill slits and greenish skin.'

The next morning I elbow my way onto an early train to London, struggle through the rush hour crush, and somehow manage to weasel my way into a seat on a train to Milton Keynes; it's full of brightly clad German backpackers and irritated businessmen on their way to Luton airport but I get off before there and catch a taxi to the cop shop. 'There is nothing better in life than drawing on the sole of your slipper with a biro instead of going to the pub on a Saturday night,' the lead singer of Half Man Half Biscuit sings mournfully on my iPod, and I am inclined to agree, subject to the caveat that Saturday nights at the pub are functionally equivalent to damp Thursday mornings at the police station. 'Is Inspector Sullivan available?' I ask at the front desk.

'Just a moment.' The moustachioed constable examines my warrant card closely, gives me a beady-eyed stare as if he expects me to break down and confess instantly to a string of unsolved burglaries, then turns and ambles into the noisy back office round the corner. I have just enough time to read the more surreal crime prevention posters for the second time ('Are your neighbours foxhunting reptiles from the planet of the green wellies? Denounce them here, free of charge!') when the door bangs open and a determined-looking woman in a grey suit barges in. She looks how Annie Lennox would look if she'd joined the constabulary, been glassed once or twice, and had a really dodgy curry the night before.

'Okay, who's the joker?' she demands. 'You.' A bony finger points at me. 'You're from—' she sees the warrant card '—oh shit.' Over her shoulder: 'Jeffries, *Jeffries*, you rat bastard, you set me up! Oh, why do I bother.' Back in my direction: 'You're the spook who got me out of bed the day before yesterday after a graveyard shift. Is this *your* mess?'

I take a deep breath. 'Mine and yours both. I'm just back down from' – I clear my throat – 'and I've got orders to find an Inspector J. Sullivan and drag him into an interview room.' Mentally crossing my fingers: 'What's the J stand for?'

'Josephine. And it's *Detective* Inspector, while you're about it.' She lifts the barrier. 'You'd better come in then.' Josephine looks tired and annoyed. 'Where's your other card?'

'My other – oh.' I shrug. 'We don't flash them around; might be a bit of a disaster if one went missing.' Anyone who picked it up would be in breach of Section Three, at the very least. Not to mention in peril of their immortal soul.

'It's okay, I've signed the Section, in blood.' She raises an eyebrow at me.

'Paragraph two?' I ask, just to be sure she's not bluffing. She shakes her head. 'No, paragraph three.'

'Pass, friend.' And then I let her see the warrant card as it really is, the way it reaches into your head and twists things around so you want to throw up at the mere thought of questioning its validity. 'Satisfied?'

She just nods: a cool customer for sure. The trouble with Section Three of the Official Secrets Act is that it's an offense to know it exists without having signed it – in blood. So us signatories who are in theory cleared to talk about such supersecret national security issues as the Laundry's tea trolley rota are in practice unable to broach the topic directly. We're supposed to rely on introductions, but that breaks down rapidly in the field. It's a bit like lesbian sheep; as ewes display their sexual arousal by standing around waiting to be mounted, it's hard to know if somebody else is, well, you know. *Cleared*. 'Come on,' she adds, in a marginally less hostile tone, 'we can pick up a cup of coffee on the way.'

Five minutes later we're sitting down with a notepad, a telephone, and an antique tape recorder that Smiley probably used to debrief Karla, back when men were real men and lesbian sheep were afraid. 'This had better be important,' Josephine complains, clicking a frighteningly high-tech sweetener dispenser repeatedly over her black Nescafe. 'I've got a persistent burglar, two rapes, a string of car thefts, and a phantom pisser who keeps breaking into department stores to deal with, then a bunch of cloggies from West Yorkshire who're running some kind of computer audit – your fault, I believe. I need to get bogged down in *X-Files* rubbish right now like I need a hole in my head.'

'Oh, it's important all right. And I hope to get it off your desk as soon as possible. I'd just like to get a few things straight first.'

'Hmm. So what do you need to know? We've only had two flying saucer sightings and six alien abductions this year so far.' She raises one eyebrow, arms crossed and shoulders set a trifle defensively. Who'd have thought it? Being interviewed by higher authorities makes the alpha female detective defensive. 'It's not like I've got all day: I'm due in a case committee briefing at noon and I've got to pick up my son from school at four.'

On second thought, maybe she really *is* busy. 'To start with, did you get any witness reports or CCTV records from the scene? And have you identified the cow, and worked out how it got there?'

'No eyewitnesses, not until three o'clock, when Vernon Thwaite was out walking his girlfriend's toy poodle which had diarrhoea.' She pulls a face, which makes the scar on her forehead wrinkle into visibility. 'If you want we can go over the team reports together. I take it that's what pulled you in?'

'You could say that.' I dip a cheap IKEA spoon in my coffee and check cautiously after a few seconds to see if the metal's begun to corrode. 'Helicopters make me airsick. Especially after a night out when I was expecting a morning lie-in.' She almost smiles before she remembers she's officially grumpy with me. 'Okay, so no earlier reports. What else?'

'No tape,' she says, flattening her hands on the tabletop to either side of her cup and examining her nail cuticles. 'Nothing. One second it's zero zero twenty-six, the next it's zero seven four-teen. Numbers to engrave in your heart. Dennis, our departmental geek, was most upset with MKSG — they're the public-private partners in the regional surveillance outsourcing sector.'

'Zero zero twenty-six to zero seven fourteen,' I echo as I jot them down on my palmtop. 'MKSG. Right, that's helpful.'

'It is?' She tilts her head sideways and stares at me like I'm a fly that's landed in her coffee.

'Yup.' I nod, then tell myself that it'd be really stupid to wind her up without good reason. 'Sorry. What I can tell you is, I'm as interested in anything that happened to the cameras as the cow. If you hear anything about them — especially about them being tampered with — I'd love to know. But in the meantime Daisy. Do you know where she came from?'

'Yes.' She doesn't crack a smile but her shoulders unwind slightly. 'Actually, she's number two six three from Emmett-Moore Ltd, a dairy factory out near Dunstable. Or rather, she was two six three until three days ago. She was getting along a bit, so they sold her to a local slaughterhouse along with a job lot of seven other cows. I followed-up on the other seven and they'll be showing up in your McHappy McMeal some time next month. But not Daisy. Seems a passing farmer in a Range Rover with a wagon behind it dropped by and asked if he could buy her and cart her away for his local family butcher to deal with.'

'Aha!'

'And if you believe that, I've got a bridge to sell you.' She takes a sip of her coffee, winces, and strafes it with sweeteners again. Responding on autopilot I try a mouthful of my own and burn my tongue. 'Turns out that there's no such farmer Giles of Ham Farm, Bag End, The Shire, on record. Mind you, they had a camera on their stockyard and we nailed the Range Rover. It turned up abandoned the next day on the outskirts of Leighton Buzzard and it's flagged as stolen on HOLMES2. Right now it's sitting in the pound down the road; they smoked it for prints but it came up clean and we don't have enough money to send a SOCO and a forensics team to do a full workup on every stolen car we run across. *However*, if you twist my arm and promise me a budget *and* to go to the mat with my boss I'll see what I can lay on.'

'That may not be necessary: we have ways and means. But can you get someone to drive me down there? I'll take some readings and get out of your face – except for the business with Daisy. How are you covering that?'

'Oh, we'll find something. Right now it's filed under 'F' for Fucking Fortean Freakery, but I was thinking of announcing it's just an old animal that had been dumped illegally by a farmer who didn't want to pay to have it slaughtered.'

'That sounds about right.' I nod slowly. 'Now, I'd like to play a random word-association game with you. Okay? Ten seconds. When I say the words tell me what you think of. Right?'

She looks puzzled. 'Is this—'

'Listen. Case-Nightmare-Green-Scorpion-Stare-Maginot-Blue-Stars. By the authority vested in me by the emissaries of Y'ghonzzh N'hai I have the power to bind and to release, and your tongue be tied of these matters of which we have spoken until you hear these words again: Case-Nightmare-Green-Scorpion-Stare-Maginot-Blue-Stars. Got that?'

She looks at me cross-eyed and mouths something, then looks

increasingly angry until finally she gets it together to burst out with: 'Hey, what *is* this shit?'

'Purely a precaution,' I say, and she glares at me, gobbling for a moment while I finish my coffee until she figures out that she simply can't say a word about the subject. 'Right,' I say. 'Now. You've got my permission to announce that the cow was dumped. You have my permission to talk freely to me, but to nobody else. Anyone asks any questions, refer them to me if they won't take no for an answer. This goes for your boss, too. Feel free to tell them that you can't tell them, nothing more.'

'Wanker,' she hisses, and if looks could kill I'd be a small pile of smouldering ashes on the interview room floor.

'Hey, *I'm* under a geas, too. If I don't spread it around my head will explode.'

I don't know whether she believes me or not but she stops fighting it and nods tiredly. 'Tell me what you want then get the hell out of my patch.'

'I want a lift to the car pound. A chance to sit behind the wheel of that Range Rover. A book of poetry, a jug of wine, a date tree, and – sorry, wrong question. Can you manage it?'

She stands up. 'I'll take you there myself,' she says tersely. We go.

I get to endure twenty-five minutes of venomous silence in the back seat of an unmarked patrol car driven by one Constable Routledge, with DI Sullivan in the front passenger seat treating me with the warmth due a serial killer, before we arrive at the pound. I'm beyond introspective self-loathing by now – you lose it fast in this line of work. Angleton will have my head for a key-ring fob if I don't take care to silence any possible leaks, and a tongue-twisting geas is more merciful than most of the other tools at my disposal – but I still feel like a shit. So it comes as a great relief to get out of the car and stretch my legs on the muddy gravel parking lot in the pouring rain.

'So where's the car?' I ask, innocently.

Josephine ignores me. 'Bill, you want to head over to Bletchley Way and pick up Dougal's evidence bag for the Hayes case. Then come back to pick us up,' she tells the driver. To the civilian security guard: 'You, we're looking for BY 476 ERB. Came in yesterday, Range Rover. Where is it?'

The bored security goon leads us through the mud and a maze of cars with POLICE AWARE stickers glued to their windshields then gestures at a half-empty row. 'That's it?' Josephine asks, and he passes her a set of keys. 'Okay, you can piss off now.' He takes one look at her face and beats a hasty retreat. I half-wish I could join him – whether she's a detective inspector or not, and therefore meant to be behaving with the gravitas of a senior officer in public, DI Sullivan looks to be in a mood to bite the heads off chickens. Or Laundry field agents, given half an excuse.

'Right, that's it,' she says, holding out the keys and shaking them at me impatiently. 'You're done, I take it, so I'll be pushing off. Case meeting to run, mystery shopping centre pisser to track down, and so on.'

'Not so fast.' I glance round. The pound is surrounded by a high wire fence and there's a decrepit Portakabin office out front by the gate: a camera sits on a motorised mount on a pole sticking up from the roof. 'Who's on the other end of that thing?'

'The gate guard, probably,' she says, following my finger. The camera is staring at the entrance, unmoving.

'Okay, why don't you open up the car.' She blips the remote to unlock the door and I keep my eyes on the camera as she takes the handle and tugs. *Could I be wrong?* I wonder as the rain trickles down my neck. I shake myself when I notice her staring, then I pull out my palmtop, clamber up into the driver's seat, and balance the pocket computer on the steering wheel as I tap out a series of commands. What I see makes me shake my head. Whoever stole the car may have wiped for fingerprints but they didn't know much about paranormal concealment – they didn't use the shroud from a suicide, or get a paranoid schizophrenic to drive. The scanner is sensitive to heavy emotional echoes, and the hands I'm looking for are the most recent ones to have chilled from fright and fear of exposure. I log everything and put it away, and I'm about to open the glove locker when something makes me glance at the main road beyond the chainlink fence and—

'*Watch out! Get down.*' I jump out and go for the ground. Josephine is looking around so I reach out and yank her ankles out from under her. She yells, goes down hard on her backside, and tries to kick me, then there's a loud *whump* from behind me and a wave of heat like an open oven door. 'Shit, fuck, shit—' I take a moment to realise the person cursing is me as I fumble at my throat for the bag and rip it open, desperately trying to grab the tiny claw and the disposable cigarette lighter at the same time. I flick the lighter wheel and right then something like a sledgehammer whacks into the inside of my right thigh.

'*Bastard . . .!*'

'Stop it—' I gasp, just as the raw smell of petrol vapour reaches me and I hear a crackling roar. I get the pigeon claw lit in a stink of burning keratin and an eerie glow, nearly shitting myself with terror, lying in a cold damp puddle, and roll over: '*Don't move!*'

'Bastard! What – hey, what's burning?'

'Don't move,' I gasp again, holding the subminiature Hand of Glory up. The traffic camera in the road outside the fence is casting about as if it's dropped its contact lens, but the one on the pole above the office is locked right onto the burning tires of the Range Rover. 'If you let go of my hand they'll see you and kill you *oh shit*—'

'Kill – *what*?' She stares at me, white-faced.

'You! Get under cover!' I yell across the pound, but the guy in the blue suit – the attendant – doesn't hear me. One second he's running across the car park as fast as his portly behind can manage; the next moment he's tumbling forward, blackening, puffs of flame erupting from his eyes and mouth and ears, then the stumps as his arms come pinwheeling off, and the carbonized trunk slides across the ground like a grisly toboggan.

'Oh shit, oh shit!' Her expression changes from one second to the next, from disbelief to dawning horror. 'We've got to help—'

'Listen, *no*! Stay down!'

She freezes in place for a full heartbeat, then another. When she opens her mouth again she's unnaturally cool. 'What's going on?'

'The cameras,' I pant. 'Listen, this is a Hand of Glory, an invisibility shield. Right now it's all that's keeping us alive — those cameras are running SCORPION STARE. If they see us we're dead.'

'Are you — the car? What happened to it?'

'Tires. They're made of carbon, rubber. SCORPION STARE works on anything with a shitload of long-chain carbon molecules in it — like tires, or cows. Makes them burn.'

'Oh my sainted aunt and holy father . . .'

'Hold my hand. Make skin to skin contact — not that hard. We've got maybe three, four minutes before this HOG burns down. Bastards, *bastards*. Got to get to the control shack—'

The next minute is a nightmare of stumbling — shooting pains in my knees from where I went down hard and in my thigh where Josephine tried to kick the shit out of me — soaking cold damp jeans, and roasting hot skin on my neck from the pyre that I was sitting inside only seconds ago. She holds onto my left hand like it's a lifesaver — yes, it is, for as long as the HOG keeps burning — and we lurch and shamble toward the modular site office near the entrance as fast as we can go. 'Inside,' she gasps, 'it can't see inside.'

'Yeah?' She half-drags me to the entrance and we find the door's open, not locked. 'Can we get away round the other side?'

'Don't think so.' She points through the building. 'There's a school.'

'Oh shit.' We're on the other side of the pound from the traffic camera in the road, but there's another camera under the eaves of the school on the other side of the road from the steel gates out front, and it's a good thing the kids are all in lessons because what's going on here is every teacher's nightmare And we've got to nail it down as fast as possible, because if they ring the bell for lunch — 'We've got to kill the power to the roofcam first,' I say. 'Then we've got to figure a way out.'

'What's going on? What *did* that?' Her lips work like a fish out of water.

I shake my head. 'Case-Nightmare-Green-Scorpion-Stare-Maginot-Blue-stars tongue be loosed. Okay, talk. I reckon we've got about two, three minutes to nail this before—'

'This was all a setup?'

'I don't know yet. Look, how do I get onto the roof?'

'Isn't that a skylight?' she asks, pointing.

'Yeah.' Being who I am I always carry a Leatherman multitool so I whip it out and look around for a chair I can pile on top of the desk and stand on, one that doesn't have wheels and a gas strut. 'See any chairs I can—'

I'll say this much, detective training obviously enables you to figure out how to get onto a roof fast. Josephine simply walks over to the ladder nestling in a corner between one wall and a battered filing cabinet and pulls it out. 'This what you're looking for?'

'Uh, yeah. Thanks.' She passes it to me and I fumble with it for a moment, figuring out how to set it up. Then another moment, juggling the multitool and the half-consumed pigeon's foot and looking at the ladder dubiously.

'Give me those,' she says.

'But—'

'Listen, *I'm* the one who deals with idiot vandals and climbs around on pitched roofs looking for broken skylights, okay? And—' she glances at the door '—if I mess up you can phone your boss and let him know what's happening.'

'Oh,' I mumble, then hand her the gadgets and hold the ladder steady while she swarms up it like a circus acrobat. A moment later there's a noise like a herd of baby elephants thudding on the rooftop as she scrambles across to the camera mount. The camera may be on a moving platform but there's a limit to how far it can depress and clearly she's right below the azimuth platform – just as long as she isn't visible to both the traffic camera out back and the schoolyard monitor out front. More shaking, then there's a loud clack and the Portakabin lights go out.

A second or two later she reappears, feet first, through the opening. 'Right, that should do it,' she says. 'I shorted the power cable to the platform. 'Hey, the lights—'

'I think you shorted a bit more than that.' I hold the ladder as she climbs down. 'Now, we've got an immobilized one up top, that's good. Let's see if we can find the controller.'

A quick search of the hut reveals a bunch of fun stuff I hadn't been expecting, like an ADSL line to the regional police IT hub, a PC running some kind of terminal emulator, and another dedicated machine with the cameras showing overlapping windows on-screen. I could kiss them; they may have outsourced the monitoring to private security firms but they've kept the hardware all on the same backbone network. The blinkenlights are beeping and twittering like crazy as everything's now running on backup battery power, but that's okay. I pull out a breakout box and scramble around under a desk until I've got my palmtop plugged into the network hub to sniff packets. Barely a second later it dings at me. 'Oh, lovely.' So much *for firewalled up to the eyeballs*. I unplug and surface again, then scroll through the several hundred screenfuls of unencrypted bureaucratic computerese my network sniffer has grabbed. '*That* looks promising. Uh, I wouldn't go outside just yet but I think we're going to be all right.'

'Explain.' She's about ten centimetres shorter than I am, but I'm suddenly aware that I'm sharing the Portakabin with an irate, wet, detective inspector who's probably a black belt at something or other lethal and who is just about to really lose her cool: 'You've got about ten seconds from *now* to tell me everything. Or I'm calling for backup and warrant card or no you are going in a cell until I get some answers. Capisce?'

'I surrender.' I don't, really, but I point at my palmtop. 'It's a fair cop, guv. Look, someone's been too clever by half here. The camera up top is basically a glorified webcam. I mean, it's running a web server and it's plugged into the constabulary's intranet via broadband. Every ten seconds or so a program back at HQ polls it and grabs the latest picture, okay? That's in addition to whatever the guy downstairs tells it to look at. Anyway, someone *else* just sent it an HTTP request with a honking great big file upload attached, and I don't think your IT department is in the habit of using South Korean primary schools as proxy servers, are they? And a compromised firewall, no less. Lovely! Your cameras may have been 0wnZ0r3d by a fucking script kiddie, but they're not as fucking smart as they *think* they are otherwise they'd have fucking stripped off the fucking referrer headers, wouldn't they?' I stop talking and make sure I've saved the logfile somewhere secure, then for good measure I email it to myself at work.

'Right. So I know their IP address and it's time to locate them.' It's the work of about thirty seconds to track it to a dial-up account on one of the big national ISPs – one of the free anonymous ones. 'Hmm. If you want to help, you could get me an S22 disclosure notice for the phone number behind this dial-up account. Then we can persuade the phone company to tell us the street address and go pay them a visit and ask why they killed our friend with the key ring—' My hands are shaking from the adrenalin high and I am beginning to feel angry, not just an ordinary day-to-day pissed-off feeling but the kind of true and brutal rage that demands revenge.

'Killed? Oh.' She opens the door an inch and looks outside: she looks a little grey around the gills, but she doesn't lose it. Tough woman.

'It's SCORPION STARE. Look, S22 data disclosure order first, it's a fucking murder investigation now, isn't it? Then we go visiting. But we're going to have to make out like it's accidental, or the press will come trampling all over us and we won't be able to get anything done.' I write down the hostname while she gets on the mobile to head office. The first sirens start to wail even before she picks up my note and calls for medical backup. I sit there staring at the door, contemplating the mess, my mind whirling. 'Tell the ambulance crew it's a freak lightning strike,' I say as the thought takes me. 'You're already in this up to your ears, we don't need to get anyone else involved—'

Then my phone rings.

* * *

As it happens we don't visit any murderous hackers, but presently the car pound is fronted with white plastic scene-of-crime sheeting and a photographer and a couple of forensics guys show up and Josephine, who has found something more urgent to obsess over than ripping me a new asshole, is busy directing their preliminary workover. I'm poring over screenfuls of tcpdump output in the control room when the same unmarked car that dropped us off here pulls up with Constable Routledge at the wheel and a very unexpected passenger in the back. I gape as he gets out of the car and walks toward the hut. 'Who's this?' demands Josephine, coming over and sticking her head in through the window.

I open the door. 'Hi, boss. Boss, meet Detective Inspector Sullivan. Josephine, this is my boss — you want to come in and sit down?'

Andy nods at her distractedly: 'I'm Andy. Bob, brief me.' He glances at her again as she shoves through the door and closes it behind her. 'Are you—'

'She knows too much already.' I shrug. 'Well?' I ask her. 'This is your chance to get out.'

'Fuck that.' She glares at me, then Andy: 'Two mornings ago it was a freak accident and a cow, today it's a murder investigation — I trust you're not planning on escalating it any further, terrorist massacres and biological weapons are a little outside my remit — and I want some answers. If you please.'

'Okay, you'll get them,' Andy says mildly. 'Start talking,' he tells me.

'Code blue called at three thirty the day before yesterday. I flew out to take a look, found a dead cow that had been zapped by SCORPION STARE — unless there's a basilisk loose in Milton Keynes — went down to our friends in Cheltenham for briefing yesterday, stayed overnight, came up here this morning. The cow was bought from a slaughterhouse and transported to the scene in a trailer towed by a stolen car, which was later dumped and transferred to this pound. Inspector Sullivan is our force liaison — external circle two, no need to know. She brought me here and I took a patch test, and right then someone zapped the car — we were lucky to survive. One down out front. We've, uh, trapped a camera up top that I *think* will prove to have firmware loaded with SCORPION STARE, and I sniffed packets coming in from a compromised host. Police intranet, firewalled to hell and back, hacked via some vile little dweeb using a primary school web server in South Korea. We were just about to run down the intruder in meat-space and go ask some pointed questions when you arrived.' I yawn, and Andy looks at me oddly. Extreme stress sometimes does that to me, makes me tired, and I've been running on my nerves for most of the past few days.

'All right.' Andy scratches his chin thoughtfully. 'There's been a new development.'

'New development?' I echo.

'Yes. We received a blackmail note.' And it's no fucking *wonder* that he's looking slightly glassy-eyed – he must be in shock.

'*Blackmail?* What are they—'

'It came via email from an anonymous remixer on the public Internet. Whoever wrote it knows about MAGINOT BLUE STARS and wants us to know that they disapprove, especially of SCORPION STARE. No sign that they've got CASE NIGHT-MARE GREEN, though. They're giving us three days to cancel the entire project or they'll blow it wide open in quote the most public way imaginable unquote.'

'Shit.'

'Smelly brown stuff, yes. Angleton is displeased.' Andy shakes his head. 'We tracked the message back to a dial-up host in the UK—'

I hold up a piece of paper. 'This one?'

He squints at it. 'I think so. We did the S22 soft-shoe shuffle but it's no good, they used the SIMM card from a prepaid mobile phone bought for cash in a supermarket in Birmingham three months ago. The best we could do was trace the caller's location to the centre of Milton Keynes.' He glances at Josephine. 'Did you impress her—'

'Listen.' She speaks quietly and with great force: 'Firstly, this appears to be an investigation into murder – and now blackmail, of a government department, right? – and in case you hadn't noticed, organising criminal investigations just happens to be my speciality. Secondly, I do not appreciate being forcibly gagged. I *have* signed a certain piece of paper, and the only stuff I leak is what you get when you drill holes in me. Finally, I am getting really pissed off with the runaround you're giving me about a particularly serious incident on my turf, and if you don't start answering my questions soon I'm going to have to arrest you for wasting police time. Now, which is it going to be?'

'Oh, for crying out loud.' Andy rolls his eyes, then says very rapidly: 'By the abjuration of Dee and the name of Claude Dansey I hereby exercise subsection D paragraph sixteen clause twelve and bind you to service from now and forevermore. Right, that's it. You're drafted, and may whatever deity you believe in have mercy on your soul.'

'Hey. Wait.' She takes a step back. 'What's going on?' There's a faint stink of burning sulphur in the air.

'You've just talked yourself into the Laundry,' I say, shaking my head. 'Just try to remember I tried to keep you out of this.'

'The Laundry? What are you talking about? I thought you were from Cheltenham?' The smell of brimstone is getting stronger. 'Hey, is something on fire?'

'Wrong guess,' says Andy. 'Bob can explain later. For now, just remember that we work for the same people, ultimately, only we deal with a higher order of threat than everyday stuff like rogue states, terrorist nukes, and so on. Cheltenham is the cover story. Bob, the blackmailer threatened to upload SCORPION STARE to the ring of steel.'

'Oh shit.' I sit down hard on the edge of a desk. 'That is so very not good that I don't want to think about it right now.' The ring of steel is the network of surveillance cameras that were installed around the financial heart of the city of London in the late 1990s to deter terrorist bombings. Look, did Angleton have any other—'

'Yes. He wants us to go visit Site Able right now, that's the lead development team at the research centre behind SCOR-PION STARE. Um, inspector? You're in. As I said, you're drafted. Your boss, that would be Deputy Chief Constable Dunwoody, is about to get a memo about you from the Home Office – we'll worry about whether you can go back to your old job afterward. As of now, this investigation is your only priority. Site Able runs out of an office unit at Kiln Farm industrial estate, covered as a UK subsidiary of an American software company: in reality they're part of the residual unprivatised rump of DERA, uh, QinetiQ. The bunch that handles Q-projects.'

'While you're busy wanking over your cow-burning nonsense I've got a ring of car thieves to—' Josephine shakes her head distractedly, sniffs suspiciously, then stops trying to fight the geas. 'That smell . . . Why do these people at Kiln Farm need a visit?'

'Because they're the lead team on the group who developed SCORPION STARE,' Andy explains, 'and Angleton doesn't think it's a coincidence that our blackmailer burned a cow in Milton Keynes. He thinks they're a bunch of locals. Bob, if you've got a trace that'll be enough to narrow it down to the building—'

'Yes?' Josephine nods to herself. 'But you need to find the individual responsible, and any time bombs they've left, and there's a small matter of evidence.' A thought strikes her. 'What happens when you catch them?'

Andy looks at me and my blood runs cold. 'I think we'll have to see about that when we find them,' I extemporise, trying to avoid telling her about the Audit Commission for the time being; she might blow her stack completely if I have to explain how they investigate malfeasance, and then I'd have to tell her that the burning smell is a foreshadowing of what happens if she is ever found guilty of disloyalty. (It normally fades a few minutes after the rite of binding, but right now it's still strong.) 'What are we waiting for?' I ask. 'Let's go!'

In the beginning there was the Defense Evaluation and Research Agency, DERA. And DERA was where HMGs boffins hung out, and they developed cool toys like tanks with plastic armour, clunky palmtops powered by 1980s chips and rugged enough to be run over by a truck, and fetal heart monitors to help the next generation of squaddies grow up strong. And lo, in the thrusting entrepreneurial climate of the early nineties a new government came to power with a remit to bring about the triumph of true socialism by privatising the post office and air traffic control systems, and DERA didn't stand much of a chance. Renamed QinetiQ by the same nameless marketing genius who turned the Royal Mail into Consignia and Virgin Trains into fodder for fuckedcompany-dot-com, the research agency was hung out to dry, primped and beautified, and generally prepared for sale to the highest bidder who didn't speak with a pronounced Iraqi accent.

However . . .

In addition to the ordinary toys, DERA used to do development work for the Laundry. Q Division's pedigree stretches back all the way to SOE's wartime dirty tricks department – poison pens, boot-heel escape kits, explosive-stuffed sabotage rats, the whole nine yards of James Bond japery. Since the 1950s, Q Division has kept the Laundry in more esoteric equipment: summoning grids, basilisk guns, Turing oracles, self-tuning pentacles, self-filling beer glasses, and the like. Steadily growing weirder and more specialised by the year, Q Division is far too sensitive to sell off – unlike most of QinetiQ's research, what they do is classified so deep you'd need a bathyscaphe to reach it. And so, while QinetiQ was being dolled up for the city catwalk, Q Division was segregated and spun off, a little stronghold in the sea of commerce that is forever civil service territory.

Detective Inspector Sullivan marches out of the site office like a blank-faced automaton and crisply orders her pet driver to take us to Site Able then to bugger off on some obscure make-work errand. She sits stiffly in the front passenger seat while Andy and I slide into the back and we proceed in silence – nobody seems to want to make small talk.

Fifteen minutes of bumbling around red routes and through trackless wastes of identical red brick houses embellished with satellite dishes and raw pine fences brings us into an older part of town, where the buildings actually look different and the cycle paths are painted strips at the side of the road rather than sep-arately planned routes. I glance around curiously, trying to spot landmarks. 'Aren't we near Bletchley Park?' I ask.

'It's a couple of miles that way,' says our driver without taking his hands off the wheel to point. 'You thinking of visiting?'

'Not just yet.' Bletchley Park was the wartime headquarters of the Ultra operation, the department that later became GCHQ – the people who built the Colossus computers, originally used for breaking Nazi codes and subsequently diverted by the Laundry for more occult purposes. Hallowed ground to us spooks; I've met more than one NSA liaison who wanted to visit in order to smug-gle a boot heel full of gravel home. 'Not until we've visited the UK offices of Dillinger Associates, at any rate.'

Dillinger Associates is the cover name for a satellite office of Q Division. The premises turns out to be a neoclassical brick-and-glass edifice with twee fake columns and wilted-looking ivy that's been trained to climb the facade by dint of ruthless application of plant hormones. We pile out of the car in the courtyard between the dry fountain and the glass doors, and I surreptitiously check my PDA's locator module for any sign of a match. Nothing. I blink and put it away in time to catch up with Andy and Josephine as they head for the bleached blonde receptionist who sits behind a high wooden counter and types constantly, as unap-proachably artificial-looking as a shop window dummy.

'HelloDillingerAssociatesHowCanIHelpEwe?' She flutters her eyelashes at Andy in a bored, professional way, hands never moving away from the keyboard of the PC in front of her. There's something odd about her, but I can't quite put my finger on it.

Andy flips open his warrant card. 'We're here to see Dr. Voss.'

The receptionist's long, red-nailed fingers stop moving and hover over the keyboard. 'Really?' she asks, tonelessly, reaching under the desk.

'Hold it—' I begin to say, as Josephine takes a brisk step for-ward and drops a handkerchief over the webcam on top of the woman's monitor. There's a quiet *pop* and the sudden absence of noise from her PC tips me off. I sidestep the desk and make a grab for her just as Andy produces a pistol with a ridiculously fat barrel and shoots out the camera located over the door at the rear of the reception area. There's a horrible ripping sound like a joint of meat tearing apart as the receptionist twists aside and I realise that she isn't sitting on a chair at all – she's joined seamlessly at the hips to a plinth that emerges from some kind of fat swivel base of age-blackened wood, bolted to the floor with heavy brass pins in the middle of a silvery metallic pentacle with wires trailing from one corner back up to the PC on the desk. She opens her mouth and I can see that her tongue is bright blue and bifurcated as she hisses.

I hit the floor shoulder first, jarringly hard, and grab for the nearest cable. Those red nails are reaching down for me as her eyes narrow to slits and she works her jaw muscles as if she's trying to get together a wad of phlegm to spit. I grab the fattest cable and give it a pull and she screams, high-pitched and frighteningly inhuman.

What the fuck? I think, looking up as the red-painted claws stretch and expand, shedding layers of varnish as their edges grow long and sharp. Then I yank the cable again, and It comes away from the pentacle. The wooden box drools a thick, blue-tinted liquid across the carpet tiles, and the screaming stops.

'Lamia,' Andy says tersely. He strides over to the fire door that opens onto the corridor beyond, raises the curiously fat gun, and fires straight up. A purple rain drizzles back down.

'What's going on?' says Josephine, bewildered, staring at the twitching, slowly dying receptionist.

I point my PDA at the lamia and ding it for a reading. Cool, but nonzero. 'Got a partial fix,' I call to Andy. 'Where's everyone else? Isn't this place supposed to be manned?'

'No idea.' He looks worried. 'If this is what they've got up front the shit's already hit the fan. Angleton wasn't predicting overt resistance.'

The other door bangs open of a sudden and a tubby middle-aged guy in a cheap grey suit and about three day's worth of designer stubble barges out shouting, 'Who are you and what do you think you're doing here? This is private property, not a paint-ball shooting gallery! It's a disgrace — I'll call the police!'

Josephine snaps out of her trance and steps forward. 'As a matter of fact, I am the police,' she says. 'What's your name? Do you have a complaint, and if so, what is it?'

'I'm, I'm—' He focusses on the no-longer-twitching demon receptionist, lolling on top of her box like a murderous shop mannequin. He looks aghast. 'Vandals! If you've damaged her—'

'Not as badly as she planned to damage us,' says Andy. 'I think you'd better tell us who you are.' Andy presents his card, order-ing it to reveal its true shape: 'By the authority vested in me—'

He moves fast with the geas and ten seconds later we've got mister fat guy — actually Dr. Martin Voss — seated on one of the uncomfortable chrome-and-leather designer sofas at one side of reception while Andy asks questions and records them on a dic-taphone. Voss talks in a monotone, obviously under duress, drooling slightly from one side of his mouth, and the stench of brimstone mingles with a mouthwatering undertone of roast pork. There's purple dye from Andy's paintball gun spattered over anything that might conceal a camera, and he had me seal all the doorways with a roll of something like duct tape or police incident tape, except that the symbols embossed on it glow black and make your eyes water if you try to focus on them.

'Tell me your name and position at this installation.'

'Voss. John Voss. Res-research team manager.'

'How many members are there on your team? Who are they?'

'Twelve. Gary. Ted. Elinor. John. Jonathan. Abdul. Mark—'

'Stop right there. Who's here today? And is anyone away from the office right now?' I plug away at my palmtop, going cross-eyed as I fiddle with the detector controls. But there's no sign of any metaspectral resonance; grepping for a match to the person who stole the Range Rover draws a blank in this building. Which is frustrating because we've got his (I'm pretty sure it's a *he*) boss right here, and there ought to be a sympathetic entanglement at work.

'Everyone's here but Mark.' He laughs a bit, mildly hysterical. 'They're all here but Mark. Mark!'

I glance over at Detective Inspector Sullivan, who is detective inspecting the lamia. I think she's finally beginning to grasp at a visceral level that we aren't just some bureaucratic Whitehall paper circus trying to make her life harder. She looks frankly nauseated. The silence here is eerie, and worrying. *Why haven't the other team members come to find out what's going on?* I wonder, looking at the taped-over doors. *Maybe they've gone out the back and are waiting for us outside. Or maybe they simply can't come out in daylight.* The smell of burning meat is getting stronger: Voss seems to be shaking, as if he's trying not to answer Andy's questions.

I walk over to the lamia. 'It's not human,' I explain quietly 'It never was human. It's one of the things they specialise in. This building is defended by guards and wards, and this is just part of the security system's front end.'

'But she, she spoke . . .'

'Yes, but she's not a human being.' I point to the thick ribbon cable that connected the computer to the pentacle. 'See, that's a control interface. The computer's there to stabilize and contain a Dho-Nha circuit that binds the Deespace entity here. The entity itself – it's a lamia – is locked into the box which contains, uh, other components. And it's compelled to obey certain orders. Nothing good for unscheduled visitors.' I put my hands on the lamia's head and work my fingers into the thick blonde hair, then tug. There's a noise of ripping Velcro then the wig comes off to reveal the scaly scalp beneath. 'See? It's not human. It's a lamia, a type of demon bound to act as a front-line challenge/response system for a high security installation with covert—'

I manage to get out of the line of fire as Josephine brings up her lunch all over the incredibly expensive bleached pine workstation. I can't say I blame her. I feel a little shocky myself – it's been a really bad morning. Then I realise that Andy is trying to get my attention. 'Bob, when you're through with grossing out the inspector I've got a little job for you.' He pitches his voice loudly.

'Yeah?' I ask, straightening up.

'I want you to open that door, walk along the corridor to the second room on the right — not pausing to examine any of the corpses along the way — and open it. Inside, you'll find the main breaker board. I want you to switch the power off.'

'Didn't I just see you splashing paint all over the CCTV cameras in the ceiling? And, uh, what's this about corpses? Why don't we send Dr. Voss — oh.' Voss's eyes are shut and the stink of roast meat is getting stronger: he's gone extremely red in the face, almost puffy, and he s shaking slightly as if some external force is making all his muscles twitch simultaneously. It's my turn to struggle to hang onto breakfast. 'I didn't know anyone could make themselves *do* that,' I hear myself say distantly.

'Neither did I,' says Andy, and that's the most frightening thing I've heard today so far. 'There must be a conflicted geas somewhere in his skull. I don't think I could stop it even if—'

'Shit.' I stand up. My hand goes to my neck automatically but the pouch is empty. 'No HOG.' I swallow. 'Power. What happens if I don't?'

'Voss's pal Mark McLuhan installed a dead man's handle. You'd know all about that. We've got until Voss goes into brain stem death and then every fucking camera in Milton Keynes goes live with SCORPION STARE.'

'Oh, you mean we die.' I head for the door Voss came through. 'I'm looking for the service core, right?'

'Wait!' It's Josephine, looking pale. 'Can't you go outside and cut the power there? Or phone for help?'

'Nope.' I rip the first strip of sealing tape away from the door frame. 'We're behind Tempest shielding here, and the power is routed through concrete ducts underground. This is a Q Division office, after all. If we could call in an air strike and drop a couple of BLU-114/Bs on the local power substations that might work' — I tug at the second tape — 'but these systems were designed to be survivable.' Third tape.

'Here,' calls Andy, and he chucks something cylindrical at me. I catch it one-handed, yank the last length of tape with the other hand, and do a double-take. Then I shake the cylinder, listen for the rattle of the stirrer, and pop the lid off.

'Take cover!' I call. Then I open the door, spritz the ceiling above me with green spray paint, and go to work.

I'm sitting in the lobby, guarding the lamia's corpse with a nearly empty can of paint and trying not to fall asleep, when the OCCU-LUS team bangs on the door. I yawn and sidestep Voss's blistered corpse – he looks like he's gone a few rounds with Old Sparky – then try to remember the countersign. *Ah, that's it.* I pull away a strip of tape and tug the door open and find myself staring up the snout of an H&K carbine. 'Is that a gun in your hand or are you just here to have a wank?' I ask.

The gun points somewhere else in a hurry. 'Hey, Sarge, it's the spod from Amsterdam!'

'Yeah, and someone's told you to secure the area, haven't they? Where's Sergeant Howe?' I ask, yawning. Daylight makes me feel better – that, and knowing that there's backup. (I get sleepy when people stop shooting at me. Then I have nightmares. Not a good combination.)

'Over here.' They're dressed in something not unlike Fire Service HAZMAT gear, and the wagons are painted cheerful cherry-red with luminous yellow stripes; if they weren't armed to the teeth with automatic weapons you'd swear they were only here because somebody had phoned in a toxic chemical release warning. But the pump nozzles above the cabs aren't there to spray water, and that lumpy thing on the back isn't a spotlight – it's a grenade launcher.

The inspector comes up behind me, staggering slightly in the daylight. 'What's going on?' she asks.

'Here, meet Scary Spice and Sergeant Howe. Sarge, Scary, meet Detective Inspector Sullivan. Uh, the first thing you need to do is to go round the site and shoot out every closed circuit TV camera you can see – or that can see you. Got that? And webcams. And doorcams. See a camera, smash it, that's the rule.'

'Cameras. Ri-ight.' Sergeant Howe looks mildly skeptical, but nods. 'It's definitely cameras?'

'Who *are* these guys?' asks Josephine.

'Artists' Rifles. They work with us,' I say. Scary nods, deeply serious. 'Listen, you go outside, do anything necessary to keep the local emergency services off our backs. If you need backup ask Sergeant Howe here. Sarge, she's basically sound and she's working for us on this. Okay?'

She doesn't wait for confirmation, just shoves past me and heads out into the daylight, blinking and shaking her head. I carry on briefing the OCCULUS guys. 'Don't worry about anything that uses film, it's the closed circuit TV variety that's hostile. And, oh, try to make sure that you are *never* in view of more than one of 'em at a time.'

'And don't walk on the cracks in the pavement or the bears will get us, check.' Howe turns to Scary Spice: 'Okay, you heard the man. Let's do it.' He glances at me. 'Anything inside?'

'We're taking care of it,' I say. 'If we need help we'll ask.'

'Check.' Scary is muttering into his throat mike and fake firemen with entirely authentic fire axes are walking around the bushes along the side of the building as if searching for signs of combustion. 'Okay, we'll be out here.'

'Is Angleton in the loop? Or the captain?'

'Your boss is on his way out here by chopper. Ours is on medical leave. You need to escalate, I'll get you the lieutenant.'

'Okay.' I duck back into the reception area then nerve myself to go back into the development pool at the rear of the building, below the offices and above the labs.

Site Able is a small departmental satellite office, small for security reasons: ten systems engineers, a couple of manager dogsbodies, and a security officer. Most of them are right here right now, and they're not going anywhere. I walk around the service core in the dim glow of the emergency light, bypassing splashes of green paint that look black in the red glow. The octagonal developer pool at the back is also dimly illuminated – there are no windows, and the doors are triple-sealed with rubber gaskets impregnated with fine copper mesh – and some of the partitions have been blown over. The whole place is ankle deep in white mist left over from the halon dump system that went off when the first bodies exploded – good thing the air conditioning continued to run or the place would be a gas trap. The webcams are all where I left them, in a trash can at the foot of the spiral staircase up to level one, cables severed with my multitool just to make sure nobody tries to plug them back in again.

The victims – well, I have to step over one of them to get up the staircase. It's pretty gross but I've seen dead bodies before, including burn cases, and at least this was fast. But I don't think I'm going to forget the smell in a hurry. In fact, I think I'm going to have nightmares about it tonight, and maybe get drunk and cry on Mo's shoulder several times over the next few weeks until I've got it out of my system. But for now, I shove it aside and step over them. Got to keep moving, that's the main thing – unless I want there to be more of them. And on my conscience.

At the top of the staircase there's a narrow corridor and partitioned offices, also lit by the emergency lights. I follow the sound of keyclicks to Voss's office, the door of which is ajar. Potted cheese plants wilting in the artificial light, puke-brown antistatic carpet, ministry-issue desks – nobody can accuse Q Division's brass of living high on the hog. Andy's sitting in front of Voss's laptop, tapping away with a strange expression on his face. 'OCCULUS is in place,' I report. 'Found anything interesting?'

Andy points at the screen. 'We're in the wrong fucking town,' he says mildly.

I circle the desk and lean over his shoulder. 'Oh shit.'

'You can say that again if you like.' It's an email Cc'd to Voss, sent over our intranet to a Mike McLuhan. Subject: meeting. Sender: Harriet.

'Oh shit. Twice over. Something stinks. Hey, I was supposed to be in a meeting with her today,' I say.

'A meeting?' Andy looks up, worried.

'Yeah. Bridget got a hair up her ass about running a BSA-authorised software audit on the office, the usual sort of make-work. Don't know that it's got anything to do with this, though.'

'A *software* audit? Didn't she know Licencing and Compliance handles that on a blanket department-wide basis? We were updated on it about a year ago.'

'We were—' I sit down heavily on the cheap plastic visitor's chair. 'What are the chances this McLuhan guy put the idea into Harriet's mind in the first place? What are the chances it *isn't* connected?'

'McLuhan. The medium is the message. SCORPION STARE. Why do I have a bad feeling about this?' Andy sends me a worried look.

' 'Nother possibility, boss-man. What if it's an internal power play? The software audit's a cover, Purloined Letter style, hiding something fishy in plain sight where nobody will look at it twice until it's too late.'

'Nonsense, Bridget's not clever enough to blow a project wide open just to discredit—' His eyes go wide.

'Are you sure of that? I mean, *really* and *truly* sure? Bet-your-life sure?'

'But the body count!' He's shaking his head in disbelief.

'So it was all a prank and it was meant to begin and end with Daisy, but it got a bit out of control, didn't it? These things happen. You told me the town police camera network's capable of end-to-end tracking and zone hand-off, didn't you? My guess is someone in this office – Voss, maybe – followed me to the car pound and realised we'd found the vehicle McLuhan used to boost Daisy. Stupid wankers, if they'd used one of their own motors we'd not be any the wiser, but they tried to use a stolen one as a cutout. So they panicked and dumped SCORPION STARE into the pound, and it didn't work, so they panicked some more and McLuhan panicked even more – bet you he's the go-between, or even the guy behind it. What is he, senior esoteric officer? Deputy site manager? He's in London so he planted the crazy blackmail threat then brought down the hammer on his own coworkers. Bet you he's a smart sociopath, the kind that does well in midlevel management, all fur coat and no knickers – and willing to shed blood without a second thought if it's to defend his position. '

'Damn,' Andy says mildly as he stands up. 'Okay, so. Internal politics, stupid bloody prank organised to show up Angleton, they use idiots to run it so your cop finds the trail, then the lunatic in chief cuts loose and starts killing people. Is that your story?'

'Yup.' I nod like my neck's a spring. 'And right now they're back at the Laundry doing who the fuck knows what—'

'We've got to get McLuhan nailed down fast, before he decides the best way to cover his tracks is to take out head office. And us.' He smiles reassuringly. 'It'll be okay, Angleton's on his way in. You haven't seen him in action before, have you?'

Picture a light industrial/office estate in the middle of anytown with four cherry-red fire pumps drawn up, men in HAZMAT gear combing the brush, a couple of police cars with flashing light bars drawn up across the road leading into the cul-de-sac to deter casual rubberneckers. Troops disguised as firemen are systematically shooting out every one of the security cameras on the estate with their silenced carbines. Others, wearing police or fire service uniforms, are taking up stations in front of every building – occupied or otherwise – to keep the people inside out of trouble.

Just another day at the office, folks, nothing to see here, walk on by.

Well, maybe not. Here comes a honking great helicopter – the Twin Squirrel from the Met's ASU that I was in the other night, only it looks a lot bigger and scarier when seen from a couple hundred feet in full daylight as it settles in on the car park, leaves and debris blowing out from under the thundering rotors.

The chopper is still rocking on its skids when one of the back doors opens and Angleton jumps down, stumbling slightly – he's no spring chicken – then collects himself and strides toward us, clutching a briefcase. 'Speak,' he tells me, voice barely raised to cover the rush of slowing rotors.

'Problem, boss.' I point to the building: Andy's still inside confirming the worst but it looks like it started as a fucking stupid interdepartmental prank; it went bad, and now one of the perps has wigged out and gone postal.'

'A prank.' He turns those icy blue peepers on me and just for a fraction of a second I'm not being stared at by a sixty-something skinny bald guy in a badly fitting suit but by a walking skeleton with the radioactive fires of hell burning balefully in its eye sockets. 'You'd better take me to see Andrew. Fill me in on the way.'

I'm stumbling over my tongue and hurrying to keep up with Angleton when we make it to the front desk, where Andy's busy giving the OCCULUS folks cleanup directions and tips for what to do with the broken lamia and the summoning altars in the basement. 'Who's – oh, it's you. About time.' He grins. 'Who's holding the fort?'

'I left Boris in charge,' Angleton says mildly, not taking exception at Andy's brusque manner. 'How bad is it?'

'Bad.' Andy's cheek twitches, which is a bad sign: all his confidence seems to have fled now that Angleton's arrived. 'We need to – damn.'

'Take your time,' Angleton soothes him. 'I'm not going to eat you.' Which is when I realise just how scared I am, and if I'm half out of my tree what does that say about Andy? I'll give Angleton this much, he knows when not to push his subordinates too hard. Andy takes a deep breath, lets it out slowly, then tries again.

'We've got two loose ends: Mark McLuhan, and a John Doe. McLuhan worked here as senior occult officer, basically an oversight role. He also did a bunch of other stuff for Q Division that took him down to Dansey House in a liaison capacity. I can't *believe* how badly we've slipped up on our vetting process—'

'Take your time,' Angleton interrupts, this time with a slight edge to his voice.

'Sorry, sorry. Bob's been putting it together.' A nod in my direction. 'McLuhan is working with a John Doe inside the Laundry to make us look bad via a selective disclosure leak – basically one that was intended to be written off as bad-ass forteana, nothing for anyone but the black helicopter crowd to pay any attention to, except that it would set you up to look bad. I've found some not very good email from Bridget inviting McLuhan down to headquarters, some pretext to do with a software audit. Really fucking stupid stuff that Bob can do the legwork on later. But what *I really* think is happening is, Bridget arranged this to make you look bad in support of a power play in front of the director's office.'

Angleton turns to me: 'Phone head office. Ask for Boris. Tell him to arrest McLuhan. Tell him, SHRINKWRAP. And, MARMOSET.' I raise an eyebrow. 'Now, lad!'

Ah, the warm fuzzies of decisive action. I head for the lamia's desk and pick up the phone and dial 666; behind me Andy is telling Angleton something in a low voice.

'Switchboard?' I ask the sheet of white noise. 'I want Boris. *Now.*' The Enochian metagrammar parsers do their thing and the damned souls or enchained demons or whatever on switchboard hiss louder then connect the circuit. I hear another ring tone. Then a familiar voice.

'Hello, Capital Laundry Services, system support department. Who are you wanting to talk to?'

Oh shit. 'Hello, Harriet,' I say, struggling to sound calm and collected. Getting Bridget's imp at this juncture is not a good sign, especially when she and Boris are renowned for their mutual loathing. 'This is a red phone call. Is Boris about?'

'Oh-ho, Robert! I was wondering where you were. Are you trying to pull a sickie again?'

'No, I'm not,' I say, taking a deep breath. 'I need to talk to Boris urgently, Harriet, is he around?'

'Oh, I couldn't possibly say. That would be disclosing information prejudicial to the good running of the department over a public network connection, and I couldn't possibly encourage you to do that when you can bloody well show your face in the office for the meeting we scheduled the day before yesterday, remember that?'

I feel as if my guts have turned to ice. 'Which meeting?'

'The software audit, remember? You never read the agenda for meetings. If you did, you might have taken an interest in the *any other business* . . . Where *are* you calling from, Bob? Anyone would think you didn't work here . . .'

'I want to talk to Boris. Right now.' The graunching noise in the background is my jaw clenching. 'It's urgent, Harriet. To do with the code blue the other day. Now you can get him right now or you can regret it later, which is your choice?'

'Oh, I don't think that'll be necessary,' she says in what I can only describe as a gloating tone of voice. 'After missing the meeting, you and your precious CounterPossession Unit will be divisional history, and you'll have only yourselves to blame! Goodbye.' And the bitch hangs up on me.

I look round and see both Andy and Angleton staring at me. 'She hung up,' I say stupidly. 'Fucking Harriet has a diversion on Boris's line. It's a setup. Something about making an end run around the CPU.'

'Then we shall have to attend this meeting in person,' Angleton says, briskly marching toward the front doors, which bend aside to get out of his way. 'Follow me!'

We proceed directly to the helicopter, which has kept its engines idling while we've been inside. It's only taken what? Three or four minutes since Angleton arrived? I see another figure heading toward us across the car park – a figure m a grey trouser suit, slightly stained, a wild look in her eyes. 'Hey, you!' she shouts. 'I want some answers!'

Angleton turns to me. 'Yours?' I nod. He beckons to her imperiously 'Come with us,' he calls, raising his voice over the whine of gathering turbines. Past her shoulder I see one of the fake firemen lowering a kit-bag that had been, purely coincidentally, pointed at DI Sullivan's back. 'This bit I always dislike,' he adds in a low monotone, his face set in a grim expression of disapproval. 'The fewer lives we warp, the better.'

I half-consider asking him to explain what he means, but he's already climbing into the rear compartment of the chopper and Andy is following him. I give Josephine a hand up as the blades overhead begin to turn and the engines rise in a full-throated bellowing duet. I get my headset on in time to hear Angleton's orders: 'Back to London, and don't spare the horses.'

The Laundry is infamous for its grotesque excesses in the name of accounting; budgetary infractions are punished like war crimes, and mere paper clips can bring down the wrath of dead alien gods on your head. But when Angleton says *don't spare the horses* he sends us screaming across the countryside at a hundred and forty miles per hour, burning aviation fuel by the ton and getting ATC to clear lower priority traffic out of our way – and all because he doesn't want to be late for a meeting. There's a police car waiting for us at the pad, and we cut through the chaotic London traffic incredibly fast, almost making it into third gear at times.

'McLuhan's got SCORPION STARE,' I tell Angleton round the curve of Andy's shoulder. 'And headquarters's security cams are all wired. If he primes them before we get back there, we could find a lockout – or worse. It all depends on what Harriet and her boss have been planning.'

'We will just have to see.' Angleton nods very slightly, his facial expression rigid. 'Do you still have your lucky charm?'

'Had to use it.' I'd shrug, if there was more room. 'What do you think Bridget's up to?'

'I couldn't possibly comment.' I'd take Angleton's dismissal as a put-down, but he points his chin at the man in the driver's seat. 'When we get there, Bob, I want you to go in through the warehouse door and wake the caretaker. You have your mobile telephone?'

'Uh, yeah,' I say, hoping like hell that the battery hasn't run down.

'Good. Andrew. You and I will enter through the front door. Bob, set your telephone to vibrate. When you receive a message from me, you will know it is time to have the janitor switch off the main electrical power. *And* the backup power.

'Oops.' I lick my suddenly dry lips, thinking of all the electrical containment pentacles in the basement and all the computers plugged into the filtered and secured circuit on the other floors. 'All hell's going to break loose if I do that.'

'That's what I'm counting on.' The bastard *smiles*, and despite all the horrible sights I've seen today so far, I hope most of all that I never see it again before the day I die.

'Hey, what about me?' Angleton glances at the front seat with a momentary flash of irritation. Josephine stares right back, clearly angry and struggling to control it. 'I'm your liaison officer for North Buckinghamshire,' she says, 'and I'd really *like* to know who I'm liaising with, especially as you seem to have left a few *bodies* on my manor that I'm going to have to bury, and this jerk' – she means me, I am distraught! Oh, the ignominy! – 'promised me you'd have the answers.'

Angleton composes himself. 'There are no answers, madam, only further questions,' he says, and just for a second he sounds like a pious wanker of a vicar going through the motions of comforting the bereaved. 'And if you want the answers you'll have to go through the jerk's filing cabinet.' *Bastard.* Then there's a flashing sardonic grin, dry as the desert sands in June: 'Do you want to help prevent any, ah, recurrence of what you saw an hour ago? If so, you may accompany the jerk and attempt to keep him from dying.' He reaches out a hand and drops a ragged slip of paper over her shoulder. 'You'll need this.'

Provisional warrant card, my oh my. Josephine mutters something unkind about his ancestry, barnyard animals, and lengths of rubber hose. I pretend not to hear because we're about three minutes out, stuck behind a slow-moving but gregarious herd of red double-decker buses, and I'm trying to remember the way to the janitor's office in the Laundry main unit basement and whether there's anything I'm likely to trip over in the dark.

'Excuse me for asking, but how many corpses do you usually run into in the course of your job?' I ask.

'Too many, since you showed up.' We turn the street corner into a brick-walled alley crowded by wheelie bins and smelling of vagrant piss. 'But since you ask, I'm a detective inspector. You get to see lots of vile stuff on the beat.'

Something in her expression tells me I'm on dangerous ground here, but I persist: 'Well, this is the Laundry. It's our job to deal with seven shades of vile shit so that people like you don't have to.' I take a deep breath. 'And before we go in I figured I should warn you that you're going to think Fred and Rosemary West work for us, and Harold Shipman's the medical officer.' At this point she goes slightly pale – the Demon DIYers and Dr. Death are the acme of British serial killerdom after all – but she doesn't flinch.

'And you're the *good* guys?'

'Sometimes I have my doubts,' I sigh.

'Well, join the club.' I have a feeling she's going to make it, if she lives through the next hour.

'Enough bullshit. *This* is the street level entrance to the facilities block under Headquarters Building One. You saw what those fuckers did with the cameras at the car pound and Site Able. If my guess is straight, they're going to do it all over again *here* – or worse. From here there's a secure line to several of the Met's offices, including various borough-level control systems, such as the Camden Town control centre. SCORPION STARE isn't ready for nationwide deployment—'

'What the *hell* would justify that?' she demands, eyes wide.

'You do not have clearance for that information.' Amazing how easily the phrase trips off the tongue. 'Besides, it'd give you nightmares. But you're the one who mentioned hell, and as I was saying' – I stop, with an overflowing dumpster between us and the anonymous doorway – 'our pet lunatic, who killed all those folks at Dillinger Associates and who is now in a committee meeting upstairs, could conceivably upload bits of SCORPION STARE to the various camera control centres. Which is why we are going to stop him, by bringing down the intranet backbone cable in and out of the Laundry's headquarters. Which would be easy if this was a bog-standard government office, but a little harder in reality because the Laundry has guards, and some of those guards are very special, and some of those very special guards will try to stop us by eating us alive.'

'Eating. Us.' Josephine is looking a little glassy. 'Did I tell you that I don't do headhunters? That's Recruitment's job.'

'Look,' I say gently, 'have you ever seen *Night of the Living Dead?* It's really not all that different – except that I've got permission to be here, and you've got a temporary warrant card too, so we should be all right.' A thought strikes me. 'You're a cop. Have you been through firearms training?'

Click-clack. 'Yes,' she says drily. 'Next question?'

'Great! If you'd just take that away from my nose – that's better – it won't work on the guards. Sorry, but they're already, uh, metabolically challenged. However, it *will* work very nicely on the CCTV cameras. Which—'

'Okay, I get the picture. We go in. We stay out of the frame unless we want to die.' She makes the pistol vanish inside her jacket and looks at me askance – for the first time since the car pound with something other than irritation or dislike. Probably wondering why I didn't flinch. (Obvious, really: compared with what's waiting for us inside a little intracranial air conditioning is a relatively painless way to go, and besides, if she was seriously pissed at me she could have gotten me alone in a nice soundproofed cell back in her manor with a pair of size twelve boots and their occupants.) 'We're going to go in there and you're going to talk our way past the zombies while I shoot out all the cameras, right?'

'Right. And then I'm going to try to figure out how to take down the primary switchgear, the backup substation, the diesel generator, *and* the batteries for the telephone switch and the protected computer ring main *all* at the same time so nobody twigs until it's too late. While fending off anyone who tries to stop us. Clear?'

'As mud.' She stares at me. 'I always wanted to be on TV, but not quite this way.'

'Yeah, well.' I glance up the side of the building, which is windowless as far as the third floor (and then the windows front onto empty rooms three feet deep, just to give the appearance of occupation). 'I'd rather call in an air strike on the power station but there's a hospital two blocks that way and an old folks' home on the other side . . . you ready?'

She nods. 'Okay.' And I take a step round the wheelie bin and knock on the door.

The door is a featureless blue slab of paint. As soon as I touch it, it swings open – no creaking here, did you think this was a Hammer horror flick? – to reveal a small, dusty room with a dry powder fire extinguisher bolted to one wall and another door opposite. 'Wait,' I say, and take the spray paint can out of my pocket. 'Okay, come on in. Keep your warrant note handy.'

She jumps when the door closes automatically with a faint hiss, and I remember to swallow – it only looks like a cheap fire door from the outside. 'Okay, here's the fun part.' I give the inner door a quick scan with a utility on my palmtop and it comes up blank, so I put my hand on the grab-bar and pull. This is the moment of truth; if the shit has truly hit the fan already the entire building will be locked down tighter than a nuclear bunker, and the thaumaturgic equivalent of a three-phase six-hundred-volt bearer will be running through all the barred portals. But I get to keep on breathing, and the door swings open on a dark corridor leading past shut storeroom doors to a dingy wooden staircase. And that's all it is – there's nothing in here to confuse an accidental burglar who makes it in past the wards in hope of finding some office supplies to filch. All the really classified stuff is either ten storeys underground or on the other side of the cellar walls. Twitching in the darkness.

'I don't see any zombies,' Josephine says edgily, crowding up behind me in the gloom.

'That's because they're—' I freeze and bring up the dry powder extinguisher. 'Have you got a pocket mirror?' I ask, trying to sound casual.

'Hold on.' I hear a dry click, and then she passes me something like a toothbrush fucking a contact lens. 'Will this do?'

'Oh wow, I didn't know you were a dentist.' It's on a goddamn telescoping wand almost half a metre long. I lean forward and gingerly stretch the angled mirror so I can view the stairwell.

'It's for checking the undersides of cars for bombs – or cut brake pipes. You never know what the little fuckers in the school playground will do while you're talking to the headmistress.'

Gulp. 'Well, I guess this is a suitable alternative use.'

I don't see any cameras up there so I retract the mirror and I'm about to set foot on the stairs when she says, 'You missed one.'

'Huh . . .?'

She points. It's about waist level, the size of a doorknob embedded in the dark wooden wainscoting, and it's pointing *up* the stairs. 'Shit, you're right.' And there's something odd about it. I slide the mirror closer for an oblique look and dry-swallow 'There are two lenses. Oh, tricky.'

I pull out my multitool and begin digging them out of the wall. It's coax cable, just like the doctor ordered. There's no obvious evidence of live SCORPION STARE, but my hands are still clammy and my heart is in my mouth as I realise how close I came to walking in front of it. How small can they make CCTV cameras, anyway? I keep seeing smaller and smaller ones . . .

'Better move fast,' she comments.

'Why?'

'Because you've just told them you're coming.'

'Oh. Okay.' We climb the staircase in bursts, stopping before the next landing to check for more basilisk bugs. Josephine spots one, and so do I. I tag them with the mostly empty can of paint, then she blasts their lenses from behind and underneath, trying not to breathe the fumes in before we move past them. There's an unnaturally creaky floorboard, too, just for yucks. But we make it to the ground floor landing alive, and I just have time to realise how badly we've fucked up when the lights come up and the night watchmen come out from either side.

'Ah, Bob! Decided to visit the office for once, have we?'

It's Harriet, looking slightly demented in a black pinstriped suit and clutching a glass of what looks like fizzy white wine.

'Where the fuck is everyone else?' I demand, looking round.

At this time of day the place should be heaving with office bodies. But all I see here is Harriet – and three or four silently leaning night watchmen in their grey ministry suits and hangdog expressions, luminous worms of light glowing in their eyes.

'I do believe we called the monthly fire drill a few hours ahead of schedule.' Harriet smirks. 'Then we locked the doors. It's quite simple, you know.'

Fred from Accounting lurches sideways and peers at me over her shoulder. He's been dead for months: normally I'd say this was something of an improvement, but right now he's drooling slightly as if it's past his teatime.

'Who's *that*?' asks Josephine.

'Who? Oh, one of them's a shambling undead bureaucrat and the other one used to work in accounts before he had a little accident with a summoning.' I bare my teeth at Harriet. 'The game's up.'

'I don't think so.' She's just standing there, looking supercilious and slightly triumphant behind her bodyguard of zombies. 'Actually the boot is on the other foot. You're late and you're out of a job, Robert. The Counter-Possession Unit is being liquidated – that old fossil Angleton isn't needed anymore, once we get the benefits of panopticon surveillance combined with look-to-kill technology and rolled out on a departmental basis. In fact, you're just in time to clear your desk.' She grins, horribly. 'Stupid little boy, I'm sure they can find a use for you below stairs.'

'You've been talking to our friend Mr. McLuhan, haven't you?' I ask desperately, trying to keep her talking – I *really* don't want the night watchmen to carry me away. 'Is he upstairs?'

'If so, you probably need to know that I intend to arrest him. Twelve counts of murder and attempted murder, in case you were wondering.' I almost look round, but manage to resist the urge: Josephine's voice is brittle but controlled . 'Police.'

'Wrong jurisdiction, dear,' Harriet says consolingly 'And I do believe our idiot tearaway here has got you on the wrong message. That will never do.' She snaps her fingers

'Take the woman, detain the man.'

'Stop—' I begin. The zombies step forward, lurching jerkily, and then all hell breaks loose about twenty centimetres from my right ear. Zombies make excellent night watchmen and it takes a lot to knock one down, but they're not bulletproof, and Josephine unloads her magazine two rounds at a time. I'm dazzled by the flash and my head feels as if someone is whacking me on the ear with a shovel — bits of meat and unspeakable ripped stuff go flying, but precious little blood, and they keep coming.

'When you've *quite* finished,' Harriet hisses, and snaps her fingers at Josephine: the zombies pause for a moment then close in, as their mistress backs toward the staircase up to the first floor.

'Quick, down the back corridor there!' I gasp, pointing to my left.

'The – what?'

'Quick! '

I dash along the corridor, tugging Josephine's arm until I feel her running with me. I pull my warrant card and yell, '*Open sesame!*' ahead and doors slam open to either side – including the broom closets and ductwork access points. 'In here!' I dive in to one side and Josephine piles in after me and I yank at the door – '*Close, damn you, fuck, close sesame!*' and it slams shut with the hardscrabble of bony fingertips on the outside.

'Got a light?' I ask.

'Nah, I don't smoke. But I've got a torch somewhere—'

The scrabbling's getting louder. 'I don't want to hurry you or anything, but—' And lo, there is light.

We're standing at the bottom of a shallow shaft with cable runs vanishing above us into the gloom. Josephine looks frantic. 'They didn't drop! I shot them and they *didn't drop!*'

'Don't sweat it, they're run by remote control.' Maybe now is not the time to explain about six-node summoning points, the Vohlman exercise, and the minutiae of raising and binding the dead: they're knocking on the door and they want in. But look, here's something even *more* interesting. 'Hey, I see CAT-5 cabling. Pass me your torch?'

'This isn't the time to go all geeky on me, nerd-boy. Or are you looking for roaches?'

'Just fucking do it, I'll explain later, okay?' Harriet is really getting to me; it's been a long day and I told myself ages ago that if I ever heard another fucking lecture about timekeeping from her I'd go postal.

'Bingo.' It *is* CAT-5, and there's an even more interesting cable running off to one side that looks like a DS-3. I whip out my multitool and begin working on the junction box. The scrabbling's become insistent by the time I've uncovered the wires, but what the fuck. Who was it who said *When they think you're technical is the time to go crude?* I grab a handful of network cables and yank, hard. Then I grab another handful. Then, having disconnected the main trunk line – *mission accomplished* – I take another moment to think

'Bob, have you got a plan?'

'I'm thinking.'

'Then think faster, they're about to come through the door—'

Which is when I remember my mobile phone and decide to make a last-ditch attempt. I speed-dial Bridget's office extension – and Angleton picks up after two rings. Bastard.

'Ah, Bob!' He sounds positively avuncular. 'Where are you? Did you manage to shut down the Internet?'

I don't have time to correct him. Besides, Josephine is reloading her cannon and I think she's going to try a *really* horrible pun if I don't produce a solution PDQ. 'Boss, run McLuhan's SCORPION STARE tool and upload the firmware to all the motion-tracking cameras on the ground floor east wing loop *right now.*'

'What? I'm not sure I heard you correctly.'

I take a deep breath. 'She's subverted the night watchmen. Everybody else is out of the building. Do it *now* or I'm switching to a diet of fresh brains.'

'If you say so,' he agrees, with the manner of an indulgent uncle talking to a tearaway schoolboy, then hangs up

There's a splintering crash and a hand rams through the door right between us and embeds itself in the wall opposite. 'Oh shit,' I have time to say as the hand withdraws. Then a bolt of lightning goes off about two feet outside the door, roughly simultaneous with a sizzling crash and a wave of heat. We cower in the back of the cupboard, terrified of fire until after what seems like an eternity the sprinklers come on.

'Is it safe yet?' she asks – at least I think that's what she says, my ears are still ringing.

'One way to find out.' I take the broken casing from the network junction box and chuck it through the hole in the door. When it doesn't explode I gingerly push the door open. The ringing is louder; it's my phone. I pull it wearily out of my pocket and hunch over it to keep it dry, leaning against the wall of the corridor to stay as far away from the blackened zombie corpses as I can. 'Who's there?'

'Your manager.' He sounds merely amused this time. 'What a sorry shower you are! Come on up to Mahogany Row and dry off, both of you – the director has a personal bathroom, I think you've earned it.'

'Uh. Harriet? Bridget? McLuhan?'

'Taken care of,' he says complacently, and I shiver convulsively as the water reaches gelid tentacles down my spine and tickles my balls like a drowned lover.

'Okay. We'll be right up.' I glance back at the smashed-in utility cupboard and Josephine smiles at me like a frightened feral rat, all sharp teeth and savagery and shining .38 automatic. 'We're safe now,' I say, as reassuringly as possible. 'I think we won . . .'

The journey to Angleton's lair is both up and along – he normally works out of a gloomy basement on the other side of the hollowed-out block of prime London real estate that is occupied by the Laundry, but this time he's ensconced in the director's suite on the abandoned top floor of the north wing.

The north wing is still dry. Over there, people are still at work, oblivious to the charred zombies lying on the scorched, soaked, thaumaturgically saturated wing next door. We catch a few odd stares – myself, soaked and battered in my outdoors gear, DI Sullivan in the wreckage of an expensive grey suit, over-sized handgun clenched in a death grip at her side – but wisely or otherwise, nobody asks me to fix the Internet or demands to know why we're tracking muddy water through Human Resources.

By the time we reach the thick green carpet and dusty quietude of the director's suite Josephine's eyes are wide but she's stopped shaking. 'You've got lots of questions,' I manage to say. 'Try to save them for later. I'll tell you everything I know and you're cleared for, once I've had time to phone my fiancée.'

'I've got a husband and a nine-year-old son, did you think of that before you dragged me into this insane nightmare? Sorry. I know you didn't *mean* to. It's just that shooting up zombies and being zapped by basilisks makes me a little upset. Nerves.'

'I know. Just try not to wave them in front of Angleton, okay?'

'Who *is* Angleton, anyway? Who does he think he is?'

I pause before the office door. 'If I knew that, I'm not sure I'd be allowed to tell you.' I knock three times.

'Enter.' Andy opens the door for us. Angleton is sitting in the director's chair, playing with something in the middle of the huge expanse of oak desk that looks as if it dates to the 1930s. (There's a map on the wall behind him, and a quarter of it is pink.) 'Ah, Mr. Howard, Detective Inspector. So good of you to come.'

I peer closer. *Clack. Clack. Clack.* 'A Newton's cradle; how 1970s.'

'You could say that.' He smiles thinly. The balls bouncing back and forth between the arms of the executive desktop aren't chromed, rather they appear to be textured: pale brown on one side, dark or blonde and furry on the other. And bumpy, disturbingly bumpy . . .

I take a deep breath. 'Harriet was waiting for us. Said we were too late and the Counter-Possession Unit was being disbanded.'

Clack. Clack.

'Yes, she would say that, wouldn't she.'

Clack. Clack. Clack. Clack. Finally I can't stand it anymore. 'Well?' I demand.

'A fellow I used to know, his name was Ulyanov, once said something rather profound, do you know.' Angleton looks like the cat that's swallowed the canary – and the feet are sticking out of the side of his mouth; he *wants* me to know this, whatever it is. 'Let your enemies sell you enough rope to hang them with.'

'Uh, wasn't that Lenin?' I ask.

A flicker of mild irritation crosses his face. 'This was before then,' he says quietly. *Clack. Clack. Clack.* He flicks the balls to set them banging again and I suddenly realise what they are and feel quite sick. No indeed, Bridget and Harriet – and Bridget's predecessor, and the mysterious Mr. McLuhan – won't be troubling me again. (Except in my nightmares about this office, visions of my own shrunken head winding up in one of the director's executive toys, skull clattering away eternally in a scream that nobody can hear anymore . . .) 'Bridget's been plotting a boardroom coup for a long time, Robert. Probably since before you joined the Laundry – or were conscripted.' He spares Josephine a long, appraising look. 'She suborned Harriet, bribed McLuhan, installed her own corrupt geas on Voss. Partners in crime, intending to expose me as an incompetent and a possible security leak before the Board of Auditors, I suppose – that's usually how they plan it. I guessed this was going on, but I needed firm evidence. You supplied it. Unfortunately, Bridget was never too stable; when she realised that I knew, she ordered Voss to remove the witnesses then summoned McLuhan and proceeded with her palace coup d'état. Equally unfortunately for her, she failed to correctly establish who my line manager was before she attempted to go over my head to have me removed.' He taps the sign on the front of the desk: PRI-VATE SECRETARY. Keeper of the secrets. Whose secrets?

'Matrix management,' I finally say, the lightbulb coming on above my head at last. 'The Laundry runs on matrix management. She saw you on the org chart as head of the Counter-Possession

Unit, not as private secretary to . . .' *So that's how come he's got the free run of the director's office!*

Josephine is aghast. 'You call this a government department?'

'Worse things happen in parliament every day of the year, my dear.' Now that the proximate threat is over, Angleton looks remarkably imperturbable; right now I doubt he'd turn her into a frog even if she started yelling at him. 'Besides, you are aware of the maxim that power corrupts and absolute power corrupts absolutely? Here we deal every day of the week with power sufficient to destroy your mind. Even worse, we *cannot* submit to public oversight – it's far too dangerous, like giving atomic firecrackers to three-year-olds. Ask Robert to tell you what he did to attract our attention later, if you like.' I'm still dripping and cold, but I can feel my ears flush.

He focusses on her some more. 'We can reinforce the geas and release you,' he adds quietly. 'But I think you can do a much more important job here. The choice is yours.'

I snort under my breath. She glances at me, eyes narrowed and cynical. 'If this is what passes for a field investigation in your department, you *need* me.'

'Yes, well, you don't need to make your mind up immediately. Detached duty, and all that. As for you, Bob,' he says, with heavy emphasis on my name, 'you have acquitted yourself satisfactorily again. Now go and have a bath before you rot the carpet.'

'Bathroom's two doors down the hall on the left,' Andy adds helpfully from his station against the wall, next to the door: there's no doubt right now as to who's in charge here.

'But what happens now?' I ask, bewildered and a bit shocky and already fighting off the yawns that come on when people stop trying to kill me. 'I mean, what's really *happened*?'

Angleton grins like a skull: 'Bridget forfeited her department, so the directors have asked me to put Andrew in acting charge of it for the time being. Boris slipped up and failed to notice McLuhan; he is, ah, temporarily indisposed. And as for you, a job well done wins its natural reward – another job.' His grin widens. 'As I believe the youth of today say, don't have a cow . . .'

AFTERWORD
INSIDE THE FEAR FACTORY

Fiction serves a variety of purposes. At its heart lies the simple art of storytelling – of transferring ideas and sequences of events and pictures and people from the storyteller's head to that of the audience solely by means of words. But storytelling is a tool, and the uses to which a tool can be put often differs from – and is more interesting than – the uses for which the tool was designed.

Fiction is spun from plausible lies, contrived to represent an abreality sufficiently convincing that we do not question what we hear – and there are different forms within fiction. Consuming fiction is fun, an activity we engage in for recreation. So why, then, do we have an appetite for forms of fiction that make us profoundly uneasy, or that frighten us?

The chances are that if you've got to this afterword, you've done so the long way round – by reading 'The Atrocity Archive' and 'The Concrete Jungle.' This book is a work of fiction, a recreational product. Nobody forced you to read it by holding a gun to your head, so presumably you enjoyed the experience. Now, at risk of demystifying it, I'd like to pick over the corpse, dissect its three major organs, and try to explain just how it all fits together.

Cold Warriors

I'd like to begin by painting an anonymized portrait of one of the greatest horror writers of the twentieth century – a man whose writing was a major influence on me when I wrote these stories.

D. was born in London in 1929, of working class parents. A bright young man, he was educated at St. Marylebone Grammar and William Ellis, Kentish Town, then worked as a railway clerk before undergoing National Service in the RAF as a photographer attached to the Special Investigation Branch.

After his discharge in 1949, he studied art, achieving a scholarship to the Royal College of Art. Working as a waiter in the evenings, he developed an interest in cooking. During the 1950s he travelled, working as an illustrator in New York City and as an art director for a London advertising agency, before settling down in Dordogne and starting to write. His first novel was an immediate success, going on to be filmed (in a version starring Michael Caine); subsequently he produced roughly a book a year for the rest of the twentieth century. D. is somewhat reclusive, and was notorious at one point for only communicating via Telex machine. He may also hold the record for being the first writer ever to produce a novel entirely using a word processor (around 1972).

D.'s work is coolly observed, with a meticulous eye for background detail and subtle nuance. His narrators are usually anonymous, their cynical inspection of organisation and situation infused with a distaste or disdain for their circumstances that some of the other characters find extremely annoying, if not ideologically suspect. The world they find themselves trapped in is a maze of secret histories and occult organisations, entities that overlap with the world we live in, hiding beneath the surface like a freezing cold pond beneath a layer of thin ice. And hovering in the background over it all is a vast grey pall, a nightmare horror of impending *Gotterdämmerung*; for the great game of D.'s protagonists, breezily (or depressively) cynical though they might be, is always played for the ultimate stakes.

D. is, of course Len Deighton, perhaps more commonly regarded as one of the greatest masters of the spy thriller (who, with such works as *The Ipcress File, Funeral in Berlin*, and *Billion Dollar Brain,* is considered by some critics to be the equal or even the superior of John Le Carré). And the background to his novels, the world that infused them with tension and provided the stakes for the desperate gambles he described, was the Cold War.

The Cold War came to an abrupt end in 1991 with the Soviet coup that led to the breakup of the Union of Soviet Socialist Republics. Today, just a decade or so after it ended with a whimper instead of a bang, it is increasingly hard to remember just what it was like to live with a face-off of such enormous proportions between two powers that represented the Manichean opposites of industrial civilization. But those of us who grew up during the Cold War have been as permanently scarred by it as any child who watched the events of 9/11 live on CNN; because the Cold War applied a thin varnish of horror atop any fictional exploration of diplomacy, spying, or warfare.

Going back to the origins of the Cold War is a difficult task; its roots grew from a variety of sources in the fertile, blood-drenched soil of the early twentieth century. What is not in question is the fact that, by 1968, the United States of America and the Union of Soviet Socialist Republics had assembled – and pointed at each other on a hair-trigger – arsenals unprecedented in the history of warfare. During the First World War, all combatants combined expended on the order of eleven million tons of explosives. This was equivalent to the payload of a single B-52 bomber or Titan-2 ICBM of the middle period Cold War, before smart weapons and precision guidance systems began to replace the headsman's axe of deterrence with a surgeon's scalpel.

Many of the children of the Cold War era grew up doubting that they'd ever reach adulthood. Annihilation beckoned, in an apocalyptic guise that was nevertheless anatomised far more precisely than the visions of any mediaeval mystic. We knew the serial numbers, megatonnage, accuracy, flight characteristics, and blast effects of our nemesis, lurking sleeplessly beneath the waves or brooding in launcher-erectors scattered across the tundra under a never-setting sun.

One of Len Deighton's skills was that he infused the personal dilemmas and conflicts of his protagonists – little men and women trapped in seedy, poorly paid bureaucratic posts – with the shadow of the apocalypse. Cold War spy fiction was in some respects the ultimate expression of horror fiction, for the nightmare was real. There's no need to hint darkly about forbidden knowledge and elder gods, sleeping in drowned cities, who might inflict unspeakable horrors, when you live in an age where the wrong coded message can leave you blinded with your skin half-burned away in the wreckage of a dead city barely an hour later. The nightmare was very real indeed, and arguably it has never ended; but we have become blasè about it, tap dancing on the edge of the abyss because the great motor of ideological rivalry that powered the Cold War has broken down and we're all business partners in globalisation today and forevermore.

Spy fiction, like horror fiction, relies on the mundanity of the protagonist to draw the reader into proximity with the unnatural and occult horrors of alienation. We are invited to identify with the likes of Harry Palmer (as Deighton named him in the film of *The Ipcress File* – significantly, he has no name in the original novel), a low-level civil servant whose occasional duties, in between filing paperwork, involve visiting nuclear test sites, shepherding weapons scientists, and hunting agents of the alien power. Slowly sucked into a ghastly plot by the slow revelation of occult, secret knowledge, Palmer is bewildered and confused and forced to confront his worst fears in a world that the novelist slowly discloses to be under a nightmarish threat from beyond the consensus reality imposed by our society.

We've also become blasè about the apocalyptic nightmares of an earlier age.

Howard Phillips Lovecraft was one of the great pioneers of the spy thriller. Born in 1890, in Providence, Rhode Island, he was the child of well-off parents. However, when Lovecraft was three years old, his father was institutionalized, and Lovecraft suffered a variety of psychosomatic ailments that prevented him attending school. Despite these problems he was self-educated, taking an interest in science as well as literature. After a nervous breakdown in 1908, Lovecraft lived at home with his increasingly deranged mother. Writing rapidly, he became a self-published amateur journalist, and in the late nineteen-teens began to send out his stories for publication.

Lovecraft brought a cool, analytical eye to the pursuit of espionage. In his writings we frequently encounter the archetype of the scholar as spy, digging feverishly through libraries and colossal archives in search of the lost key to the cryptic puzzle. In *At the Mountains of Madness* Lovecraft prefigures the late twentieth-century techno-thriller brilliantly, with his tale of highly trained agents of an imperial power infiltrating a forbidden icy continent – not a million miles from the brooding ice plateaux of Siberia – in search of secret knowledge, at peril of death at the hands of the vigilant defenders of the new order should they come to their attention. Echoes of Lovecraft's obsessions abound in the more developed thrillers of the Cold War, from Alistair MacLean's *Ice Station Zebra* to the fervidly luscious garden of biological horrors in Ian Fleming's *You Only Live Twice* (the book, not the film).

Are we confused yet? Just in case, I'll summarise. Len Deighton was not an author of spy thrillers but of horror, because all Cold War-era spy thrillers rely on the existential horror of nuclear annihilation to supply a frisson of terror that raises the stakes of the games their otherwise mundane characters play. And in contrast, H. P. Lovecraft was not an author of horror stories – or not entirely – for many of his preoccupations, from the obsessive collection of secret information to the infiltration and mapping of territories controlled by the alien, are at heart the obsessions of the thriller writer.

(Before I stretch this analogy to breaking point, I am compelled to admit that there *is* a difference between the function and purpose of horror and spy fiction. Horror fiction allows us to confront and sublimate our fears of an uncontrollable universe, but the threat verges on the overwhelming and may indeed carry the protagonists away. Spy fiction in contrast allows us to believe for a while that the little people can, by obtaining secret knowledge, acquire some leverage over the overwhelming threats that permeate their universe. So, although the basic dynamics of both horror and spy fiction rely on the same sense of huge, impersonal forces outside the control of the protagonists, who might initially be ignorant of them, the outcome is often different.)

The Game of Spy and Dagon

The fictional spy is very unlike the spy in real life.

Every so often, Western intelligence agencies advertise in public for recruits. The profile of the professional agent is that of a government employee: quiet, diligent, punctilious about filling out forms and obeying procedures. Far from having a mysterious past, prospective employees of secret agencies have to provide a complete and exhaustive list of everywhere they've ever lived, and their background will be picked over in detail before the appointment is approved. Far from being men of action, the majority of intelligence community staff are office workers, a narrow majority of them female, and they almost certainly never handle weapons in the line of duty.

The picture changes when you contemplate non-Western organisations such as the Iraqi Mukhabarat, agencies of states that contemplate internal subversion with the cold eye of totalitarian zeal. It changes in time of open warfare, and it changes again when you examine Western agencies concerned with counter-terrorism and organised crime duties, such as the FBI. But the key insight to bear in mind is that in reality, the James Bond of the movie series (and, to a lesser extent, Ian Fleming's original literary wish-fulfillment vehicle) is an almost perfect photographic negative of the real intelligence agent. He is everything that a real spy cannot afford to be – flashy, violent, high-rolling, glamorous, the centre of attention.

So why are spies such fascinating targets of fiction?

Answer: because they know (or want to know) what's really going on.

We live in an age of uncertainty, complexity, and paranoia. Uncertainty because, for the past few centuries, there has simply been far too much knowledge out there for any one human being to get their brains around; we are all ignorant, if you dig far enough. Complexity multiplies because our areas of ignorance and our blind spots intersect in unpredictable ways – the most benign projects have unforeseen side effects. And paranoia is the emergent spawn of those side effects; the world is not as it seems, and indeed we may never be able to comprehend the world-as-it-is, without the comforting filter lenses of our preconceptions and our mass media.

It is therefore both an attractive proposition (and a frightening one) to believe that someone, somewhere, knows the score. It's attractive when we think they're on our side, defenders of our values and our lives, fighting in the great and secret wars to ensure that our cosy creature comforts survive undisturbed. And it's terrifying when we fear that maybe, just maybe, someone out there who *doesn't like us*, or even *doesn't* think *like us*, has got their hands on the control yoke of an airliner and is aiming dead for the twin towers of our *Weltanschauung*.

That's not just a tasteless metaphor, by the way. One comment that surfaced a lot in the second half of September 2001 was, 'I thought at first it was like something out of a Tom Clancy novel.' Tom Clancy is one of the leading exponents of the mega-scale techno-thriller, the bigger-is-better offshoot of the spy novel and its obsession with gadgets and tools of the trade. For an instant, the fabric of the real world seemed to have been ripped aside and replaced with a terrible fiction – and indeed, the 9/11 hijackers thought that they were *sending a message* to the hated West. It was a message that shocked and horrified (and maimed and murdered); and part of the reason it was so painful was that it struck at our assumption that we knew the score, that we knew what was going on and that our defenders were awake and on the ball.

Sometimes the paranoia can strike too close to home: writing in the near future is a perilous proposition. I began writing 'The Atrocity Archive' in 1999. For Bob's trip to California and his run-in with some frighteningly out-of-their-depth terrorists, I went digging and came back with an appropriately obscure but fanatical and unpleasant gang who might, conceivably, be planning an atrocity on American soil. But by the time the novel first came into print in the pages of the Scottish magazine *Spectrum SF*, it was late 2001 – and editor Paul Fraser quite sensibly suggested I replace Osama bin Laden and al-Qaida with something slightly more obscure on the grounds that, with USAF bombers already pounding the hills of Afghanistan, bin Laden didn't appear to have much of a future. (In retrospect, I got off lightly. Who can forget the wave of late-eighties cold war thrillers set in the USSR in the mid-nineties?)

As for the war in Iraq, I make no apologies. The novel was written in 1999–2000, and should be taken as set in 2001, *before* the events of 9/11.

On the other side of the narrative fence from our friend the spy stands our enemy, the destructive Other. The Other comes in a variety of guises, but always means us ill in one form or another. It might be that the Other wants to conquer and subjugate us, enforce our obedience to a religion, ideology, or monarch. Or the Other might simply want to eat our brains, or crack our bones and suck our marrow. Whatever the goal, it is defined in terms profoundly incompatible with our comfort and safety. Sometimes ideology and alienation overlap in allegory; the 1950s classic *Invasion of the Body Snatchers* was superficially about invading aliens, but also served as a close metaphor for Cold War paranoia about Communist infiltrators. Meanwhile, *The Stepford Wives* tore away the mask of an outwardly utopian vision of a conformist community with everyone in their place to reveal a toe-curlingly unpleasant process of alienation worming its way beneath the skin.

There is this about horror: it allows us to confront our fears, dragging the bogeyman out of the closet to loom over us in his most intimidating guise. (The outcome of the confrontation depends on whether the horror is a classical tragedy – in which the protagonist suffers their downfall because of a flawed character and hubris – or a comedy – in which they are redeemed; but the protagonist is still tainted with the brush of horror.)

And there is this about spy fiction: it allows us to confront our ignorance, by groping warily around the elephant of politics until it blows its trumpet, or perhaps stamps one gigantic foot on the protagonist's head. (Again, the outcome depends on the tragicomic roots of the narrative – but it still all hinges on ignorance and revelation.)

And now for something completely different.

HAX0R DUD35

The fictional hacker is not a real computer geek but a four-thousand-year-old archetype.

There have been trickster-gods running around administering wedgies to authority figures ever since the first adolescent apprentice took the piss out of his elder shaman. From Anansi the spider god through to the Norse trickster-god Loki, the trickster has been the expression of whimsy, curiosity, and occasional malice. Our first detailed knowledge of polytheistic religions comes from the first agricultural civilizations to leave written records behind. Early agricultural societies were conservative to a degree that seems bizarrely alien to us today: they balanced on a Malthusian knife-edge between productive plenitude and the starvation of famine. Change was deeply suspicious because it meant, as often as not, crop failure and starvation. The trickster-god is the one who makes a constant out of change; stealing fire, stealing language, stealing just about anything that isn't nailed down and quite a lot that is, he brought our ancestors most of their innovations.

Let's fast-forward to the present day, where a bewildering rate of change is actually a norm that can be counted upon to continue for decades or centuries. While we don't have trickster-gods and death-gods and crop-gods anymore, we *do* have narratives that serve the purpose of accustoming us to the idea of almost magical social dislocation.

The hot core of recent technological innovation – 'recent' meaning since 1970 – has been the computer industry. Driven by the inevitable progression of Moore's law, we've seen enormous breakthroughs, the likes of which haven't been seen since the rapid development of aviation between 1910 and 1950. Computers are a pervasive technology, and wherever they go they leave a sluglike trail of connectedness, information-dense and meaning-rich with the distillate of our minds. Unlike earlier technologies computers are general-purpose tools that can be reconfigured to do different tasks at the press of a button: one moment it's a dessert topping, the next it's a floor wax (or a spreadsheet, or an immersive game).

Hackers, in fiction, are the trickster-gods of the realm of computing. They go where they're not supposed to, steal anything that isn't nailed down (or rather, written down in ink on parchment with a quill plucked from a white goose), and boast about it. There is a refreshing immediacy to their activities because they move at the speed of light, cropping up anywhere they wish.

In reality, nothing could be further from the truth. Real hackers – computer programmers in the sense that the word was coined at MIT in the 1960s – are meticulous, intelligent, mathematically and linguistically inclined obsessives. Far from diving in and out of your bank account details, they're more likely to spend months working on a mathematical model of an abstraction that only another hacker would understand, or realise was an elaborate intellectual joke. All engineering disciplines generate a shared culture and jargon. The computing field has generated a remarkably rich jargon, and a shared culture to go with it. In some cases the sense of tradition is astonishingly strong; there are clubs and mutual support groups, for instance, for those people who choose to lovingly nurse along the twenty-year-old mini-computers they rescued from scrapheaps, rather than abandon them and move what software they can to a new generation of hardware.

At the other end of the spectrum are the script kiddies and warez dudes, the orcish adolescent *otoaku* who trash other people's work machines and try to take over chat networks in a fit of aso-cial misspelled pique. These are the real and mildly destructive hackers who generate most of the newspaper headlines and out-rage – tweaking the codebase of moronic email viruses, hanging out online and moaning endlessly, swallowing the image reflected back at them by the magic mirror of the tabloid press.

But if we return for a moment to the fictional hacker, not only do we discover the archetype of the trickster-god lurking just round the corner, but we also discern the outline of our spy/horror protagonist hunched over their keyboard, trying to dig down into the network of dreams and fears to understand what's really going on.

Every science-fictional depiction of a hacker at work seems to be about pulling away the rug to reveal a squirming mass of icky truths hiding beneath the carpet of reality. From John M. Ford's *Web of Angels* onward, we've had hackers exploiting networks to find the truth about what's really going on. Sometimes the hacker archetype overlaps with the guy-with-a-gun (as in Ken MacLeod's *The Star Fraction* or William Gibson's *Johnny Mnemonic*), or the gamer-with-a-virtual-gun (in film, Mamoru Oshii's *Avalon*), or even both (Hiro Protagonist, in Neal Stephenson's *Snow Crash*). Mao remarked, 'power grows from the barrel of a gun' – both in real life and in fiction – and if guns are about power, then hacking is about secret knowledge, and knowledge is also power. In fact, when you get down to it, what the fictional hacker has come to symbolize is not that far away from the fictional spy – or the nameless narrator of one of H. P. Lovecraft's strange tales of explor-ation and alienation.

Hacking the Subconscious, Spying on Horror, Revealing Reality

There's an iron tripod buried in the basement of the Laundry, carved with words in an alien language that humans can only interpret with the aid of a semisentient computer program that emulates Chomsky's deep grammar. Unfortunately the program is prone to fits of sulking, and because it obeys a nondeterministic algorithm it frequently enters a fatal loop when it runs. There is no canonical translation of the inscription. Government linguists tried to de-cypher the runes the hard way; all those who tried wound up dead or incarcerated in the Funny Farm. After a systems analyst suggested that the carving might really be the function binding for our reality, and that pronouncing it with understanding would cause a fatal exception, Mahogany Row decided to discourage future research along these lines.

The metafictional conceit that magic is a science has been used in fantasy – or science fiction – several times. James Gunn's *The Magicians* is explicitly based upon it. Rick Cook managed to squeeze several books from the idea of a socially clueless programmer stranded in fantasyland and forced to compete with the magi by applying his unfair expertise in compiler design. There is something *about* mathematics that makes it seem to beg for this sort of misappropriation: an image problem deeply rooted both in the way that the queen of sciences is taught, and in the way we think about it – in the philosophy of mathematics.

Plato spoke of a realm of mathematical truth, and took the view that unearthing a theorem was a matter of discovery: it revealed its truth to us like a shadow cast upon the wall of a cave by a light source and a reality invisible to our eyes. Later Descartes used similar reasoning and a weasely analogical excuse to split the world into things of the spirit and of the flesh. If the body was clearly an organic machine, *someone* had to be in a driving seat controlling it through a switchboard located (he believed) in the pineal gland.

The history of nineteenth- and twentieth-century medical

research was a disaster for the idea of an immortal soul. Mind-body dualism sounds good, until you realise that it implies that the body's sensory nerves must in some way transfer information to the soul, and the soul must somehow affect the dumb matter with which it is associated. When the best microscopes could barely resolve nerve fibres, this was not a problem: but the devil lies in the detail, and with electron micrographs taking us down to the macromolecular level of cytology, and with biochemistry finally beginning to explain how everything works, the brain was revealed for what it is – a mass of fleshy endocrine cells squirting their neurotransmitter messages at one another in promiscuous abandon. There is precious little room left for a soul that can remain hidden but nevertheless influence the flesh.

But. Let us take Plato's realm of mathematical abstraction seriously; and with it, let us adopt the Wheeler model of quantum cosmology – that there exists an infinity of possible worlds, and all of them are *real*. Can we, by way of the Platonic realm, transfer signals between our own sheaf of human-friendly realities and others, infinitely distant and infinitely close, where other minds might listen? What if, in other words, the multiverse is leaky? What sort of people might first discover such information leakage, and to what use would they put it, and what risks would they encounter in the process?

This is the twentieth (and early twenty-first) century, an age of spooks and wonder, of conspiracies and Cold War, an age in which the horror of the pulp magazines lurched forth onto the world stage in trillion-dollar weapons projects capable of smashing cities and incinerating millions. This is not the era of the two-fisted hero-scientist putting the finishing touches on his spherical exploration machine before setting off on a flight to Galaxy Z. Nor is it the age of the mad scientist in his castle basement, laboriously stitching together the graveyard trawl while Igor flies a kite from the battlements to bring the animating power down to the thing on the slab. It *is* the decade of the computer scientist, the fast-thinking designer of abstract machines that float on a Platonic realm of thought and blink in or out of existence with a mouseclick.

We can get some ideas about the lives and occupations of these people by extrapolating from the published material about the intelligence services. James Bamford's *Body of Secrets,* a deep and fascinating history of the US National Security Agency, offers some hints from outside – as do other histories of the cryptic profession, such as David Kahn's *The Codebreakers* and Alan Hodges's masterful biography of Alan Turing – for if any agency gets its hands on tools for probing the Platonic realm, it will be a kissing cousin of the kings of cryptography.

We can draw some other conclusions from the unspoken and unwritten history of the secret services. Why, for example, was the British Special Operations Executive disbanded so suddenly in 1945? One version is that the rivalry between SOE and the established Secret Intelligence Service was bitter, and after the 1945 election SIS lobbied the new government to disband SOE. But we know that when other similar organisations have disbanded they have left ghosts behind. US Secretary of State Henry Stimson disbanded the Black Chamber in 1929, with the immortal phrase, 'gentlemen do not read each other's mail,' but that didn't stop the Black Chamber's secrets ending up in Room 3416 of the Munitions Building, there to become the core of the Army's new Signal Intelligence Service.

British governments are less forthcoming – many of Whitehall's deepest secrets are stored in boxes labelled for release no less than a hundred years after the events they describe – but we can guess at similar revenants of SOE surviving the winter of the war, just as we know that many of the secrets of Bletchley Park's codebreaking operation ended up in Cheltenham, at the new (and unimportant-sounding) Government Communications Headquarters. SOE was deeply engaged with resistance operations against the Nazi occupation of Europe during the Second World War; if by some chance the Ahnenerbe-SS *were* sheltering ghastly secrets, it is unlikely that the subsequent custodians of such knowledge would have joined their comrades mustering out of service at the end of the conflict.

We can extrapolate somewhat from the post-1945 growth of

the intelligence agencies. Back in 1930, when William Friedman became the first chief of the US Army Signal Intelligence Service, the new successor to the Black Chamber had just three employees. By the year 2000, Crypto City – the NSA headquarters in Maryland – had a population of 32,000 regular workers and an annual budget on the order of seven billion dollars. The much smaller Government Communications HQ (GCHQ) – Britain's equivalent of the NSA – still has a budget measured in the high hundreds of millions. Information is power, and these agencies wield it without much restraint on the purse strings and without substantial external oversight. We can assume that even a relatively small 1945-vintage occult intelligence operation would have grown over the years into a sprawling organisation with either a huge central office or, possibly, multiple secure sites dotted around the country.

Finally, this brings us back to the Laundry. The Laundry squats at the heart of a dark web, the collision, between paranoia and secrecy on one hand, and the urge to knowledge on the other. Guardians of the dark secrets that threaten to drown us in nightmare, their lips are sealed as tightly as their archives. To get even the vaguest outline of their activities takes a privileged trickster-fool hacker like Bob, nosy enough to worm his way in where he isn't supposed to be and smart enough to explain his way out of trouble. Some day Bob will grow up, fully understand the ghastly responsibilities that go with his job, shut the hell up, and stop digging. But until then, let us by all means use him as our unquiet guide to the corridors of the Fear Factory.

Afternote: Two Frequently Asked Questions

While I was writing 'The Atrocity Archive,' my friend Andrew Wilson (science fiction reviewer for *The Scotsman*) kept telling me: 'For God's sake, don't read *Declare* by Tim Powers until you finish the novel.'

Powers is a remarkable writer, and in *Declare* he explored an arcane world remarkably close to that of 'The Atrocity Archive.' The points of similarity are striking: rogue departments within SOE that survive the end of the war, operations in the British secret intelligence community that focus on the occult and run independently of anything else for a period of decades – even a protagonist who, with a special SAS team, tries to take on a supernatural horror.

Luckily for me, I listened to Andrew. He was right: if I'd read *Declare* it would have derailed me completely. And that would have been a shame, because in tone and attitude the two novels are very different. *Declare* is perhaps best read as an homage to John Le Carré, whereas the outlook of 'The Atrocity Archive' is perhaps closer to Len Deighton, by way of Neal Stephenson. *Declare is* about disengagement and the abandonment of former responsibility; 'The Atrocity Archive' is more interested in coming of age in a world of ghosts and shadows. *Declare* is about the secret services that waged The Great Game; 'The Atrocity Archive' is about the agencies that fought the Wizard War. The two novels are sufficiently far apart that they stand on their own merit. I'll just leave the topic by saying, if you liked this book, you'll probably enjoy *Declare*.

About six months *after* the scare over *Declare* another friend said, 'Hey, have you ever heard of Delta Green?'

I used to be big on role-playing games, but it's been close to two decades since I was last involved in the scene to any extent. So the whole Chaosium phenomenon had passed me by. It turns out that Lovecraft's horrors have found a fertile field (or swamp) in the shape of the game *Call of Cthulhu*. In *Call of Cthulhu*, gamers role-play their way through one or another 1920s-era scenario that usually involves solving bizarre mysteries before something hideous sucks their brains out through their ears with a crazy straw. 'Delta Green' is an almost legendary supplement to *Call of Cthulhu* that attempts to bring the mythos role-playing game up-to-date. There's a rogue intelligence agency battling to prevent infestations of extradimensional horrors . . . sound familiar?

All I can say in my defense is, no: I hadn't heard of 'Delta Green' when I wrote 'The Atrocity Archive.' 'Delta Green' has such a markedly American feel that 'The Atrocity Archive' is right off the map. (Which is odd, because in tone if not in substance they feel a lot closer than, say, *Declare*.) So I'll leave it at that except to say that 'Delta Green' has come dangerously close to making me pick up the dice again.

Charles Stross
Edinburgh, UK
April 2003

GLOSSARY OF
ABBREVIATIONS,
ACRONYMS, AND
ORGANISATIONS

BA British Airways [UK]
BLACK CHAMBER Cryptanalysis agency officially disbanded in 1929, secretly retasked with occult intelligence duties [US]
CESG Communications Electronics Security Group, division within GCHQ [UK]
CIA Central Intelligence Agency [US]
CMA Computer Misuse Act, the law governing hacking [UK]
COTS Cheap, Off The Shelf – computer kit; a procurement term [US/UK]
CPU Counter-Possession Unit, a specialised team operating across departmental lines within The Laundry [UK]
DARPA Defense Advanced Research Projects Agency, formerly ARPA, a government scientific research agency affiliated with the Department of Defense [US]
DEA Drug Enforcement Agency [US]
DERA Defense Evaluation and Research Agency, privatised as QinetiQ [UK]
DGSE Direction Générale de la Sécurité Extérieure, the external intelligence organisation (French equivalent of CIA) [France]
DIA Defense Intelligence Agency [US]
EUINTEL European Union Intelligence Treaty – fictional [EU]

FBI Federal Bureau of Investigation [US]

FO Foreign Office [UK]

FSB Federal Security Service, formerly known as KGB [Russia]

GCHQ Government Communications HQ (UK equivalent of NSA) [UK]

GCSE General Certificate of Secondary Education – high school qualification; not to be confused with CESG [UK]

GRU Russian Military Intelligence [Russia]

HMG Her Majesty's Government [UK]

JIC Joint Intelligence Committee [UK]

KCMG Knight-Commander of the Most Distinguished Order of St. Michael and St. George – honours service overseas or in connection with foreign or Commonwealth affairs [UK]

KGB Committee for State Security, renamed FSB in 1991 [Russia]

LART Luser Attitude Readjustment Tool – see *The New Hacker's Dictionary*, edited by Eric S. Raymond, MIT Press, ISBN 0-262680-92-0 [All]

THE LAUNDRY Formerly SOE Q Department, spun off as a separate organisation in 1945 [UK]

MI5 National Security Service, also known as DI5 [UK]

MI6 Secret Intelligence Service, also known as SIS, DI6 [UK]

NEST Nuclear Emergency Search Team (US equivalent of OCCULUS) [US]

NKVD Historical predecessor organisation to KGB, renamed in 1947 [USSR/Russia]

NSA National Security Agency (US equivalent of GCHQ) [US]

NSDAP Nationalsozialistische Deutsche Arbeiterpartei – National Socialist German Workers Party, aka Nazi Party [Germany]

OBE Order of the British Empire – awarded mainly to civilians and service personnel for public service or other distinctions [UK]

OCCULUS Occult Control Coordination Unit Liaison, Unconventional Situations (UK/NATO equivalent of NEST) [UK/NATO]

ONI Office of Naval Intelligence [US]

OSA Official Secrets Act, the law governing official secrets [UK]
OSS Office of Strategic Services (US equivalent of SOE), disbanded in 1945, remodelled as CIA [US]
Q DIVISION Division within The Laundry associated with R&D [UK]
QINETIQ See DERA [UK]
RIPA Regulation of Investigatory Powers Act, the law governing communications interception [UK]
RUC Royal Ulster Constabulary, the paramilitary police force deployed in Northern Ireland during the Troubles [UK]
SAS Special Air Service – British Army special forces [UK]
SBS Special Boat Service – Royal Marines special forces [UK]
SIS See MI6 [UK]
SOE Special Operations Executive (UK equivalent of OSS), officially disbanded in 1945; see also The Laundry [UK]
TLA Three Letter Acronym [All]

extras

orbit
www.orbitbooks.net

extras

about the author

Charles Stross is a full-time science fiction writer and resident of Edinburgh, Scotland. The author of six Hugo-nominated novels and winner of the 2005 and 2010 Hugo awards for best novella ("The Concrete Jungle" and "Palimpsest"), Stross's works have been translated into over twelve languages.

Like many writers, Stross has had a variety of careers, occupations and job-shaped-catastrophes in the past, from pharmacist (he quit after the second police stake-out) to first code monkey on the team of a successful dot-com startup (with brilliant timing he tried to change employer just as the bubble burst). Along the way he collected degrees in Pharmacy and Computer Science, making him the world's first officially qualified cyberpunk writer (just as cyberpunk died).

He's currently working on a variety of novels, including the fifth volume of the Laundry Files, *The Rhesus Chart*. In 2013 he will be Creative in Residence at the UK-wide Centre for Creativity, Regulation, Enterprise and Technology, researching the business models and regulation of industries such as music, film, TV, computer games and publishing.

Find out more about Charles Stross and other Orbit authors by registering for the free monthly newsletter at www.orbitbooks.net.

Prologue
Game Face

This is not the end of the world, Ross told himself.

He closed his eyes as a low hum began to sound around him, heralding the commencement of the scan. The effect was more white-out than black-out, the reflective tiles filling the room with greater light than the fine membranes of his eyelids could possibly block.

He should look upon all of it as a new start; several new

starts, in fact. Yes: multiple, simultaneous, unforeseen, unwanted and utterly unappealing new beginnings. Welcome to your future.

As he lay on the slab he conducted a quick audit of all the things that had gone wrong in the couple of hours since he'd stepped off his morning bus into a squall of Scottish rain and a lungful of diesel fumes on his way to work. He concluded that it wasn't a brain scan he needed: it was a brain transplant. Nonetheless, as the scan-heads zipped and buzzed above him, for the briefest moment he enjoyed a sense of his mind being completely empty, an awareness of a fleeting disconnection from his thoughts, as though they were a vinyl record from which the needle had been temporarily raised.

'Hey Solderburn, are we clear?' he asked, keeping his eyes closed just in case.

There was no reply. Then he recalled the capricious ruler of the Research and Development Lab telling him to bang on the door if there was a problem, so he deduced there was no internal monitoring.

He opened his eyes and sat up. It was only a moment after he had done so that he realised the tracks and scan-heads were no longer there. He did a double-take, wondering if the whole framework had been automatically withdrawn into some hidden wall-recess: it was the kind of pointless feature Solderburn was known to spend weeks implementing, even though it was of no intrinsic value.

There was still no word from outside. Solderburn probably had a lot of switches to flip, so Ross was patient, and as he didn't have a watch on, he only had a rough idea how long he'd been sitting there. However, by the time the big hand on his mental clock had ticked from 'reasonable delay' through 'mild discourtesy' into 'utterly taking the piss', he'd decided it was time to remind the chief engineer that his latest configuration included a human component.

The bastard had better not have sloped off outdoors to have a fag. Seriously, was there any greater incentive to stop smoking than having to do it in the doorway to this dump, looking out at the rest of the shitty Seventies industrial estate surrounding it?

Ross got to his feet and extended a fist, but before he could deliver the first of his intended thumps, the door opened, though not the way he was expecting. Instead of swinging on its hinge, the entire thing withdrew outwards by a couple of inches, then slid laterally out of sight with the softest hiss of servos.

WTF?

Beyond it lay not the familiar chaos of the R&D lab, but merely a grey wall and the grungy dimness of a damp-smelling corridor.

So Solderburn *was* taking the piss, but not in the way Ross had previously believed. This was the kind of prank that explained why the guy had ended up working here in Stirling, rather than winning a Nobel Prize. He must have slid some kind of false wall into place outside the scanning room. Ross walked forward, stepping lightly because he suspected Solderburn's practical joke had some way to go before it reached the pay-off stage.

He looked left and right along the passageway.

All right, so maybe it was time to revise the practical joke hypothesis.

There was a dead end to the left, where the way was blocked by three huge pipes that emerged from the ceiling and descended through a floor constructed of metal grilles on top of concrete, into which sluice channels were etched in parallel. There was a regulator dial on the right-most tube, sitting above a wheel for controlling the flow. A sign next to it warned: 'DO NOT MESS WITH VALVE'.

It was a redundant warning in Ross's case: he wasn't going near it. Even from a few yards away, he could feel the vibration of flow in the pipes, indicating that enormous volumes of fluid must be passing through the vessels. It sounded like enough to power a small hydroelectric station. Even Solderburn couldn't fake up something like that.

In the other direction, the corridor went on at least twice the length of the lab, condensation beading its walls. He could hear non-syncopated pounding, its low echo suggesting something powerful and resonant that was being dampened by thick walls. This thought prompted him to glance at the ceiling, which mostly comprised live rock, occasionally masked off by black panels insulating lines of thick cable.

He began to make his way along the corridor. Light was provided by strips running horizontally along the walls, roughly two feet above head height. Ross assumed them to be inset, but if so it was a hell of a neat job. They looked like they could be peeled right off and stuck wherever they were required.

There was another light source further ahead, a dim blue-green glow coming from behind a glass panel set high in the wall on the left.

The corridor trembled following a particularly resonant boom from somewhere above. Ross could feel the metal grates rattle from it, the air disturbed by a pulse of movement. It felt warm, like the sudden gust of heat when somebody has just opened an oven door. There was still no rhythm, no pattern to the sounds, and yet Ross found something about them familiar.

As he approached the panel, he could see a play of coloured light behind the glass, constant but fluid, as though there might be a team of welders on the other side of it. Please, he thought, *let* there be a team of welders on the other side: hairy-arsed welders with bottles of Irn-Bru and Monday-morning hangovers, toting oxyacetylene torches and forehead-slappingly obvious explanations for what was going on. Perhaps he had ended up at one of the factories on the estate, somehow?

The panel was high, so Ross had to stand close and stretch to get a look through the glass. As soon as he did, he caught a glimpse of someone on the other side and promptly threw himself back down low, out of sight.

It wasn't a welder; or if it was, it was one who had utterly lost it at some point and started grafting stuff to his own face.

In his startlement and panicked attempt to hide, Ross tumbled backwards to the deck, a collapse that felt less painful but sounded altogether more clangingly metallic than he was expecting. If the hideous creature behind the wall hadn't seen him as he peered through the glass a moment ago, then he had surely heard him now.

He had to get moving, and hope there was more than one way out of this corridor. It might be prejudiced to assume that the man he had seen meant him any harm purely on the basis of his unfortunate appearance, but it was difficult to imagine anybody with a penchant for soldering things to his coupon being an entirely calm and balanced individual. Besides, Ross's alarm hadn't been inspired purely by the fact that the guy would have a bastard of a time getting his face through airport security; it was the look Ross had briefly glimpsed in that nightmarish visage's eyes: wild, frantic, unhinged and, most crucially, searching.

It was as he uncrumpled himself from a heap on the floor that he discovered any attempt at flight was futile, and for a reason far worse than that this mutilated horror might already have cut off his escape. His eye was drawn, for the first time since emerging from his cell, to his own person rather than his surroundings, and a glance at his limbs showed them no longer to be clad in what he remembered pulling on that morning. Gone were the soft-leather shoes, moleskin jeans and charcoal shirt, replaced by a one-piece ensemble of metal, glass and bare skin, all three surfaces scarred by scorch-marks and gouges.

He looked in terrified disgust at his forearm, where two light-pulsing cables were visible on the surface, feeding into his wrist at one end and plunging beneath an alloy sheath at the other. His legs were similarly metal-clad, apart from glass panels beneath which further fibre-optic wiring could be seen intermittently breaking the surface of skin that was a distressingly unhealthy pallor even for someone who had grown up in the west of Scotland.

His chest and stomach had armour plates grafted strategically to cover certain areas whilst retaining flexibility of movement by leaving other expanses of skin untouched, and there were further transparent sections revealing enough of his interior to suggest he wouldn't be needing a bag of chips and a can of cream soda any time soon.

Trembling with shock and incredulity, he hauled himself upright, finding his new wardrobe to be impossibly light. His movement was free and fluid too, feeling as natural as had he still been wearing what he'd turned up to work in.

Was it some kind of illusion, then?

No. Of course. He had fallen asleep during the scan. It was a dream.

Except that normally the awareness of dreaming was enough to dispel it and bring him to.

Ross looked himself up and down again. There was no swirling transition of thoughts and images bringing him to the surface, no dream-logic progress linking one bizarre moment to the next.

He approached the glass again. He could see two vertical shafts of energy, one blue and one green, seemingly unchannelled through any vessel, but perfectly linear, independent and self-contained nonetheless. Reluctantly, he pulled his focus back from what was behind the glass to the reflecting surface itself.

Arse cakes.

He looked like he had faceplanted the clearance sale at Radio Shack. It was still recognisably his own features underneath there somewhere: even that little scar on his cheek from when he'd fallen off a spider-web roundabout when he was nine. He recalled what a fuss his mum had made when he needed stitches. Everything's relative, eh Mammy?

Another muffled boom sounded, moments before another shudder rippled the air. He could hear lesser percussions too, like it was bonfire night and he was indoors, half a mile from the display. It was hardly an enticement to proceed down the corridor, but what choice did he have?

He strode forward on his augmented legs, surprised to discover his gait felt no different, his tread lighter than the accompanying metal-on-metal thumps suggested. There was absolutely nothing about this that wasn't absolutely perplexing, not least the aspects that felt normal. For instance, as he followed the passageway around a bend to a T-junction leading off either side of an elevator, he was disturbed to find that he seemed instinctively to know where he was going. Was there something in all this circuitry that was doing part of his thinking for him? He wasn't aware of it if so; though the fact that he probably wouldn't be aware of such a process was not reassuring.

He stepped on to the open platform of the elevator and pressed his palm to the activation panel. A light traced around his atrophied fingers at the speed of an EKG and the platform began to rise.

He looked again at the leathery grey of his hand. It gave a new meaning to the term dead skin. He thought of all the times Carol had ticked him off for biting his nails, of her rubbing moisturiser on his cracks and chaps in wintertime.

Carol. No. Not yet.

He put her from his mind as the elevator reached the top of the shaft, where his faith in instinctively knowing where he was going was put to the test by his arriving somewhere he was dangerously conspicuous. No narrow passageway this time: he had reached some kind of muster point or staging area, and was rising up into the centre of it like it was his turn on *Camberwick Green*.

He got there just in time to see a group of figures – each of them similarly dressed by the Motorola menswear department – march out through a wide doorway. They moved briskly and with purpose, two halves of the automatic door closing diagonally behind them as the elevator platform came to a stop, flush with the floor.

The booms were louder here. The smaller ones sounded like muffled explosions somewhere beyond the walls, but the big ones seemed to pulse through the very fabric of whatever this place was. He could tell when one was coming, as though the entire structure was breathing in just before it; could sense something surge through all those pipes lining the walls. It was like being inside a nose that was about to sneeze.

He was absolutely sure of which way to head next, but it wasn't to do with any weird instinct or control by some exterior force. It was simply a matter of having observed in which direction the platoon of zombie-troopers had shipped out and of proceeding in precisely the opposite.

They'd had their backs to him so he couldn't get a clear view of what they were all carrying, but the objects had been metal and cylindrical, and he considered it unlikely they were some kind of cyborg brass section that had just been given its cue to hit the stage. Given how little sense everything else was making right then, it was always possible that the latter was the case and they were about to strike up 'In the Mood', but Ross strongly suspected that the only thing they were in the mood for was shooting anybody who got in their way.

He proceeded towards his intended exit at what he realised was an incongruously girly trot: hastened by his eagerness to get away but slowed short of a run in case it should be conspicuous that he was making a break for it. His head spun with awful possibilities, trying to piece together what could have happened. It had to have been the scan, he deduced. Whether intentionally or not, it had left him in a state of suspended animation and his body had been stored until the advent of the technology that currently adorned and possibly controlled him.

Neurosphere. Those amoral corporate sociopaths. This was their doing. There was probably a clause in his employment contract that covered this shit, and as he'd never bothered to read the pages and pages of legalese, he'd had no real idea what he was signing. Now he could be working for them forever, part of a manufactured army. But in that case, why hadn't they erased or at least restrained his memory? Why was he not a compliant drone like the others he'd seen? Perhaps something had gone wrong with the process and he was the lucky one – retaining his memory and his sense of self and thus able to testify to Neurosphere's monstrous crime. Or perhaps he was the really *un*lucky one, trapped in this condition but not anaesthetised by merciful oblivion, and unlike the others he'd be conscious of every horror he was about to witness, or even effect.

He had no idea what year it was, or even what century. Chances were everyone he ever knew was gone. There might be nothing in the world he would recognise.

The big doorway opened obligingly as he approached, its two halves sliding diagonally apart to reveal another corridor, brighter than he'd seen before. Light appeared to be flashing and shimmering beyond a curve up ahead, and with nobody to observe him, he ran towards it.

'Oh,' he said.

The source of the flashing and shimmering on the far side of the passageway turned out to be a huge window opposite, easily twelve feet high by twenty feet wide, through which Ross could see what was outside this building. He hadn't thought he could ever look into another pane of glass and see a more unsettling sight than the one that had met him only a few minutes ago when he glimpsed his own reflection. Clearly it was not a day to be making assumptions.

The first thing he noticed was the sky, which was a shade of purple that he found disturbing. It wasn't so much that there was anything aesthetically displeasing about the colour itself; it was, to be fair, a quite regally luxuriant purple: deep, textured and vibrant. It was more to do with his knowledge of astronomy and subsequent awareness that, normally, the sky he looked up at owed its colour to the shorter wavelengths and greater proportion of blue photons in the type of light emitted by the planet's primary energy source. What was disturbing about this particular hue was not merely that it could not be any sky on Earth, but that it could not be any sky beneath its sun.

Worse, its predominantly purple colouration wasn't even the most distressing thing about the view through the window: that distinction went to the fact that it was full of burning aircraft. There were dozens of them up there, possibly hundreds, stretching out all the way to the horizon. It looked to be some kind of massive extraterrestrial expeditionary landing force, and its efforts were proving successful in so far as landing was defined as reaching terra firma: all of the craft were certainly managing that much. However, controlled descents executed without conflagration and completed by vessels comprising fewer than a thousand flaming pieces were, quite literally, a lot thinner on the ground.

Ross felt that inrush again, that sense of energy being channelled very specifically to one source, then heard the great boom once more, and this time he could see its source. It was a colossal artillery weapon, sited at least a mile away, but evidently powered by the facility in which he was standing. Its twin muzzles were each the size of an oil tanker, jutting from a dome bigger than St Paul's Cathedral, and its effect on the invasion force was comparable to a howitzer trained on a flock of geese. Each mighty blast devastated another host of unfortunate landing craft, sending debris spinning and hurtling towards the surface.

He had no sense of how long he had been standing there: it could have been thirty seconds and it could have been ten times that. The spectacle was horrifyingly mesmeric, but the car-crash fascination was not purely vicarious. Everything Ross saw had unthinkable consequences for himself. Instead of being merely lost in time, he now had no idea which planet he was even on.

He could see buildings in the distance, only visible because they were so large. The architecture was unquestionably alien, as was the very idea of building vast, isolated towers in an otherwise empty desert landscape. And still something inside him felt like he belonged here, or at least that his environment was not as alien as it should have been.

'It's an awe-inspiring sight, isn't it?'

When Ross heard the voice speak softly from only a few feet behind him, he deduced rather depressingly that he must no longer have a digestive system, as this could be the only explanation for why he didn't shit himself.

He turned around and found himself staring at another brutally haphazard melange of flesh and metal, one he decided was definitely the estate model. The newcomer was a foot taller at least, and more heavily armoured, particularly around the head, leaving his face looking like a lost little afterthought. He looked so imposingly heavy, Ross could imagine him simply crashing through anything less than a reinforced floor, and couldn't picture walls proving much of an impediment either. Wherever he wanted to be, he was getting there, and whatever he wanted, Ross was giving him it.

'Yes,' Ross agreed meekly, amazed to hear his own voice still issuing from whatever he had become.

'You could lose yourself in it,' the big guy went on. His tone was surprisingly soft, perhaps one used to being listened to without the need to raise it, but not as surprising as his accent, which was a precise if rather theatrical received pronunciation. Clearly, as well as advanced technology, this planet also had some very posh schools.

'Perhaps even forget what you were supposed to be doing. Such as joining up with your unit and getting on with fighting off the invasion, what with there being a war on and all.'

His voice remained quiet but Ross could hear the sternest of warnings in his register. There was control there too, no expectation of needing to ask twice. Very bizarrely, Ross was warming to him. Maybe it was the programming, same as whatever was making him feel this place was familiar.

'Yes, sorry, absolutely … er … sir,' he remembered to add. 'My unit, that's right. Have to join up. On my way now, sir.'

'That's "Lieutenant Kamnor, sir",' he instructed.

'Yes, sir, Lieutenant Kamnor, sir,' Ross barked, eyes scanning either way along the corridor as he weighed his options regarding which direction Kamnor expected him to walk in.

He turned and made to return to the staging area. Kamnor stopped him by placing a frighteningly heavy hand on his shoulder.

'Are you all right, soldier?' he asked, sounding genuinely concerned. 'You seem a little disoriented. Do you know where your unit even is?'

Ross decided he had nothing to lose.

'I have no idea where *I* even am, sir. I don't know how I got here. I have no memory of it. I'm not a soldier. I'm a scientific researcher in Stirling. That's Scotland, er, planet Earth, and this morning, that being an early twenty-first-century morning, I had a neuroscan as part of my work. I was still totally biodegradable; I mean, an entirely organic being. When I stepped out of the scanning cell, I found myself here, looking like this.'

Kamnor's face altered, concern changing to something between alarm and awe, and everything that it conveyed seemed amplified by being the only recognisable piece of humanity amidst so much machine.

'Blood of the fathers,' he said, his voice falling to a gasp. 'You're telling me you were a different form, in another world?'

'Yes sir, lieutenant, sir.'

'Blood of the fathers. Then it truly is the prophecy.'